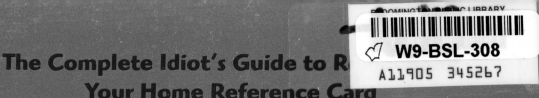

The Complete Idiot's Guide to Remodeling Your Home Reference Card

How to Map Your Electrical Circuits

1. First, turn on all your lights, radios, TV, etc. throughout your house (every outlet must be accounted for).
2. Next, have someone monitoring each room.
3. Begin removing fuses or flipping circuit breakers, one at a time.
4. Carefully record which lights, outlets, and appliances are affected by each fuse or breaker.
5. Attach your recordings to the door of your fuse box or electrical panel.

The Ten Biggest Remodeling Mistakes

1. Remodeling without a plan
2. Neglecting to take out permits for the work
3. Failing to check out your contractor's credentials
4. Imposing an unrealistic schedule on your project
5. Not doing essential repairs and maintenance first
6. Drawing up an unrealistically low budget for the job
7. Relying on oral agreements with contractors rather than written ones
8. Opening your house to the weather for an extended period of time
9. Neglecting your family or spouse during the remodeling
10. Adding more value to your house than your neighborhood can possibly support when resale time comes

alpha
books

Sure Signs That You Should Consider Remodeling Your House

- ➤ Your family is growing and you don't want to leave the neighborhood.
- ➤ You're getting tired of chopping wood for your Abraham Lincoln–era kitchen stove.
- ➤ The last time your bathroom saw new fixtures was when your house was built—in 1945.
- ➤ Not a winter goes by that your windows don't ice up on the inside of your house.
- ➤ The neighbors anonymously send you advertisements for sales at Remodelers-R-Us.
- ➤ You've got so much equity in your home that you could spend $100,000 on remodeling and still come out ahead.
- ➤ The knotty pine paneling covering the downstairs walls is giving you cabin fever.
- ➤ Your kitchen is so small that you can't chop vegetables and boil water at the same time.

Remodeling Money Savers

- ➤ Make careful plans and stick to them; change orders are expensive!
- ➤ Look for close-outs on plumbing fixtures, lights, and carpet which can be used for your project.
- ➤ Shop around for the best remodeling financing package.
- ➤ Think twice before installing expensive, high-maintenance items like hardwood floors in bathrooms. Would you be better off with an alternative material?
- ➤ Negotiate with your contractor to do some of the basic work—such as demolition and hauling—yourself.

Ten Problems/Expenses You Can Run Into When Remodeling

1. Hidden wood rot
2. Insect or rodent nests
3. Drainage problems
4. Previous work not done to code
5. Contractor delays
6. Backordered materials
7. Unforeseen structural problems
8. Lead-based paint and asbestos removal on old houses
9. Disagreements with a building inspector
10. More fast food consumption than you ever imagined

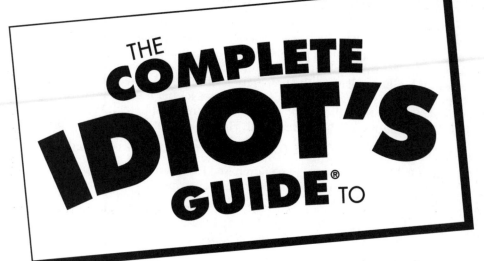

THE COMPLETE IDIOT'S GUIDE® TO

Remodeling Your Home

by Terry Meany

alpha books

A Division of Macmillan General Reference
A Pearson Education Macmillan Company
1633 Broadway, New York, NY 10019-6785

Alpha Development Team

Publisher
Kathy Nebenhaus

Editorial Director
Gary M. Krebs

Associate Publisher
Cindy Kitchel

Associate Managing Editor
Cari Shaw Fischer

Acquisitions Editors
Jessica Faust
Michelle Reed

Development Editors
Phil Kitchel
Amy Zavatto

Production Team

Development Editor
Doris Cross

Production Editor
Stephanie Mohler

Copy Editor
Heather Stith

Cover Designer
Mike Freeland

Photo Editor
Richard H. Fox

Cartoonist
Jody P. Schaeffer

Designers
Scott Cook and Amy Adams of DesignLab

Indexer
Tonya Heard

Layout/Proofreading
John Bitter
Jerry Cole
Natalie Evans
Terri Sheehan

Contents at a Glance

v

Contents

Part 4: Get a Fresh Start: Interior Changes   183

Part 5: Street Appeal: Exterior Upgrades   233

19 Taking Sides: Your Exterior Walls   235

20 Porches and Decks: Your Outdoor Rooms   247

Foreword

It all seems so simple, doesn't it? Flip on the TV and you can build a deck. Crack a magazine and you've got a new bedroom extension. Log on and you're halfway to the soaring ceiling of your new great room. So much that's being presented today skates across the reality of renovation, instead selling tools and materials by making it all seem, well, easy.

We aren't fooled.

We've tried to put in nothing more than a new doorknob and suddenly we've been faced with questions about levers vs. knobs, brass plate vs. chrome, $2^3/_4$- vs. $2^3/_8$-inch backset. We've grappled with drilling and mortising and chiseling and then, finally, at the end of the day, the dang thing still didn't latch.

We know about renovation.

What we want to know is the truth, the opinionated truth about the one particular project we're ready to do. That is where this book shines. It has a comprehensive discussion of just about any project you might consider. It gives you the inside track on everything from decks to kitchens, plumbing to contracts, and restoration to renovation. And it does it in the usual *Complete Idiot's Guide* fashion: smart-alecky remarks, funny cartoons, and a lot of simple, easy-to-understand information.

Let's face it: The materials, tools, and technology exist to do practically any project. What's missing is the owner's insight. This book helps you understand the materials, the design considerations, and the cost ramifications before you set off for the home store or call up the deck guy.

Think of this book as your retired contractor uncle who's got the time to set you straight and point you in the right direction. That's all we really need.

John Rusk

John Rusk is founding president of the American Renovation Association and author of *On Time and On Budget: A Home Renovation Survival Guide* (Doubleday, 1996). He has run Rusk Renovation since 1986, and recently launched Quick-Cote, the first nationwide interior painting service designed to assist real estate professionals in organizing their clients' painting needs.

Introduction

The design, size, and style of a home is as individual as its owners. Features which were perfectly acceptable to the previous occupants may send you running back to the drawing board—or maybe for a chain saw and a sledge hammer. Remodeling is in our human programming. Put our DNA under a really powerful microscope and you'll find nucleic acid shaped like a tool box.

We all bring ideas along when we move to a new home. Some call for a gourmet kitchen with nuclear-powered appliances and freezers so cold that NASA could use them to test their spacecraft. Other are as simple as replacing a 1940s bathroom. Your schemes and dreams should reflect your own needs, tastes, and budget, not the picture-perfect projects shown in high-end home design magazines.

Older homes sometimes beg for remodeling, but even new houses can benefit from finished basements or the addition of a sun room. What do you see when you walk through your home? Two small, unused bedrooms might become a master suite. A utility room can be extended and converted into a home office. Enclose an old porch and the kids get a warm, cozy playroom.

Don't worry if you don't know a roof rafter from white-water rafting. We'll walk the house, from the bottom up, so you'll know what you're looking at and how your home is put together. You'll learn how to make a plan and a budget, and realistically decide how much work you want to do yourself and how much you want to contract out. Most important, you'll learn the ins and outs of the remodeling process so you can control it, instead of having it control you!

Many people tell remodeling horror stories of unforeseen structural repairs, skyrocketing costs, schedules that change weekly, and not-quite-old-world craftsmanship on the part of some contractors. This doesn't have to happen to you. Will you run into the unexpected? Of course, but, in some cases, you might be pleasantly surprised: A job might go faster than you expected, or the floor of an attic you're converting to living space may not need additional bracing after all. Some people have even torn walls open only to find a pair of the original sliding doors and hardware tucked away and waiting to be used again.

Remodeling involves more than the work and materials themselves. A certain enlightenment—it's too noisy to be a Zen exercise—comes along with the process. Budget restraints, for instance, will compel you to come up with creative solutions and alternatives.

Maintaining a sane family life—assuming it wasn't already insane to begin with—can be a challenge. Your new second-story addition, along with its noisy and long work hours, can take on a life of its own, but don't let it separate you from your family and friends.

Projects can seem overwhelming, but breaking them down into doable tasks, and following a well-laid-out plan, can get you through with flying colors.

Finally, you're looking for good, well-crafted results, not the perfection of the Hope Diamond. Your home is to be lived in, not treated like a museum exhibit kept under glass. Your improvements should add greater comfort and convenience to your life—not just be for show!

How to Use This Book

Remodeling can be like a romantic relationship: Lots of fun at the start, but then the real work begins. Tearing into a room, shopping for materials, cutting a hole in the side of the house, all have a big cartoon dialog balloon over them saying, "Hurray, we're getting started, we're getting something done. Get out of the way and watch the dust fly." A few hours later, reality sets in and you realize it may take longer than a weekend to add that enclosed Olympic-size swimming pool you've been pining for.

This book is set up to take you through all stages of remodeling, regardless of your skill level. It will provide you with plenty of information and give you the means to decide if you really want to start a project, live with what you have, or even move to a house more to your liking.

The only rules you must follow are safety and building code regulations. The rest is up to you.

How this book is organized:

- **Part 1: Does Your Home Need a Makeover—or Reconstructive Surgery?**

  Before you do any remodeling, you need a sense of what shape your house is in now and what shape your finances are in to pay for any improvements. You'll need to examine your house with an eye towards detail, repairs, maintenance, and future plans.

- **Part 2: Making Big Plans First**

  Remodeling without a plan is like traveling without a map: You'll probably get there eventually, but you'll spend way more time and money along the way than you'd thought you would. Plans, budgets, and realistic time frames will keep you on the main road and get the job done faster—and without too many stops at roadside burger joints!

- **Part 3: Quit Planning and Get to Work**

  Time to take off your homeowner's hat and put on a hard hat. This part will show you how to evaluate the skills you'll need to do different projects, the scope of the work itself, and when to hire a contractor.

- **Part 4: Get a Fresh Start: Interior Changes**

  The real reason you bought this book! Part 4 will show you, step-by-step, what it takes to build a knock-out kitchen or an at-home office tucked under the stairs. You can take these ideas and adapt your own versions or scale down if your needs are more modest.

- **Part 5: Street Appeal: Exterior Upgrades**

  The outside of your house needs attention, too, especially if you want it to stand up to all the weather it puts up with.

- **Part 6: And Baby Makes Three: Additions to Your Home**

  Adding a room is almost like building your house in miniature; you'll use many different skilled trades to do the job.

- **Part 7: Fantasy Time: Your Dream Projects**

  The fun, rewarding jobs that come after the main work is completed.

Extras

Some ideas need to stand out so they don't get missed, and others add interest to a subject. In the four types of boxes described below, I've highlighted information that provides easy problem solving, explains terminology, warns you of difficulties or dangers you may face, and offers bits of history and background on remodeling and remodelers.

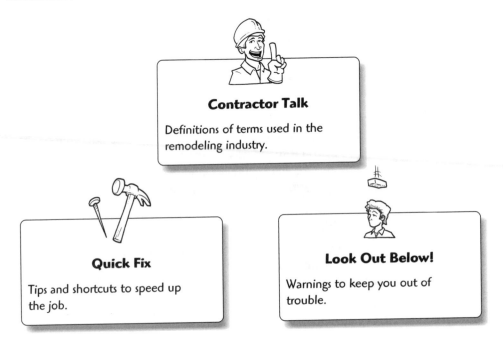

Contractor Talk

Definitions of terms used in the remodeling industry.

Quick Fix

Tips and shortcuts to speed up the job.

Look Out Below!

Warnings to keep you out of trouble.

Tales From the Scaffold

Stories based on my on-the-job experiences, and intriguing trivia of all kinds.

Acknowledgements

Books are collaborative efforts and mine is no exception. A number of friends, colleagues, and even complete strangers generously gave of their time and expertise in the writing of this manuscript.

I would like to thank Steve Appolloni of Appollini Designs and John Yost of Marble Street Studio for providing many of the color photographs, as well as Stickney, Murphy, and Romine Architects; Lorne McConachie, AIA; Luther Hintz, AIA; and Dan Thane of Thane Construction for various photos used throughout the book. Susan Guidry provided real estate figures and Michael and Karen Friend allowed me to shamelessly photograph and exploit their basement remodeling.

At Alpha Books, I would like to thank everyone who gave me the go-ahead as author and helped shape this into a finished book including Gary Krebs, Editorial Director, and Doris Cross, long-suffering Development Editor.

A special nod to Sam, our cairn terrier, who reminded me to turn off the computer from time to time and get out of the office—even if getting fed was his main motivation.

Special Thanks to the Technical Reviewer

Richard L. Feller's construction experience has ranged from road building in Oregon to restoring historic apartment buildings in Seattle. Through it all, he's juggled job specifications, subcontractors, and architects with an eye for details and a wry sense of humor. He has my thanks for reviewing this text.

I also want to thank Don Harper of Harper Electric; John Havekotte, also known as Hooper the House Doctor; and the Miller Paint Company for their technical expertise.

Trademarks

All terms mentioned in this book that are known to be or are suspected of being trademarks or service marks have been appropriately capitalized. Alpha Books and Macmillan General Reference cannot attest to the accuracy of this information. Use of a term in this book should not be regarded as affecting the validity of any trademark or service mark.

Part 1

Does Your Home Need a Makeover—or Reconstructive Surgery?

Beauty is in the eye of the beholder. You might see your cozy, Craftsman-period bungalow with its honey-colored, shellacked woodwork and hexagonal bathroom floor tile as a precious relic of another era. Your designer cousin might see a house just waiting to be torn apart and brought into the 21st century. You see antique brass lights; she sees antique wiring. What do you do?

Historically, we've never had safer, more comfortable, or better-constructed houses than the ones we're building now, but that shouldn't stop us from casting a critical eye on our surroundings. Older homes often need updates to bring them into line with the java-fueled, Internet-crazy lifestyles of the '90s. We expect more bathrooms, larger kitchens, and family rooms that our parents and grandparents didn't have in their houses. We want cable access, second phone lines for fax machines, and a dozen shower heads in the bathroom. New houses don't have complete bragging rights over old ones: They're often a little short in the storage department and lack finishing touches, such as wide baseboards and tile fireplaces.

Walk around your home. Do you need a new kitchen, or would opening up a wall and adding a few cabinets to your existing one do the trick? Would a new addition off the back give you the office space you need, or would you be better off finishing your existing basement, the one you're currently using as a big storage bin? The chapters in Part 1 will help you grapple with these questions as you get to know your home from top to bottom. You'll start looking at your remodeling ideas with a more critical eye. You'll learn just how your home is put together, how to identify essential repairs, and how to establish a remodeling budget. You'll also get closer to turning your remodeling dreams into reality.

Chapter 1

Your Home Is Your Castle—Keep It That Way!

In This Chapter

➤ Take care of your house, and it will take care of you

➤ Turn today's maintenance into tomorrow's dollars

➤ Remodeling projects that pay off—and those that don't

➤ Is this the right time for you to remodel?

The issue of home maintenance brings back childhood memories of parents cajoling us to clean our rooms or put away our toys. Warnings that our bicycles would rust if we left them out in the rain weren't taken too seriously because our parents normally brought them into the garage if we didn't. They paid for them, after all. We knew they were right, but there were never any real consequences. That's too bad; if we'd had a bike that rusted out, we'd probably be taking better care of our homes today.

It's easy to ignore a few missing roof shingles or a drafty window, but these small problems can lead to bigger ones. A little preventive maintenance now can save you money and time in the long run, and a well-maintained house is more comfortable to live in and more valuable if you decide to sell.

Maintenance is one thing, but what about remodeling? Where do you draw the line on additions and improvements to your home? This chapter will help you define the issues and decide on the approach that's best for you and your household—sometimes it's best to just leave your house alone and move. If you intend to stay put, it's time to look after your house a little more than you did your childhood bicycle and bring it in from the rain.

Keeping Your Rambler from Rambling

If your home could be kept hermetically sealed and stored in a huge, climate-controlled warehouse, it probably wouldn't need any maintenance. The container might need a dusting now and again, but your house would last forever. Of course, you'd be out in the cold and rain, but you'd never have to pick up a hammer or call a plumber. Your home is a home first and an investment second. For many people, it's the biggest investment they'll ever make, so it makes sense to protect it. You wouldn't knowingly allow someone to pilfer your bank account, would you? Ignoring maintenance and remodeling is even worse than watching your bike rust.

Resale aside, you have to consider these factors when maintaining and improving your home:

➤ Comfort and convenience

➤ Safety

➤ Building code requirements

Look Out Below!

A job change or family situation may force you to sell your home in a hurry. Under those circumstances, who has the time to catch up on maintenance and repairs that have been put off? A well-cared-for home will not only be easier to sell, it'll also bring a better price just when you'll probably need the cash most.

Comfort Zone

Fresh safety issuesair is great when and where you want it. Fresh air blowing through your leaky windows and doors during a record cold snap is another matter. Water in the shower is OK. Turning your floors into an obstacle course of pots, pans, and buckets to catch water dripping through the ceiling isn't OK. The inconvenience of walking around containers isn't the only problem; the major problem is the damage that things like leaks can cause to other parts of the house.

Houses don't ask for much, so when they do, we need to listen. It's to our benefit. A clogged furnace filter means the furnace has to work harder to do its job. Furnace filters are cheap; diminished furnace efficiency is not.

Safety Pays

A well-maintained house is a safe house for everyone in your household and for your guests. Consider:

➤ A light installed over an unlighted stairwell may run $100 to 150 in electrician fees. What would be the cost of hospital care for any injuries resulting from a fall down those stairs in the dark?

➤ Regular chimney cleanings can help prevent chimney fires. A chimney fire, if allowed to burn on its own, can take your entire house with it.

➤ Checking your hot water heater settings (making sure they're set no hotter than 120 degrees) can prevent the severe scalding that would occur if a child were to accidentally turn on the hot water full blast.

➤ In 1997, the chairman of the Consumer Products Safety Commission stated that home death by electrocution could be cut by up to one half if *GFCIs (ground fault circuit interrupters)* were installed in all homes.

➤ Outlets and light switches that are unusually warm or even hot to the touch suggest an unsafe wiring condition that could lead to a fire.

Quick Fix

A replacement washing machine hose costs around $10. An old one (anything that's been on longer than five years) can burst and leak, spewing out up to 500 gallons of water an hour. A simple examination of your hose for swollen areas or pinhole leaks can potentially save you thousands of dollars in damages. Better yet, install an extended life hose(about $30), which will stand up to water pressure a lot longer.

➤ A loose deck railing or improperly spaced balusters can result in serious injury from falls, especially for young children.

A little maintenance goes a long way when it comes to your comfort and safety, not to mention your financial well-being!

Play Now, Pay Later

Simple routine maintenance that any homeowner can do will prevent bigger repairs later. For instance, ignoring deteriorated or missing caulking and grout around bathtubs and showers is an invitation for water to get in behind tile or the tub surround and cause major damage to areas of your walls. Recoating the varnish on your front door once a year is easier, and less expensive, than having to completely refinish the door because you let it go too long. Routine maintenance pays, big time.

Contractor Talk

GFCI stands for *ground-fault circuit interrupter.* If it detects a short or irregularity in the circuit, it shuts off power to outlets almost instantaneously. GFCIs are required for outlets in bathrooms, kitchens, and outdoors.

Quick Fix

An outside metal railing in need of repainting will eventually start rusting, meaning more work and a larger repair for you.

Keeping Resale in Mind

Think about the house-hunting you did when you bought your current home. Which homes were most attractive to you? Probably not the ones with missing shingles, broken glass, and an interior that hadn't been painted since disco was hot. Houses like that appeal only to bargain-hunting renovators who feel lost if they're not remodeling something. You were probably attracted to a clean, well-kept house with a modern kitchen, a color scheme you could live with, and water that ran out of faucets without sputtering. Houses kept in this condition get top dollar when they're sold. To a weary buyer who wants to move right in and has trooped through dozens of marginal homes, such as house will look like the Holy Grail.

Big Repairs: In the Beginning

Big repairs evolve the way life does: Something invisible to start out with subdivides and grows until it's a wailing, demanding baby. Put off the repairs long enough, and eventually you'll have a rebellious, nose-ringed adolescent on your hands. Tune out the problem, and soon you'll be looking at the equivalent of a fading centenarian who's no longer able to function.

For an example, let's turn to the world of wildlife. Birds, termites, rodents, carpenter ants, and other life forms may also see your home as a great place to live. Sure, nature is a wonderful thing, as long as it stops at your doorstep. Termites can cause thousands and thousands of dollars worth of damage to the structure of a house if they're not zapped in their tracks by an exterminator. If you live in an area known for some kind of insect infestation, regular inspections will prevent big surprises later.

Ignorance of the law isn't considered an excuse for breaking it (somehow that seems a little extreme when it comes to something as incomprehensible as the tax code), and ignorance of your house's problems doesn't mean that you won't have to pay for them at some point. You may not know that you have a leaky roof, but it's your responsibility to poke around once in a while to be sure everything's OK. A little quality time with your home now will give you more time to enjoy it later.

The Mundaneness of Maintenance

No one ever said owning a home would be a thrill-a-minute experience; the thrill is buying it and looking forward to moving in and setting it up. The reality is that you have to take care of it. Once you accept home maintenance as a necessity, like dental checkups, you can make it easier on yourself:

➤ Schedule your monthly chores over a single block of time, do them all at once, and then treat yourself to something fun.

➤ Figure out what it would have cost to hire someone to do each job you do yourself, set that money aside, and use it towards a vacation later in the year.

➤ Pay your kids, as they become old enough, to do as many of the jobs as possible. Don't even think about expounding on the character-building virtues of the work, because it's clear you don't want to do it either. Just pay.

Nothing Lasts Forever

Sometimes, despite your best efforts and those of your well-paid children, you may still face some major repair or maintenance issues. For example, roof shingles can last only so long before you need to cover or replace them. Things eventually wear out. Keep this fact in mind, and you won't be shocked when you have to replace an expensive item such as your hot water heater when it just can't cut it anymore.

Some rules of thumb for maintenance/replacement cycles include the following:

➤ Exterior paint: 7 to 10 years

➤ Interior paint: up to 10 years, less for bathrooms and kitchens

➤ Wood floor finish: roughly 10 to 15 years

➤ Hot water heater: up to 15 years

➤ Furnace: 20 to 25 years

➤ Roof: 15 to 30 years for composition shingles, depending on the grade of shingle

Knowing when these big repair costs will come up gives you plenty of time to budget and prepare for them. Now that you know, you won't be caught by surprise!

People Will Paint

The life of exterior paint depends on several factors, such as the quality of the paint job and the paint used, weather exposure, gutter maintenance, and the moisture content of the siding. Typically, the western and southern sides of a house receive the most weather-related damage, so paint tends to fail there earlier.

Look Out Below!

If you have to remove bird droppings, remember that they are toxic, and you need to take precautions. Wear long rubber gloves and a respirator, both available at your local paint store. When you have removed the droppings, clean the area with a strong soap and bleach solution.

Quick Fix

You can sometimes avoid repainting the entire outside of your house by repainting only the truly weathered sides. Keep the other sides clean with a yearly wash and rinse—use a pressure washer or house washer that attaches to a garden hose—and put off the BIG paint job.

Interior paint doesn't have weather to deal with, but fading and the scrapes and blows of daily life do eventually add up. And after you've looked at the same Fawn Mist bedroom walls for a few years, you just get an itch to paint them whether they need it or not. Paint's main purpose in life (besides making money for paint manufacturers) is to protect the surfaces to which it's applied. If that were the only factor, interior paint would rarely have to be recoated, but personal tastes, visual appeal, and the need for change take precedence. From my observations, after about seven years or so, homeowners start itching for a change of color.

What's Your Dream Theme?

From a survival standpoint, most of our homes far exceed what we need: a roof and walls to keep the weather out, a source of heat, and maybe a Jacuzzi. Because we've evolved so far beyond basic survival, we can take another look at our dwellings and see how they can provide even greater comforts. This is where remodeling fantasies take root, but they may not grow into actual remodels if they can't survive a reality check: How much will the remodel cost, and will it be feasible in my neighborhood? A street full of one-story bungalows, for instance, probably will not support the resale value of a three-story Tudor conversion with a swimming pool and private helicopter pad.

Still, we need to consider our dream projects to see if they make any sense in light of other work we need to do on our homes. By understanding what we must do, such as replace a malfunctioning furnace, we can then decide to put off other, nonessential projects until a later time.

Supersize Your Floor Plan

Extra floor space is often a plus, especially in smaller homes with one or two bedrooms. According to some surveys, adding a third bedroom will bring more added value for the money invested than adding a fourth bedroom will. It's always easier, unless everything beyond the foundation of your house is marshland, to go for a ground-floor addition. Even an inexperienced homeowner can do a fair amount of this work in conjunction with a contractor (see Chapter 6, "Fixing Your House Without Breaking the Bank").

Rooms with Views

Oddly enough, some older homes were not necessarily built to take advantage of killer views. Today, views are a major consideration. There are all kinds of ways to open up your home to those views you're dying to see: building dormers, opening up the attic, or even adding a second story. These renovations are major investments, so think about whether you'll stay in your home long enough to recoup your costs.

Roman Bath Without the Romans

We're Americans, and we love our bathrooms, an affection not always understood in other parts of the world. Everyone wants more bathrooms; some higher-end homes have more of them than bedrooms!

Bathroom remodels require many different skilled workers: plumbers, carpenters, tile layers, wallpaper hangers, and cabinetmakers. Adding a full or partial bathroom (see Chapter 16, "Bathrooms with Bragging Rights") to a one-bath house is usually a plus when it comes to resale, though some surveys show that it's better to have one updated, tastefully done bathroom than two mediocre ones.

Fast-Food Kitchen, Gourmet Tastes

The kitchen is usually the most expensive single room in the house to remodel (see Chapter 15, "Cooking Up a Storm: Reworking Your Kitchen"). Some residential ones put commercial restaurant kitchens to shame. How far can it go? How far do you *want* it to? Gold sink fixtures, marble counter tops, cherry wood cabinets, and maple floors can all be yours for the right price.

It's easy to get carried away with a kitchen remodel, so remember what it's for: a place to prepare, and probably eat, food. The more of an art piece you turn it into, the more upset you'll be when you see the first scratch on the floor or nick in a cabinet. You can have a very suitable, appealing kitchen without spending the kids' college funds.

Dreams Guide; Budgets Decide

Unless you have an inexhaustible trust fund backing you up, you'll have to work with a remodeling budget (see Chapter 6, "Fixing Your House Without Breaking the Bank"). Here's where you enter the tangled world of wants, desires, credit, loans, resale value, and delayed gratification. Don't throw up your hands: You can get through this with grace and aplomb and end up with results you can be proud of. Don't forget to affix your name and the date to the bottom corner of a wall in any room you worked on.

Look Out Below!

Before you decide on any second-story-view additions, find out whether your neighbors have any remodeling plans, especially if there's a vacant lot between you and the view. You could spend a great deal of money on a view addition and end up looking at your neighbor's second story.

First Things First

Comfort jobs are the fun ones: A new kitchen that finally has some real counter space or a playroom for the kids with soundproof walls. These jobs are the ones we want to do, even though we can live without them. They're the ones that stretch budgets and break hearts (see Chapter 6, "Fixing Your House Without Breaking the Bank"), so you have to think them through, and do them only after you've dealt with the big stuff.

Tales from the Scaffold

I once had a client who owned a fabulous house that had some natural springs running under the property. He never had the foundation checked, because he couldn't see any apparent problems. After he completed a very expensive dream kitchen, some of the cabinet molding separated from the ceiling. He had it repaired; it separated again. Instead of having an engineer look at the foundation under the kitchen, he just kept half-following the English proverb, "Hope for the best, but prepare for the worst." As far as I know, the shifting is still going on.

As a rule of thumb, you should approach your remodeling in this order:

➤ Emergency jobs first

➤ Core jobs second

➤ Comfort jobs third

Emergency jobs include dangerous structural problems, such as an unstable front porch. They also include furnaces that don't combust properly, thereby allowing carbon monoxide into the house; nonfunctioning water heaters; and collapsing chimneys. If you have a dead tree in your yard dropping large branches at will, you can include that, too.

Core jobs, such as replacing your electrical service or installing a new roof, are the not-so-fun tasks that have to be done before other work can even be contemplated. A new kitchen just won't work if you've still got the original four-circuit, wooden fuse box. These are not projects you can always warm up to—it's tough to get the same kick out of a new $5,000 roof as you do from your new media center with the giant-screen TV. But you won't enjoy watching TV from your new leather couch if rainwater is dripping all over it because you didn't replace the roof.

Is It Worth It?

Worth is a multifaceted word. There's market-place worth: Will all of your expense and improvements pay off when you sell your house? Will you break even or make a profit? There's also subjective worth: Will these improvements make your life more comfortable? Will they be worth the unsettling and time-consuming process you'd have to go through?

The world of statistics can be of some help in determining marketplace worth, but only if you understand how the statistics were gathered. Every year, surveys are done to determine the financial return from various remodeling projects. Because they can all use different criteria, direct comparisons can be difficult, but they will give you an idea of which projects will bring the highest return.

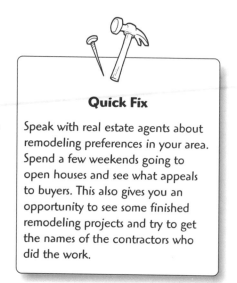

Quick Fix

Speak with real estate agents about remodeling preferences in your area. Spend a few weekends going to open houses and see what appeals to buyers. This also gives you an opportunity to see some finished remodeling projects and try to get the names of the contractors who did the work.

One of the most thorough surveys is done by *Remodeling Magazine* (202-736-3444; One Thomas Circle, NW, Suite 600, Washington, DC 20005). Their 1997–98 Cost vs. Value Report, gathered by Bruce Snider and Cary Haney, covers 12 popular home improvement projects in 60 cities nationwide. Cost estimates for each city were gathered from construction cost-estimating guides and software (Craftsman Books, HomeTech Information Systems, and R.S. Means). Real estate agents in those same cities then estimated how much these projects would add to the price of a mid-priced house in an established neighborhood, assuming the house was sold within one year of completing the work. Even if you're not going to sell that soon, the survey is a good gauge of the return on your investment.

Results of the 1997–98 Remodeling Magazine Cost vs. Value Report

Project	Return
Minor kitchen remodel	102 percent
Additional bathroom	92 percent
Major kitchen remodel	90 percent
Second-story addition	87 percent
Master bedroom suite	87 percent
Attic bedroom	86 percent
Family room addition	86 percent
Bathroom remodel	77 percent

Results of the 1997–98 *Remodeling Magazine* Cost vs. Value Report (cont.)

Project	Return
Deck addition	73 percent
Siding replacement	71 percent
Home office	69 percent
Window replacement	68 percent

There's another factor to consider when you calculate your return: Will a particular remodeling project hasten the sale of your home? Skylights, for example, don't offer much of a return given their cost, but they may brighten up an otherwise dark interior, thus speeding up the sale of your house. If time is of the essence, or if you've already moved and are committed to another mortgage, your skylights are suddenly a great investment.

We're not quite done yet. One more factor is the general economy. If the economy is contracting and money is tight, the resale prices of homes may drop in many markets. Depending on where you live, your state-of-the-art, $40,000 kitchen may not pay for itself at all. In a buyer's market, you may have to overdo your remodeling just to sell your house.

Keep these guidelines in mind when you're figuring the return on your remodeling projects:

➤ The cost-to-resale benefits are more important if you plan on moving in a few years; you'll want to concentrate on projects that give you the highest return of capital.

➤ The longer you stay in your home, the greater your return from remodeling projects.

➤ Kitchen and bathroom remodels bring the most return, but hold your spending to no more than 10 percent of your home's value when remodeling either one of these rooms.

➤ Unless you're planning on staying in your current home for years and years, be sure your projects don't overimprove for your area.

➤ Regional preferences matter. In areas with cold winters, for example, a garage is a real plus, but a swimming pool, with its limited use and ongoing maintenance, could be seen as a liability.

➤ Keep the value of your improved property within the 15 to 20 percent range of your neighbors; buyers who can afford more than that will probably buy in a more expensive area.

➤ If you're thinking of resale, radical style is out; stick with *neutral* colors and design.

➤ Quality design, materials, and construction will always win out over amateur work.

➤ Unless you're doing work you have to do to sell your home and get your cash out of it, remodeling should be done with your future comfort in mind.

Some improvements don't bring much of a financial return simply because a buyer expects certain features on a house. According to the *Better Homes and Gardens* Real Estate Service, a new furnace or increased house insulation can return only a fraction of their costs because a buyer expects these things to be there. A fireplace, on the other hand, can return 100 percent because it's a very desirable feature to many prospective buyers.

Look Out Below!

Your home is a nonliquid asset; that is, it's not easily converted to cash. In uncertain economic times, you don't want so much money tied up in your house that you don't have at least a six-month supply of cash readily available for living expenses. Even in good times, you don't want to be house-rich and cash-poor.

Middle Ground

By now, you're wondering if you should even consider picking up a hammer or paint roller at all! It's not that bad. Just because a dollar spent remodeling doesn't yield a dollar back at resale—remember, it's not that easy to determine such a yield—doesn't mean you need to live with the lime green tile in your bathroom or the orange and black shag carpet in your den. Life's often a compromise, so strike one with your home.

If you're not sure how long you'll be living in your house, but are pretty sure it won't be more than five years, scale back your remodeling dreams. Do a minor facelift in the kitchen, paint the downstairs, and refinish the floors. Instead of landscaping the yard to look like the Hanging Gardens of Babylon, install a small deck, some outdoor lighting, and some perennials.

Where you draw the line will depend upon these factors:

➤ Your financial limits

➤ Your desired return on investment

➤ How long you expect to be living in your home

➤ The personal benefits of the improvements

Contractor Talk

In real estate parlance, *neutral* means inoffensive. Color-wise, it usually means some shade of white or beige. Design-wise, it means no fake wooden paneling.

13

Tales from the Scaffold

I once had clients whose interior designer prompted them to install hardwood floors in their 1930s kitchen. The designer insisted that they not be installed over the existing floors because the kitchen floors would be higher than those in the dining room, requiring a slight threshold between them to serve as a transition. Mind you, no one but the designer would have been bothered by this (and she wasn't living there), but it added at least 50 percent to the cost of the installation. Vinyl anyone?

After you've mulled over all of these factors, remodel accordingly. Whatever you do, stick with your decision. The worst thing you can do is stop short of doing your remodel just the way you want it, and be dissatisfied enough to decide to redo it afterward. If the cost of your project is going to keep you strapped financially, then think about putting it off or even scrapping it entirely before you get started. The prospect of soaking in a marble bathtub complete with whirlpool jets is hardly worth it if you spend your soaking time fretting about how you're going to pay off your bank loan. Take yourself to a day spa instead—it's cheaper, and someone else will clean up after you!

Moving Away from Your Problems

Sometimes the simplest remodel of all is to move to a different house. Skip the dust, noise, fast-food meals, and agonizing over tile patterns and find a place more to your liking—preferably one that doesn't need any remodeling! That house may not exist, but you could come close, especially with a newer home.

The factors you should weigh in making the decision to move versus remodel include:

➤ The cost of moving versus the cost and return on investment of remodeling

➤ Recovering the cost of moving

➤ The desire to change neighborhoods

➤ Appreciation factors of both houses

Architect Greg Gibson notes in his book, *Remodel*, that if you can't recover at least 75 percent of your remodeling costs, you should consider moving to a house that would approximate yours after remodeling. There's more to moving than simply dollars and cents, but sometimes it's the only thing that makes sense. Use this worksheet to weigh the financial costs of moving versus remodeling:

1. Current value of your home:_____
2. Remodeling costs, including financing:_____
3. Estimated value after remodeling:_____

Some remodeled houses go well beyond recovering their remodeling costs. This is especially true with "fixer-upper" houses which can dramatically increase in value after major remodeling jobs. Now, compare your post-remodeling home value with the costs of moving and selling your house as-is.

Costs to move and purchase another house:

1. Real estate selling commissions:_____
2. Cost of new house:_____
3. Total loan costs (origination fees, appraisals, etc.):_____
4. Moving costs:_____
5. Added commuting costs, if applicable:_____

As you can see, these costs really add up! You'll have to calculate whether your money is better spent increasing the value of your current house or moving. Keep in mind that your remodeled house may not appreciate in value as much as a house in a different neighborhood or as much as a newer house.

You can estimate the financial costs easily enough. But what about the emotional costs? Moving will break most of your day-to-day ties with your neighbors and nearby friends. This break can be especially difficult for your children. On the other hand, if your neighbors include heavy metal rockers who practice nightly in their garage, you may be more than ready to move on. Scrutinize all of these factors before you make any decisions.

Quick Fix

Be sure to look at your career path before you go too far with the moving versus remodeling debate. If you see an income increase or relocation due to work coming within a few years, it may be better to hold off on any decision until that time. You don't want to move any more often than you have to!

The Least You Need to Know

➤ Regular, timely maintenance is the best and easiest investment you can make in your home.

➤ Small maintenance issues can quickly become big, expensive problems if left unattended.

➤ Critical repair work should always be done before any other remodeling jobs.

➤ You must figure the true financial and emotional cost of any remodeling before you start the work.

➤ If your current house isn't worth remodeling for your purpose, consider moving.

Chapter 2

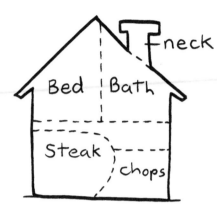

The Anatomy of Your Home

In This Chapter

➤ Getting to really know your house, warts and all

➤ Taking note of defects

➤ Reconsidering your wiring, plumbing, and heating

➤ Going on a room-by-room discovery tour

➤ Putting it all together

Some homeowners have very little understanding of how their houses work, let alone how they're put together. They'll call an electrician when a fuse blows or a circuit breaker trips instead of investigating the problem. If the gutter is overflowing, they'll call a roofer. I've had these homeowners as clients. They were all well educated in their respective fields, but they were uninformed when it came to their houses.

The best way to get better acquainted with your house is to tour it as though you were a house inspector, poking around from bottom to top and taking notes as you go. If you read Chapter 1, "Your Home Is Your Castle—Keep It That Way!," you were reminded of the important maintenance and repair jobs that come along with home ownership. You mused over remodeling projects and started thinking about costs. In this chapter, you'll gather more information about your house to help you with repair and remodeling decisions.

Remember as you walk through your house that no house is perfect. Even people who have homes custom-built end up wishing they had made some different decisions about certain features. Your goal is to see your house for its possibilities (at least the ones that fit your budget) and decide where to follow through.

Get Your Hiking Boots: A Walk Through Your House

Weekends are a great time for touring your house. Warm, sunny days will make your chore that much easier. Put on your grubby clothes, a pair of comfortable shoes, and grab a notebook and pen, or if you prefer gabbing, take along a small tape recorder.

You'll need a few small tools: a flashlight, a pocketknife, and measuring tape.

➤ A flashlight will allow you to peer into those corners and crevices you can't walk or crawl into.

➤ Your trusty pocketknife is good for poking and probing any suspicious-looking piece of wood that may be rotted or damaged by moisture or termites.

➤ Use your measuring tape to record the approximate dimensions of each area of your house. These measurements will be useful later if you plan on painting or carpeting, for instance, and you want to figure the amount of material you'll need.

Quick Fix

If you have a friend or relative with more homeowner or remodeling experience than you have, by all means invite him or her along to help you inspect. Bribery always helps, so offer dinner at a good restaurant. Especially helpful are individuals who have gone through extensive remodeling and worked with contractors. Find someone whose house is about the same age as yours.

Be sure to measure the height of unfinished basement and attic spaces you're thinking of converting into living space (minimum height—explained later—is required for these conversions).

No Need to Be an Expert

There are people who inspect homes for a living. Some of them are quite good; others are a few appliances short of a kitchen. This was true of our house inspector (and he was inspecting a new house!), who was wrong on two out of three items in his report. You may not know what everything you're looking at is, but you'll know if something doesn't seem right and will at least have some good questions to discuss with a contractor or architect.

An easy way to keep track of your findings is to set up a checklist in your notebook. Don't worry if you have a lot of checks; many of them will be minor concerns.

Sample Checklist

Item	Good	Acceptable	Forget It	Comments
Furnace	XX			Two years old
Plumbing			XX	Replace
Windows		XX		OK

Information Is Power

Once you're armed with your checklist, you can start researching problems you've identified. Ask friends if they've ever run into similar situations and discuss alternate solutions. You may have your heart set on adding some dormers to your upstairs, but then you discover during your house tour that your wiring needs to be replaced first. That may blow your budget, but it's better to find out about it and fix it before you start tearing holes in your house.

Your Targets: Leaks, Squeaks, and More

Besides revealing the obvious problems, like ceiling lights that flicker your name in Morse code every time you hit the switch, your inspection tour will give you an overall impression of your house's condition. You've probably been aware of some of these typical annoyances, and just learned to live with them. Now it's time to record them on your checklist.

As you walk through your house, do you notice:

➤ Squeaks in the floors?

➤ Sticking doors?

➤ Drafts?

➤ Mold or mildew?

➤ Tight quarters?

➤ Wall cracks?

➤ Not enough outlets or lights?

Older homes mean more checks on your checklist. Don't worry; we'll tackle each project one at a time!

Creaky Enough for a Haunted House

Floors creak and squeak for several reasons, but the main one is that one piece of wood is not secured tightly to another and is therefore rubbing against it. This isn't a structural problem, but it can be irritating.

Note possible sources of squeaks in this typical wood floor system:

1. *Between joist and underlayment.*

2. *Between hardwood and underlayment.*

3. *Between hardwood floor boards.*

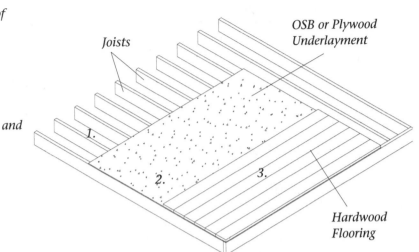

Some wood floor noises have low-tech solutions, such as sprinkling the wood with talcum powder or powdered graphite. Others need more involved repairs, such as shimming the floor boards or underlayment (see Appendix G, "Repairs"). For right now, record the locations of the squeaks so you can fix them once and for all.

Sticking Doors

Try all your doors during your tour, even closet doors. A sticking door can be a minor problem, such as a bit of swelling, or it can be indicative of the bigger problem of the house settling.

Is It Windy in Here?

Even when the thermostat reads 70 degrees, you will feel cold if you're sitting near a draft. Multiply this feeling by a house full of drafty windows and doors, and you can be freezing—no matter what the thermostat says. To compensate, you inch the temperature up a few degrees, and when you see the heating bills, you wonder if you'll ever be able to save for retirement.

If you haven't spent a winter in your home yet (and you're doing this survey in the summer), you won't know where your drafts are, but you can make some educated guesses. Look for the following:

➤ Windows and doors that don't seal or close tightly

➤ The presence or absence of vinyl, rubber, or metal weather-stripping around the doors and windows

➤ Insulation in the attic

➤ In an older house, whether the windows are original to the house or have been replaced

Short of wrapping the whole place in a huge plastic bag, what can you do? Appendix G points out weather-stripping options any homeowner can handle.

Use Your Nose: Rot and Mildew

Rot favors damp, preferably dark, resting places, as did Dracula, which may account for his creepy behavior.

While you're snooping around, you may have to look into some disagreeable places, such as your crawl space. Drainage problems, lack of ventilation, and wood in contact with soil are the main culprits in promoting rot and decay in crawl spaces. Also look for tell-tale green mildew stains across bathroom ceilings; they're a sure sign of ventilation problems.

Look for these signs of rot in crawl spaces or with other wood structures:

➤ Soft, spongy wood you can easily stick a knife into

➤ Wood with a white, powdery surface

➤ A crumbling, checked pattern on the surface of the wood

Keeping Track of Cracks

Any wall can develop a crack. They're not dangerous, but they may indicate that the house is settling or pressing down and compacting the soil under the foundation, which may have to be looked at.

Most interior walls are covered with either plaster or plasterboard (also referred to as drywall or Sheetrock). Applying plaster is a big job that requires skilled journeymen plasterers. It produces a wonderful wall, but it costs at least twice as much as the installation of plasterboard (see Chapter 23, "The Big Leagues: Adding a Room").

Nothing a Gallon of Paint Won't Fix

Painting can be a contagious process. I once painted our daughter's room, which, along with the rest of the house, had been painted seven years earlier. It looked great when I was through, all bright and clean, the usual marks and scrapes of life covered up. Then I looked at the hallway, the dining room, the office—you get the picture. I repainted everything. Fortunately, we moved before I could be seized by the impulse again.

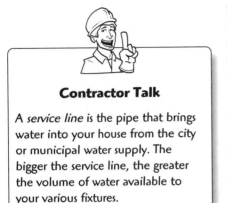

Contractor Talk

A *service line* is the pipe that brings water into your house from the city or municipal water supply. The bigger the service line, the greater the volume of water available to your various fixtures.

Note the condition of your paint. Is it faded? Does it have black marks on it from briefcases or gym bags rubbing against it? Are you tired of the color? These are all legitimate reasons to consider doing the least expensive house remodeling of all: A simple repaint.

Feeling Cramped?

As you go on your tour, get a feel for traffic flow. Is everything going OK until a wall or a narrow doorway gets in your way? Maybe you've run into your own in-house gridlock. Think back to your last dinner party. Did you run into bottlenecks trying to get the food served because everyone was squeezed into the kitchen between the counters and the refrigerator?

The expensive solution is to build an addition onto your kitchen. The cheaper and easier way (if it's feasible) would be to remove a wall and combine the kitchen with an adjoining room.

Behind the Scenes: Furnaces, Plumbing, Wiring

Compared with our ancestors, we have it easy. Heating systems are more efficient than ever. Plumbing is safer (lead pipes were still being used into the 1920s), and modern wiring allows more power into our individual homes than was once available to the entire state of Wyoming. We take these invisible helpers entirely for granted until something goes wrong, like a furnace dies on Christmas Eve.

You should be aware of your house's mechanical systems: heat, plumbing, and electrical. A room that stays too cool in the winter may have a problem with a furnace duct or steam pipe. An old electrical system may have to be updated. Plumbing upgrades can be a major expense. The more information you have, the better your remodeling decision-making will be.

Pipes and Potability

Plumbing is simple in principle: Clean water comes in; waste water goes out. As long as the plumbing is running and isn't leaking, you're usually happy with it. You can't exactly look inside your walls and examine your pipes and drain lines, but you can look for clues regarding their health.

Plumbing red flags you should watch for include:

➤ Low water pressure, which may indicate clogged pipes, clogged aerators, or an undersized *service line*

➤ Obvious leaks and drips

➤ Slow-draining sinks and tubs

Keeping the Home Fires Burning

We never think about our furnaces in the summer, and that's too bad, because that's the perfect time to get them inspected and serviced for the coming winter. Furnace technicians are easier to schedule in July than during December snow storms. Regardless of the type of heat you have, you'll need some degree of maintenance (see Chapter 4, "Paintbrush or Work Crews? Fixing the Immediate Stuff" and Chapter 14, "Clear the Air: Heat and Air Conditioning").

You need to be aware of these heating system issues:

Look Out Below!

Asbestos is a nonflammable, fibrous mineral material previously used in the building industry to insulate hot water pipes and furnace ducts. Due to safety and health considerations, it is no longer in use for these purposes, and must be removed according to legal abatement regulations.

➤ Uneven heating throughout your home

➤ Upgrading old (non-programmable) thermostats

➤ Filters needing regular replacement

➤ Old systems that may have asbestos-wrapped ducts or pipes

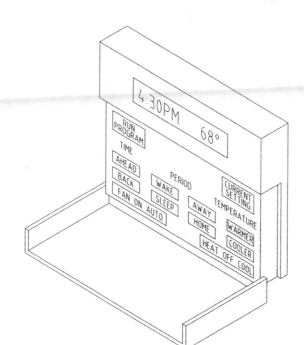

A modern thermostat with multiple settings.

Old thermostats had just one setting and had to be manually adjusted to increase or lower the temperature beyond pre-adjusted settings. You can now buy slick, digital thermostats with multiple settings to turn the heat on and off according to pre-selected times. Is your thermostat a candidate for replacement?

Power Shortage: Enough Outlets and Lights?

When electrical wiring was first introduced to residential housing in the late 19th century, it was a big deal to have one light and one outlet in every room. Current code, to put it simply, calls for one outlet within six feet of wherever you can stand against a wall. Doors, closets, and fireplaces are considered breaks in the wall and not part of the 6-foot rule. Ground fault interrupter outlets or circuits (GFIs) are required in bathrooms, kitchens, and outdoors. Overhead lights are required in all living spaces. How does your home stack up?

Sometimes new electrical service is installed in a home along with some new circuits, but some old wiring (pre-1965, when modern, grounded cable was introduced) may remain. Old wiring doesn't necessarily have to be replaced, but you should note it on your list anyway. You're still fact gathering, not planning a new electrical service.

Your service will be either an old fuse box, a modern panel or circuit-breaker box, or possibly a combination of the two. The combination would consist of the original fuse box and perhaps a smaller sub-panel box added later.

Tales from the Scaffold

What was quaint in 1900 is a nuisance today. Most homes have had some upgrading over the years (some of it done by a past owner's uncle Fred who thought he knew something about wiring), but many older homes still lack sufficient outlets and lights for our gadget-filled lifestyles.

Old systems consist of fuse boxes and either knob-and-tube wiring or BX cable (see Chapter 12, "Refusing Fuses"). Although there's nothing inherently dangerous in a fuse-based electrical system, there is danger in frayed and brittle wiring, particularly where it's tied into an outlet or light.

The biggest dangers to electrical systems old and new are improperly done modifications by homeowners and contractors. Adding or extending circuits must be done in

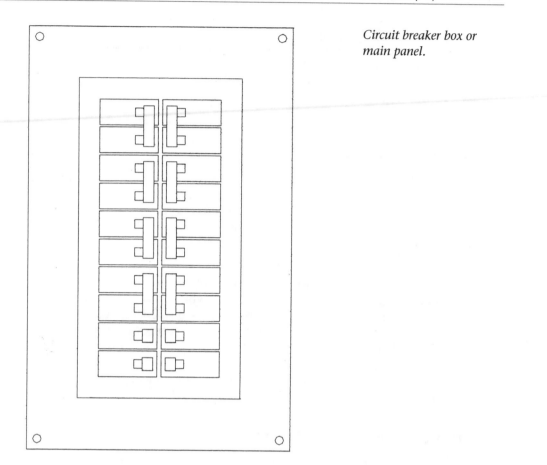

Circuit breaker box or main panel.

accordance with standard National Electrical Code rules and guidelines. Obviously, you can't tell from a surface inspection what has been done behind the scenes, or the walls in this case, but at some point, you can map out your wiring system and get a better idea as to how the circuits are set up.

Setting up a wiring map of your house is simple, with a little help from your friends:

1. Station at least one person in every room and hallway in your home.
2. Turn on all the lights and appliances in the house; plug a lamp or radio into every outlet and turn them on as well.
3. Turn one circuit breaker off, or unscrew one fuse, at a time; as the power is shut off to different rooms, have your friends shout out which rooms are affected.
4. Designate someone to record the information and post this sheet on your panel or fuse box.
5. Serve pizza.

Sample Circuit Map

Fuse or Circuit Breaker	Controls
#1	Clothes dryer
#2	Stove
#3	Kitchen outlets
#4	Furnace

In large, old houses, mapping the circuits can be interesting, if not bewildering, as you discover that your hallway light is hooked up to the circuit for your garage door opener. In the case of our last house, some clever homeowner connected the washing machine to the basement light circuit. Maybe it was an omen that the washing machine would die three months after we moved in.

The size of your electrical service (the amperage or amps) will determine how many toys and contraptions you can comfortably run and have power to spare. Some old fuse systems were as low as 30 amps, which is what it takes to run a modern clothes dryer. Modern homes should have at least a 150-amp service, but 200 is better. If you're considering installing a new service, look at it this way: It requires no more labor to install a 200-amp service than it does to install a 150-amp one. The difference in cost for the equipment is, at that point, negligible, so don't try cutting any costs here. For more information on how much load individual circuits can carry, see Chapter 12, "Refusing Fuses."

A Room-by-Room Tour

Now that you're an expert on house construction, you can begin your tour in earnest! Don't worry; the more you familiarize yourself with your home, the clearer these concepts will become.

Quick Fix

In crawl spaces, it's especially critical to check for wood damage, the presence of vents in the walls, and any exposed dirt, which should have plastic laid over it.

Bottoms Up: Basements and Crawl Spaces

Basements act as a great collection box for holiday decorations, old bicycles, and everything you didn't unpack from the last move. They're also a convenient space to put the furnace and its ducting, the electrical panel, the main water shut-off, pipes, wiring, and the hot water heater.

Based on what you've learned, you'll want to do the following on your tour of your unfinished basement:

➤ Check for dampness, puddles, or water seeping in around the foundation.

➤ Look at the installation date on your furnace. Has it been converted from oil to gas? Is there any asbestos present? Check the age of the water heater as well.

➤ Find your main water shut-off and test it by trying to close it; if it doesn't close all the way, or if it sticks, it will have to be freed with penetrating lubricant.

➤ Is your wiring old knob-and-tube or modern cable? Are both types present (they will be running through holes in the overhead floor joists)?

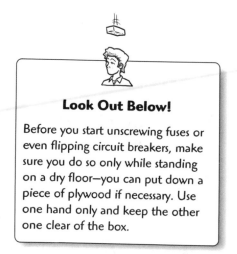

Look Out Below!

Before you start unscrewing fuses or even flipping circuit breakers, make sure you do so only while standing on a dry floor—you can put down a piece of plywood if necessary. Use one hand only and keep the other one clear of the box.

➤ Poke and probe any wood resting on the foundation with your pocketknife; you're looking for soft or weak pockets that may indicate rot or insect damage.

If you have a finished basement, you can't check the overhead wires or pipes, but you can check for dampness and any leaks around doors and windows.

Consider Your Kitchen

Modern kitchens have plenty of cabinet space, newer appliances (including garbage disposers and built-in microwave ovens), and up-to-code wiring. Check your outlets; they should all be GFIs (ground-fault interrupters). Is there enough counter lighting to do your cooking chores? Are there enough counters, for that matter? How's the water pressure?

The kitchen is a main gathering place in most homes; everyone squeezes in. Could you use some more room or a different traffic pattern? Mark it on your list.

A Bathroom Down the Hall

Bathrooms are the second most frequently remodeled rooms in the house after kitchens. Some of the same issues hold true for bathrooms as kitchens. Does yours have a GFI outlet? Good water pressure?

Look at the walls and floor. Is the paint stained or just plain in need of a recoat? Mildew on the ceiling or walls would suggest you have ventilation problems, which can be resolved with either an operable window or a good exhaust fan. Take a peek at the base of your toilet. Any presence of water can indicate that the toilet may need a new wax seal. Is your bathroom warm enough in the winter? Many older ones aren't and are good candidates for small in-wall heaters (see Chapter 14, "Clear the Air: Heat and Air Conditioning").

Common Rooms: Living, Dining, and Family

In the common rooms, you're looking for the availability of lights and outlets and the condition of the walls, paint, floors, and windows. Is the carpet worn? Do the wood floors need refinishing? Are you getting tired of looking at the tangerine-colored paint?

Per Chance to Sleep: Bedrooms

Look at these rooms just as you did the previous three. Closet space is always a consideration in bedrooms. Do you need more, or do you need to organize your existing closet with additional shelves and storage? Is it feasible to combine two bedrooms into one master suite? Mark down the condition of the rooms, and add some side comments for possible future changes.

Attics and Third Floors

Unfinished attics and third floors offer many opportunities to expand and add usable finished living space. Remember, you need a minimum of $7^1/_2$ feet of ceiling height over 50 percent of the floor space in order to convert an attic to a living area. Look at your attic from the outside of your house as well to get some idea of possible views if you decide to open the space up.

Some older homes have finished third floors; view them as any other bedroom during your tour. Look for available lighting and outlets and evaluate the condition of the walls, floor, and windows.

Garages: More Than Car Storage

Garages also offer opportunities for expanded use. Some people turn their attached garages into finished office spaces or playrooms. You can pull this off in a mild climate, but I wouldn't recommend it if you live through Minnesota winters and drive a car that will never forgive you for leaving it out in the snow.

Look into the electrical situation: Is there adequate lighting? A GFI outlet? Does the garage need shelves or cabinets for neater storage? Now that you're about to become an ace remodeler, is there space in your garage for a workshop?

The Cool-Down After the Walk-Through

You've seen it all now, from the spiders and dirt in the crawl space to the dust in the attic. Maybe you have writer's cramp and are a bit overwhelmed by all your notes. Trust me, you'll be glad you have all of this information later when you decide to start your remodeling projects.

Don't Call the Builder Just Yet

You still have some more work to do in the chapters ahead before you start interviewing general contractors. You may have some big repairs to attend to first (see Chapter 4, "Paintbrush or Work Crews? Fixing the Immediate Stuff") before you start any of your dream projects. You'll have to establish a budget (see Chapter 6, "Fixing Your House Without Breaking the Bank") and draw up some plans (see Chapter 7, "Prepare First; Remodel Later"). Then there's always the question, is it worth it to you to remodel at all?

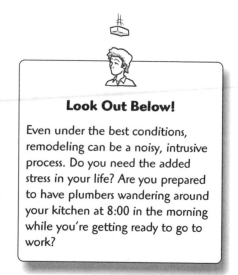

Look Out Below!

Even under the best conditions, remodeling can be a noisy, intrusive process. Do you need the added stress in your life? Are you prepared to have plumbers wandering around your kitchen at 8:00 in the morning while you're getting ready to go to work?

Learning to Live with It

Part of our birthright as Americans is never to be satisfied with anything we choose not to be satisfied with, even if, by many standards, it's a pretty good deal. When it comes to our homes, we constantly fuss and change things and often move on when we're through, only to start the process all over again.

Before you remodel anything, ask yourself:

➤ Can the money be better spent elsewhere? Do I really want to take on this additional debt?

➤ Will the results justify the process, including having part of my house torn up while the work is being done?

➤ Do I have any alternatives to these projects?

The more thought you give to these questions, the better decisions you'll make.

The Least You Need to Know

➤ A thorough inspection of your house is a prerequisite to any major remodeling project.

➤ Information gathered during your inspection will guide any remodeling decisions.

➤ The older your house, the more likely you'll have to consider upgrading major systems such as plumbing and wiring.

➤ After you factor in all the costs and time involved, choosing not to remodel can sometimes be the best decision.

Chapter 3

Judging a House by Its Cover

It's easy to ignore the outside of your house, unless the color it's painted is so garish that your neighbors are trying to get an ordinance passed to prohibit its use. But it is the first thing we see every time we hit the driveway and the first thing a prospective buyer sees, so it's important that it look its best.

Some interior problems, such as leaks, infestation by insects and rodents, and poor fireplace draft, start outside, and the roof, siding, and windows are your main protection from the elements. Both of these points are good reasons to keep the outside of your house in top repair. Like mail carriers, house exteriors are exposed to rain, sleet, snow, wind, and extreme heat. They need to be looked after and tended. This chapter will start you off by showing you how to find and identify conditions that need attention, from your roof to the foundation.

Before you embark on any big remodeling projects, it pays (trust me) to address the major exterior features: The roof, chimney, foundation, and everything else that makes up the outside of your house. As fun as it might be to build a handball court in your basement, replacing a leaky roof on its last shingles gets priority. The same goes for

Look Out Below!

In a wet climate, yard drainage isn't something to be taken lightly. You don't want water accumulating against your foundation and seeping through. This situation can cause your house to settle, which can require expensive repairs to correct.

repairing a chimney that's beginning to look like the Leaning Tower of Pisa, a foundation in need of drains, and siding that has more mold on it than paint.

As a homeowner, you can do much of this exterior work yourself or contract out the really messy jobs, such as replacing the roof. Approach the outside of your home the same way you did the interior, with an inquisitive eye and a notebook in hand, ready to record your observations.

A Walk Around the Homestead

During your outside tour, you won't have to be mucking around any dark crawl spaces or cramped attics. Your task will be essentially the same as it was for the interior: To observe and record the conditions of your house and, in this case, the yard and garage.

Why look at the yard? You study the yard because:

➤ You may have trees in need of trimming, or even removal if they block views or sunlight.

➤ Some crawling vine-type plants may be growing under the siding and into the house.

➤ Some plants may be too close to your house, facilitating the growth of mildew behind them.

➤ Tree roots can be pushing up against your sidewalks.

You should observe conditions on both a dry day and a wet, rainy one. On a rainy day, you can check the gutters, downspouts, and drainage system. A series of wet days may tell you that water is collecting in soggy spots in your yard instead of draining away as it should.

To keep track of your observations and notes as you go along, set up your notebook the same way you did for your interior tour.

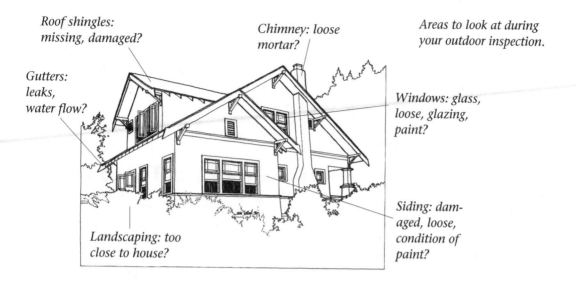

Roof shingles: missing, damaged?

Chimney: loose mortar?

Areas to look at during your outdoor inspection.

Gutters: leaks, water flow?

Windows: glass, loose, glazing, paint?

Landscaping: too close to house?

Siding: damaged, loose, condition of paint?

Sample Notebook Entries

Item	Condition	Comments
Roof	Fair	Composition shingles
Siding	Good	Cedar, three loose pieces, south side
Paint	Poor	Needs extensive stripping and repainting
Porch	Fair	Repair stairs
Rear deck	Very poor	Replace

The Lay of the Land

You don't have to be a professional surveyor or landscaper to know whether your home is pushing the boundaries with the next door neighbors' or being crowded on its own lot by too much vegetation. Take a good look around your house and do some investigating, and the problems (and possibilities!) will become apparent.

Building codes control how a building is situated on a piece of property. Your local code has regulations regarding the following issues:

➤ The limits on a building's size, that is, how much of the lot it can cover

➤ Setbacks, or how close to the property lines a building can be constructed

➤ The placement of any future additions

➤ A building's height

33

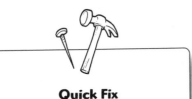

Quick Fix

Measure your lot or look at the lot description you received when you purchased your house. Then measure the square footage of the house, garage, and attached deck. Figure the percentage of your lot that's available for building. Before you consider any ground floor additions, ask your local building department if you can build on any of the available space.

Vegetation is another matter to look at. What shape is your yard in? Do you have a clump of rhododendrons the size of a school bus? Does your grass look like a sea of yellow every summer when the dandelions bloom? Yard remodeling, or landscaping, can be very expensive and time-consuming. Let your imagination run wild enough, and you won't have any money left over to remodel your house!

Inside Problems That Start Outside

The most obvious interior problem that gets started outside your house is leaking, usually from the roof. Windows can also leak through the glass, overhead flashing, and sill. In any case, you don't know you have leaks until you've seen some kind of water stain inside your house. Even then, finding the source of the leak isn't easy, especially on a dry day.

You can get a general idea of your roof's condition by examining it with binoculars. If your house is two or more stories tall, ask your neighbors if you can look at it from one of their upstairs windows. When you examine a roof, look for the following:

➤ Missing shingles

➤ Shingles beginning to curl at the edges

➤ Deteriorated *flashing*

➤ Moss

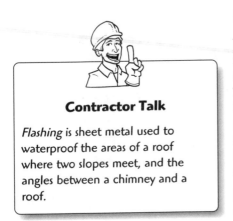

Contractor Talk

Flashing is sheet metal used to waterproof the areas of a roof where two slopes meet, and the angles between a chimney and a roof.

Windows Leak, Too

Water leaks through or around windows are a little more easily detected than roof leaks, even on dry days. Check for breaks in the seals around the glass. The worst offenders are old, wood windows in which the glass is either held in with wood stops or glazing compound, a clay-like material that hardens after it's applied around the edge of the glass. You can easily handle most window leak repairs yourself (see Appendix G, "Repairs").

If you have a brick house, look at the window sills (the sloped, horizontal piece of wood at the bottom of the window); they tend to cup and curl, allowing water to wash through when it rains. Typically, the damage to the inside is water-stained plaster under the window. These sills should be replaced (see Appendix G, "Repairs").

Chimneys

Chimneys are one part of your exterior that can really benefit from an up-close inspection. If your binocular observation shows loose and missing mortar (the cement mixture that holds the bricks together at their joints), or if the chimney is leaning, you need to schedule some repairs. Even if it's an inactive chimney with no prospects for future use, it can be dangerous if the bricks are loose.

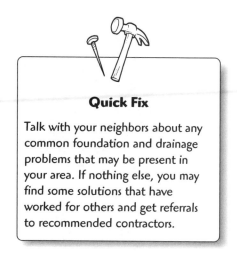

Quick Fix

Talk with your neighbors about any common foundation and drainage problems that may be present in your area. If nothing else, you may find some solutions that have worked for others and get referrals to recommended contractors.

Can you remember the last time your chimney was cleaned? If not, call a chimney sweep and have it inspected at the same time as the cleaning. The frequency of chimney cleanings will depend on how much you use it, the type of fuel you burn, and how much creosote build-up there is. Chimney fires occur all too frequently and are mostly preventable with proper chimney maintenance.

Who Knew It Was Swamp Land?

In some parts of the country, water infiltration and drainage aren't big issues (Arizona comes to mind). But chances are that if you're a homeowner, you have to be sure that water is draining away from your house and not toward it.

Water problems around foundations include the following:

➤ Lack of proper drainage

➤ Soil not sloped away from the foundation

➤ Downspouts not carrying water away from the house

If water doesn't drain away from your home's foundation, it will try to find a way to undermine it. It can force its way through any cracks or openings in the concrete, and percolate up between the floor and the walls. Look for obvious signs of poor drainage, such as excessively soggy soil or sunken depressions in the dirt.

What's the Buzz?

"The birds and the bees" mean one thing when you explain reproduction to your kids, but quite another when they're living inside your walls and roof. You won't necessarily

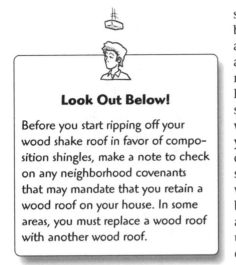

Look Out Below!

Before you start ripping off your wood shake roof in favor of composition shingles, make a note to check on any neighborhood covenants that may mandate that you retain a wood roof on your house. In some areas, you must replace a wood roof with another wood roof.

see them flying in and out during your inspection, but look for wasps or bees that may be hovering around any porch columns or roof overhangs. Birds also tend to favor secluded parts of an overhanging roof. Whatever you do, after you've noted that you have nonpaying guests living in your house, don't simply plug the holes and trap them inside! Wasps will find a way out, even if it means eating through your walls. Birds can die and decompose. Bees may die, but they will leave honey behind, which won't smell so sweet after it starts to deteriorate. You want these critters out of your house, dead or alive, before you start patching up the holes they used for access. Same for squirrels, rats, and mice. If you're uncomfortable with dealing with them, call an exterminator.

A Pretty Picture or Not?

As you walk around, consider the general impression your house makes. How would you react if you were a prospective buyer? Whether you're selling or not, what can you do to improve its appeal?

When you look over your survey and start to plan your remodeling projects, you'll be distinguishing between cosmetic jobs, such as painting, and critical jobs, such as roof replacement. This distinction applies to outside work as well.

When Roofs Go Bad

While you're examining your roof with binoculars or by climbing on top of it and walking around, take a closer look. What kind of roof do you have? Wood shakes or shingles? Tile? Composition shingles?

Each type of roofing comes with its own considerations:

➤ Wood shakes and shingles are a traditional material, but they require the most maintenance of the three.

➤ Tile is heavier and longer-lasting than other roof material, but it's also more difficult to install.

➤ Composition shingles are the most commonly used roofing material. They require little maintenance and are easily repaired.

Slipping Away: Gutters and Gravity

Most new gutters are made from continuous aluminum. An installer arrives at a job site and cranks up a special extruding machine. Flat-sheet aluminum goes in one end, and your new gutters come out the other. Each gutter is cut to the exact length needed, per section of your house. This means you'll have very few seams, which is good because seams are always potential points for leaks.

Wood gutters require regular cleaning and sealing. They can be repaired and kept in good shape, but they require more work than aluminum ones, which simply need to be cleaned and rinsed out from time to time.

While you're doing your inspection, check for loose gutters pulling away from the edge of the

Quick Fix

To maintain wood gutters, clean and rinse them out thoroughly, allow them to dry completely, and then apply a generous amount of pure linseed oil. This process should be a yearly event. Some tar-like products are sold as substitutes for linseed oil, but I don't recommend them. After a few years, these products dry out and crack, water gets trapped beneath them, and the gutters deteriorate faster.

roof, and be sure your downspouts are securely attached to the gutters. On rainy days, check for leaks or overflows; if your gutters are overflowing, better schedule a cleaning.

Siding Sadness

Siding's job is to keep water out first and be attractive to look at second. Quite a variety of exterior siding products tries to fulfill these functions, including the following:

➤ Wood siding (usually cedar)

➤ Wood shingles

➤ Aluminum siding

➤ Vinyl siding

➤ Manufactured wood siding

➤ Brick

➤ Stucco

Wood is used everywhere; it's kind of the all-purpose siding material around the country. Properly maintained (painted and sealed), it can last indefinitely. Wood shingles can also be long-lasting if they're maintained, though they have a tendency to cup or curl on the weathered sides of a house.

With either wood siding or wood shingles, watch for the following problems:

➤ Split, cracked, or missing pieces

➤ Cupped or curled pieces

➤ Peeling, chipping, or blistering paint

Most homeowners can easily do siding and shingle repairs (see Chapter 31, "Restoration or Remodeling?").

Aluminum siding, the no-maintenance, just-hose-me-off product of the '50s and '60s, has been replaced by its polymer successor, vinyl siding. These are truly low-maintenance products, although many people are put off by their aesthetics, or lack thereof.

The most infamous of the manufactured siding products is L-P siding, L-P standing for Oregon-based Louisiana-Pacific. Between 1985 and 1995, L-P siding, a product developed, according to a former CEO, without "a nickel's worth of research" was installed on approximately 800,000 homes nationwide. Slowly, as mold, mushrooms, and deterioration spread across the land of L-P siding installations, the company began regretting that they hadn't coughed up that nickel for research, especially in light of the huge class-action lawsuit that followed.

L-P siding has a rough grain appearance and a slight wave to its bottom edge, especially on very long pieces. If you even suspect that you have such siding on your house, call the L-P Claims Administrator at 800-245-2722 and request an information packet and claim forms.

Quick Fix

Aluminum siding removed during restoration projects is a recyclable product. It's worth some money! A two-story house might yield a few hundred dollars, depending on aluminum prices, which should take some of the sting out of all the work required to remove the siding and cart it away.

Brick is not quite the carefree product it appears to be, especially in cold climates. Bricks are held together with mortar, a cement-based material that hardens and seals the joints between bricks. Over time, especially when exposed to winter freeze cycles, the mortar can loosen, deteriorate, and begin to recede. Scrape your mortar and see how easily it crumbles. If it's quite loose, you may have to consider having it all tuck-pointed, a process by which a mason finishes the joints between bricks with mortar.

When you're checking your stucco, look for:

➤ Failing paint

➤ Cracks

➤ White, powdery deposits, or *efflorescence*, especially near the base, indicating that water is passing through the stucco

An especially troublesome stucco finish called EIFS (Exterior Insulation Finish System) has been the subject of lawsuits and some outright bans by various building departments. If your house is less than 20 years old and has a stucco finish, see Chapter 19, "Taking Sides: Your Exterior Walls," for more information.

Windows with Problems

Windows serve a three-fold purpose in our homes: They provide natural light, ventilation, and means of escape in case of fire. They come in three flavors: wood, metal, and vinyl. Vinyl is becoming the material of choice for most new residential window installations. If that's what you have, about your only concern is keeping them clean. Metal residential windows are either

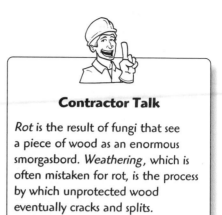

Contractor Talk

Rot is the result of fungi that see a piece of wood as an enormous smorgasbord. *Weathering*, which is often mistaken for rot, is the process by which unprotected wood eventually cracks and splits.

aluminum or steel. Older versions of metal windows are usually low maintenance except for the openers and hardware, which can break or go out of adjustment. You probably already noted any of these problems when you toured the inside of your home.

Wood windows, even new ones, are subject to deterioration unless they're kept painted and sealed. On the *weathered* sides of your house, this can be almost a yearly chore, depending on the quality of the painting.

Porch and Deck Health

Porches are similar to interior rooms. They have solid floors, ceilings, lights, and usually some furniture. Unlike your interior rooms, though, porches are open to all kinds of weather and wood-loving fungi and insects who take your welcome mat quite literally. Concrete porches eliminate some of these issues, but they come with one of their own: Particularly massive concrete porches can pull away from the house as the soil underneath them compresses and can throw any porch columns out of alignment.

Tales from the Scaffold

Wood decks are, in a word, dumb, but many of us have them (me included; it came with the house). Porches are at least covered and somewhat protected from the weather. Decks are an open challenge to the rain, sun, and snow gods who regularly pelt them with wood-destroying heat and water throughout the year. As a result, decks require more routine maintenance than other exterior wood surfaces.

Wood porches are subject to rot from below if they:

➤ Do not have any ventilation in their crawl space

➤ Have wood-to-soil contact

➤ Are infested with termites or other wood-destroying insects

If you have an old wood porch, inspect underneath it the same way you checked your other crawl spaces (you'll need your flashlight). Probe any wood that has come in contact with soil with your pocketknife and check for deterioration. While you're down there, be sure to brush any soil away from the porch framing.

After you look underneath your porch, walk all over it to be sure there aren't any soft spots. Such spots would suggest some wood decay or other damage. If you have wood steps, stand on each one and rock back and forth. Loose treads, the flat surface you walk on, are common and should be secured with either galvanized nails or deck screws (see Chapter 20, "Porches and Decks: Your Outdoor Rooms").

During your tour of your deck, check for:

➤ Loose decking boards, railings, and steps

➤ Damaged wood of any kind

➤ Dirt and mildew, indicating a cleaning is needed

➤ Condition of the finish

➤ Contact between deck posts and soil

As a rule, wood decks need to be cleaned and sealed once a year if they're to have any chance of living even a moderately long life. Decks must follow building code regulations to ensure structural strength and integrity (see Chapter 28, "Deck Your House with Decks").

Look Out Below!

A painted deck is a deck asking for trouble, unless it's scrupulously maintained. Peeling deck paint allows water to seep into the wood underneath, causing even more paint to peel. Painting over a deck that needs cleaning and sealing is simply compounding your maintenance.

Your Garage: More Than Dead Storage

Garages can have the same rot, insect, paint, and structural problems as any other part of your home. They're handy, and I certainly recommend keeping them in decent repair, even expanding them if it suits your purposes.

Give It a Rest

You're done; you've seen it all. Maybe your checklist is a mass of scribbles, but who's thinking about remodeling now? Relax, and take the process one step at a time in some kind of logical order. Look over your list. Is anything so absolutely crucial that it must be done right now? Your roof may look bad, but if it still has a few years left in it, you can put it off while you do more critical work.

Your gutters leak, but do they need to be replaced, or simply patched and sealed? The distinction can save you hundreds of dollars or thousands, in the case of a roof. Your paint may be intact on three sides of the house, but not on the most weathered side. Why paint it all if you have budget considerations? Paint the side that's most in need of it and put off the rest until it's really showing some wear and tear.

Drainage problems or water leaking into the basement need to be dealt with soon. Go through both your inside and outside lists and decide what has to be done now. Then you can concentrate on the fun remodeling.

The Least You Need to Know

➤ Examine the exterior of your house with as much scrutiny as the interior.

➤ Inspect your house during a rainy day as well as a dry one. Rainy days will disclose leaky gutters and drainage problems.

➤ Ignoring major outside problems such as roof repair or poor drainage can lead to inside problems later.

➤ Weather damage is the biggest single factor in outside maintenance.

➤ Maintaining good paint coverage is the best way to preserve the exterior of your home, especially wood sections.

Chapter 4

Paintbrush or Work Crews? Fixing the Immediate Stuff

In This Chapter

➤ Repair first; remodel later

➤ Determining the scope of the job

➤ When to hire it out

➤ Putting the jobs in logical order

➤ Covering the big systems

By now, you may be wondering just when you can get going on that room addition or state-of-the-art, Martha Stewart-eat-your-heart-out kitchen remodel. I could counsel patience and try to pass off bits of wisdom such as the Chinese proverb, "Patience, and the mulberry leaf becomes a silk gown," but what does that have to do with your house? The simple truth is that before you can start your remodeling projects, you or a Mr./Ms. Fix-It for hire will have to pick up some tools and do some repairs.

Fixing existing problems and maintaining your house is one stage of the preparatory part of the remodeling process. This stage is where you can get hands-on experience without getting into too much trouble and start to assess your ability to complete the more complex tasks that lie ahead. Doing some painting or repairing your deck will give you some instant feedback on your skill levels.

As you get more comfortable with hammers and plaster and troubleshooting your spongy floors, you'll start eyeing the jobs you've been considering, such as adding new lights or even whole rooms. But first you must assess what should be done now and decide which jobs you can do yourself. A lot of the work you'll have to do is already on your house inspection lists, so there won't be too many surprises.

You're More Talented Than You Think

If you can cut with a knife, sign your name, or change a tire, then you can hold a tool or two. Expertise comes with time. How long did it take you to learn how to handle a knife and fork or chopsticks? Or write with a pen? The first time you try to brush a smooth line of paint next to a pane of window glass it won't be as clean and smooth as it will be the 50th time.

I guarantee you that your comfort level will improve the more often you use your tools and attack a few repairs around your house.

Not as Easy as It Looks

Sure, you can do most of these jobs, but remember: Every practiced professional makes a task look easy. They do their jobs so well you can doubt that it's all that challenging, until you remember your childhood piano lessons, and how you barely got through book number one of "Say Hello to Mr. Piano."

When to Bow Out

Time restraints, general frustrations, and amateurish results are legitimate excuses for pulling out of doing the work yourself and hiring contractors. If the work isn't going well, there's no point in trying to be a hero. There are many opportunities in life for character-building experiences, and remodeling doesn't have to be one of them.

Quick Fix

This is your apprenticeship—take your time! Working when you're tired or frustrated means making mistakes, some of them dangerous ones. Besides hitting your thumb with a hammer, you can fall off a ladder or cut yourself with a saw. Making too many mistakes? Stop for a while, even a day or two. The work will still be there waiting for you.

Contractors Just Seem Expensive

Figuring up your true remodeling costs, especially if you hire a contractor to work on your house, is a complicated task. It isn't just dollars and cents; it's also the use of your time, the quality of the results, the emotional costs, and the difference between pre-tax and after-tax dollars.

A painting contractor can come into your home while you're at work, lay out a pile of drop cloths in your bedroom, turn those lime green walls that came with the house into champagne gray, clean up, and be gone before you walk in the door. What's this worth to you? Three hundred dollars? Four hundred dollars? The alternative means you have to:

➤ Buy all the materials, including paint, tools, sandpaper, drop cloths, Spackle, rags, and so on

➤ Spend two or three nights doing the work or do it over a weekend

➤ Clean up after the job

How does that $300 to $400 price tag look now? If it's still high, then you've established a value for your time and decided that you should do your own painting. But the issue isn't always a matter of dollars. I've had clients who found remodeling almost therapeutic after a day of looking at a computer monitor or writing legal briefs. You have to set your own criteria. What about quality? Floor finishers get called in all the time to redo floors done by homeowners who let the floor sanders get away from them. You can't do everything well, so decide when it's in your best interest (aesthetic or otherwise) to call in a contractor.

We'll get into the emotional costs of remodeling in Chapter 8, "Everything You Didn't Think About," but they're pertinent when you consider a contractor's fee. Say you have a stressful, time-consuming occupation that demands long hours and high productivity. How stressed will you get if you use the little spare time you have to rebuild your front porch steps? If your significant other starts scanning the personal ads looking for dates with strangers, it's probably wise to hire a carpenter to build the steps. There are times when a sense of relief is worth the cost.

Finally, think of your remodeling costs in terms of pre-tax and after-tax dollars. If you're in the 28 percent tax bracket, every $500 you earn leaves you with $360 after taxes. Now that painter seems more expensive than ever! If you're in the 28 percent tax bracket, every dollar you pay a contractor requires you to come up with almost $1.40 in income.

Making Dirt and Dust Your Friends

If you work in an office, as so many of us do these days, working on your house will introduce you to an entirely different world. You'll trade a climate-controlled, clean environment for dust, noise, fumes, and a blister or two. You'll also be working in cold, wet winters and hot, humid summers, sometimes into the early morning hours. Bet you can't wait to get started!

Look Out Below!

Just because you're feeling harried over your remodeling, don't throw all logic out the window. Go someplace relaxing and think the thing through. Break the scenario down into small pieces and deal with them one at a time, deciding which jobs you'll do yourself and which you'll hire out. You can avoid rash decisions by stepping back and getting some perspective on the project.

Quick Fix

Buy some extra-heavy-duty plastic trash bags if you have odds and ends of construction debris to remove, and pick up some sturdy cardboard boxes at your supermarket.

You're going to be messy (if you're doing much of the work yourself) and/or living in a mess (if you're hiring someone to do the work) until the job is finished. If you have perfect acrylic fingernails, you can count on breaking them on a regular basis, and forget about that high-maintenance hairstyle.

Wear work gloves except when using power tools (they can get caught in spinning saw blades and drill bits), keep the work site clean, and wear inexpensive, disposable paper suits (available at paint stores). Latex dishwashing gloves are great when you're dealing with paint, putty, or caulking. Heavier work gloves, available at any hardware or lumber store, will keep blisters and splinters at bay when you're hammering wood, digging, or tearing out walls. We wear shoes to protect our feet; why not protect our hands, too?

A clean work site is a safe work site and psychologically encouraging, especially if things are beginning to get out of hand. The best vacuum cleaner I found for most job clean-ups is the Eureka Mighty Mite. I've used it to pick up everything from sawdust to drywall screws. Mighty Mite doesn't recommend these practices, but mine lasted for years, and you can get one today for only about $80.

Jack and Jill of All Trades

OK, you're ready to get started. Now it's time to distinguish between what has to be remodeled and what you can achieve with simple repairs and maintenance. What if you could repair your old windows instead of having to replace them? A paint job can change your whole attitude towards your living room. Are your doors feeling a little breezy? Can you add some weather-stripping instead of installing a new door? Looking into repair options may help you avoid some of the remodeling you thought you needed to do.

Do-it-yourself stores abound, from your local hardware store to stadium-size home improvement centers. They all carry the tools and materials you'll need to get you started.

Anyone Can Paint

As simple as painting seems to be, it can be as much a science as an art. Chapter 9, "Painting: Your House Is Your Canvas," goes into it in great detail. Painting comes down to a few simple basics:

➤ Preparing the surface thoroughly

➤ Protecting all floors and furnishings

➤ Choosing the correct paint for the job

➤ Applying paint carefully

Painting is the least difficult and least expensive remodeling/maintenance task you can do. Dollar for dollar, a fresh, bright, new coat of paint will give you a greater result in less time than just about any other job. (OK, having your kids clean up their rooms may have even more of an impact.)

Tracking Your Wall Cracks

Walls give our homes some sense of definition and order. They also serve as giant display boards for paintings, family photographs, and Most Improved Speller awards from third grade. Over time, in addition to the holes we make, walls develop cracks on their own.

Quick Fix

Paint colors look different at different times of day because they're affected by changes in natural light. That medium gray that looks so cool in the morning may be depressing in the early evening or during short winter days. Look at your color samples at various points in the day before you make your final choice.

Chances are (unless you live in a cave or log cabin) your interior walls are covered with plaster or drywall, also known as plasterboard. Plaster itself comes as a powdered mix containing gypsum, a cementing agent. It's rarely used in house construction any-more, because drywall is so much easier to install. Drywall is basically a sheet of pre-formed gypsum-based plaster sandwiched between two pieces of paper or cardboard. It's nailed or screwed to the studs, and the joints are sealed with drywall tape and compound.

As the house settles over time, cracks can appear in either material. Cracks in plaster can occur anywhere, but are often in corners; drywall will crack or separate only at the *seams.* Both plaster and drywall cracks can be easily repaired (see Chapter 31, "Restoration or Remodeling?") with a caulking gun and a tube of inexpensive latex caulking. Small holes can be filled with pre-mixed and ready-to-use Spackle applied with a small putty knife.

Why Painting Matters

Regular painting and wall repair are signs of a well-kept home that is pleasing to us as occu-pants and attractive to potential buyers. Al-though painting isn't a structural issue and can

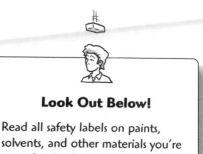

Look Out Below!

Read all safety labels on paints, solvents, and other materials you're using for the first time. Don't take any chances with your sight or hearing by ignoring recommenda-tions to wear safety equipment such as ear plugs or safety glasses. Take extra precautions around power tools, especially electric saws.

Tales from the Scaffold

Because just about anyone can be a self-designated painter and take out a contractor's license, the quality within this trade varies tremendously. I've seen a good number of superlative paint jobs and even wallpapering done by homeowners. I had one client who was so meticulous that she chemically stripped all of her old woodwork before painting it. As you can imagine, it looked fabulous.

be done anytime, clean, bright paint can significantly change your home environment. And you can do this work yourself without spending a lot of money or having exceptional skills.

Working Windows

Windows are one of your house's most noticeable architectural elements, both inside and out, especially the old wood ones. When old wood windows are removed and replaced by renovators, building owners can be denied historic tax credits. I should know; I wrote a book about wood window repair (see Appendix I, "Resources"). But many homeowners write off their old windows, believing that their only choice is to replace them, which they often do with vinyl—not a great fit with the style of an older home. Don't do it! Anyone can do basic repairs and weather-stripping of wood windows (see Appendix G, "Repairs"); in fact, fewer and fewer carpenters and contractors even bother with them. This is a perfect homeowner project and a big money saver.

Contractor Talk

There are three levels of work in the drywall trade: *Stockers* deliver the drywall, *hangers* install it, and the *tapers* fill the joints and nail or screw holes to produce a finished product.

Put on a Floorshow

Floor repairs run from fixing squeaks to refinishing to installing new carpet. Squeaks can be annoying, especially when you get caught sneaking out of the kitchen in the middle of the night with the last piece of cheesecake. Fortunately, they're easily repaired, and you don't need any fancy tools to do the job.

Carpet installation is no day at the beach. Why would you want to bother? If the carpet isn't stretched just right, it lies loose and wears out faster. Despite what some do-it-yourself-you-don't-ever-need-to-hire-anyone authors advise, carpet installation is not a homeowner job.

Keep the Home Light Bulbs Burning

A modern, 200-amp electrical service (see Chapter 12, "Refusing Fuses") is more than adequate to serve the power needs of all of our computers, megawatt CD players, and retro-hip lava lamps. Electrical appliances, such as stoves, dryers, and water heaters, are the big power draws. Even if you have gas appliances, a 200-amp service is a good idea because it can cover most unanticipated future power needs.

New houses with new services and wiring should keep just about anyone happy, although you may find places where you want to add extra lights or outlets after you've lived in your home for a few months. If your house has an old system, it doesn't necessarily have to be replaced, but it's a good idea to do so if you're planning major remodeling later.

Upgrading old electrical systems consists of these tasks:

➤ Installing a new electrical service panel

➤ Upgrading major circuits (stove, laundry, water heater)

➤ Installing new circuits as needed, or rewiring the entire house, bypassing and replacing all the old circuits

Do-it-yourself installations of new panels are not for the faint-of-heart. Adding new circuits or even replacing much of the old wiring and leaving the final connections to an electrician are certainly doable homeowner projects.

Minor Work for Minor Repairs

You may not be prepared to replace your entire electrical service, but adding circuits or individual outlets and lights are projects a homeowner can handle, as long as they're done with care. Electricity's reputation as a force understood only by medieval magicians or the writers of the National Electrical Code is certainly exaggerated. Dealing with electricity is like most other life relationships: Respect it and it can be your friend. Chapter 12, "Refusing Fuses," spells out the operation of your home's electrical system.

Look Out Below!

Any faulty electrical work done without a permit and an inspection can come back to haunt you. If it results in a fire or other damage and your insurance company can prove the work was done illegally, your claims can be disallowed.

Contractor Talk

A *circuit* is the path of electricity. It starts at a source, your panel or fuse box, and travels via one wire to a *load*, a device that requires its use. It then travels back to the source via a second wire. If this loop of electricity gets interrupted, you have a *short circuit.*

Unplugged: Simple Solutions

Electrical *circuits* can provide only so much juice before they shut things down by blowing a fuse or tripping a circuit breaker (see the information on electrical *loads* in Chapter 12, "Refusing Fuses"). If you keep blowing fuses or tripping breakers, the best solution is to install an additional circuit or upgrade the existing one. Not ready for that? Unplug something, or at least don't turn it on when you're running other electrical toys. Lack of power is usually a problem in kitchens and bathrooms where electrical devices draw a lot of power. If you want to go with this simple solution, you'll have to change your routine around a little. Try mixing your protein shake in the blender first and toasting the bagels second instead of running both appliances at once.

When Wiring Problems Get Out of Hand

Unless you have constant fuse failure or circuit breakers tripping, you won't have any obvious signs of electrical shortcomings. It's also impossible to see what's going on inside the walls. If a past owner or contractor replaced a 15 amp fuse with a 20 amp one—a really, really bad idea—in a misguided attempt to stop a fuse from burning out, you probably wouldn't be aware of it. A 15 amp circuit runs 14 gauge wire; a 20 amp circuit runs 12 gauge, which is thicker. If you try to run 20 amps' worth of electricity through a wire designed to carry 15 amps, you'd better start looking for smoke.

When you took your house tour, did you find any exposed, old knob-and-tube or BX cable running through your unfinished basement? Was the insulation on some of the wires frayed? Did it look like more than one past owner had tied in an additional outlet or two or more? Unscrew an old light fixture. What shape are the wires in? Are the ends brittle; is the insulation worn? These are signs that you should consider replacing the system.

Your Plumbing: Pipe Dreams or Nightmares?

Like electricity, plumbing is a behind-the-scenes major component of your house. These problems bring it to your attention:

➤ The water comes out very slowly or not at all

➤ Faucets or pipes drip or leak

➤ Water drains out too slowly due to clogged drain lines

➤ Anything whatsoever goes wrong with a toilet

Plumbing is often more intimidating to work on than wiring, with good reason: A few wrong turns of a pipe wrench and you can have water gushing out in all the wrong places. With electricity, if you've made an error, you can always turn one individual circuit off. When it comes to plumbing, you may have to live with all the water shut off until you've completed the repair.

Drips, Drains, and You

You can handle most small plumbing repairs with the help of a plunger and a few hand tools (see Appendix G, "Repairs"). These jobs include:

➤ Cleaning clogged drain lines and toilets

➤ Making minor faucet repairs

➤ Adjusting a stuck garbage disposal

➤ Replacing toilet parts

➤ Repairing small pipe leaks

Look Out Below!

Check that your main shut-off valve is working properly. If you're leaving town during freezing weather, consider turning off your water completely.

Most people don't want to mess with their plumbing, but do you know how much a plumber costs at 10:00 p.m. when your toilet is overflowing? Call a plumber when things are really out of hand—a frozen pipe bursts, for instance, or you want to run new pipes and drain lines for an additional bathroom. You could learn to do that kind of work, too, but I've rarely run into anyone who wanted to, except plumbers, of course.

Cold Prevention: A Working Furnace

If you want to freeze in the winter, ignore your furnace or boiler. If you prefer warmth, read on. As a homeowner, your main concerns about your heating plant are the following:

➤ Is it working safely?

➤ Am I spending more on heat because of inefficiency?

➤ Is it dependable?

A licensed heating technician can easily determine your furnace's safety and dependability. Older furnaces won't be as efficient as newer ones, which begs the question: Am I better off upgrading? If so, do I go with a standard furnace or a more expensive, high-efficiency model? This decision is a matter of costs, not comfort.

Furnace replacement is not a project for a homeowner, but furnace maintenance is. Yearly furnace maintenance by a heating technician will include:

➤ A system check

➤ A check for carbon monoxide leaks

➤ Cleaning or replacing filters

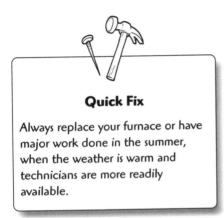

Quick Fix

Always replace your furnace or have major work done in the summer, when the weather is warm and technicians are more readily available.

The only other maintenance your furnace needs is replacement or cleaning of the filters every 30 to 60 days, depending on usage.

I'm a realist: Most people aren't going to fuss with their radiators or boilers. Far better to budget for a yearly inspection than go without heat on a cold day. Replacing an aging heating system in the summer is also a good idea.

Keeping the Rain Outside: Roof Repairs

A roof (see Chapter 11, "The Messiest Job: Replacing Your Roof") will last for years with some basic maintenance. Most of the repairs are pretty simple, and you can do them yourself if you're comfortable climbing around on top of a roof. Repairs generally call for replacing a missing shingle or two that probably flew off during a big wind storm or patching leaks with roof cement. The big problem is finding the leaks, especially if they're not consistent every time it rains. That means you've got leaks from wind-driven rain, which are a lot harder to locate. If you cannot find the source of a leak (you may have noticed some when you toured your house), then call a roofing contractor. If it's time to replace the roof, you definitely should call a roofer.

Underwater: Basement and Foundation Leaks

As we've moved through this chapter, we've gone from the easiest tasks, painting and spackling holes, to the toughest ones, repairing roofs and foundations. Both can leak, and both have to be taken care of. The water may not bother you that much, but you'll have a tough time convincing a potential buyer that it's no big deal.

Basement and foundation leaks (see Chapter 10, "Floundering Foundations") are due to water working its way in through cracks or holes in the concrete. Sometimes the source is clear. For example, your gutters may be overflowing and dumping an excess amount of water against your foundation.

Don't be a wise guy and coat the inside of your foundation walls with some weird waterproofing material; even if it worked, which it might temporarily, it wouldn't solve the problem, because the water would still be trying to get inside. Investigate first (see Chapter 10, "Floundering Foundations"), and then call a contractor if necessary.

Where Do You Start?

Always start with the most pressing matters: leaking roofs, dying furnaces, and adding a second bathroom for your family of five are important projects. These aren't the fun projects, so you may decide to hire them out and make up the costs by doing the fun stuff yourself. Replacing a roof, for example, is not fun for anyone, including the roofers.

The other top-priority jobs are the basics that affect just about every remodeling project: wiring, plumbing, heating, and foundation work. There's no point in doing a first-class painting, wallpapering, and floor refinishing job in your downstairs if you haven't yet put in the additional outlets the rooms need.

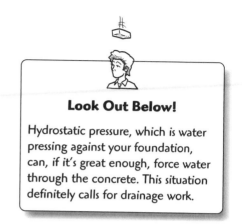

Look Out Below!

Hydrostatic pressure, which is water pressing against your foundation, can, if it's great enough, force water through the concrete. This situation definitely calls for drainage work.

Remember the order of events: Do any destructive work, such as tearing into walls, pulling up old carpet, or replacing windows, before you do any finish work. If you need to replace the gutters, do it before you paint the house, and be sure to paint the area behind the gutters before they're installed. You have a lot to consider, and all you wanted to do was spruce up your house! Don't worry; you're learning and increasing your skills, and that will make for better, faster remodeling when the time comes.

The Least You Need to Know

➤ The more you practice, the more you'll improve and refine your remodeling skills.

➤ Remodeling is a messy business, but it's easy to keep the mess to a minimum.

➤ Put your misgivings aside. Most homeowners can learn to do basic jobs around the house without calling in a contractor.

➤ Do the big jobs first, even if you'd rather avoid them. Ignoring them can come back to haunt your future projects.

Chapter 5

You Say Condo; I Say Home

In This Chapter

➤ Remodeling in condominiums and co-ops

➤ Neighborhood restrictions

➤ The limitations of living in a designated historic district

➤ Working on your home if you rent

➤ Your rights in common property situations

Being a homeowner doesn't necessarily mean owning a house; condominiums and co-ops are an attractive alternative because they are usually affordable and secure. Unlike most independent houses, however, condominiums and co-ops come with restrictions on everything from pets to hanging political campaign posters in your windows.

Condos and co-ops aren't the only form of housing to put the kibosh on your remodeling fantasies. In some neighborhoods, homes also come with restrictions in the form of covenant agreements that are usually written into the deeds. These covenants limit such things as housing style or size and can put a damper on that miniature golf course you wanted to build in the front yard.

Among the most restrictive neighborhoods are historic preservation districts. If you live in a historic district and want to make changes to the outside of your house, you'll need to get a variance from your local historic board, which can be a tedious process.

What if you want to redo the apartment or house you're renting? Most leases don't allow such work unless it's approved by the owner. Even repainting your bedroom can

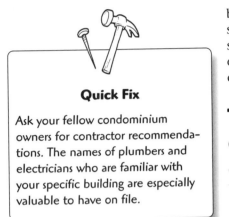

Quick Fix

Ask your fellow condominium owners for contractor recommendations. The names of plumbers and electricians who are familiar with your specific building are especially valuable to have on file.

be fraught with landlord/lady reprisals if you do something like cover the owner's special hand-stenciled (but spectacularly ugly) wall border. This opens a real can of legal worms that I'll discuss in this chapter.

The Ups and Downs of Group Living

Condominiums and co-ops have become an alternative for a great number of people who don't want to take on the responsibility of a separate, detached house or are downsizing from one. In some places, you don't have much choice: Just try to find a nice, three-story colonial in downtown Manhattan. Living in a condo or co-op can definitely complicate your remodeling plans.

Co-op or Condo: What's in a Name?

There's a clear distinction between co-ops and condominiums. Co-ops or co-operatives are often set up as corporations in which you buy shares and receive a proprietary lease to a specific apartment. You can remodel, but must abide by the corporate regulations.

In a condominium, you have individual ownership of a specific unit, your exclusive use area, and individual interest in the common areas such as the hallways and parking lot. Essentially, you own everything from the drywall and hardwood floors up to the cobwebs in the ceiling. Unfortunately, this ownership doesn't give you free reign to do whatever you want inside your unit.

Redecorate, Yes; Remodel, Maybe

Some law firms specialize in condominium bylaws and disputes, and they have no shortage of business in places such as Florida and Hawaii. Suppose you live in an older building where you pay a share of the electric bill because the units don't have individual electric meters. You decide you want to install your own washer and dryer because you're getting tired of schlepping down to the basement laundry room, and besides, you don't want everyone to know you wear Donald Duck underwear.

Your remodeling project is already running into roadblocks:

➤ Other owners may complain about your demands on the wiring and force a hearing with the owners' association to contest your proposed changes.

➤ How will the building's plumbing handle the new demands?

➤ Your appliances may be too noisy for surrounding neighbors, especially anyone living below.

You are potentially changing the conditions of the building. Can you do this according to the association's bylaws? To go ahead with a project without approval, simply hoping it will pass, is an almost guaranteed ticket to an ongoing battle with your board of directors.

Your remodeling restrictions won't stop at adding major appliances. Your neighbors or board of directors may frown on any of your attempts to rearrange your floor plan if it involves removing interior walls, whether they're *bearing* or *nonbearing* ones. Homeowners' associations and boards need to see documentation that your project won't have any adverse effect on the building.

Contractor Talk

A *bearing wall* supports the floor above it. It's a critical part of the building structure and cannot be removed unless an equivalent support in the form of posts and a beam are installed in its place. A *nonbearing wall* is a partition wall that's there to define a smaller space.

It's critical to understand the difference between remodeling and decorating, at least insofar as your building covenants define it (be sure you've read them thoroughly). Potentially, remodeling can have an effect beyond the confines of your living unit. Here are some examples of projects that can have such an effect:

➤ Installing major appliances that were not present when you purchased the unit

➤ Installing an additional bathroom

➤ Adding a small exterior sun porch with access doors

➤ Adding skylights

➤ Adding a fireplace

➤ Removing interior walls

Look Out Below!

Before you do any remodeling project you might deem questionable—and you'd better question most of them—check with your board and research your building's regulations. Some people (with more money and ego than good sense) automatically go to the mat over every pet project. Don't follow their example.

Plenty of projects fall into the realm of decorating, or non-invasive remodeling; that is, they don't affect anyone beyond the individual unit. These projects would only update existing features:

➤ Painting and wallpapering

➤ Refinishing wood floors or installing carpet

➤ Updating a kitchen or bathroom without increasing demands on the building's plumbing or electrical systems

➤ Installing tile in a bathroom or kitchen

➤ Replacing existing light fixtures

If you're seeking a variance to the rules, remember that it can take months of negotiations, depending upon the responsiveness of your board. Be prepared to back up your request with drawings and photographs of similar projects, and solicit the support of your neighbors (petitions show that you have the blessings of other owners).

Tales from the Scaffold

I once had clients who installed their own washer and dryer in a second-floor condominium unit housed in an old Victorian mansion. Everything was fine until a badly balanced load sent the washing machine dancing across the floor. Old Victorian plaster being what it is, the washing machine managed to dislodge part of the dining room ceiling in the unit below. Unfortunately, at the time, the downstairs owners were serving beef Wellington to 12 guests.

A final note: Once your project is approved, inform surrounding neighbors, including those above and below, of any work you're going to be doing that might involve a lot of noise. Floor refinishing, with its relentless machine sanding, is one good example. Give them a chance to plan their schedules around your work or at least prepare for disruptions. If you hire a contractor, be sure to establish working hours before the job begins. Hammering on a Sunday morning isn't a good way to win friends or influence people.

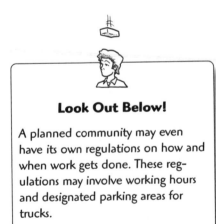

Look Out Below!

A planned community may even have its own regulations on how and when work gets done. These regulations may involve working hours and designated parking areas for trucks.

Freedom of Expression Stops at Your Door

When you're inside your unit, your imagination can run wild. I had a client who painted most of her unit in midnight blue, which sounds a bit macabre, but she pulled it off, and it had a certain charm. Others have stripped and bleached woodwork, added miles of track lighting, and, in the case of one New York City architect, painted oak floors with high-gloss, black marine enamel. But once you reach your front door (or windows for that matter), you have to leave your imagination behind, because the group mind takes over.

Living by Committee

One way you can ensure some reasonableness on your board is to run for office. Volunteers for these positions are always wanted, and your offer to run will be welcome. That doesn't mean that you'll get special treatment; the board's job is to be fair and give all requests an open hearing. But you will have an opportunity to influence changes in regulations and rules.

By now, you may be thinking that neither condo nor co-op life is right for you. Give me a house, you say, where I can be free to be me and keep old cars in the driveway, the ones I keep swearing to restore—after I get all those old washing machines running. But what if your house is in a neighborhood with its own rules?

Living in the 'Hood: Covenants and Restrictions

Some developers establish covenants when they build new residential areas so they can maintain some control over the quality and design of the housing. These restrictions are written into the deeds to each property and basically limit your full use of it. These covenants usually deal with the following issues:

➤ Minimum lot size

➤ The style and size of each house

➤ The materials used in house construction

➤ The minimum and maximum lot size

➤ Exterior features, including fences, paint color, satellite dishes, air-conditioning units, and even mailboxes

Seaside, Florida, a planned community built in the early 1990s, limits exterior painting options by providing homeowners with a list of allowable paint colors and their manufacturers. Need to replace your roof? If it's got wood shakes or shingles, you can expect to have to replace it with the same material. A community may allow small additions to your home, often recommending that you use the original architect or another firm they favor to do the planning.

If you're a homeowner in a restricted neighborhood, membership is mandatory. Essentially planned communities with their own zoning ordinances do everything possible to keep them that way; they may even have restrictions on changes you can make to your home's interior. The tradeoff for accepting these restrictions is a uniform and well-kept environment that some people find desirable.

If you're thinking of moving into a neighborhood with covenants, be prepared to live within their boundaries and limitations. Neighborhood associations go to great pains to explain them to prospective new residents. Don't move in believing you can challenge the rules by installing your own private cellular phone tower in the front yard.

Read your deed carefully. Ask a lot of questions. Take a good long look at the house you're considering buying and at yourself. If you decide that you want to do the least amount of remodeling possible, a very restrictive deed could be a blessing in disguise; now you're in a situation where you can't remodel—talk about a built-in excuse! You can tell your friends that you really want to add that third-story combination observatory/billiards room, but those darn covenants won't let you.

Historic Districts

By European standards, our ideas of preservation aren't all that marvelous. After all, they operate pizza parlors in 17th century buildings. When you compare that to saving a 1920s craftsman bungalow, it isn't too impressive. Nevertheless, there are efforts all across the country to save what we have, and these efforts can affect your remodeling plans.

There are varying degrees of historic designation for old buildings and homes, including listing in the National Register of Historic Places, location in a historic preservation district, and falling under city or state historic registration. Historic designation and its influence on future use and remodeling of individual buildings can be bewildering. Local and national building codes easily conflict with the restraints imposed when a building is registered as historic.

Tales from the Scaffold

The National Register of Historic Places is a list of properties acknowledged by the federal government as worthy of preservation for their significance in American history and culture. National Register properties include districts, buildings, sites, and objects of significance to their local community, state, or the nation. The National Register is maintained by the Secretary of the U.S. Department of the Interior and administered by the National Park Service.

Designation Don'ts

In a sense, historic designation or registration imposes the same types of restrictions that neighborhood covenants do. Instead of being based on a developer's rules and tastes, they're based on the historic origins of the building itself. Unlike planned community rules, historic details are all too often a matter of interpretation, if not a bit of caprice.

I once worked on a building in Seattle's historic Pioneer Square district. The owner wanted to strip the paint (appropriately enough, a brick-red color) off the exterior brick and return it to its original, unpainted condition. The historic board turned him down on the grounds that it had been painted longer than it had been unpainted! "We want you to maintain the historic fabric," he was told. "But I want to take it back to the way it was when it was built before someone put all this stupid paint on it," he said. "Sorry," was the answer he got, "we don't like your version of historic fabric."

Generally, on the exterior of your home, you will be restricted as to:

➤ Additions to your home

➤ Paint colors

➤ Selection of roofing materials

➤ Selection of siding

➤ Window replacement

Contractor Talk

Restoration is returning a building to a state as close as possible to its original condition. *Rehabilitation* is preserving the building's architecturally distinctive points while adapting it to new or current use.

Tax Credits Where They're Due

At one point, generous tax credits made commercial historic restoration a big business. It was, and still is, important to adhere to strict rehabilitation standards in order to retain those tax credits. A number of projects lost big money when, for example, developers replaced original windows with new ones that in no way matched the originals.

If you're a residential owner, federal government largesse in the form of tax credits isn't available to you, but in some cases, state tax credits may be. Call your state historic preservation office (any local historical organization will have the phone number) in case your house and neighborhood qualify for tax credits.

Painting Impediments

You will also be restricted as to how you do some work, especially exterior painting. Preparation is one of the most important steps in painting. Inadequate preparation can blow the whole job. With old houses, you have the additional liability of lead-based paint, which must be contained; there are lots of guidelines on this (see Chapter 31, "Restoration or Remodeling?") if it gets stripped or scraped off during preparation work. Then, there's the issue of what constitutes appropriate preparation work on a historic building—no wonder it's called hysterical restoration!

There are two schools of thought when it comes to paint preparation for old buildings:

➤ The more paint you remove, the better, because you're getting rid of a lot of build-up that can hinder future painting.

➤ Remove only loose and flaking paint to the next sound layer using the least abrasive method possible. Old, intact paint is considered part of the historic character of the building.

The second approach is the official stance of the Department of the Interior and associated agencies that oversee historic restoration. It's highly subjective: How do you define the next sound layer, and how long do you expect it to be sound? This approach guarantees that you'll be repainting more and more often as that now intact old paint fails.

Tales from the Scaffold

Some restorations can be surprising. I worked on an abandoned 1920s hotel in which every pane of glass had been broken out. The windows had been exposed to the weather for years, as had the interior. Unexpectedly, the windows were the best-fitting units I'd ever worked on, despite their neglect.

More Hassles with History

Replacement siding and roofing shingles must match the originals. This requirement is a given. Windows and window replacement are not such clear issues, however. Any original wood window in an older building can be repaired, even though it may require going to ridiculous lengths to do so in some cases. I should know, I repaired close to 4,000 of them in my past life as a restoration contractor.

Historic guidelines basically allow you to replace your windows if you can prove that more than 50 percent of them cannot be repaired using reasonable measures. Once you get the approval, don't be in any hurry to call Happy Vinnie's Vinyl Window Emporium. You'll have to replace the windows with like material, that is, new wood windows of a similar pattern and appearance to the old ones. These windows are quite expensive.

Especially if you're a homeowner surrounded by houses in compliance with historic regulations, you're not going to get much leeway. You may be able to add on rear decks or skylights, provided they can't be seen from the street. (Visibility, or more correctly, lack thereof, is very important.) Before you get beyond the planning stage with any of these projects, check them against local restrictions. If your proposed changes can be seen from the street, it could be virtually impossible to get them passed by a historic board.

On the Bright Side

The other side of living under the controls of a historic designation is knowing that your neighborhood will stay relatively intact. No stuffing two skinny houses on one lot, no vinyl windows stuck into a classic Greek revival, and no weird additions that don't match the house, but do match the limited building skills of the owner. And with a historic home, you'll never lack for remodeling or maintenance projects to work on.

Landlords: The Best Remodeling Is No Remodeling

We all have horror stories about past landlords. From a legal standpoint, a property owner who rents you a dwelling must meet safety regulations and minimal standards of cleanliness and livability. Some of these standards are open to interpretation, certainly, but once they're met, a landlord/lady isn't going to be particularly interested in remodeling a rented unit unless it will yield more rent or retain a favored tenant.

As a residential tenant, your lease or rental agreement precludes you from doing any alterations to your dwelling, even painting, without the owner's permission. Often, a casual agreement is reached between a tenant and an owner allowing the tenant to do a prescribed amount of work to a rental unit in lieu of rent if it's major work or if the owner provides the materials (paint usually). Either way, it can be a bad idea for both parties.

Renters' Risks

From a legal standpoint, the moment you pick up a paint brush or a saw and hammer in exchange for money or rent, you've entered into a contract. What happens if:

➤ You fall off of a ladder or are otherwise injured?

➤ You damage the property?

➤ You do substandard work that isn't discovered until a later date, possibly after causing some damage or injury?

From the owner's standpoint, you've created a real mess. Would you be considered an employee because you did the work for money? If so, to keep it legal, taxes and Social Security would have to be taken out, as well as state department of labor costs. What if you consider yourself an independent contractor? Fine, where's your license? And your bond?

> **Quick Fix**
>
> Historically accurate hardware, moldings, and other components of your house are expensive if you depend on new duplications. Look around for an architectural salvage yard or, better yet, a building the same vintage as yours that is going to be demolished or modernized. Ask the owner if you can salvage some materials.

Granted, these types of work arrangements are made all the time (often on low-rent properties), but only at the owner's peril. Large, well-established property owners never allow this kind of work to be done by tenants, which means that, when it comes to remodeling your rental space, you could be out of luck.

How You Can Pull It Off

You don't need to give up your remodeling fantasies completely, however. First, be an exemplary tenant. Pay rent on time and keep the premises clean. Present your case to your landlord/lady. Take along some drawings of your proposed changes and explain how they'll benefit the space (without increasing your rent, of course). Many owners are reasonable and will try to meet you halfway. Some proposals, such as adding some bookshelves, probably don't present much potential legal jeopardy if you're doing it for your own satisfaction without any expectation of payment. Remember, you're renting. You don't want to overimprove the place and then turn the results of your labor over to the owner and the next tenant.

Renter Danger Zone

Any work you do on your unit—even if it greatly improves it—can be held against you when you vacate the unit if it was done without the owner's permission. At the least, it provides a reason, in the mind of a vindictive owner, to withhold your rental deposit. If you do something major, such as adding a deck or widening a doorway between a living room and a dining room, you can really have problems.

Your lease is a legal agreement. If you don't like the terms, change or negotiate them before you sign. Making unilateral remodeling decisions after you move in is an invitation to trouble.

The Least You Need to Know

➤ Be sure you understand the restrictions your condominium or co-op situation imposes on your remodeling activities.

➤ Secure any necessary permission from your homeowners' association before you start any remodeling.

➤ Strictly adhere to covenants and restrictions in planned communities when making any changes to your home.

➤ Compliance in designated historic districts is often a matter of interpretation.

➤ As a renter, any remodeling you do on your unit is best avoided, because it can draw you into all kinds of leasing and legal issues.

Chapter 6

Fixing Your House Without Breaking the Bank

In This Chapter

➤ Developing a remodeling budget

➤ Funding the job

➤ Knowing where the money goes

➤ Figuring up whether remodeling is worth it to you

➤ Living with cutbacks in your plans

When it comes to remodeling, rationality can go flying out your new third-story window in a hurry. There's no shortage of magazine articles and even popular movies about people who buy fixer-upper houses that eat up money with the ferocity of wolverines. Why? Because when it comes to our homes, we become very emotional. We'll compare prices on frozen orange juice to save 15 cents, but won't think twice about spending hundreds of dollars more than we budgeted on a cool kitchen sink and faucet combination.

Unless you have a huge trust fund or sit on piles of stock options from hot, new Internet companies, budgets are a reality, but they don't have to be all that restrictive. When you have only so many dollars to spend, imagination and good design can go a long way. Most of a remodeling budget goes for labor and materials and more than a few fast-food dinners. You can cut down on labor costs by doing much of the work yourself, but keep in mind that your time is worth something, too. Finally, as satisfying as the results of remodeling can be, there's more to life than your house. Maintaining it as a shrine works only if you have no children, pets, or guests, and you confine

Quick Fix

Be realistic about what you need and what you'll use. Do you cook enough to warrant a five-star restaurant kitchen? Will you enjoy a tub with multiple whirlpool jets enough to justify the cost? Budget your money for improvements you need or will take full advantage of.

yourself to using the basement, hardly much of a home life. Do the work without going overboard, keep the budget reasonable, and sit back and enjoy the results.

The *B* Word: Budget

The idea of a budget conjures up visions of bespectacled bookkeepers who never throw a pencil out if it's more than an inch long. As Americans, we want instant gratification; we like to jump in now and deal with the consequences later. The problem is that (if you live through the remodeling) later always comes. It's easy to get carried away with the creative and adventurous aspects of remodeling; a sober budget can keep things from getting out of whack. Budgets go hand in hand with plans. Plan well and allow enough money for those pesky problems that pop up unexpectedly, and your house won't become the poorhouse!

Look at your budget as an important tool for getting the job done. Just when your enthusiasm (even obsession) could be leading you to financial disaster, having a budget and sticking to it gives you a reality check. When you plan, think through some alternatives: New five-paneled doors and keep the old carpet, or clean up the doors you have and get some outrageously thick, comfortable carpet? Or live with the old doors and carpet and put a little more money into your kitchen?

Don't be too conservative with your budget. Anticipate cost overruns during the course of a project, especially the more elaborate kind, and build them into your budget up front(more on this later). Here's a typical worksheet for estimating costs:

Sample Kitchen Remodel Estimate Sheet

1. Install new oak cabinets. Cost of materials: _____ Cost of labor: _____
   Alternative: Refinish existing cabinets and install new brass hardware.
   Cost of materials: _____ Cost of labor: _____

2. Replace all counters with new maple butcher block. Cost of materials: _____
   Cost of labor: _____
   Alternative: Install new plastic laminate (Formica brand) over existing counters.
   Cost of materials: _____ Cost of labor: _____

3. Install oak parquet flooring flooring. Cost of materials: _____
   Cost of labor: _____
   Alternative: Install new Armstrong vinyl flooring. Cost of Materials:_____
   Cost of labor:_____

4. Install new appliances, GE Monogram series. Cost of materials: _____
   Cost of labor: _____

   Alternative: Install Hotpoint appliances. Cost of materials: _____
   Cost of labor: _____

5. Update wiring to include two 20-amp small appliance circuits and circuits for refrigerator and disposer. Cost of materials: _____ Cost of labor: _____

6. Install six recessed ceiling lights with white rims. Cost of materials: _____
   Cost of labor: _____

   Install one 4-foot fluorescent light fixture with oak trim.
   Cost of materials: _____ Cost of labor: _____

7. Install new oak center island with marble countertop. Cost of materials: _____
   Cost of labor: _____

   Alternative: Install new oak center island with laminate countertop.
   Cost of materials: _____ Cost of labor: _____

8. Replace existing sink with American Standard, double-bowl, enameled steel sink with a Delta single-handle Gourmet faucet. Cost of materials: _____
   Cost of labor: _____

   Replace existing sink with American Standard single-bowl stainless steel sink and K-12175 Koehler Fairfax model faucet. Cost of materials:_____
   Cost of labor:_____

9. Install Pella Designer Series sliding wood windows. Cost of materials: _____
   Cost of labor: _____

   Refurbish existing wood windows. Cost of materials:_____
   Cost of labor:_____

10. Patch and paint all walls and woodwork. Cost of materials: _____
    Cost of labor: _____

11. First choice total for materials: _____

12. First choice total for labor: _____

13. Deductions per alternative chosen (itemize separately): _____

14. New total cost (materials plus labor): _____

15. Contingency amount (10 to 15 percent of total cost): _____

16. **Final total budget:** _____

Costs add up quickly, and that's why it's important to reflect and consider:

➤ What you really want

➤ What you're willing to live with

➤ How far you're willing to stretch your financial resources

Look Out Below!

Before you go into any debt to remodel your house, be sure your finances are in good order. Make sure you have an emergency account of three to six months' worth of living expenses set aside, a recommendation made by many financial advisers. The last thing you need in the middle of a big remodeling project is a financial crisis.

Remember, you'll have to come up with the money for all of this work.

What's It Worth to You?

If you take money out of savings or other investments, you'll forego any further return on it in order to pay for lumber, paint, and drywall hangers. Do you expect the results of the work to be worth giving up this financial security?

What about going into debt? Calculate your interest payments into your bills from the contractor and the Lumber-R-Us store for a true total cost. Do you still want to proceed?

Making Friends with Your Banker

If you do decide to borrow, you have several loan sources available to you, some more onerous than others. I'd stay away from big guys in the pool halls who have even bigger guys as collection officers. Banks offer the following ways to get money:

➤ Mortgage refinancing

➤ Home-equity loan

➤ Home-improvement loan

➤ Refinance-remodel loan

➤ Unsecured, personal line of credit

Other sources of money include:

➤ 401(k)

➤ Credit cards

➤ Family or friends

An unsecured personal line of credit establishes that you are truly creditworthy. A credit line is well worth establishing for use in an emergency, regardless of whether you need one for remodeling. The drawback is that the interest is not tax-deductible.

In some parts of the country, homes have been riding a market wave of higher prices for the past few years. At the same time, interest rates have been dropping. Refinancing is one source of remodeling money, but be sure to work out the figures:

➤ There are refinancing fees to pay that add to your cost basis for the loan and, ultimately, your remodeling costs.

➤ When you refinance, you're starting out with a fresh mortgage again, that is, at year one of a 15- or 30-year loan.

➤ You'll need to figure out how many months it will take you to make up for the new loan fees with the savings you'll get from a lower interest rate and lower monthly payments.

➤ You're wiping out most of the equity you've built in the house by taking it out in cash.

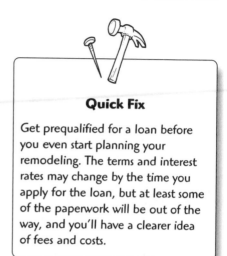

Quick Fix

Get prequalified for a loan before you even start planning your remodeling. The terms and interest rates may change by the time you apply for the loan, but at least some of the paperwork will be out of the way, and you'll have a clearer idea of fees and costs.

Homeowners can also take out a home-equity loan, which is essentially a second mortgage. These loans are based on your percentage of equity versus mortgage debt. There are many advantages to these loans in that you're only incurring enough additional debt to pay for the specific remodeling, rather than refinancing your entire loan. Like total refinancing, home-equity loans are currently tax-deductible.

Home-improvement loans are set up for smaller amounts of money, say $15,000 to $20,000, and are based on an "as will be" value of your home after the project is finished. In other words, the bank will base its loan amount on the anticipated value of your home, based on their own assessment and estimates, after the improvement.

Refinance-remodel loans are an interesting animal. They also work on an "as will be" basis. These programs pay off your first mortgage and then directly pay off the remodeling costs as the work is completed. The lending institution keeps a tight rein on the money; they never pay out more than the finished work is worth as a percentage of the loan. These loans typically have higher fees and costs than regular mortgages.

More Than One Source of Funds

Some people are willing to borrow against their retirement plans to remodel their homes, even though there are risks involved. I'm not a big fan of this approach, but it can be appropriate under some circumstances. Borrowing from your 401(k) might make sense if:

➤ It's a short-term loan

➤ If the house is sold, the remodeling yields a positive return equal to or in excess of what it may have earned in your retirement account

Credit cards are a tremendous convenience and a great way to get free use of the issuer's money for a few weeks if you pay the balance in full every month. Otherwise, you're paying a hefty fee for charging those power tools at Home Depot.

Your Insurance Agent Would Like a Word with You

You have to have enough insurance coverage on your house to cover replacement value if there's a total loss from a fire or other calamity covered by your policy. It doesn't do you much good to find out you're only covered for 85 percent of its replacement value. What do you do, rebuild without a bathroom?

Remodeling often adds value to your home and will call for increased coverage and premiums. Call your insurance agency and apprise them of your plans so they can recalculate your coverage.

Figuring It All Up

By now, you may be tired of the whole remodeling process, and all you've lifted is a pencil! Dealing with money and costs is fatiguing, and these are only the first steps. So far, you've had to figure how much you're able, or willing, to pay for remodeling your home, where and how you can get the money and financing, and what's the best deal for your circumstances.

Circumstances determine everything. What's the rest of your debt load like? How long do you plan on staying in your house? Are interest rates dropping or heading up to the stratosphere? What if you discover the day after the contracts are signed that the family you were planning to have is going to show up earlier than expected.

Where Those Dollars Will Go

Your remodeling dollars will be spread across a broad cross-section of America and the world economy. Potentially, you'll be supporting local contractors, tile designers, foreign nail factories, guys who drive drywall delivery trucks, paintbrush manufacturers, and numerous national fast food outlets that feed all of these people.

Does your state have a sales tax? Figure that in, too. Suddenly your $25,000 budget will get cut down a notch or two. Dozens of insidious costs and delays sneak up on every remodeling project: late material deliveries that delay a contractor who goes off to another job and can't get back to yours for two weeks, unseen structural problems that require more money than you budgeted, and the owner fatigue factor. This last item means that, after a while, you'll throw just about any amount of money at the job to get it finished and get your pre-remodeling life back.

The Two P's: Plans and Permits

Well-thought-out plans will more than pay for the time it takes to write and draw them up, especially on complicated remodels. Plans ensure that all your contractor bids are based on the same assumptions, as long as the plans are referenced in your contracts. In other words, if the contract calls for solid-core oak doors, a contractor cannot come back to you and say, "Hey, I bid this to use plastic-coated cardboard. What's your problem?" Plans protect you and allow a bidding contractor to point out potential flaws or problems.

Plans for simple projects, such as adding additional kitchen counter space, or building a small deck, don't have to be all that elaborate. You can draw them up yourself by making a list of the measurements, materials, and finishes. No drafting skills? Relax. Simple sketches will work on small jobs, as long as your accompanying description is clear, as in the following example:

Project: Kitchen Island/Workspace

Dimensions of base cabinet

Length: 48 inches
Width : 24 inches
Height: 34.5 inches

Dimensions of countertop

Length: 60 inches
Width: 38 inches

Details: Base cabinet is to be done in oak plywood, cabinet grade, to match existing kitchen cabinets. Include two doors and two drawers to match existing cabinets and one adjustable shelf of high-density particle board. Install base shoe, and stain and lacquer cabinet to match existing cabinets. Countertop will be $3/4$-inch, high-density particle board covered with Formica pattern D-456 Gray Pebble. Countertop will be edged with oak strip to match existing cabinets.

More elaborate plans—anything calling for major structural changes, for instance—should be drawn up by a professional (an architect or a designer/builder). See Appendix E, "Hiring and Working with a Contractor," and Appendix F, "Contracts," for guidelines on finding reputable professionals and structuring your agreements.

The Second P: Permits

All kinds of remodeling work gets done without permits from local building departments. The reasons are usually the same:

➤ This is a small job; we don't need one.

➤ They're too slow in issuing permits.

➤ It's none of the building department's business.

Some jobs, such as adding kitchen cabinets or upgrading your windows, usually don't require permits because they don't structurally change your house or mess with the wiring, plumbing, or furnace. The final determinant as to whether you need a permit for your proposed work is your local building code. If you're not certain, give the building department a call. Before you decide to skip the permits, consider what can happen:

➤ Any damage to your home as a result of faulty, uninspected work does not have to be covered by your homeowner's insurance policy.

➤ You can be fined, and the job can be delayed if a building inspector discovers what you're doing.

➤ You must disclose any improvements done to the house when you go to sell it and whether they were done without permits.

Overall, permits are to your advantage. Either you or your contractor can get them, but it's to your advantage to have the contractor do it and keep more of the liability for the job and its code compliance in his or her court, not yours. If the contractor agrees to take out the permits, be sure you see them posted before the work begins.

A Materials World

There are materials, and then there are budget-busting materials. You can have sliding vinyl windows or the finest new wood double-hung windows with solid brass hardware. You may not have much choice when it comes to meeting code requirements, but you're in the driver's seat when it comes to many of the materials.

Choosing materials is a matter of needs versus wants and where the two should meet. Can you get along without that self-heating toilet with the built-in CD player? It's easy to get carried away with materials, so consider your budget along with your desires and work out some compromises.

Look Out Below!

If a contractor tries to talk you out of a permit when one *is* clearly required, watch out! Your house can get caught in the middle, especially if the job *is* shut down by a building inspector until the necessary permits and inspections are obtained.

Hired Hands: Contractors

Hire a contractor, and you're trading your money for someone else's time and expertise. Fees are strictly supply and demand, a system we readily accept when the demand is up for the work we do, but when a plumber quotes $40+ per hour, we start considering price controls. With the exception of some very high-end materials or special order items, your biggest expense when remodeling will be hired labor.

Some contractors offer two prices: One if you pay by check and request receipts, another if you pay in cash. Cash prices usually exclude sales tax, because the whole point is for the contractor to avoid paying taxes on the income. I'm not going to moralize here. You can always claim you paid for the work and what the contractor did afterwards was none of your business. But before you adopt the New Hampshire license plate motto, "Live Free or Die," think about what could happen to you:

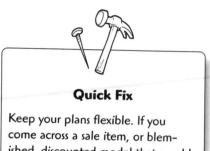

Quick Fix

Keep your plans flexible. If you come across a sale item, or blemished, discounted model that would suit your purposes, consider substituting it for your first choice and grab the savings.

➤ Without any receipts for the job, you can't prove that the work was done and therefore added value to your home.

➤ If the employees or suppliers of the contractor used on your job ever sue for lack of payment, the contractor can always claim not to have been paid by you; you could be held liable instead. Even when everything is above board and you have proof of payment to your contractor, you can still be liable for lack of payment to others.

➤ You could be hit up for unpaid sales tax on the work performed and materials purchased.

The cash economy is alive and well all over the world, but it is not without its consequences; think hard before you take this path.

Hidden Expenses

The best-laid plans can't anticipate everything (see Chapter 8, "Everything You Didn't Think About"). What other costs can there be to your remodeling besides labor, materials, plans, and permits? Well, where would you like to start?

Let's start with financial costs; I'll hit the personal ones later. If you're doing the work yourself, you'll need to buy, borrow, or rent tools. There are dump fees for the refuse and debris. In Pierce County, Washington, disposal fees run $96 a ton! You've already figured in the materials, so no surprises there, except that you may have to make more trips to the store than you figured on.

If you have to move out of your home, you have to live somewhere, and that may involve rent or moving in with friends or relatives (which in some ways could cost you more than renting). Of course, there are the surprises you run into during the course of the job: rotted floor joists, drainage problems, and a dormer that's attached to the rest of the house with carpet tacks. You should always add a contingency percentage—10 to 15 percent of the cost of the project is good—to your estimated costs to cover these not-so-fun discoveries.

Reality Check: Estimated Expenses Times Two

There's one well-worn notion that the only way to figure the real cost of remodeling is to take your best estimate and double it. This is a fun piece of folklore, but if you do your homework first, it's a great exaggeration. You'll never estimate a large project to the penny, but you and your contractor can get it close enough.

Many jobs go over budget because owners start changing the original plans once the job gets started. When it's no longer drawings on paper, and the reality sets in, owners see things differently. Change orders can be costly, especially if a contractor is using them as a profit center. Once the job is going and a price is set, any changes can be priced proportionally higher than if they been included in the original scope of the work. Figure out what you want from the beginning, and you'll stick closer to your budgeted costs.

Is It Worth It?

How do you decide if your remodeling is worth it to you? You can measure this worth personally and financially. No one can assess the personal payback but you. Ask yourself:

➤ Will I enjoy myself? After all the work is done, will the quality of my home life improve enough to warrant the expense?

➤ Will this ever be worth all the stress I'm going through now?

➤ Am I doing this for the right reasons (for example, because I want to stay here and remodel, not just make my spouse/partner happy)?

Measuring the financial worth of a remodeled house is a lot easier: Once you're finished, will it be worth more than the accumulated debt you've incurred? Will you make money if you sell it? This is when a good real estate agent can provide some market guidance.

Decisions, Decisions

You're looking at expenses, dust, and a disrupted life when all you wanted was a nice house with an extra bathroom. You may have to borrow money to do the work, and you've heard nothing but horror stories about contractors. One paint store clerk tells you to use water-based polyurethane, and another says you'd be nuts to do that, and just who would ever suggest such a thing?

The process can be overwhelming, especially if you haven't had much exposure to remodeling. Of course, that's why you bought this book! Step back for a moment, and try to look at the job objectively, as though you don't own the house, but are the project manager. Does what you were considering look any different to you?

Downsizing That Remodel

You can always do less than you planned and still get a high-quality product. You don't need the very finest grade material to get acceptable results. Still, be honest with yourself: Will you be satisfied if you cut back, or would you be better off waiting until you can afford to do the work you really want? There's no point in reducing your expectations only to look at those vinyl floors—when you wanted tile—every day and hate them.

Quick Fix

Your least expensive projects, such as repainting, adding shelves, or stripping a fireplace mantle, can give you an immediate sense of accomplishment. If money is tight, these jobs let you know that things are moving forward.

The Least You Need to Know

➤ A realistic budget is one of your best remodeling tools.

➤ When you figure up your budget, consider the hidden costs, such as taxes and unexpected change orders.

➤ Clear, well-defined plans are another critical remodeling tool and should be completed before any work begins.

➤ It's much less expensive to rethink the project before you get started than implement changes during the course of the work.

➤ Personal costs and stress will also be part of your remodeling efforts and should be anticipated in your planning.

➤ A beautiful house is fun to live in, but don't make it the most important thing in your life.

Part 2
Making Big Plans

You've walked in, around, and through your house. You know your budget limitations and are slowly figuring out what you want to do. The indoor pool is out and probably the racquetball court. You've narrowed down your remodeling desires to a new bathroom and finishing the basement. Vague notions of marble bathtubs and a new media room float around your head, but how are you going to pull this off? Where do you start? The first thing you need is a plan.

Remodeling without plans is something like putting together a holiday dinner with whatever food you happen to have around the house: It might work out, but canned spaghetti and Jell-O is no substitute for stuffed turkey with all the trimmings. Planning, timing, and scheduling are as important to your project as your budget and financing. You won't avoid all the pitfalls that normally accompany these projects, but you won't have to fall in too deep.

Even small projects such as painting a couple of bedrooms require some planning. You have to choose colors, purchase paint and supplies, clear out the rooms, schedule time to do the work, and possibly do wall and woodwork repairs. You also have to decide who's going to do the work, you or your checkbook. If it's you, be prepared to lose a weekend of your free time. Hiring it out? You have to find a painter, review estimates for the job, and schedule the work. This job is more than just showing up with a can of paint and a paintbrush, even if someone else is doing most of the painting.

The bigger your project, the more you can expect the unexpected. You're dealing with more suppliers, contractors, and dollars. For the first time, you'll fully understand your high school math term "exponential" as things start multiplying. Don't worry; you'll be "based" and ready once you've read the next few chapters.

Chapter 7

Prepare First; Remodel Later

In This Chapter

➤ Starting with ideas and ending up with plans

➤ Doing the basics first (so you can do the fun jobs later)

➤ Finding inspiration

➤ Scheduling beforehand to get the upper hand

➤ Dealing with remodeling roadblocks

➤ Creative ways to find and buy building materials

It's easy to get carried away with your remodeling dreams. If you follow in the very misguided steps of your author, you'll start tearing into everything—as I did with my first house—and not finishing anything. All right, eventually I did get it done, but only after going through more dumb ways of doing things and more stress than I ever needed to. It doesn't exactly do wonders for a marriage, either.

This chapter will help you keep those regretful experiences to a minimum when you remodel. You've already been introduced to the idea of writing up remodeling plans; now learn how to broaden your visions and focus on turning them into realities. You can't plan for everything, but the more information you have, the more exposure to other people's projects and ideas, the better prepared you'll be for your own work. Learning from other people's remodeling experiences can be one of your best investments. Why find out the hard way that kids and wooden kitchen floors aren't the best combination in the world (unless you go for that scratched look)?

Lots of Ideas, but not a Clue

Page through *Sunset Magazine, Metropolitan Home,* or the tonier *Architectural Digest,* and remodeling looks easy. You see the results, but rarely see the process. The pictures show a gleaming bathroom the size of a garage with polished brass faucets, multiple shower heads in the tub, a gas fireplace, and maybe an android towel attendant or two. Pictures of the process would show a gutted room, a plumber telling the designer where to get off, and a tile installer working under spotlights until 1:00 a.m. (on what had been a Sunday night) to finish before the painter showed up first thing Monday morning.

Never hesitate to throw all your remodeling ideas on the table and look at them by the light of day. You can drive stakes through the hearts of a few of them right away, like the three-story rock-climbing wall complete with waterfall. What about the ones that are hazy? How do you know what this project will be like until you've done it? Can you truly predict what a lemon-yellow bedroom will look like from a color swatch?

> **Look Out Below!**
>
> If you write a contract with an absolute final completion date but start adding change orders, your contractor no longer has to stick with the original time frame. Keep this in mind when you request changes, because they can mess up your deadlines in a big way.

Perfect Remodels—on Paper

A picture may be worth a thousand words, but all the pretty pictures in the world can't convey the experience of living in the remodeled space. We're three-dimensional creatures. We have to walk through the room, look at the colors for a while, and mix a few margaritas on the kitchen counter. We have to know if it's all going to fit and feel right. You should ask yourself these kinds of questions:

➤ How practical are certain finishes and styles around young children (if you have or are planning to have kids)?

➤ Do I want to bother with a new wood-burning fireplace when a gas model is so convenient?

➤ Am I willing to maintain a ground-level, wooden deck for years to come or would a stone or concrete patio be more suitable?

➤ Should I choose a fiberglass tub and shower combination that can get scratched or a tile surround that's more durable but needs more upkeep, and can leak?

You can never know for sure, but there are ways to shed light on how well your future renovations will work out.

You Can Walk It Out

Walk around the space and do your best to envision how the changes or additions will look or feel. Pepper yourself with questions about how well the room will work with your life:

➤ With three Labrador Retrievers and two cats that play chase all day, should I reconsider installing antique pine floors in the living room?

➤ Is a 3-foot-wide moat around my computer enough to keep the kids away from it when I'm not home?

➤ Will we miss having a kitchen if I use the space to extend the garage? Isn't this why pizza delivery was invented?

➤ Should we reinforce the section of the floor where I'll be displaying my antique brick collection?

Visit Some Remodeling Veterans

Everyone knows someone who's done some remodeling work on his or her home. You may have watched your parents or a colleague go through it or seen the telltale collection of pick-up trucks and vans surrounding a neighbor's house. Maybe you learned about social hibernation when some old friends you hadn't been able to reach for months invited you to their remodeled house to ooh and ah. The homes of people you know who've been there, done that, are a great resource for the following reasons:

➤ You can see finished results.

➤ They can tell you what to avoid and what to expect.

➤ You'll learn the names of competent and incompetent contractors.

➤ If you kept in contact with the owners during the remodel, you'll have a better idea of the stress levels the work can produce.

Compare results. Does one paint job look okay while another one absolutely sparkles? Look at the *finish carpentry*. Did one contractor get by with a simple, strictly functional approach while another went to great pains to produce something more appealing?

Contractor Talk

Finish carpentry refers to the installation of wood casings around doors and windows, baseboards, base shoe, wood edges on countertops, and installing doors. Basically, it's work involving the installation of a finished wood product or trim.

Snooping Around Open Houses

Go to weekend open houses where there's been new construction; it's a great way to see different designs and styles up close. Look at houses in the price range of your own and go up from there.

Internet Inspirations

The Internet offers all kinds of opportunities to explore home design and remodeling ideas. One of the easiest ways is to go to the Web site of a particular manufacturer and check out their online showrooms and product displays.

Don't have a particular product in mind? No problem, just do a Web search for cabinets, plumbing fixtures, designer homes—whatever broad category you're looking for. You can also go to http://remodeling.hw.net/guide and check out its extensive list of products, along with links to different company Web sites.

Software Gives You the Edge

Many architects and designers use CAD (computer-assisted design), a wonderful by-product of the computer revolution. These programs allow you to see finished rooms with a seemingly infinite combination of finishes, trim, window treatments, and floor finishes. Full-scale CAD programs are very expensive and not appropriate for a homeowner to purchase for a simple remodel. Consumer-friendly, scaled-down versions of these programs, however, can present you with endless remodeling options. Macmillan Digital Publishing offers Imagine Your Complete Home & Landscape software package that uses photographs of our own home, and goes from there, combining hundreds of wallpaper, carpet and color samples.

What Do You Want to Remodel Today?

Given your druthers, you probably want to start right in constructing the killer master bedroom suite, complete with a mini-kitchen, sunken hot tub, and media center. That's something like polishing and waxing your car when the brakes are shot. There's always time to install the new bathroom, but check that you don't need to replace the hot water heater first.

Once you decide what you need to do first, you then need to decide when to do it. In many parts of the country, summer is the ideal time for work on the outside of your house, but winter may be the best time for you to do some inside repairs.

There Really Is an Order to This

The following is a rough guideline to putting your job priorities in order:

➤ If it leaks, sparks, smokes, is falling down or sinking fast, fix it first.

➤ Major upgrades, such as wiring, plumbing, roofs, furnace, or water heater, should be done second.

➤ If it squeaks, sticks, drips, or has a hole, tear, or scratch in it, fix it third.

➤ Anything that improves your comfort, but you could live without, such as new rooms, remodeled kitchens and bathrooms, or new flooring, can be done last.

You're moving from the big issues—pipes that are doing an imitation of Old Faithful, for instance—down to the small stuff like squeaking floor boards. Finally, you move into your wish list. Individual jobs will have their own order of events, moving from the rough work of demolition to the finish painting. You'll find details on specific projects in Parts 3, 4, and 5.

Tales from the Scaffold

I once did a major restoration on an older, high-end apartment building in Seattle. The job superintendent had an unusual understanding of the effects of one subcontractor's work on another. When all the major work was finished, and after the first coat of primer and paint had been applied, he had the hardwood floors installed, sanded, and finished with one coat of sealer. With the dusty part of their job over with, he then had the floors covered with heavy construction paper while the painters finished up. After all the work had been done, the floor crew came back, removed the paper, and applied the final coat of finish. It was a beautiful job.

Even the most experienced contractors and project managers go out of sequence sometimes due to circumstances beyond their control. A subcontractor may not be available, materials are delayed due to factory shortages, and even weather changes can throw a job schedule out of whack (those darn hurricanes). But with flexible planning and plenty of lead time, you can usually avoid major slowdowns.

It's Summertime, and the Working Is Easy

You should be mindful of the weather and how it will affect your project. If you can't do everything in the warmer months, at least do the following:

➤ Roof replacement

➤ Drainage and foundation work

➤ Any work where an exterior wall of the house gets opened up for a room or door addition

➤ Exterior framing, siding, and painting

➤ Window replacement or restoration

➤ Digging out crawl spaces to add or extend a basement

The one drawback to summer scheduling is that summer is the busy season for most contractors (furnace technicians excepted, so it's a good time to get hold of them).

Contractor Talk

To contractors, the *critical path* is the portion of the work that must be done in a timely manner because too much other work depends on it. Thus, electricians are important to the critical path.

Make arrangements as far ahead of time as possible and be prepared to adjust your timetable if your contractor gets backed up (or you get bumped temporarily because a more profitable job came up).

In the colder months, go ahead and work on any interior projects you weren't able to get to sooner. Time them around the holidays so you're not taping drywall and trying to wrap presents at the same time. Remember, the only time you need to be in a hurry is when you're adding on a room or replacing a roof, and the weather gets bad. Otherwise, your patience will pay off later if you take your time and do the job right.

Ideas Guide; Plans Decide

Every homeowner has ideas about changes they'd like to see in their homes, but without a concrete, well-drawn plan, they'll just stay ideas. In terms of remodeling, *planning* refers to the entire preparatory process prior to and the follow-up during the remodeling process. *Plans* are the physical drawings that outline and display the work to be performed. Without some kind of plan, your project can become a freeform sculpture, changing with your whims on a daily basis (I've had clients like this).

Plans accompany specifications. The specifications list the materials to be used, the installation procedures to follow, and the quality that's expected from the job. They're a how-to reference for whoever is doing the work.

Specifications for a new deck, for example, could include:

➤ 12 × 12–inch pier blocks under each post

➤ Posts, beams, and joists all are pressure-treated lumber

➤ Use 6 × 6–inch posts; reseal any cut, exposed ends with wood preservative

➤ Decking consists of number-one cedar two-by-fours, fastened with $3^1/_2$-inch deck screws

➤ Railing and balustrades consist of number-one cedar two-by-fours and two-by-twos, as per plan

Tales from the Scaffold

Plans take care of all the nonartistic underpinnings of the work, such as the location of wires, structural details, and the slope of the roof. They also dictate the finer points, such as the brass hardware on the French doors or the style of molding to be used around the windows. Plans and specifications are your authority of last resort if you have a dispute with your contractor: Just be sure *you've* read them over, too.

Drawing Up the Plans

Can you draw up your own plans and specifications? Certainly, people do it every day and show up at their local building department to take out permits for their remodeling projects. The building department will tell you quickly enough whether your plan is acceptable. Among other things, your plans will show:

➤ Room dimensions

➤ Plumbing and electrical changes

➤ Structural changes, including new walls, removal of existing walls, adding windows or doorways, extending or strengthening a foundation, or changing a roof line

➤ Any changes to your heating/air conditioning system

What if your ideas are more elaborate, such as adding a room or even a second floor? Chances are you may be a little rusty when it comes to calculating the additional load a second story can have on your existing framing and foundation. Call in a professional.

Calling a Professional

Short of looking in the phone book for Plans-R-Us, who do you turn to come up with plans and specifications for your remodeling job? You have several choices, including:

➤ Architects

➤ Architectural draftsmen

➤ General contractors

Architects have the most formal training and will normally have the highest fees. An architectural draftsperson is comparable to a legal aid or a physician's assistant in their respective fields, that is, they have sufficient knowledge to deal with most common problems. Some general contractors—known as design/builders can produce adequate plans for certain jobs, but they will work with architects on more complicated projects.

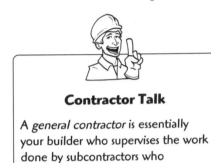

Contractor Talk

A *general contractor* is essentially your builder who supervises the work done by subcontractors who specialize in single trades, such as plumbing.

Got Any Change?

Plans and specifications are not set in stone, but put on your safety glasses if you have to start chiseling away at them too much. Changes can be expensive and frustrating to the progress of the job. They can also cut back the scope of work if you have to start tightening up on your budget (eliminating the separated heated garage for your snowmobiles, for example).

If you're going to deviate from the plans:

➤ Be prepared for delays and additional costs.

➤ Discuss these deviations with your contractor and designer first.

➤ Ascertain whether your changes are even feasible.

Tales from the Scaffold

The ultimate in unplanned homes is the Winchester House in San Jose, California. Sarah Winchester, widow of the heir to the Winchester rifle fortune, was told by a psychic to build a house for the spirits of all those who ever found themselves on the wrong end of a Winchester rifle. The spirits would not haunt Sarah as long as the house was being built; they even directed the building via nightly seances. Starting with an eight-room farmhouse, carpenters worked 24 hours a day for 38 years until Sarah's death in 1922. The result was a house with 160 rooms, 47 fireplaces, doors that opened into walls, staircases to nowhere, and a $1/2$-inch deep storage cabinet.

Schedules Rule

Airlines, physicians, and appliance repair persons all try to stick to a schedule, more or less. Schedules are great on paper, but reality rears its ugly head as planes arrive late, your doctor gets stuck with a hypochondriac, and the appliance guy is three hours late. Your remodeling experience will go the same way, whether you do everything yourself or hire it all out.

From a general contractor's standpoint, the following must be done:

➤ Permits must be taken out, and start and finish dates of the job must be established.

➤ All the materials have to be ordered to ensure they'll arrive in time for installation and be compatible with each task (you don't want framing nails to show up when you need finish screws).

➤ The subcontractors must complete their work in such an order that no single subcontractor holds up another one.

➤ All materials and labor must be paid for in a timely manner.

➤ Inspections must be arranged with the local building department.

➤ Meetings must be held with the owner and architect during the course of the project to discuss progress and any problems that might arise.

That's a lot to do! If you're going to be doing some of the work yourself, you'll have to complete your end of the work in a timely manner so you're not holding anyone up. What if you're doing everything yourself? Take the general contractor's list of scheduling responsibilities and add the task of arranging both your free time and your normal work time to do things like file for permits, take deliveries, and meet inspectors. All of these happen during business hours—your business hours.

A simplified schedule, assuming permits are in hand, for a one-month kitchen remodel might look like this:

Day 1: Demolish existing cabinets and countertops; remove debris.

Days 2 and 3: Remove appliances and sink; strip old vinyl floor.

Days 4 and 5: Run wiring for two 20-amp circuits, disposal circuit, and refrigerator circuit; wire new recessed ceiling lights; schedule initial electrical inspection.

Day 6: Begin patching walls; cabinets arrive on job site.

Days 7 through 9: Finish wall patching.

Days 10 and 11: Prime and paint walls; electrical work is inspected.

Days 12 and 13: Install cabinets.

Days 14 and 15: Install countertops and laminate.

Day 16: Install sink and disposal; replace old trap; call for inspection; new appliances delivered.

Day 17: Finish electrical work by installing outlets and new light fixtures; call for final electrical inspection.

Day 18: Mask off cabinets and counters; apply finish coat of paint to walls.

Day 19: Install new vinyl floor.

Day 20: Install prefinished or painted trim; complete any finish carpentry; plumbing inspected; final electrical inspection.

Days 21 and 22: Do final paint coat; finish trim.

Day 23: Install new appliances; do final cleaning.

All right, this schedule isn't so much exaggerated as idealized. No remodeling or construction project ever goes completely according to schedule, but schedules help keep us on track.

Get Real

When you imagine the remodeling process, your project goes quickly, without snags, and turns out just like the photos you see in the glossier magazines. Reality is another matter. Regardless of how fast or proficient you may believe yourself to be, allowing too little time to perform the job will prove nothing but frustrating and can compromise your results (I'll deal with specifics in Chapter 8, "Everything You Didn't Think About").

Quick Fix

Figure out the very latest date you have to be finished with the job and then start as early as you can. This strategy should give you more than enough time to complete your work in case something extreme comes up, such as a family emergency. Short, tight schedules are great in theory, but not always in practice.

Have you ever painted a closet or a bathroom? These areas are not very large, and you may think they could be painted pretty quickly. In fact, they are disproportionately time-consuming for their size. Uncertain about your skills and how much time you'll need to do different jobs? Pad your schedule. Think two days instead of one, five instead of three. Finished ahead of time? Good for you; take the evening off or push on in case you run into snags on the next part of the job. As you get more experienced, you'll learn to schedule more accurately.

Finally, keep a log of the actual amount of time you spend on your remodeling. Don't leave out extra chores or trips to the store; you want to be able to look back and accurately assess the true cost of the job, both in terms of your money and your time. The next time you remodel, you'll have a better idea of when to hire work out and when to do it yourself.

Another Saturday at the Lumberyard

When you're working full time, a big remodeling job takes up a lot of evenings and weekends. In addition to doing the work, you'll have to select and buy the materials. When you're hiring the job out, the contractor does all of the running around and ordering, hence the contractor's markup on most materials.

Look Out Below!

If contractors are booked up and your planning is off by a day or two, you may not see them again for weeks!

What can you expect if you're doing your own hunting and gathering of lumber, paint, and floor coverings? If you've never done this before, you'll discover a strange, but oddly compelling, world away from your desk or computer as you walk among aisles of plywood, hand tools, vinyl adhesive, and every type of nail and screw imaginable.

Beyond Home Depot

All-purpose home centers like Home Depot are great for seeing a lot of materials, hardware, and fixtures in one place. They're a good start for viewing limited versions of model kitchens and bathrooms, carpet samples, and color charts, but don't stop your research there.

Check your phone book for plumbing retail showrooms and suppliers, retail kitchen cabinet and equipment showrooms, and stores specializing in lighting fixtures. Look under "cabinetmakers" for bookshelves and storage systems for offices and family rooms. Visit paint stores, especially the ones contractors go to, for additional information on different painting systems and wallpaper selections.

Got Storage?

Great, you're bringing home kitchen sinks and bundles of oak trim—now what? You haven't even started the job yet. Follow a few simple storage rules:

➤ Do not store materials in the room you're going to be working on; keep the area clear, and bring in the materials when you need them.

Quick Fix

After you narrow down your paint color selections, always get a sample of the paint before committing to the color. Sometimes the sample color card and the actual color are quite different, especially under various lighting conditions. If you're trying to custom-match a color you already have elsewhere, in a piece of fabric, for instance, paint stores will try to secure a match for you.

➤ Keep everything dry and protected; outdoors, store materials on palettes or strips of lumber to avoid contact with the ground or concrete floor.

➤ Store materials in the order they will be needed so you don't have to dig through them.

➤ Use inside storage if you can.

If you have a shortage of storage room, convince your friends and family to help you out. Tell them you'll include their names on a dedication plaque in your new kitchen.

Salvage

Don't rule out salvage stores if you're looking for period pieces or trying to match old fixtures. Reproduction materials are usually available, but they are usually expensive. Check your phone book for architectural or historical salvage stores, and call contractors who specialize in demolition and modernizing old homes to see if they'll set some things aside for you.

The Least You Need to Know

➤ Before you do any remodeling, formulate a plan, budget, and work schedule.

➤ Anything can delay a schedule, so maintain some flexibility with your project.

➤ Look at as much new construction and as many remodeling projects as you can to clarify your own design ideas.

➤ A hold-up in one part of your remodeling work can have a snowball delaying effect on the rest of the project.

➤ Keep an open mind when buying materials; watch for lower-priced close-outs that can cut your costs.

Chapter 8

Everything You Didn't Think About

Remodeling is only an exact science on paper. All houses have some surprises. They don't always amount to much, but you'd never know it by the horror stories you hear. Take these stories with a grain of salt; it's human nature to stress the sensational and ignore the many projects that get completed in a less-dramatic fashion. We're all actors at heart, and a harrowing remodeling story gives us our moment on stage.

The truth is, even the best-laid plans can't anticipate everything you or a contractor may run into. Before you dig out your crawl space for a new basement, you assume you're on dry land. After digging through two feet of dirt, you discover an underground stream. Speaking of underground, who could have known that your old, unused oil tank had been leaking for years? Now that you've decided to remove it, your contractor tells you the good news: It's another $1,000 to remove the contaminated soil.

Some delays and problems aren't quite so sensational. Your electrician might be off a day or so from the estimated completion time, a sink may have to be returned due to blemishes, or you may decide the chateau mauve paint color in the bathroom just isn't going to do it. This chapter will give you some ideas about what to expect and how to deal with these time- and money-consuming annoyances. When you know what could happen, you have a chance of heading it off or at least heading out to dinner and forgetting about it for a while.

If It's Not One Thing . . .

The list of things you don't plan on has no limits. Extremes do exist. Airliners have been known to drop unexpected debris through someone's roof into the dining room. Who's going to expect something like that?

The bizarre aside, you can divide these surprises into two basic categories:

➤ Unforeseen conditions in and around your home that will affect your work

➤ Unexpected delays, including the human factor, after you start the work

Tales from the Scaffold

Sometimes remodeling and demolition bring pleasant surprises. One carpenter I met was tearing apart a staircase and found $350 in old currency. He turned it over to his client who cheerfully used it to pay some of the carpenter's fees. He even had him do some additional work, now that his budget had increased.

What You Can't See Can Cost You

Some unforeseen conditions include:

➤ Insect infestation and subsequent damage

➤ Previous work not done to code

➤ Collapsed drain lines

➤ Structure affected by rot

➤ Inadequate foundation and foundation drainage

Insects can range from termites to yellow jackets. Every contractor, especially painters, has stories to tell of disturbing a nest of ornery critters that came flying out with their stingers set on maximum stun power. An exterminator or a can of pesticide can send them to the great insect kingdom beyond, but you'll have to patch up any damage they've caused. Termites and other wood-loving little guys can be pretty damaging.

You don't have to bring your entire house up to code when you remodel. Building codes, both the national Uniform Building Code and your local code, spell out the current standards for all phases of new construction. These standards must be met for a builder to be in compliance; otherwise, all work can be stopped until they are.

You only have to have pertinent areas in compliance. An electrical service has to be able to support the demands of a new kitchen, for

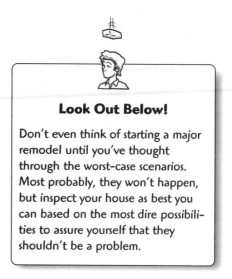

Look Out Below!

Don't even think of starting a major remodel until you've thought through the worst-case scenarios. Most probably, they won't happen, but inspect your house as best you can based on the most dire possibilities to assure yourself that they shouldn't be a problem.

instance. What if you have a disposal and a dishwasher already and are only going to replace them with new models? You might assume that their wiring was run properly and you won't have to install new circuits, only to discover that they're tied into your garage door opener and you've got to rewire it all.

Your best bet if you've got old wiring, meaning a fuse box instead of circuit breakers, is to include the cost of a new electrical panel in your budget. You don't necessarily need to rewire your entire house (that could be overkill), but you'll be ready for any future projects that may require new wiring. Besides, both your insurance company and your future real estate listing agent will reward you for this change. Insurance companies like upgraded electrical systems, and any agent will tell you that its presence will make the house an easier sell.

Drain lines and poor drainage have to be addressed, too. Just because drainage is out of sight doesn't mean it's not affecting your house. Foundations can be undermined by lack of drainage. Have it checked out; if for nothing else, you don't want a potential buyer's house inspector to make the discovery for you.

An inadequate foundation would be one that won't support your plans for an addition unless you beef it up, which may be a cost you hadn't considered. When you're in the planning stage, an evaluation by an architect or builder would let you know early on if your budget will need beefing up as well.

The more preparation work you do—inspecting for insects, checking for rot, digging around your foundation to confirm drainage, and cutting into walls to inspect for structural problems—the better you'll be able to predict whether your proposed plans, schedule, and budget will work out as you expected. When possible, it's always better to find out about such problems in advance!

Delays That Defer

Your house is inanimate, or should be. Haunted, poltergeist-ridden residences are not the province of this book; I'll leave that to Stephen King. Once human beings are involved in your remodeling, anything can happen. For the most part, people come to work and do their jobs, materials show up roughly on time, and the project gets done. But people also get sick, deliveries get misrouted, labor disputes pop up, and even technology can run amok (Y2K tip: *Don't* start your remodeling on December 31, 1999).

Delays can include:

➤ Slowdown in permits being issued

➤ Contractors starting late

➤ Individual tasks taking longer than estimated

➤ Work not passing inspection

➤ Materials not being available

➤ Weather-related delays occuring

➤ *Change orders* being made

Permits, including the building permit and those for plumbing, electrical work, mechanical work, and even insulation, are doled out by your local building department. It's easier to get a prompt response and a permit issued for projects that aren't too far afield from normal remodeling jobs. Remodel your kitchen and knock out a back wall? Fine. Add a three-story, pyramid-shaped breakfast nook? That's going to take a while. Some building departments are slow, regardless of your request.

Unless you're going to be doing your own work, don't take the permit out in your own name. Have your general contractor do it and include its cost in his or her fees. If you're only hiring subcontractors such as plumbers and electricians, have them supply the necessary permits. Your building department will require that your contractors be licensed, bonded, and insured. You should require proof of this as well, but the extra assurance from the building department is always welcome.

Whatever you do, don't proceed with any work that requires a permit until you have it in hand. You want the approval of, and the inspections by, your building department; this approval helps ensure that the work is done properly and according to code. In the long

Contractor Talk

A *change order* spells out a mutually agreed to change in the original scope of the work as spelled out in the contract. Change orders usually suggest more expense, but they can also cut back on the scope of work by, for example, substituting less expensive hardware for what was originally specified.

run, it's better that some work *not* pass inspection and be corrected than not to be inspected at all.

Contractors don't always start on time. An existing job may be taking longer than expected; yours could, too. Allow some flexibility in your starting dates, but don't let it get out of hand. Your contract will state a start date and spell out any cause for delay. Reputable contractors usually stick to their start dates.

Many jobs can be estimated accurately and completed in a timely manner. Estimates are based on the past experience of each contractor, but some jobs offer new problems. I watched a very frustrated window washer (who ultimately walked off the job) struggle to clean hundreds of multipaned windows, only to discover early on that a silicone sealer had been used around the glass. He assumed that what he was looking at was normal construction dust and grime.

Quick Fix

Building inspectors do a good job, but they're not perfect. The thoroughness of an inspection will depend on the inspector's interpretation of the building code, qualifications for the job, and workload at the time of your inspection. If possible, be present for any inspections. You can learn what an inspector looks for and get any of your own questions answered as well.

Someone else eventually cleaned them, but it took much longer than expected. If you're doing the work yourself and have little experience, you will really be guessing.

Weather can affect the job inside as well as outside your house. A week of unexpected damp weather during the summer means all your interior finishes will take longer to dry and cure. A sudden cold snap stalls the installation of your new landscaping. And forget about roofing during a wind storm.

Spare Changes?

Change orders are probably the main cause of remodeling delays. Every time you change your mind about anything, such as cabinet style, tile selection, or paint color, you're adding time to the project. You should make all of these decisions up front when you write up your plans and specifications. In addition to outlining the design of your project, plans and specs will list materials by manufacturer and brand name and colors and finishes.

You can avoid costly change orders by doing your homework. Look at as many sinks, faucets, paint colors, carpets, and plastic laminate samples as you can so your decisions are final before the job starts. Not only will you incur costs from changes in materials, your contractor will add an overhead charge as well (some charge a flat additional fee for any change order).

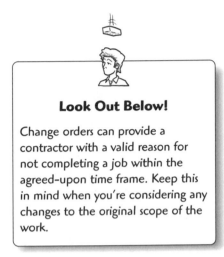

Look Out Below!

Change orders can provide a contractor with a valid reason for not completing a job within the agreed-upon time frame. Keep this in mind when you're considering any changes to the original scope of the work.

Practice Your Writing Skills

Always, always, always get change orders in writing. Casual conversations won't cut it. A written change order should detail the work you request or the contractor has discovered will be necessary. The change order should also include specifications, any necessary drawings, the amount of time needed to complete the work, and the fee. Putting these orders in writing keeps everyone honest, including you in case you happen to forget your discussion with your contractor.

There will always be some changes, but you want to keep them to a minimum. Phrases like, "Hey, what if we . . .," or "I've got a great idea," are real budget and schedule killers.

Word for the Day: Backorder

In addition to change orders, there's another order you should know about: the backorder. A backorder occurs when a supplier is out of something you need for your job and has to order it from a manufacturer. It could be anything from special fasteners to cabinet hardware. You may be able to speed up its delivery if you're willing to pay extra for separate shipping and possibly a handling fee. The earlier you order fixtures and materials specific to your job, especially if they're custom or unusual orders, the better the chances are that they'll be there when you need them.

Everything Starts Out Small

After you've lived in your house for a year or so, you decide you want an additional bathroom. How much trouble can that be? You'll just build it on the other side of your existing one to keep the costs down. It's not like you're adding a new floor to the house or anything.

Your new bathroom will introduce all kinds of people into your life, including:

➤ Plumbers and plumbing fixture suppliers

➤ Electricians and lighting suppliers

➤ Carpenters, drywall hangers, and tapers

➤ Tile setters and tile suppliers

➤ Painters and paint suppliers

➤ Vinyl floor installers and flooring suppliers

➤ Building department workers and building inspectors

Any project that involves more than a paint-brush will be more complicated than you expected. I'm not trying to be depressing; I just want to remind you of the importance of good planning. Knowing what you're getting into makes the whole process easier.

Old Houses Are the Worst

The monthly magazine *Old House Journal* extols the virtues of old houses and the rewards of restoring them. These often-beautiful homes have detail work rarely even approached in new construction. Along with the beauty comes the beast in the form of suspicious-looking past remodeling, old wiring, and cranky heating systems.

Quick Fix

You can avoid surprises by doing preliminary planning months before you would even consider doing any work. Finding out six months in advance what a bathroom addition will entail (you'd have to draw up the plans anyway) will help you prepare for the inevitable.

The older the house, the more likely that it's been changed by past homeowners, often without permits. You can run into just about anything. Contractors usually put some kind of contingency language in their bids to deal with these unknowns. X-ray vision would help, but the last time I looked, Superman wasn't in the remodeling business.

A Little Rot Goes a Long Way

Rot and deterioration aren't limited to old houses; new homes can have problems, too. Improperly flashed and sealed siding can allow water to seep into your house for years

I thought the plaster looked OK.

before it's discovered. In some cases, it's the siding itself or its installation that's the problem. Louisiana-Pacific's L-P Siding (see Chapter 3, "Judging a House by Its Cover") and various synthetic stucco products are the most notable examples.

Bathrooms are another fine source of rot, typically behind tub and shower walls that haven't been completely sealed, or whose seals haven't been maintained. Toilets whose wax seals have deteriorated are another source of leaking water that wreaks havoc on wood floors and joists. You come along expecting to replace a few fixtures only to find that you have wall and floor repairs to do as well.

Blame the Last Guys

Past homeowners—and you'll eventually be one unless you never move—can be a blessing or a curse when it comes to your remodeling project. I had a client who wanted me to sand down a deck built by the previous owner of his house so he could repaint it. We discovered that the decking was the cheapest wood available: #3 pine boards. The boards cost less than my fee to sand them!

Tales from the Scaffold

A local condominium homeowners' association was having problems with leaks coming through the outside walls of their 10-year-old building. Apparently, the exterior had never been properly flashed and caulked. As the contractor dug into things, he discovered that the wall framing was rotting because it had had so much water seepage. The more he worked, the more seepage he found—on every floor! Talk about unexpected surprises. The only way he would do the job was by the hour. He told the owners they'd be better off demolishing the building, but they kept going with the project, hoping it would eventually get better. It never did.

The worst problems you'll run across with past remodeling is work that wasn't done to code in existence at the time. Structural issues are big ones. I know of a one-room addition that is about to be torn down because it was built so poorly, but the house was sold with it in that condition nevertheless. So much for bank appraisals.

Those Darn Kids (and Spouses, Too)

If it were just you and your house, you could declare one or two rooms off-limits oases to contractors, dirt, and construction materials and get along just fine with the remodeling process. At the end of your normal work day—or if you're doing the work yourself, when you're tired of sanding woodwork—you could close the door behind you and relax. Couples and families can't pull it off quite so easily.

Kids and spouses, even when you're both doing or supervising the work together, want their house back and they want it now. You probably do, too, for that matter. While you spend the evening hours and on into early morning taping drywall, the family wants your company. It's tough to come home from work and try and get a few hours in on your bedroom addition if your kids want you to take them to the movies. Family and spousal needs and demands on your time don't change because part of your house is torn apart.

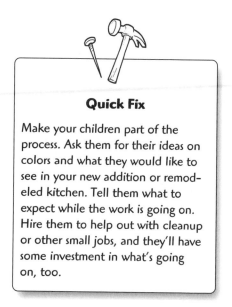

Quick Fix

Make your children part of the process. Ask them for their ideas on colors and what they would like to see in your new addition or remodeled kitchen. Tell them what to expect while the work is going on. Hire them to help out with cleanup or other small jobs, and they'll have some investment in what's going on, too.

It's easy to get caught up in remodeling projects. We justify the time we're spending doing the work and ignoring the family by the savings on contractors (maybe), and it really isn't taking that long, is it? (Yes, it is.) When we do our own remodeling work and mom the painter becomes mom the cook, chauffeur, and bedtime story reader more often than dad, equal parenting duties fall by the wayside. Dads, by my observations, have a harder time putting the hammers away when they should.

Remember Why You're Doing This

Tempers flare up pretty easily during remodeling work, especially if it's a large job that regularly adds floating dust to your morning breakfast cereal. Even if you've hired all the work out, there's a certain weariness to living with the process, regardless of whether you're staying in your house or camping out elsewhere. Most of us are creatures of habit—children certainly are—and we want to be home in our own beds at night, not rolled up in sleeping bags at the in-laws' house.

Make no mistake about it: There will be dust everywhere when you do major work on your house. Hammering, sawing, floor sanding, and demolition will produce and loosen dust that will take on a life of its own as it travels and settles all over your house. Plastic over the doorways helps, but daily cleanup will take extra time, too.

In the midst of the noise, dust, and unprecedented checking account activity, remember why you started this in the first place. You're doing this work to give yourself and your family a more comfortable home. Remember, it's not an end in and of itself and shouldn't end up consuming your life.

The Most Expensive Remodel of All

Remodeling projects can bring out the worst in anyone, and sadly, some couples' marriages don't survive it. The problems usually revolve around:

➤ Decision-making

➤ Costs

➤ Doing your share of the work

Tales from the Scaffold

Married clients of mine had just moved from a houseboat into their first house, a turn-of-the-century classic Seattle box. The inside was beautiful and had been completely remodeled. They told me that the last owners had done all the work and promptly divorced and sold the house—to the new owners' benefit. They were happy with the house, of course, but they commented that if they were ever to get a divorce it would be over something more important than remodeling. Fifteen years later, they're still married and living in the same house. Of course, all they've had to do was repaint the outside.

There are dozens of decisions in any remodeling project. A couple who hasn't learned how to compromise can be at loggerheads with each other over everything from the floor finish to the lighting fixtures. This is not the time to start working on your communication skills. Have you heard so many horror stories that you're not sure how you'll do? Consider starting small. Redo your master bedroom closet, for instance. See whether you can jointly select the shelves, choose the paint color, and maybe install an overhead light. Then move on to something else. If you and your spouse can't finish the closet without more than a few arguments, you'd better hold off on redoing the downstairs.

The simplest thing to do is to have regular family meetings to discuss the process of the job with everyone involved. Let them get their gripes out in the open, and address them together. Put all those communications seminars you had to sit through at work to good use at home; you probably never used them at work anyway.

Costs can always be stressful, especially when they begin to escalate. Part of the problem goes back to decision-making. He wants marble countertops; she thinks plastic laminate is more practical. She thinks they should add more windows to the new family room now that it's framed in and seems too dark; he doesn't want the expense of the change order. You really want to see the sparks fly? Make a unilateral decision and sign off on the additional cost without telling your spouse. Regular discussion is essential; it's right up there with planning.

Your Turn

You were painting until midnight; she quit at 6:00 p.m. He took Saturday morning off while you hauled framing lumber up to the second floor. Two people will never exactly split the work down the middle, but resentment can build in a hurry if a mutually agreed-upon remodel isn't worked on mutually.

You can avoid this problem if you:

➤ Draw up a list of tasks and agree on who will do what.

➤ Re-evaluate responsibilities from time to time, especially if one or another party is feeling put off.

➤ Understand that one partner may be doing "invisible" work, such as running out for materials, meeting with lenders, and scheduling inspections, but that it's work nevertheless.

➤ Have each partner recognize his or her own strengths and work appropriately.

Balancing Acts

I bring up the personal hardships and the effects of remodeling on a marriage for the same reason I emphasize thorough planning. Both give you advance knowledge. If you understand the stresses ahead of time, then you can better recognize the warning signs (such as your spouse pouring a can of midnight blue paint on your head and announcing that you'll be finishing the room alone). I figured out a long time ago that if a marriage can make it through a top-to-bottom remodel, it will make it through just about everything. That said, I wouldn't intentionally tear the house apart as a test. Try something less dangerous, like extreme snow-boarding or bungee-jumping.

Knowing When to Call It a Day

You think to yourself, just another hour or two. Suddenly it's midnight, and you still have to get up early for work the next morning. You have to know when to put your tools away, clean up, and go do something else, like eat or sleep. What are the signs? You'll know it's time to stop when:

➤ You start dropping or spilling things

➤ Your work starts looking sloppy

Quick Fix

As long as it's unskilled work that has to be done, think about getting it over with even if you're tired. It may mean you can sleep in the next morning.

➤ You start making mistakes

➤ Your children no longer recognize you

There are also practical reasons to stop. Daylight begins to fade, and you can't see your work as clearly as you would like. Local noise ordinances kick in (usually between 7 p.m. and 9 p.m.), legislating that you put your power tools away. And you shouldn't be painting the exterior of your house if the evenings are turning cool and moist.

Before you close up shop, look ahead to the next day. Spending an extra half-hour cleaning up or hauling the old doors or bathroom fixtures out to your trash pile, even if you're exhausted, may put you in a much better starting place when you return to the work.

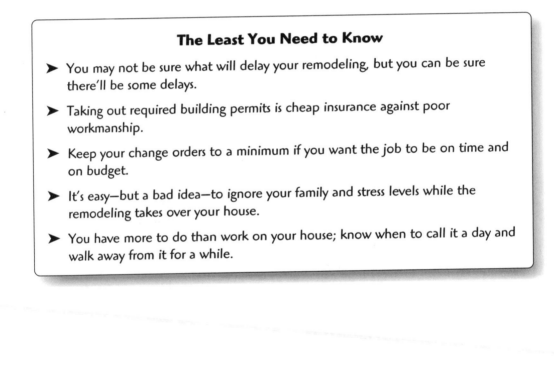

The Least You Need to Know

➤ You may not be sure what will delay your remodeling, but you can be sure there'll be some delays.

➤ Taking out required building permits is cheap insurance against poor workmanship.

➤ Keep your change orders to a minimum if you want the job to be on time and on budget.

➤ It's easy—but a bad idea—to ignore your family and stress levels while the remodeling takes over your house.

➤ You have more to do than work on your house; know when to call it a day and walk away from it for a while.

Part 3
Quit Planning and Get to Work

There comes a time when you have to quit the designing and actually remodel something! You know what that means: You must first do the jobs that keep you and your house dry and warm, light your way as your walk around, and give you clean water out of every tap.

Much of your remodeling work depends on doing these basics. Your beautiful new bathroom with six shower heads will look like a real waste of budget dollars if water only dribbles out of your old pipes. Leaky or missing gutters will make hash out of a new outside paint job in no time. These are not the fun jobs! You won't take your friends out to the garage to show them your new electrical panel or your foundation repairs.

The basics have to be planned, scheduled, and budgeted just like your other projects. You can't just slap a furnace in without thinking about new duct work, a choice of fuel (a change to gas, for instance, means a gas line will have to be run to your house), and even the type of thermostat. The chapters in this section will help you wade through the world of painting, roofs, foundations, wiring, plumbing, and heating/air conditioning, and keep your home drier, warmer, and brighter.

Chapter 9

Painting: Your House Is Your Canvas

In This Chapter

➤ Choosing the right paint for the job

➤ The conditions that will affect your painting

➤ Preparation: Your most important step

➤ Tools and techniques for a professional job

➤ Cleanup: The last step

A carpenter I once knew used to say that every time Boeing, Seattle's behemoth airplane company, had a lay-off, a few hundred new painting contractors would show up on the scene. Painting gets no respect—I mean, anyone can paint, right?

There's more to painting than meets the eye. Many homeowners spend more time agonizing over color selection than choosing the right kind of paint. Preparation time, the part no one likes to talk about, is woefully underestimated by first-time painters. But this is one job you can learn to do competently, neatly even, with a little practice and a free weekend or two.

Quality finishes, the right tools, and plenty of preparation work will give you great results, and you'll never paint yourself into a corner. This chapter tells you how to find your way around a paint store, roll out your walls, spiff up your siding, and spin your brushes clean at the end of the day. You will, however, have to pick your own colors.

So Many Paints, So Little Time

Before rollers and sprayers were introduced, painters used brushes of all types and sizes for everything. Can you imagine painting all the walls in your home with brushes instead of rollers? No? Well, that's how the walls in the Empire State Building were painted when it was built!

Paint and finishes now come in a confusing assortment of oils, latex, epoxies, and polyurethane, to name a few. Each type is made for specific purposes. Make the wrong choice, and you could be worse off than if you hadn't painted at all! Detailed information on types of paint can be found in Appendix B, "Paint and Painting."

Common Uses of Paint

Type of Finish	Where to Use
Latex paint	Interior walls, woodwork, exterior siding, trim, stucco
Alkyd and oil paint	Interior woodwork, wood floors, metal, exterior trim, windows, doors, porch floors
Solid body stains, semi-transparent stains	Exterior wood siding
Polyurethane	Interior woodwork, furniture, wood floors, exterior doors
Varnish	Interior woodwork, furniture, exterior doors
Danish oil	Interior woodwork furniture
Epoxy	Masonry, floors, plywood decks
Interior wood stain	Interior woodwork, floors, furniture, exterior doors (if coated with varnish or polyurethane)

Wade through the paint can labels, and you've got only two grades of paint available: cheap quality and good quality. Cheap paint is no bargain, unless your idea of fun is putting on a second coat when one should have sufficed. The solids content of paint will determine how well it covers the area you're painting (the higher percentage of solids the better). You want coverage, not extra work.

Making It Stick

Painting is pretty simple once you understand a basic principle or two. One important principle is what paint chemists call inter-coat adhesion. In plain English, this is the ability of one coat of paint to stick to another. Doesn't paint always stick once you brush it on? Sure, but you want it to stick around for the longest time possible, so the conditions have to be just right.

The factors that affect paint adhesion include:

➤ The condition of the surface you're applying it to

➤ The type of paint you're painting over

➤ The temperature

➤ Moisture

Sand or Strip?

Paint likes to be applied over a clean, slightly *toothy*, or coarse, surface so it has something to bite into. This means that the existing surface will require some form of preparation, anything from a light sanding to complete stripping. Old homes (see Chapter 31, "Restoration or Remodeling?") have special considerations to address before you can even pick up a paintbrush, such as multiple coats of paint, some of it lead-based, and severely deteriorated surfaces.

What's on First?

Beliefs regarding the suitability of coating one type of paint with another differ, so I'll make it easy:

➤ You can always coat one paint with another paint of the same type (alkyd over alkyd, latex over latex, and so on).

➤ You can usually apply latex over oil or alkyd if the surface is dull, or you can dull it by thoroughly sanding or deglossing it, and then coating it with primer.

➤ Alkyd paint is the universal cover-up specialist; it can stick to all kinds of interior finishes, including latex, shellac, varnish, and polyurethane, without extensive preparation work.

If you have a newer home, paint compatibility on the woodwork is a little trickier. More and more, interior woodwork is being painted with very fast-drying finishes containing exotic solvents and resins that allow the painter to apply several coats in one day. These surfaces will have to be well-sanded and possibly primed (depending on the original material) before you repaint.

Do a Temperature Check

Good preparation will solve most compatibility problems, but what can you do about the temperature? It's more of a concern with exterior painting, but for most types of paint, 65 degrees is considered the lowest optimum temperature, indoors or out.

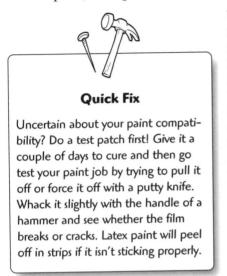

Quick Fix

Uncertain about your paint compatibility? Do a test patch first! Give it a couple of days to cure and then go test your paint job by trying to pull it off or force it off with a putty knife. Whack it slightly with the handle of a hammer and see whether the film breaks or cracks. Latex paint will peel off in strips if it isn't sticking properly.

Varnish and polyurethane like warm (70 degrees or more), dry temperatures. If it's too cool(do a test patch first on a piece of scrap wood), the resin starts to solidify in small chunks while you're applying the material, and no amount of brushing will keep them from forming. Your varnish job will look like it's got a case of acne. Hint: If you do any interior varnishing in the winter months, don't open a window near your work; the cool breeze will mess up your finish.

Painting outdoors when it's too hot can get you into trouble, too. Applying paint in direct, hot sunlight can cause the paint to form a skin or film before it's completely dry. The solvents in the paint still want out, and they'll come kicking through the paint film in the form of blisters and bubbles.

If you have to paint outdoors in hot weather, follow these guidelines:

➤ Start early in the day.

➤ If there isn't any dew on your house, paint the most shaded side (which is usually the north side) first.

➤ Follow the sun around your house as you paint.

Extra Dry, Please

Moisture is more of a concern outside, but you don't want to paint the bathroom two minutes after you've taken a steamy shower. Dry is the order of the day. Exterior wood also has to be dry before you paint it, otherwise the moisture forms blisters or bubbles on your newly painted house.

Get Hep with Prep

"I still can't start painting?" you're saying to yourself. Sure you can, and you'll have the opportunity to paint again sooner than you expected if this coat of paint doesn't last as long as it should.

Preparation is key to a first-rate, lasting paint job. Preparation includes:

➤ Cleaning

➤ Scraping

➤ Sanding or otherwise deglossing existing paint

Paint sticks best to clean surfaces; it doesn't like kitchen grease, crayon marks, grit, or grime. It also isn't too fond of being applied over glossy, peeling, or flaking paint. Preparation work is so vital that I've devoted Appendix C, "Paint Preparation," to the subject. Don't paint anything until you read about preparation.

A Primer on Primer

There's a difference between paint and primer. Primer is applied to new, unfinished material, such as wood, metal, and drywall, to both seal it and provide a slightly coarse surface for the paint to adhere to. Without the primer, the paint would soak into the surface and not form a complete protective film. You can use either latex or oil-based primer on wood (latex primer is almost always used on plaster and drywall). Oil-based primer can be covered with latex or alkyd paint. On new wood, latex primer works well, but oil-based primer often holds better on older homes with sections of bare, worn wood.

Primer Chart

Finish Material	Kind of Primer to Use
Latex paint	Can use either latex or oil primer, depending on application
Alkyd oil paint	Oil Primer
Interior stain	No primer
Exterior Stains	No primer
Varnish, polyurethane	First coat is diluted to seal wood

The Right Tools

Every time you paint with them, cheap tools remind you that they're cheap and so were you when you bought them. The brushes leave loose bristles as calling cards, hold less paint, and are not terrific for doing close detail work. It doesn't pay to skimp on paint roller covers and the rollers themselves either(those spinning things that you slip the roller cover over, more correctly known as roller frames). Think of painting the way professional painters do: The fewer times they have to dip a brush or roller into the paint, the faster the job gets done.

Most rooms require both roller and brush work to do the job. The tools you should buy—or borrow if you're on good terms with friends or relatives—include:

➤ Drop cloths

➤ 2$\frac{1}{2}$- to 3$\frac{1}{2}$-inch cut in brushes

➤ Roller tray, roller, and roller cover

➤ Roller extension

➤ 6-foot step ladder

➤ Blue masking tape

➤ Empty 5-gallon bucket

➤ Razor blades

➤ Spackle

➤ 1$\frac{1}{2}$-inch putty knife

➤ Latex caulking

➤ Caulking gun

➤ Screwdriver with changeable heads

➤ Sandpaper

➤ Paint stirrer/mixer

It sounds like a lot of stuff, but most of it you can use and reuse for years if you keep it clean and are careful about whom you loan it out to! You're probably familiar with most of these tools, but we'll do a quick review.

Drop That Cloth

Drop cloths protect furniture and floors. Painters use very heavy-duty drop cloths that prevent normal paint spillage from soaking through. You can substitute a roll of builder's plastic that's 6 millimeters or so thick and cover it with an old sheet.

Brush 'n' Roll

Brushes come with synthetic bristles (either nylon or polyester) for latex paints and natural bristles (boar's or ox hair usually) for alkyd. Each type of bristle likes the paint it was intended to be used with, so buy the appropriate brush.

The most common size for paint rollers is 9 inches. Roller covers come with different naps, or textured surfaces, from smooth to coarse. The surface you're painting will determine the required nap of the roller. For a textured wall, for example, a medium nap is more efficient. Like cheap brushes, cheap roller covers will leave bits of themselves behind in your paint, so buy good ones. You'll also need a roller tray and a roller extension, which allows you to paint ceilings easily and gives you some leverage on walls.

Mask It

Masking off a room is the process of applying masking tape, paper, and plastic over areas you're trying to avoid splattering with paint. Masking tape comes in various grades and quality. It isn't meant to stay taped to a surface indefinitely. The longer it's kept on, the better the chance it won't tear off very easily, especially if it's exposed to sunlight. The blue tape has a different adhesive than standard masking tape and can be safely be left in place for up to two weeks. For speed-challenged painters, it's well worth the extra money.

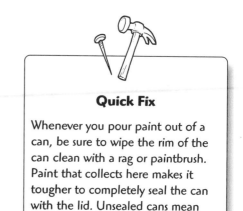

Quick Fix

Whenever you pour paint out of a can, be sure to wipe the rim of the can clean with a rag or paintbrush. Paint that collects here makes it tougher to completely seal the can with the lid. Unsealed cans mean dried-out paint.

Clean It and Caulk It

Use single-edge razor blades to remove paint (new or old) from window glass. Spackle is the eponymous name for a soft, putty-like material used to patch small holes in wood, drywall, and plaster. (Filling larger holes and other wall repairs are covered in Appendix G, "Repairs.") Latex caulking is the universal crack filler; DAP has a huge line of caulking available everywhere.

Undo It

Finally, you need the screwdriver to remove window and door hardware, whatever you don't want to paint around or cover with masking tape, and the plastic, metal, or ceramic electrical switch and outlet covers on the walls. You can also use it to open your paint cans. You need sandpaper to rough up the surface paint.

Time for an Inside Job!

By now, maybe you've decided it's easier to live with your home the way it is and just wait until your avocado-green walls hit the top of the paint popularity chart again. Once you get going, you'll be amazed at how much a room can change from something as simple and inexpensive as a fresh coat of paint. We'll start with your interior.

You've decided what type of paint you want, latex or alkyd, and the degree of sheen or gloss (see Appendix B, "Paint and Painting"). The color's another matter, so look at as many color chips and samples as you need until you've found the one that says, "Hey, this is me; I'm Ruby Red and proud of it."

How much paint should you buy? Buy more than you think you'll need; you can return unopened cans of off-the-shelf colors. Now that you have your paint, you have to learn a little about painting techniques before you're ready to break out the brushes and rollers.

Painting Progress

Before you pry open that paint can, you need to understand the order of painting events:

1. Empty out the room (just cover the grand piano).

2. Cover every inch of the floor and any furniture or cabinets with plastic or drop cloths. It is an axiom of painting physics that the one square you don't cover will be where you drip paint. This was the main focus of Einstein's work before he got sidetracked by relativity.

3. Fill any holes in the walls or painted woodwork with Spackle or Red Devil according to the directions on the can.

4. Sand the woodwork and any Spackle (after it's dried and hardened), vacuum the dust, brush off the wood surfaces with an old, clean paintbrush, and wipe the surfaces with a moist rag dipped in the appropriate solvent for the paint you're going to use.

5. Caulk any noticeable seams or cracks.

6. Cover any stains, bare surfaces, or areas of Spackle with primer.

7. After the primer and caulking have dried, you can begin painting.

Where to Start

There are a few simple rules to follow when you paint (brush and roller techniques are outlined in Appendix B, "Paint and Painting"). Stick to these and you'll be way ahead of most amateur painters:

➤ Start painting from the top down (ceilings first, baseboards last).

➤ Paint your walls and ceiling before you paint your woodwork.

➤ Don't load up either your brush or your roller with an excessive amount of paint (you'll know because it will drip all over).

➤ Check back on your work periodically and catch any paint drips before they dry.

➤ Don't apply your paint too thickly to try and cover in one coat when you really need two.

➤ When you paint your doors and windows, start at the top and work your way down.

➤ Send your cat away with friends for the day.

The biggest mistake people make when brushing paint is not painting in long, continual strokes, following the direction of the wood. Too much dab and stab and brushing crosswise without smoothing out the paint is a definite sign of an amateur job.

Wallpaper Woes

What if you have wallpaper? Can you paint over it? Do you have to strip it? A lot of old wallpaper has been painted over and the results leave a lot to be desired. One technique that will both cover existing wallpaper and smooth out your wall at the same time is called skim coating or skimming. This is the application of a coat of drywall compound over an entire wall, in effect giving you a new surface for painting (see Appendix C, "Paint Preparation," and Chapter 31, "Restoration or Remodeling?").

Quick Fix

Paint is ready to use out of the can and normally doesn't need any diluting or thinning. As the job goes on, if your paint doesn't seem to flow quite as easily as it did at the start, add a small amount of solvent. It doesn't take much, just a tablespoon or two per gallon (water for latex or mineral spirits for alkyd) thoroughly mixed into the paint.

You can paint over wallpaper if you don't want to skim the walls, but some preparation work will be necessary first (sound familiar?). Appendix C, "Paint Preparation," describes different types of paper and how to paint over them and even remove them from your walls. Keep in mind if you do remove your wallpaper, you may have to deal with newly uncovered wall repairs.

It's an Outside Job

Outside painting isn't all that different from interior painting: You still have to clean and prep the area you're going to paint, pick out the right material for the finish, and apply it carefully so you won't have to paint again for the next couple of presidential elections. Exterior paint has a tough job because it has to stand up to rain, snow, hail, heat, and cold. (So do mail carriers, but they get to come inside once in awhile.)

The main difference between interior and exterior painting is getting at it. Your 6-foot step ladder just isn't going to do the job if you've got a three-story monster house to paint. Because I consider ladder selection and safety to be so important—even life-saving—I've included a separate section in Appendix D, "Ladders," to discuss the ins and outs (the ups and downs?) of ladders.

Your outside painting steps include:

➤ Washing the exterior with either a pressure washer or a house washer

➤ Sealing and caulking the windows and doors

➤ Nailing loose siding

➤ Scraping and sanding any loose paint

➤ Repairing and caulking all cracks

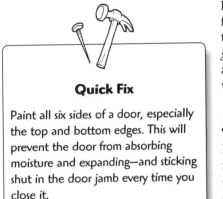

Quick Fix

Paint all six sides of a door, especially the top and bottom edges. This will prevent the door from absorbing moisture and expanding—and sticking shut in the door jamb every time you close it.

Look for any gaps between your window and door frames and the surrounding wall or siding and caulk them with a paintable silicone caulk. On older *single-glazed windows*, lightly scrape away any loose material and apply new glazing compound, allowing at least a week for curing before applying any paint.

Sidle Up to Your Siding

Loose siding should be nailed with 6d (or 6 penny, indicating its length of 2 inches) siding nails or an equivalent galvanized finish nail. Galvanized nails are coated with zinc to resist rusting.

On new houses, much of the wood siding is rough-textured, especially the manufactured siding products. These kinds of siding rarely need any scraping because they hold paint so well. Ironically, the most expensive siding, clear, smooth cedar, will not hold paint as well as rougher wood. Scrape and sand the wood until all loose paint has been removed and you have a smooth surface.

Stuck on Stucco?

On stucco siding, fill minor cracks with paintable silicone caulking. Minor holes in stucco can be filled with any number of fillers, such as DAP Elastomeric Patch. For larger holes, contact your local masonry materials supplier for an appropriate stucco mix. Think of stucco as an exterior grade plaster, and you can apply the same plaster repairs outlined in Appendix G, "Repairs."

Contractor Talk

A *single-glazed window*, sometimes called *single pane*, contains one piece of glass. An insulated window containing two pieces of glass panes is *double-glazed*, with an air space between the glass panes for heat retention.

Stroke by Stroke

You'd be surprised how much painting you can get done—if you're doing brush work—by devoting one or two hours a day to it after you get home from work. Change your clothes, spin out the brush you've got soaking in water (see Appendix B, "Paint and Painting," for brush and roller cleaning), and paint some siding. By the time the weekend comes along, you've done the equivalent of one long day's work without knocking yourself out. I speak from experience. I painted our first house this way and got it done in good time. This method only works if you do the work during the summer months when it's warm into the early evening, and you don't have foggy or otherwise moist conditions at night while the paint is drying.

Gardens of Good and Evil

Plants and landscaping are very civilizing and very much in the way when you paint. Think twice before you plant those prize perennials if you see a major paint job coming up anytime soon. There aren't a lot of easy ways to protect your botanical beauties from ladders, paint spatters, and dropped tools. I've watched painters throw sheets of plastic over plants in hot weather only to have every last flower wilt in the heat of the day. Usually they'd revive before the client got home, but sometimes the painter had some explaining to do.

Look Out Below!

After you wash your house, let it dry completely for three days in warm weather before you paint. You don't want to trap any moisture in the wood, because moisture is guaranteed to blister your paint job.

Shrubs, bushes, and trees planted too close to the house—not a good idea anyway because they retain moisture against your siding—are the worst painting obstacles. You need to get them out of the way by:

➤ Trimming them back as much as possible

➤ Tying them into a bundle

➤ Wrapping a rope around the trunks or branches and pulling them away from your house, tying the other end of the rope to a tree or stake some distance away

Paint Time

You've tied back the landscaping, examined your ladders, and given your house a nice shower with a pressure washer or house washer. What happens next depends on how you want to paint. You can use either brushes and, when appropriate, rollers or a paint sprayer.

Brushes and rollers are low tech, but you can control the flow and direction of paint, which is a big consideration on windy days. You won't need to mask off windows or trim, just paint away and cut in as you go. Rollers work well on stucco, plywood, and any form of siding where one piece is flush against another, such as ship lap or vertically installed siding. A 3½- or 4-inch brush is a good size to use for most siding. A wider brush will hold more paint, but it will also get heavy in a hurry if you're not used to it.

Look Out Below!

Treat a paint sprayer like a handgun: Never, ever point it at anyone, including yourself. The paint is under so much pressure that it can be injected under your skin and into your bloodstream.

Let It Spray

There are two types of sprayers: airless and conventional. Airless sprayers are used on large-volume jobs like the exterior of houses and on any new construction, inside and out. They atomize paint and pump it out at a fantastic rate and under great pressure. You'll use more paint than you would with a brush, but the speed will amaze you. Your hands will develop an immediate allergic reaction to ever handling a brush again, at least until you consider:

➤ All the masking that has to be done

➤ The paint that doesn't land on your house gets carried off to land somewhere else

➤ Somewhere else includes all of your plants, your roof shingles, your car, and your neighbor's car

Spraying also means more safety and protective equipment for you including:

➤ A respirator (available at your paint store)

➤ Disposable paper suit

➤ Gloves and head covering (called a painter's sock, also at your paint store)

Unless you own your own spray equipment (unlikely if you're not a painter), you'll need to rent everything, which means no leisurely painting for you. You'll be going for volume as quickly as you can so you don't run into high rental costs.

Before you test out your spraying skills on the top of your three-story classic Craftsman, practice handling the equipment. You can even run clear water through and spray your lawn (test that the gun is clean of paint first by spraying into an empty trash can) until you're use to the force of the gun. Then, spray out your garage until your familiar with the spray pattern of the paint. With some practice, you'll be ready to go onto the main stage and do your house.

Spray painting comes in handy on two types of exteriors:

➤ Shingles

➤ Painted brick

No one can brush out brick or shingles as cleanly and quickly as they can be sprayed. Spraying also has a big edge when it comes to painting soffit, the underside of the roof that overhangs the sides of your house. This part of a house is a big nuisance to paint.

Take It from the Top

Regardless of the painting method you choose, the order of painting events is the same:

1. Prepare the old paint.
2. Repair and caulk siding, trim, windows, and doors.
3. Mask where necessary.
4. Start painting from the top down.

Spraying the siding will get paint on your windows, trim, and *fascia* (the horizontal boards that run along the edge of the roof), so you'll have to backtrack and paint these when the siding is finished. Otherwise, if you're brushing out your house, you can start with the fascia, which is the highest point of a house, and work your way down. You want to make the fewest possible trips up the ladder and move it as little as possible. Finish one side at a time and move on.

The Wet Look

Exterior stains soak into wood and start setting up, or drying, very quickly. Coat the entire length of a board at one time to maintain an even color. You need to maintain a wet edge where you last painted, brushing over where you stopped to blend in the new section. This makes staining from a single ladder pretty tough and is an opportune time to set up a plank between two ladders. You should try and maintain a wet edge with paint, too, for a consistent look. It's easier to do this if you paint out of direct sunlight, which you should be doing anyway.

The Dark Side

There are no restraints to your color selection (unless your neighborhood covenants specify certain paint colors, see Chapter 5, "You Say Condo; I Say Home"), but keep a few things in mind. Dark colors fade faster than light ones. They also absorb more heat and tend to bubble and blister if there's any problem with the underlying paint. Light colors also fade, but not as noticeably.

The more accent colors you choose, the longer it will take to paint your house. That means more ladder set-ups as you return and paint out the areas you're accenting. Your house may look very slick, but there's a price to pay for your artistry. This type of paint job will also extend your rental time and your fees for ladders and planks.

Hired Hands

Exterior painting involves a lot of steps and expenses: Ladders, spray guns, gallons and gallons of paint, pressure washing, rental costs, and your time. You might consider hiring your local home-for-the-summer-looking-for-a-job collegiate neighbor to give you a hand or even do the whole job. It's tempting; most of us have been on one side or the other of those transactions, but in a litigious world, it's not a very good idea.

Anyone working on your house who takes a tumble can end up as your responsibility. If you hire anyone, be sure they're a licensed and bonded painting contractor. Follow the recommendations for hiring contractors discussed in Appendix E, "Hiring and Working with a Contractor".

Cleanup Time

It would be great if you could throw all your paintbrushes and rollers into the dishwasher, but paint cleanup doesn't quite work that way. If you want to brush and roll another day with these same tools, you'll have to rinse, clean, and store them properly. See Appendix B, "Paint and Painting," for cleaning techniques to keep your tools looking like new.

The Least You Need to Know

➤ Modern paints and the right tools can turn every homeowner into a house painter.

➤ Without the right preparation work, you're wasting your time doing any painting at all.

➤ You should be aware of the best use and means of applying each separate finishing material you buy before you open the can.

➤ Big paint jobs won't disrupt your life too much if you do a little bit of work on them every day.

Chapter 10

Floundering Foundations

In This Chapter

➤ Concrete basics

➤ Problems below: When concrete and water don't mix

➤ Giving your house a raise with floor jacks

➤ Wood-loving insects and your framing

Foundations keep our houses (and us) up from and off of the ground. That's a lot of weight to carry, and once in a while, a foundation can slip a little—or a lot. Some settling isn't unusual, but it can get out of hand. When your furniture starts sliding to one corner of the room, it's safe to say that one side of your house is way too low.

This chapter covers the ins and outs of foundation construction and problems. You may never have to think about your foundation, but few houses are completely immune to soil problems, wayward drainage, or bugs that find the underside of your home the ideal place to raise their family. You won't become a foundation expert, but at least you'll know what's holding your house up.

Concrete Jungle

Concrete was a great discovery that we now take entirely for granted. New York City's population would be spread out about a hundred miles in each direction if it weren't for all of those tall concrete buildings everyone is crammed into. For such a simple mix of ingredients—cement, sand, gravel, and water—concrete is an awesome construction material. It's tough stuff and forms the foundations of new homes. But unlike duct tape, concrete isn't an absolute miracle material. Before you can understand what can go wrong with a foundation, you need a quick lesson in the fun world of concrete.

Solid Facts

Concrete can put up with the weight of your house because it has great compression strength, but it's lacking in tensile strength, which is the ability to withstand longitudinal stress. Think of taking an unsharpened pencil, standing it upright, and trying to break it by pushing down on it (compression). That's a lot tougher than trying to break it by snapping it in half with your hands (longitudinal stress). To make up for this lack of tensile strength, rebar (or steel reinforcing bars) is added to concrete foundations.

Tales from the Scaffold

The Romans were big-time users of concrete, constructing over 5,000 miles of roads with a primitive mix of mortar, gravel, coarse sand, hot lime, water, and even animal blood from time to time.

Wet concrete is poured into wood forms, which act like spring-form pans: They hold the concrete in place until it's set, and then they're removed. Concrete cures and gains strength over a period of days and even weeks, depending on the size of the pour (the structure itself). In hot weather, the concrete is lightly sprayed with water or covered with wet tarps, so it doesn't cure prematurely.

Quick Fix

At only a few dollars a bag, concrete is cheap. If you're doing a small project, such as setting fence posts, get an extra bag or two so you don't run out. As with many other materials, you'll go through more of it than you expect to.

Concrete Notions

Concrete foundations are far stronger than older stone or brick foundations done years and years ago. New foundations consist of these two parts:

➤ Footings or piers
➤ Stem wall

A concrete slab or floor is sometimes poured as well, but this slab isn't holding the house up.

A footing, which is shaped like an inverted *t*, is buried into the ground below the frost line and acts as the

Footing, wall, and slab.

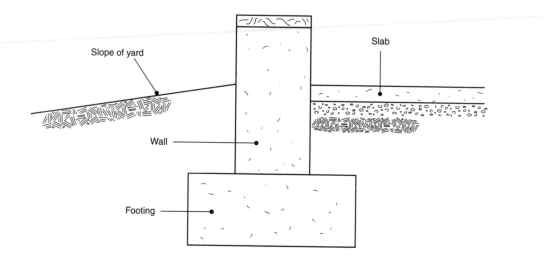

base for the foundation wall. A footing's dimensions are based on the load to be carried. On uneven surfaces such as hillsides, concrete piers (usually cylindrical) are used in lieu of footings.

House Support

We think about our foundations about as often as we do our roofs, which is almost never. Foundations don't get our attention until they cause problems, such as:

➤ Leaks

➤ Cracked and buckled walls

➤ Unlevel floors

➤ Badly sticking doors

➤ Sticking windows

➤ Nails coming loose from drywall

➤ Cracking drywall

➤ Cracks around fireplace

➤ Noticeable cracks in bricks and mortar

A footing.

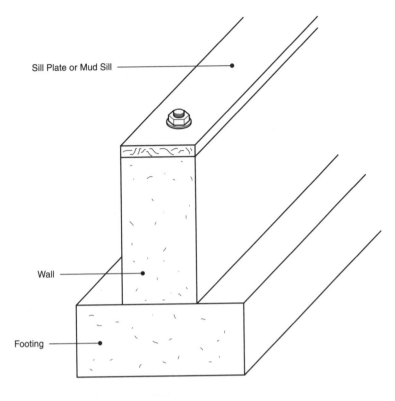

Sill Plate or Mud Sill

Wall

Footing

Look Out Below!

Just because a door or window is sticking, don't jump to the conclusion that you have a foundation problem. The wood itself may not be completely sealed and can swell up due to a change of seasons. Look for other signs of damage before you assume you have foundation problems.

What's with This Settling?

You take a look at your foundation and see the telltale signs of settling: cracks. You wonder what's going on. After rejecting the possibility that your kids are playing an elaborate trick, you conclude that your house has settled.

Settling occurs when the soil under the concrete contracts, expands, or shifts, usually due to a change in water content. Soils differ: Clay is expansive; sandy soil collapses. Eliminate the water, and you usually stop the settling (see Chapter 3, "Judging a House by Its Cover"). That said, different parts of the country present different soil conditions where this advice may not apply. Local builders and architects should be able to advise you about appropriate construction methods.

Sometimes these cracks are a big deal, but usually they're normal behavior. In most cases, common wall cracks don't suggest any kind of foundation failure and are only

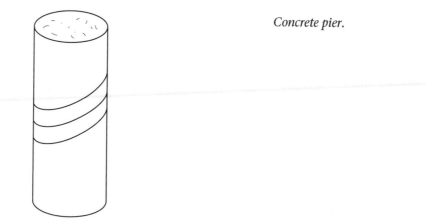

Concrete pier.

superficial in nature. Cracks also can occur from shrinkage in the concrete itself during the curing process. Cracks *can* be a problem if they allow water from the soil to trickle into your basement or crawl space; they can be a bigger problem if they allow water in as the weather turns cold. The water turns to ice and expands, and the cracks becomes bigger. One recommended building practice to help stave off water penetration is waterproofing the exterior side of any newly poured basement wall.

Tales from the Scaffold

Former clients had to install a drain line on one side of their house and weren't relishing the idea of doing the digging. Instead, they combined this work with the installation of a new gas line, which they conveniently had located on the same side of the house where they had a drainage problem. The gas company did all the digging, and my clients got two jobs done at the same time without lifting a single shovel-full of dirt!

In the Trenches

Digging a ditch or trench, even a short one, is tough work. You can say good-bye to any plant life in the digging area and hello to blisters on your hands (wear some work gloves). Extensive digging means piles of dirt for days and days on end and plywood or some kind of protective barrier around the trench so no one falls in. Before grabbing your shovel, get a few bids from contractors specializing in drainage systems. You may be setting yourself up for more work than is needed to solve your water problems.

For digging, picks and shovels do the trick, but slowly. There aren't a lot of ways to speed up the job, but here's one: If you're digging in the summer months and the ground is dry, try soaking it with a hose a few hours before you start digging. This will soften up the soil and make it easier to dig. In some cases, you may want to consider using a small Rototiller to break up the soil before digging it out with a shovel.

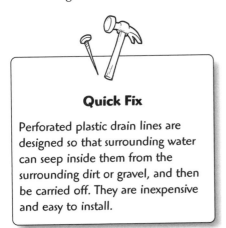

Quick Fix

Perforated plastic drain lines are designed so that surrounding water can seep inside them from the surrounding dirt or gravel, and then be carried off. They are inexpensive and easy to install.

The modern choice, if you have enough room next to your house, is a ditching machine, such as one of the Ditch Witch walk-along machines. Check with your local rental store and see what it recommends.

Ditch digging is a great job to hire out. Find a licensed landscaper and see how much it would cost to hire one of the employees to do the digging. Try one of your local temporary employment agencies, such as Manpower—just be sure the agency sends someone ready to dig all day!

Plugging the Leaks

Examine your exposed foundation wall. See any cracks? You'll need to inject a water-activated urethane resin, available at a masonry supply store, into the cracks and holes. The urethane resin reacts with any water present to form a flexible waterproof gasket. If the wall moves again, the gasket moves too, without breaking the seal. This repair is more effective than trying a traditional patch with new concrete or mortar. Urethane has been used to repair dams, tunnels, and subways; it should hold up easily for residential work. Now that you've plugged the leaks, you have to divert the water away from your house.

Look Out Below!

When you're digging, be sure you're nowhere near your water service line or telephone lines. These utilities usually have a number you can call to find out exactly where these lines are. If you don't check before digging, you may run into old drain tiles, which will have to be removed, or even your sewer line—something you definitely don't want to disturb.

French Drains, Oo La La

A French drain (don't ask me how it got its name) is a pit or trench full of gravel and covered over with regular yard plants or grass. It has to be located far enough down slope from your house to collect and hold all the water that's been going into your basement. A perforated, plastic drain line set in gravel will run from your trench out to the drain. The distance and size of the drain will be determined by your yard and the amount of water you're dealing with. The point of a French drain is to allow the water it collects to slowly pass into the surrounding soil. Placing it 15 or 20 feet from your trench would not be unreasonable.

Bigger Problems

What about those cracks around the chimney and walls and the buckling floors? Maybe you've got a bigger foundation problem, and drainage is only part of the solution. Your house may have settled, and its foundation may no longer be moving, but the house itself still needs to be leveled out. An out-of-level house can be apparent in several areas; for example, trim over doors and windows may show a definite slant.

Your first order of business is to determine where your house is no longer level. We're not talking minor adjustments here, but drops of a couple of inches, enough to throw your doors, windows, and floors out of whack. Rolling a marble on hardwood floors is the classic way to determine where you need to do your leveling work (the marble will roll on its own toward a corner if the floor is out-of-level). When you sell your house, you don't want some wise-guy buyer's agent pulling a marble out while you're negotiating a selling price. If you raise your house, maybe you can raise your price.

An Upraising Experience: House Jacks

Short of hoping a friendly alien spaceship with a killer suction beam might come along and lift your house up while you level it, what do you do? Raising a house is serious business. House leveling is accomplished using a series of jacks, including screw jacks—so-called because they adjust with a screw mechanism. These jacks are available at rental stores and have the capacity to lift tons and tons of weight (such as your house).

The jacks are placed on a firm foundation, such as your basement floor or foundation slab. A heavy piece of lumber, (a six-by-six post, for instance) is placed on top of the jack, which will push it against the floor joists overhead (a couple of two-by-six boards are placed at the top of the six-by-six). The house rises as the pressure from the jacks pushes against the post.

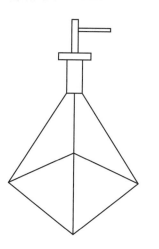

Screw jack.

Inch by Inch

Raising your house with jacks is a slow process that can take weeks. You only want to raise your house a small bit at a time (with a screw jack, it's just a turn or so) and then let it sit for at least a few days or even a week.

Raising a house is a creaking experience. It will creak and stretch as it's being raised, and you'll wonder if you're doing the right thing. What you're doing is structurally kind of traumatic and is a great way to start cracking window glass and plaster. Your house will gradually adjust until you've leveled it out as best as can be done.

Once you've raised your house, you'll have to brace it with new posts and beams in select spots. An architect or structural engineer can pinpoint the appropriate locations for new supports.

Tales from the Scaffold

Before you get discouraged about resolving a leveling problem, look at what house-moving companies do. With a great deal of digging and liberal use of screw jacks and cribbing (a framework of lumber used as a support), these companies manage to raise and remove very large homes and transport them to new building lots. Raising your house up a few inches is child's play by comparison.

Do You Hire It Out?

The idea of leveling a house and knocking out main support beams can be intimidating, but if you're not comfortable doing it, hire it out.

House leveling is typically done by the same contractors who move houses. Some general contractors will tackle it as well, but check their references from past jobs. You want an experienced hand here, not someone who is still learning the process.

When You're Really Bugged

Water problems aren't your foundation's only menace. An array of creepy crawlers may be subletting your basement or crawl space. Not only are they not paying any rent, they're eating the place up. These tenants-from-hell include:

➤ Termites

➤ Wood-boring beetles

➤ Carpenter ants

➤ Powder-post beetles

Termites often cause their damage long before they're discovered, because they tend to eat wood from within. According to the Orkin Exterminating Company, termites cause more damage to American homes than storms and fires combined. After all, they've been around for over 250 million years, work 24 hours a day, and can have up to 1 million members per colony (the termites, not Orkin).

Unless you live in termiteless Alaska, your house has the potential to be termite food. A termite or general bug inspection is always recommended, and in some areas is mandated, when a house changes hands. If an inspection finds evidence of termites or other house-eating pests in your house, you need to call an exterminator.

Repairing the Damage

After the extermination is finished, you have the fun job of repairing any damage. Cellulose-loving insects can compromise the very posts and beams that hold your house up. They can also munch away on the *sill plates*, the bottom member of a framed wall that's attached to the foundation.

Any single piece of your house is replaceable. Some pieces are more of a nuisance to replace than others. In order to replace a damaged section of sill plate, for example, you have to raise the house slightly with jacks, carefully cut out the plate, and insert a new piece of pressure-treated lumber (the type that resists moisture damage). The replacement section should be glued and toe-nailed into the existing wall studs.

Posts are even more important to replace. You *could* cut out the damaged section and splice and secure a new piece of pressure-treated wood, but this is a misguided frugality. Buy a new post, put in some temporary bracing while you remove the old one, and install the new one.

An Ounce of Prevention

Once the bugs are gone, you want them to stay out. An annual inspection by your exterminating service will help keep them in check, but it's important to eliminate the conditions they thrive in. Termites need moisture to survive, making basements and crawl spaces their perfect home. Install vents in your crawl space to keep the moisture down. Outside, seal off all the cracks and gaps that say "Welcome Termites."

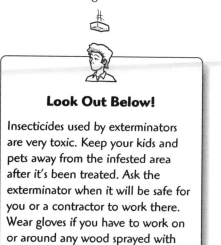

Look Out Below!

Insecticides used by exterminators are very toxic. Keep your kids and pets away from the infested area after it's been treated. Ask the exterminator when it will be safe for you or a contractor to work there. Wear gloves if you have to work on or around any wood sprayed with insecticide.

129

And do your own checking now that you know what could be living downstairs from you.

Laying a New Foundation: Additions

New ground-floor additions call for concrete work. When your addition is going over a flat, level yard, you'll have to decide whether you want a concrete slab floor or a wood floor. A sloping, uneven yard almost always calls for a wood floor over a concrete foundation. A level yard can go either way: You can do a one-pour slab with perimeter footings or dig down to accommodate a wood floor and a crawl space so your addition is level with the ground floor of your house.

Concrete is harder on your feet, but it's easier and less expensive to install. You just level out and prepare the ground, build your foundation wall, and pour in the slab floor. Concrete also has the advantage of never squeaking or being eaten by termites. A wood floor requires that a framing system of joists be built over a vapor barrier, with a subfloor attached on top of the joists.

Because a wood floor doesn't have direct contact with the ground, it will be warmer than a concrete floor. This is one of those comfort-versus-expense decisions. If your addition is only a laundry/utility room, then by all means go with a concrete floor. Family rooms are another matter. Even the thickest carpet can't completely disguise the fact that you and the kids are playing over a hard, concrete floor.

Tales from the Scaffold

Pouring and forming concrete is hard enough, but removing it due to a change of plans is even worse. A recent story in the *Seattle Times* indicated that our local baseball team decided they wanted a deeper whirlpool in their new stadium, which is still under construction. The concrete had been in for months and had to be jackhammered out at considerable cost. All this for a less-than–illustrious team, I might add.

Although a concrete floor is easier to install than a wood floor, concrete work isn't just a matter of pouring and walking away from it. Forms have to be built, ditches have to be dug, rebar has to be installed, the ground has to be prepared and compacted for slabs, the correct concrete has to be purchased (different temperatures and other conditions demand different mixes). Concrete floors also have to be finished by screeding and floating. You also have to calculate the load on the concrete and pour the correct dimensions to carry that load. Concrete work is another of those jobs you should consider hiring out.

The Least You Need to Know

➤ Concrete makes a very strong foundation, but it can be affected by drainage and water problems.

➤ Some house settling is inevitable, but major cracks or out-of-square doors and windows are a sign that it's extreme.

➤ Taking care of your drainage problems is the first thing you should do when repairing your foundation.

➤ Termites and other pests are the second big structural problem many houses face.

➤ A lot of preparation work goes into new concrete work; you may want to hire a contractor specializing in it rather than do it yourself.

Chapter 11

The Messiest Job: Replacing Your Roof

In This Chapter

➤ Replacing or covering over your old roof

➤ So many roofing materials, so little roof

➤ Repairing the small stuff

➤ Skylights: Overhead windows

➤ Gutters: Your roof's partners

How often do any of us think about our roofs? They don't exactly rank as a topic for dinner conversation, unless rain is dripping onto our plates (and we remember how simple it would have been to inspect the roof during the summer, when life was warm and dry). Leaks can be harbingers of bigger things to come, like having to replace the roof, or they can just make us notice that we need to repair a missing shingle or bad flashing.

Our parents and grandparents had few choices in roofing materials, but today we have all kinds of exotic compositions available; even sheet metal roofs are gaining in popularity. Nevertheless, roof failure is a given. Even the sturdiest materials, such as slate, cement, and clay tile, will eventually have to be replaced (it may take a few centuries with slate, though). You have to choose what the best material is for you, your house, and certainly your budget. A copper roof looks awesome, but it costs more pennies than most of us can afford.

Although it's unlikely you'll want to replace your roof by yourself, I'll run through the steps so you'll know what's involved. Small repairs, such as patching or replacing a few shingles, can be done by any homeowner who doesn't suffer from vertigo and is smart enough to do the work before the rainy season starts. Gutters come along with the roofing territory, and you'll read about those, too. You'll be surprised at how long they can last with some regular cleaning and maintenance.

Good Roof, Bad Roof

What are the signs of a bad roof? Shingles blowing up and down in the wind like the wings of a crazed seagull are definitely a bad sign, but you shouldn't see anything quite that dramatic. Finding more mineral granules in the gutters than on the shingles themselves is a more common bad sign. Each type of roof will show different symptoms of wear and tear.

Elements of a roof.

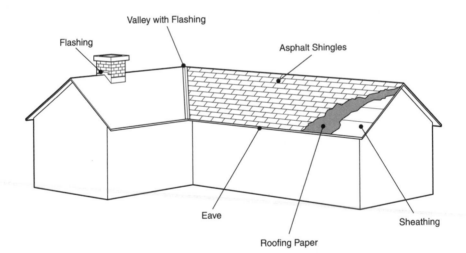

Easy Roof, Nuisance Roof

Types of roofing materials include:

➤ Asphalt shingles

➤ Wood shakes and shingles

➤ Tile

➤ Metal

➤ Slate

Most roofs on American homes are covered with asphalt shingles, which are also known as composition shingles. The best are made from fiberglass, asphalt, and mineral or ceramic granules. These shingles are relatively easy to install, long-lasting, and low maintenance. Architectural grade asphalt shingles are thicker and longer-lasting than the standard three-tab shingle, which is the less expensive of the two types.

The best wood shakes and shingles are usually made from cedar and are a sorry choice for a roofing material in my opinion. Wood is high maintenance (in some climates, it should be cleaned and treated every two to three years) and has mediocre fire resistance. If you don't believe me, ask the California firefighters who watched house after wood-roofed house go up in flames during these past few years of fire outbreaks. Periodically spraying fire-retardant chemicals on wood shake roofs increases their fire resistance only marginally and even then for only a limited period of time.

Fire departments and insurance companies like tile, metal, and slate because they don't burn. Homeowners like them because they're long-lasting, low-maintenance materials.

Roof Warnings!

The following are some warning signs you may have seen during your inspection of your roof:

➤ Asphalt composition shingles: Missing; thin, excessive loss of granules, or bare spots; curling ends; previous patch work

➤ Wood shakes or shingles: Missing, warping, splitting, cracking, moldy

➤ Tiles: Cracked or missing

➤ Metal: Rust, old patching; signs of leaks on interior

➤ Slate: Scaling or brown stains indicating deterioration

Consider the age of your house and roof. A composition roof lasts roughly 15 to 20 years, sometimes more, depending on the grade of the shingle. If your house was built in the early 1980s, you should start thinking about a new roof a few years down the road. Is the weathered, or south side, of your house in worse condition then the rest? Sunlight is a big enemy of composition and wood roofs.

How many layers of composition roofing do you have now? Three is the limit before you need to start stripping off the old roof before replacing it. Total removal greatly increases your cost, so if you can simply install another layer of shingles over the existing ones, do it. Look for structural sagging, such as rafters that start bowing, which is a sure sign that you have too many shingles on your roof.

How does the workmanship on your roof strike you? Do the edges of the shingles line up straight? Do you see roof vents? A lack of vents indicates a lack of ventilation in unfinished attic spaces, and that indicates problems.

Roofing's biggest seller: The asphalt three-tab shingle.

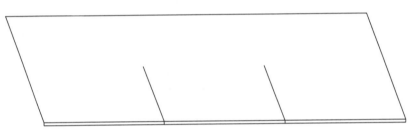

Full of Hot Air

Attic spaces need to be ventilated; otherwise, the moisture buildup can damage the roof from the inside. Moisture results from daily activities such as cooking, showering, and breathing. Every time we breathe, we release moisture, and it has to go someplace. Heat carries it to the top of the house where it can come into contact with cold roof *sheathing*. A vented attic will prevent heat and moisture buildup and damage to the sheathing. A general recommendation (though it can vary) calls for 1 square foot of venting for every 150 square feet of ceiling space. The roof *soffit* is also vented.

Contractor Talk

Roof *sheathing* is plywood that is nailed to the roof rafters, and various roofing materials are nailed to it. Wood shingles and shakes are attached to *skip sheathing*. A *soffit* is the underside of the roof.

Along with escaping heat, moisture can be the culprit in the development of ice dams. An *ice dam* (you Floridians can skip this paragraph) forms when melting snow runs down from a warm area of the roof and freezes, usually at the eaves or lower edge of the roof where it overhangs the outer walls. As the ice forms, it traps water that can work its way under the shingles and damage them as well as the sheathing. If the water stops at the gutter, it can accumulate there and cause the gutter to deteriorate or even pull away from the house.

A well-ventilated attic allows both accumulating moisture and warm air to escape in a controlled manner rather than heating the roof. If you see a lot of melted snow on your roof in the winter, it means that you need to check out the attic ventilation and insulation, both of which prevent warm air from escaping.

Strip Down or Add Another Layer of Shingles?

You've decided you need to replace your roof. If you have a composition roof, the easy way out is to nail another layer of shingles over the old ones and walk away from it. You can usually have up to three layers of composition roofing or a combination of composition shingles over original wood shingles, before your house yells "uncle" and wants you to start taking off this stuff.

Stripping off an old roof (known as doing a *tear-off*) is not a genteel activity. Think this through before you even consider replacing your own roof. Roofing is a dirty, hot, and dangerous job, especially if your roof has a steep pitch or slope to it. It must be done in a timely manner, none of this,

Quick Fix

Even careful roofers will drop nails and bits of old roofing as they work. If you have garden beds close to the house, consider laying some plastic down over them when roofing work is being done. Be careful, though, because too much heat buildup underneath the plastic can destroy your plants.

"I'll spend an hour or two after work every day until it's done." You never want to expose your house to the elements for any longer than necessary. I can guarantee you that in rainy Seattle, roofs are installed really fast. If you've had some experience in installing roofs, See Appendix G, "Repairs," which outlines the steps involved. I don't recommend that any amateur homeowner install a new roof; I do recommend roofers.

Why We Have Roofers

Roofers have the dirtiest job in construction, particularly when it comes to installing new flat commercial roofs. These roofs are the so-called "built up" roofs consisting of multiple layers of material, including a flood coat of tar-like material that has to be mopped on. Residential roofers work long hours because an occupied home cannot be exposed to the weather any longer than necessary. If a sudden storm shows up, plywood sheathing alone just isn't enough to keep all the water out.

A roofing contractor will bid a job based on the pitch of the roof (steeper roofs cost more), the amount of old material to be removed, the number of *squares* of roofing material required, and any repairs needed. If you do the work yourself, you'll have to rent or buy ladders and roof jacks, order the materials, arrange for trash disposal, and take delivery of the shingles. At least you won't have to haul them up to the roof: The delivery trucks come with extended conveyor belts that deliver the shingles right to your roof!

You've probably figured out that I *really* recommend that you hire a roofing contractor. You'll still have a role in the job though (besides writing a check); you get to choose the new roofing.

Contractor Talk

A *square* equals 100 square feet of roofing. A roof requiring 20 squares of material needs 2000 square feet of shingles. A roofing bid will often indicate a certain dollar amount per square of installed material.

My Shingles Are Better Than Your Shingles

There are more choices in roofing materials than ever before. If you decide to replace your composition shingles with, say, concrete or tile, you'll have some structural limitations, because your existing rafters may not be strong enough to carry the weight. That doesn't mean you can't have an interesting roof.

Shingles come in different colors, styles, shapes, and materials. In addition to the standard asphalt composition shingles, there are fiber-reinforced Hardishake cement shingles, and metal shingles made from either steel or aluminum, coated with acrylic, and covered with stone chips for protection from sunlight. These products are manufactured to resemble costlier, and far less practical, wood shakes, but have a *Class A fire rating*. These higher-tech materials come with longer warranties (up to 50 years) and a higher price tag than composition shingles. No one stays in one house for 50 years any longer (all right, the Queen of England may be an exception), so weigh the cost of these more exotic materials carefully. You probably won't get it back when you sell the house.

An increasingly popular option is the use of *standing seam steel*, sheets of steel precoated with a colored finish. A lightweight material, metal roofing is expensive but long-lasting, and it comes with that coveted Class A fire rating (as long as it's not installed over an existing roof).

Look Out Below!

Some recent composite roofing materials have been like some recent composite siding products: terrible. With any new product, always inquire about problems and manufacturer recalls.

Take a look at different roofing patterns and materials. Most roofing suppliers will have small displays at their stores. Find something you like and ask if they've installed it on a house nearby so you can take a look at it in action.

Shingles? What Shingles?

Flat roofs, used on commercial and some residential buildings, are kind of misnamed. They really just have a very low *pitch* or slope. The less slope, the harder it is to shed water.

The problem with flat roofs is *ponding*, or the development of depressed spots that water loves. Most of these roofs are Built Up Roofs (BURs) consisting of layers of bitumen asphalt, felt or fiberglass sheeting, more bitumen, and then gravel. Newer versions of flat roofs include polymer-modified bitumen (a more elastic material than the original) and sprayed polyurethane foams coated with special sealers.

Flat roofs generally need recoating about every five years, which is an easy, but stinky, job for a homeowner. Check for low spots and build them up with extra material so water won't accumulate. If your flat roof is cracked, blistered, and full of soft spots, call a roofer.

Contractor Talk

The *pitch* of a roof is the number of inches in height the roof rises for every 12 inches in horizontal length, the rise over run. A 6:12 roof, for example, means that for every 12 inches of horizontal measurement, the roof slopes or rises 6 inches.

First Rate with Slate

Slate is both extremely durable and fragile; walk on it the wrong way, and you can easily damage it. It is very long-lasting, though some types aren't the best choice for roofs in wet climates. When your slate roof needs attention, call a roofer who regularly installs this material.

Hiring a Roofer

When hiring a roofer, follow the practices you would use when hiring any contractor, outlined in Appendix E, "Hiring and Working with a Contractor".

Roofing is noisy work. Try and stay away for a few days unless you like the sound of hammering for hours on end. Do your roofers a favor and leave out some cold juice or soda and a cooler of ice. They'll remember you for it.

While You're at It: Skylights and Other Changes

What better time to install a skylight or two than when you're re-roofing your house? Skylights can brighten up any room, but they are especially useful in hallways and rooms that windows forgot. Before you get carried away and plot a skylight for every room in the house, consider this: Erratically placed skylights may be terrific inside, but they look terrible on the outside of your house.

Skylights come in various flavors. Ask yourself:

➤ Do I want a fairly flat skylight or more of a dome style?

➤ Do I want plastic or glass?

➤ Should it open? Would the extra ventilation be welcome?

➤ Who's going to install it?

➤ Don't they leak all the time?

Skylight, open and closed.

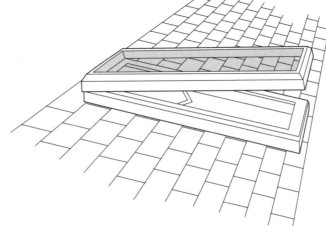

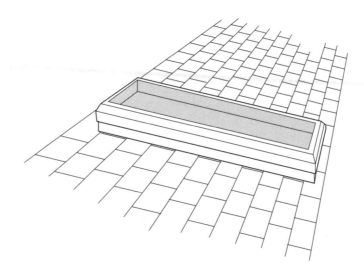

Skylights have been around for a long time. New versions are models of tight engineering and shouldn't leak unless they're badly installed or a small meteor crashes through them. One popular innovation is the self-flashing skylight, which saves the trouble of installing separate metal flashing between it and the roofing shingles.

There's an advantage to having a roofer or other contractor install a skylight: If it *does* leak, you're not responsible. You don't necessarily want to practice your newly developing carpentry skills on skylight installation. Your time can be better spent planning skylight locations and checking out styles.

A Little Off the Top: Changing Your Roof Line

The ideal time to reconfigure your roofline (add some dormers, for example) is at the same time you're replacing the roof. Even if you were thinking of making these changes a few years down the road, but your roofing can't wait, consider framing them in anyway so you won't be tearing into your nice new roof later on. You'll need a building permit for any such additions.

As Long as You're Up There

Your original house inspection called for you to look over your chimney. What shape was it in? Is the mortar loose? Is the chimney leaning? You don't want to start pulling your chimney apart all over your new roof, so have a mason look at it before you start re-roofing.

Gutters Anyone?

Gutters have been around since some clever people decided it was a good idea to make all that water running off the roof go somewhere besides down the sides of their homes. The gutter network is not just a nuisance item that gets added to your fall cleaning list every year; it's a drainage system, and it's important to the health of your house. Gutters direct water away from your foundation and basement. They also keep water off your siding, which means less painting for you.

Quick Fix

It's worth scooping the leaves out of your gutters once in a while to prevent water from overflowing; it will keep your paint intact longer.

Did your house inspection show leaking, worn gutters, and downspouts beyond repair? When you filled them with water did it flow easily towards the downspout or did it pond up because the gutter wasn't properly sloped? Replacing gutters is another one of those tasks I think are best left to specialized contractors, but you'll have a hand in the job just as you did with your roof.

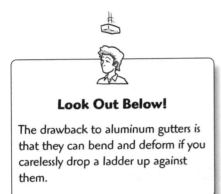

Aluminum Wins Every Time

Wood gutters were the traditional choice for American homes for years, mostly because there wasn't much choice. They were followed by steel, copper, aluminum, and plastic. Copper, a very long-lasting material, is found on higher-end homes and particularly on older Tudor-style houses.

Look Out Below!

The drawback to aluminum gutters is that they can bend and deform if you carelessly drop a ladder up against them.

Without regular maintenance, wood gutters rot out, and metal gutters rust. Aluminum gutters, on the other hand, just seem to keep going and going, demanding only the regular cleanings that all gutters require. Installed in sections that cover the full length of a house, seamless aluminum has fewer places to leak. Aluminum is the material of choice for both new house construction and gutter replacement.

Plastic gutters, a do-it-yourself specialty, are more fragile than aluminum ones because they can crack and they also deteriorate from exposure to ultraviolet radiation. They are easy enough to install, but you have a lot of pieces and sections to deal with and I don't recommend them. Before you install plastic gutters, compare their cost with those of continuous aluminum. The difference in price will be less than you might think.

The Swinging '60s and Integral Gutters

Integral gutters, which gained some popularity in the 1960s, were essentially troughs lined with built-up roofing material at the end of the rafters and fascia. Not the best idea, this gutter system requires regular inspection and repair of the lining. Look into replacing it with a regular gutter system the next time you re-roof your house.

Roof and Gutter Fixes

Replacing your roof and gutters is an expensive proposition. The longer you can put it off—without damaging your house—the better. You can easily make repairs without going nuts and re-roofing the whole place.

Roof repairs usually mean patching or replacing a shingle and sealing the flashing. First you have to find any leaks, sometimes a frustrating job at best since they only show themselves during rainy weather or during thaws. Gutters need holes and seams patched, fasteners tightened, and regular cleaning. You need only a few tools, including:

➤ Ladder

➤ Hammer and roofing nails

➤ Prybar, utility knife, and putty knife

➤ New shingles and roofing cement or tar

Remember, you're no longer on terra firma. Wear shoes with non-slip soles, and tie yourself to the chimney for extra security. If you're not comfortable up there, by all means get off the roof. The last thing you need is to take a fall because you were embarrassed about your discomfort with heights.

Shingle Surgery

Shingles need to lie flat to repel water properly. If a composition shingle is cupped or the corners are sticking up, smear some tar or cement under them, nail them down with roofing nails, and coat the nail heads with tar. It's better to be liberal with your use of roofing tar and cement than to apply too little.

Don't use the putty knife to apply the tar or roofing cement unless you wrap the blade in plastic first, or else use something like a paint stirrer instead. You want easy cleanup, and both tar and roofing cement are a nuisance to clean.

To replace a missing or badly damaged shingle, follow the steps in Appendix G, "Repairs."

Wood Roof Repairs

Wood shakes and shingles are repaired the same way as composition shingles: Carefully remove the old material, insert a new shake or shingle, and nail it in place (you'll need longer wood shake nails for roofing). One important difference in the repairs is your shoes. Special strap-on, spiked shoes called *corkers* are recommended for walking on wood shake roofs. They're available at some rental shops or through roofing suppliers and are an especially good idea if you have to walk around on a wet shake roof.

> **Quick Fix**
>
> A simple way to patch broken shingles is to smear roofing cement on the back of a piece of sheet metal or stiff plastic and then slip it under the damaged shingle. Be sure the metal is galvanized or painted with rust-resistant paint.

Wood is especially susceptible to rot and deterioration from water, so you need to keep a wood roof clean of leaves and other fun stuff that falls off trees by sweeping it with a broom, blowing it off with a yard blower, or hosing it off with a garden hose as often as needed. Moss control requires some chemical intervention. If you're living in a damp climate or your roof is shaded by large trees, clean it off once a year with a commercial cleaner and moss killer for wood roofs. It's not a bad idea to also spray on a commercial sealer after the roof has dried.

Lashing Out at Your Flashing

Flashing, the sheet metal that joins roofs at chimneys, valleys, and skylights, is also vulnerable. Nails can loosen, and the metal itself can rust. Secure any nails (you may need to pull them out and use longer ones) and fill in any gaps at the edge of the flashing with roofing tar. Here's one cheap trick: Spray any suspect flashing with a can of automobile undercoat. This coating both protects and seals the metal. One warning: Copper flashing must be secured with copper nails. Anything else causes a nasty chemical reaction and, ultimately, corrosion.

In the Gutter Again

All gutters need regular cleaning; you can prevent some of this by trimming tree branches that overhang your house. Some advocate installing gutter screens to prevent leaves and twigs from clogging up the works, but I'm no fan of them. Gutter screens keep the large debris out, but smaller stuff still gets in; and just try cleaning the small stuff out with those stupid screens in the way. A small downspout screen (available at many hardware stores), however, is a good idea; it will prevent debris from going down the downspout and keep your drains clear of gutter garbage.

In addition to cleaning, gutter and downspout maintenance consists of:

➤ Sealing any leaking seams

➤ Checking that all fasteners are tight

➤ Being sure the water is draining off away from the house

Look Out Below!

Wear latex gloves when you scoop out your gutters. The granules from asphalt shingles can give you a rash on your hands. Besides, some of the junk in your gutters can be pretty disgusting.

A leaking seam will present itself on a wet day, of course, or you can force the issue by using a garden hose to fill your gutters with water and check for yourself. Apply a thick bead of waterproof polyurethane caulking to these seams when they're completely dry, and test them again for leaks after the caulking has cured.

The Demands of Wood Gutters

Wood gutters can last indefinitely if you're vigilant. In the good old days, the recommended maintenance included regular cleanings and coating the inside of the gutters with linseed oil once a year. The oil sealed the wood and prevented water damage. You can relive this fun ritual of yesteryear, but your wood gutters may need a little more tender loving care first.

Check the bottom of the gutters for cracks and splits. They must be repaired to prevent further deterioration. I pour liquid fiberglass or epoxy into a damaged, clean, dry gutter, allow it to dry, and then coat the gutter with linseed oil. There are some tar-like products sold for coating wood gutters, but I don't recommend them. The material eventually dries out and lifts at the edges, forever trapping water under the patch and making a bad situation worse.

Just like wood shake roofs, wood gutters are very attractive and impractical. If you keep yours, be prepared for a labor of love.

The Water Has to Go Somewhere

Remember, your gutters and downspouts are a drainage system. You want to be sure the water is draining away from the house, not toward it. The very best system has downspouts connected directly to your storm sewer. The second best drainage is into a *French drain*, a gravel or rock-filled pit located far enough from the house to absorb water runoff from your downspouts and keep it away from your basement. Plastic drain lines connected to the bottom of your downspouts carry the water to the French drain.

The least preferred system uses *splash blocks* at the end of your downspouts to direct water away from your house. Splash blocks are cheap, rectangular plastic or concrete blocks, cut at an angle to provide a slope for water to run off. Splash blocks are better than nothing, but they don't carry the water very far from your house.

The Least You Need to Know

➤ All roofs eventually fail, but you can read the warning signs ahead of time.

➤ Replacing a roof is a big, time-consuming, messy job that's best left to a roofing contractor.

➤ Simple roofing repairs can be done by most homeowners and will easily prolong the life of your roof and your bank account.

➤ Gutters and downspouts make up a critical drainage system designed to protect your siding and foundation.

➤ Wood shake roofs and wood gutters have a lot of aesthetic appeal, but they are highly impractical for modern homeowners.

Chapter 12

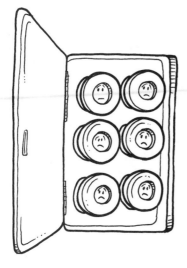

Refusing Fuses

In This Chapter

➤ You deserve a lot of power

➤ Overcoming your wiring fears

➤ Light up the night with outdoor lighting

➤ Wiring the weird spaces everyone forgets

Electricity is central to our lives. We heat, cook, listen to music, and see our way around the house with it. If we didn't have it, I'd be doing this manuscript with a manual typewriter or, worse yet, in longhand, a truly ugly notion, Catholic school penmanship lessons notwithstanding.

Few people understand electricity, and many are afraid to tackle wiring upgrades themselves. Fortunately, electrical wiring is a logical process, but there's an art to it as well. Trained electricians bring an elegant method of problem-solving to the job. Do-it-yourself work may be a little clunky, but it will still be safe and up to code if you follow proper wiring procedures.

I'm a great advocate of electrical conveniences. I want lights and outlets anywhere and everywhere (including crawl spaces and closets) that I may have to go and be in need of a light or source of power. Why mess with flashlights and extension cords if you don't have to? Older houses particularly can benefit from electrical upgrades. This chapter explains the basics of electrical work and shows you how to get wired.

Wiring That Your Grandparents Installed

The earliest electrical wiring most of us are familiar with is the knob and tube variety. This wiring passed through and around ceramic tubes and knobs while winding its way through a house. When it was first introduced, people didn't have much to run on it: One or two lights per room and, later on, a radio and some small appliances. These days, an electric clothes dryer demands more electricity than an entire house once used.

Knob and tube systems are controlled by fuses. If you overload a circuit, the fuse blows, as it should. Fuses are the built-in protectors in old wiring systems. If you demand more electricity from them than they're designed to carry, they burn up. This result is most visible in the old, glass, screw-in type fuse. When the circuit is overloaded, a small copper strip inside the glass fries and turns black.

Old wiring isn't automatically bad wiring, but it can probably stand an update. Older systems can't always handle the demands of modern households. On top of that, they usually feature a chronic shortage of outlets, unless you count those multiple-outlet, plug-in power strips homeowners buy to make up for their system's shortfall.

> **Quick Fix**
>
> You need a permit for any change to your electrical system. Replacing a light fixture doesn't change the wiring, but adding a light does. To justify the cost of the permit, have as much of your electrical work done at one time as you can; you don't want to have to take out a permit every time you add an outlet or two!

> **Look Out Below!**
>
> Never, ever, ever replace a fuse of one amperage with a larger amp fuse. This will allow more electricity to pass through the wire than the wire was designed to handle. The wire will overheat before the fuse does, which is a good way to start a fire. Don't put a penny in as a temporary fuse, either—this is an even worse idea.

New Is Better

Fuses are no longer used in residential construction. They've been replaced with circuit breakers, a technology introduced in the 1950s. A circuit breaker is reusable: After it's tripped, which is the modern equivalent of blowing a fuse, it can be reset and used for, essentially, the life of the system.

Wiring in newer houses, installed to meet the National Electrical Code, is much superior to what you'll find in an old house. Wire is now wrapped in tough, plastic casing, unlike the old combinations of rubber and cloth insulation used in knob and tube wiring. Plastic boxes, which, unlike the old ungrounded metal ones, cannot conduct electricity, now house switches and outlets as well as fixture wiring. And all new houses have buried power lines that are safer and

148

less prone to damage during storms. This doesn't mean that you won't have any ideas for changes and improvements, however.

No Emergency, But . . .

The components of old wiring systems are the usual cause of trouble, not the systems themselves. Residential electrical circuits are three-wire systems, made up of:

➤ A black or hot wire that carries electricity from the panel to the point of usage

➤ A white or neutral wire that carries the current back to the panel

➤ A bare copper ground wire that helps keep you safe

Old two-wire systems (black and neutral only), such as knob and tube or BX cable, keep the wires separate from each other as they run through your house. The problems occur when they meet up at switches, outlets, and light fixtures.

After years of having currents and heat running through it, wire becomes stiff and brittle (I call it chronic electron fatigue syndrome), especially at the ends. This is why short circuits occur when someone replaces a switch or light and isn't careful with the old wire. If your house has old wiring, you don't have to replace everything—that's a big, expensive job on a large house—but you should at least have your system examined by a qualified electrician for some advice on its current condition.

Tales from the Scaffold

One attorney customer of mine (who was also a licensed plumber from his college days) wired his house with the future in mind. He installed two 200-amp services, which is twice as much as a typical new 2,000 square foot house would have. He and his family were ready for anything. They had a good size, but not huge, house, and he never wanted to do any major wiring again. I don't know if they ever fully used their new electrical toys, but their electrical system was very impressive for a residence.

Bright Ideas

Just about every remodeling project can involve your electrical system if you want it to. Building a trash can holder? If you had an outside light, wouldn't it be easier to see what you're doing when you take out the trash at midnight? How about an outlet for that electric garage door opener you got for your wedding anniversary from your

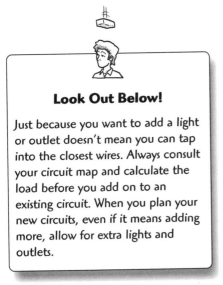

ever-so-practical spouse? Adding wiring changes to existing rooms is time-consuming and expensive, but if you're adding on new rooms, take the opportunity to wire them up like the NASA Space Center, with outlets and gadgets everywhere.

Wiring is kind of a one-time deal: Once you have it where you want it, you don't have to redo it as you do paint colors or worn carpet. Outlets and lights just keep going and going through years of decorating changes. It's a one-time investment to make your life more comfortable.

Thinking Ahead: Wiring for Future Projects

If there's one remodeling rule that is routinely ignored it's this one: Think ahead. Little things, like ordering extra window hardware or cabinet hinges to have around as spares, can make your life or that of a future owner a lot easier if something breaks later on. When you install a new electrical service, keep the future in mind.

For instance, you can run a circuit or two up to your unfinished attic. You or your electrician will just dead-end the cable into a junction box and there it will wait in case you later decide you want a third-floor bedroom or office. It's always easier to do these kinds of things while you're tearing up walls and you have an electrician handy.

What size of electrical service should you install? I think anything less than a 200-amp service in a detached house is a waste of time and money to install. You can't predict future needs; what if you decide to go into business for yourself and install a portable microchip factory in the basement just to show Intel who's boss? It's faulty economics to save a few bucks on the cost of a smaller service, say 125 amps, only to find out a few years down the road that you need more power. Smaller services are fine for apartments and condominiums. Developers sometimes install them in track housing because developers deal in volume, and the savings really add up for them—but not for you.

Forgotten Spaces and More

While you're remodeling, consider adding a few more wiring chores to your electrical list. Some possibilities are:

➤ Crawl spaces

➤ Closets

➤ Attic spaces

➤ Special office needs

➤ Outdoor lighting

Crawl spaces? Whoever puts lighting there? No one, and that's exactly my point. Periodically, someone has to snoop around in a crawl space to check for bugs or leaks. Just how much trouble would it be for a builder of new homes to put a light or two in? A lot, apparently, but that's no reason you shouldn't do it if you're already adding more circuits or a new service.

Your Clothes Might Match if You Had Some Light

New master bedroom closets typically have overhead lights installed, but secondary bedrooms don't always have this feature. Old homes rarely had closet lights, although some very elegant systems of automatic lights that go on whenever the closet door opens can be found in some higher end, older homes. If you or your electrician are crawling around in an attic space anyway to install new lights or outlets in existing bedrooms, think about adding some closet lights, too. Something as simple as a pull chain fixture can make a world of difference.

Attics

Attic spaces are another area we don't think about until we have to start crawling around in them. You don't have to be up there very often to appreciate having some light. In my last house, after one too many trips to the attic to run wires or check for a persistent leak in the old roof, I got so annoyed I wired up three lights in the area. When we sold the house, the purchaser's inspector even commented on how much easier the lights made his job, if just for a few minutes.

The Home Office: Computer Circuits That Don't Byte

Some futurists seem to believe that just about everyone will be telecommuting in the future and never leaving their home office. That may be fine for socially maladroit techno-geeks who sit around thinking up this stuff, but most of us want some human contact during the day and will continue to seek it through work. Still, a home office is a reality for many people, including me.

Offices come with office toys including:

➤ Computers

➤ Fax machines

➤ Copiers

➤ Printers

➤ Scanners

151

Tales from the Scaffold

In my last house, I succumbed to the reality of urban life—yes, even in the latte land of Seattle—and installed an alarm system. Residential alarm systems are low-voltage equipment, and my model was installed by plugging it into the nearest available electrical outlet. I didn't want to look at an electrical cord stapled to the baseboard, so I installed an outlet in the closet where the alarm controls were going to be. The installer was very surprised that I would go to this trouble and pleased that he could leave a neater-looking job.

Not every piece of equipment needs its own circuit, though copiers usually do, but you may want to think about it for your computers. If your office circuit also runs to an adjoining room, you don't have any control over who plugs in what. Even if you're using an auto-save feature, why take a chance on losing some of your brilliant prose because little Jimmy tripped the circuit when he stuck the vacuum cleaner hose in the toilet and flooded the motor? A dedicated circuit is one that powers only a single end user, usually an appliance such as a stove or garbage disposal. You can install dedicated circuits for any specialty uses where you don't want power interrupted by other users.

Lighting Up the Outdoors

Outdoor lighting opens up all kinds of possibilities. You can install pagoda-shaped yard lights, motion detector security lighting, even porch ceiling lights that can be bright enough for reading. Outdoor outlets (always GFCIs) are a great convenience and well worth installing.

You can take two approaches to outdoor lighting:

➤ Attach all your lights to the house itself

➤ Run some lights in the yard, along sidewalks, and in gardens

Lights attached to the house are wired like any interior lighting; all the wiring will run inside your walls. The difference is that the fixtures themselves are made to withstand rain and temperature changes. Lights in the yard require digging because the cable has to be at least 18 inches underground. Special underground cable with a tough sheathing is made for this purpose, or you can run regular house cable inside a conduit (plastic or metal piping made to carry electrical cable).

Keep It Subdued

Outdoor lighting takes some planning, just like any remodeling project. You don't want so much light that airplanes attempt to land on your driveway, and you don't want to antagonize the neighbors with your poorly placed spotlights. You want enough light to make your home a welcoming place, especially for guests coming over on wet, dark winter nights. You also want enough light to convince people who may otherwise wander around your house at night to go somewhere else.

Solar Lighting

Solar-powered yard lights are a weak alternative to hard-wired lights on a regular circuit. They're kind of like mood lighting for your yard as long as your mood calls for dim lights. Go and look at some installations (at night, of course) before you slap down your credit card and cart any home.

Quick Fix

Install any spotlights or security lighting high enough off the ground, porch, or deck so that the bulbs cannot be easily unscrewed. You'd be surprised how often these lights are installed near the top of a door, making it easy for the bad guys to remove the bulbs and defeating the whole purpose of installing them.

A Primer on Power

Now that you're ready to fill every room of your house with lights, dedicated circuits, and automatic window blinds, how do you do it? What's the logic behind all of those wires running out of your electrical panel? Should you be concerned when the electrician on a remodeling job is nicknamed Sparky?

A modern residential electrical system is based on a series of rules. The rules determine amps, watts, wire size, the size and scope of a circuit, and even the size of the light bulbs in your bathroom vanity light. Follow the rules, and you won't get hurt.

Problems pop up when a handy-guy type decides to add an outlet or a light without knowing whether the system can handle it. Your big concern is whether you have enough circuits to power your house the way you want to and whether each circuit is safe. A circuit is nothing more than one complete loop of electricity. It starts at your electrical panel, passes through a light, outlet or appliance, and then heads back. You want to be sure it's traveling the high road and meeting the electrical code while it's doing its job.

Keeping Both Feet on the Ground

All new electrical outlets come with three holes, one for each prong on a three-pronged plug. This number of holes indicates that the system is grounded, and that's a good

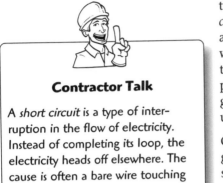

Contractor Talk

A *short circuit* is a type of interruption in the flow of electricity. Instead of completing its loop, the electricity heads off elsewhere. The cause is often a bare wire touching a second bare wire or other piece of metal.

thing. Grounding means that, in the case of a *short circuit*, the system will guide any wayward electricity away from you. This doesn't mean you can stand in a water-filled metal bucket and challenge your friends to drop a plugged-in toaster at your feet. Grounding provides reasonable protection, but that's pushing the grounding envelope. Old two-wire systems aren't usually grounded.

One improvement to the grounding system is the ground-fault circuit interrupter (GFCI). This highly sensitive outlet detects short circuits far faster than an ordinary circuit can. Any circuit can trip or shut off if there's a short circuit, but it may not shut off fast enough to prevent you from getting injured. A GFCI shuts power off in a fraction of a second, quick enough to keep you out of trouble. GFCIs are required in bathrooms, kitchens, and outdoors (all that water and those metal bathtubs, you know). GFCI circuit breakers are also available for service panels.

It All Adds Up

If you want to know about your electrical system, you have to run some numbers. A circuit's current is measured in terms of amps or amperes. Each circuit breaker or fuse is marked with its amperage rating (15 amps, 20 amps, and so on). A 15-amp circuit carries 15 amperes of electricity. If you demand more than 15 amps—say, by plugging two or three toasters into the same circuit—the fuse or circuit breaker senses this excessive demand and shuts the power off.

Quick Fix

GFCI outlets should be tested every month to make sure they're in working order. The test is simple: Press the black test button, watch the red reset button pop out, and then press the reset button. If it doesn't pop out, your outlet may be defective and need replacement.

If the circuit breaker didn't shut off electricity, more electricity would travel through the wires than they are designed to carry, and something would have to give. In this case, the wire would start to fry, because in its attempts to resist this additional flow of electricity, it would produce heat, like the red-hot coils in your toaster. Heat in your toaster is great, especially around breakfast time; bagels aren't quite the same when they're not toasted. The same kind of heat inside your wall, however, can start a fire.

How do you know if you're demanding more power than your 15-amp circuit is up for? The power used by every electrical appliance, light, and gadget in your house is measured in watts. Watts demand amps. To figure out the power demand, you also need to know about volts (don't worry, this jargon ends soon).

Be an Electrical Engineer for a Day

The currents of electricity flowing through your house are either the 120 or 240 volt variety (stoves, dryers, water heaters, and some other high-demand appliances and tools require 240 volts; all other house circuits will use 120). Volts are often described as units of pressure, that is, the electromotive force required to move a current of electricity through the resistance offered by wiring. Just think of it as electricity with an attitude, being really pushy as it works its way down the wire.

Look Out Below!

You're always better off figuring your circuit allocations conservatively, especially if you're an amateur electrician. This is not an area of remodeling where you want to push the envelope and think, "just one more ceiling light, what can that hurt?"

To figure your power usage, use this formula: Watts divided by volts equals amps. To find out the number of watts you're drawing, look on the back of your appliances and on top of light bulbs. When you get the number of amps, you'll know whether you're demanding more than the circuit can provide. For example, the numbers for figuring out the amps that a kitchen circuit requires might stack up this way:

Toaster: 800 watts

Food processor: 600 watts

Coffee maker: 900 watts

Total watts: 2300 watts

2300 watts divided by 120 volts: 19.167 amps

Kitchen circuit: 20 amps, or 2400 watts maximum

Hey, you have .833 amps to spare! Well, not quite. You should figure on drawing only 80 percent of a circuit's capacity during periods of continual loading or use. How come? It's all about heat buildup. If you try to draw the maximum power from a circuit for hours on end, the wire and circuit breaker will just keep heating up. Before things get out of hand, the breaker will trip for a cooling-off period. Running at only 80 percent capacity means you have much less chance of tripping a breaker or blowing a fuse. This is one reason kitchens have two 20-amp circuits in them for small appliances, as well as dedicated circuits for large ones. All of those juicers demand a lot of juice!

If you're blowing fuses or tripping circuit breakers regularly, the simplest solution is to redistribute your power load. With an old kitchen circuit, this redistribution may mean running the toaster and coffee maker first, and then running the blender. Use your circuit map from Chapter 2, "The Anatomy of Your Home," to figure out whether you're overloading any individual circuit.

A circuit map will give you a clear idea of how far an existing circuit can be extended and how many circuits you can add to an existing service. If you have an old fuse box, you'll probably want an electrician to step into the wiring fray in order to add circuits.

Tales from the Scaffold

Code requirements for electrical wiring have been in force since the turn of the century. Building departments started taking electricity very seriously shortly after the advent of the electric light bulb and the development of the first power plants. Electrical fires result when the code is ignored or a system is abused.

Call Me Sparky

A committed homeowner who follows code requirements and maintains good workmanship standards can do a number of wiring and rewiring tasks around the house. My brother wired his dental office—a complicated job that had to meet the tougher commercial electrical code—and passed his inspection with flying colors. The only work he had to correct was the wiring done by the original contractor not too many years earlier.

Doing your own electrical work will include some of the following tasks:

➤ Planning the work and calculating the electrical loads for the proposed job

➤ Taking out a permit and arranging one or even a series of inspections

➤ Buying electrical cable (wire), tools, and other supplies

➤ Stringing (installing) the cable by drilling through floor joists and wall studs

➤ Cutting out sections of drywall or plaster if rewiring an existing room

➤ Installing fixtures, outlets, and light switches

➤ Patching your walls and cleaning up

So much for adding a quick couple of outlets in the kitchen! On top of this, you'll have to deal with an inspector who will probably review your work with a more critical eye than if you were an electrician. Is this an important enough area to save some money, or is your interest in learning to do the work high enough, to go through all of this?

An electrician knows how to mix new wiring with old, even if it means tapping into an old knob and tube system. Are you prepared to do this? I'm not trying to scare you, and I'm not on the payroll of any national electricians' council, but wiring is serious business, and you have to be prepared to educate yourself before you do the work.

When You Need an Electrician

Any service change or upgrade should be done by a qualified electrician. Few homeowners are prepared to do this themselves. I won't even do it, and I've done more than my share of house wiring. Wiring individual circuits is another matter. After the panel has been installed and inspected, and if you follow the rules, you can safely run new circuits and replace existing ones yourself. So can an electrician, of course, and probably faster than you could, but an electrician's hourly rates are considered high in some circles.

Look Out Below!

Be prepared to do your own wall patching after an electrician is through wiring an existing room and has cut into the drywall or plaster. They don't do this work! They wire and leave. The rest is up to you.

Doing your own wiring is like any other remodeling job: A trade-off between your time and your money. Knowing how to run and calculate the circuit is the knowledge part of the job, and you can learn the basics from any number of electrical wiring books. But wiring an existing structure involves a lot of drilling and wire pulling, not exactly activities that require advanced skills. One hint: It's easier with two people doing the work, but it means that you're now tying up two people's time instead of just one person's time. If you're trying to figure out whether doing the work yourselves is truly financially advantageous, calculate the value of your combined time on the job.

Electricians aren't perfect, which will come as a shock to the ones I know. The best trained and most conscientious will do the best work. As in any trade or profession, the best will also be the toughest to schedule; despite the fact that they never advertise or solicit work, they're always busy. These contractors are worth waiting for, so contact them way in advance of the time you need the work done.

Another World of Wiring

We have more than just electrical wiring in our houses now. A few other gadgets have worked their ways into our lives, including:

➤ Stereo systems

➤ Multiple telephone lines

➤ Alarm systems

➤ Cable TV

➤ Internet access cable

These are all low-voltage systems that must share the walls with your electrical wiring and must be kept separate from your electrical wiring as they run through your walls, floors, and ceilings. You can't drill one series of holes and try and pull all different types of wire through them. Well, you can, but you'll mess up the low-voltage stuff, especially the phones, if you do.

Separate the two systems by a good 12 inches as they run through your house. If you're hiring both an electrician and other wiring specialists, such as alarm installers, stereo technicians, and so on, they'll need to coordinate their work before starting the job. This coordination will save them and you the frustration and expense of getting in each other's way when they could be assisting each other.

The Least You Need to Know

➤ Upgrading an old wiring system is a first step in many remodeling projects.

➤ Rewiring your house is an exact science. Respect the rules, and you'll stay safe.

➤ A modern electrical system should make every room in your house more comfortable by increasing the lighting and the number of convenient outlets.

➤ Your yard and the outside of your house offer fabulous lighting possibilities, far beyond basic security; careful planning will open them up to you.

➤ Low-voltage wiring systems (such as cable television and alarm systems) must be installed compatibly with your high-voltage system.

Chapter 13

Plumbing the Depths of Your Plumbing

In This Chapter

➤ Coping with water pressure and hoping for more

➤ More lead problems

➤ Choosing your pipes

➤ Getting fixed on the right fixtures

➤ Plumbing for the future

➤ Tanking up: Water heaters

Plumbing has been with us ever since the Romans built systems to carry drinking water in and waste water out (Romans weren't the first, just the most prominent). Unfortunately, they used lead pipes, and some scholars think that lead poisoning may have had something to do with the decline and fall of Rome. They do admit that the Goths showing up in A.D. 410 to sack the place may have helped things along a little bit.

We're the beneficiaries of greatly improved plumbing systems that are greatly unappreciated—until we have problems. A leak or a broken toilet will suddenly bring on a new-found interest in plumbing. When you're remodeling, your thinking will go beyond the occasional plumbing problem to building new bathrooms, selecting fixtures, and hiring plumbers. Plumbing is one of those specialties that requires a lot of on-the-job training; if you mess up your plumbing, you can find yourself slogging through the results, mop in hand. This is one reason plumbers are paid so handsomely.

Before the actual work, you'll have some decisions to make: Plastic pipes or copper? Functional fixtures only or elaborate ones? How many bathrooms do you really need?

Upgrading your plumbing is one of those one-time expenses that's well worth the investment. You'll enjoy it while you add to the value of your house. This behind-the-scenes stuff needs to get done before you do any fancy finishing work. You'll have plenty of time to wallpaper the bedroom later.

An End to Scalding Showers

Everyone who's ever lived in an old apartment building and had roommates knows the terror of a shower scalding when someone flushes a toilet or turns on the tap at the sink. Your plumbing is only doing its job: Providing water on demand. In the world of economics, when there's too much demand and not enough supply, you get scarcity. With plumbing, you get a sudden change of shower temperature. The water is just doing its best to satisfy all users.

Tales from the Scaffold

If you think your plumbing is bad, consider the White House, the nation's number one address. According to *Plumbing and Mechanical Magazine* (July 1989), the White House had no running water until the 1830s even though it was available in private mansions and hotels by that time. The president still made do with servants, buckets, and a water source several blocks away. By 1833, iron pipe was laid from a bubbling spring to the White House; the water was pushed through with the help of a pumphouse. Hit-and-miss repairs and additions over the years compelled Harry S Truman, who discovered his bathtub sinking into the floor, to authorize a multimillion-dollar reconstruction of the White House.

Why does plumbing behave like this? Your plumbing serves two basic purposes:

➤ It provides clean, potable water, under pressure, through a system of various-sized pipes for use at various fixtures and faucets.

➤ Using the force of gravity, it removes waste water through a separate system of drain lines.

If you had big enough pipes, both the shower and toilet, as well as the sink, dishwasher, and washing machine, would have enough water to do their jobs without causing problems elsewhere. Unless you're on a private well, your local municipality or county (parish for all you Louisiana folks) supplies your water via the water main. This pipe is really big because it has to supply every-one else's house, business, and rent-it-by-the-hour hot tub place as well. Between you and the water main is your water meter (so the water company can bill you for service) and your service line. The service line is part of the reason you get a shower surprise.

At your end of the service line is the main shut-off valve for all the water in your house. Newer plumbing systems will also have individual shut-off valves for individual fixtures (look under your sinks and behind the toilet). Past your shut-off valve, your water branches off into two lines, one for cold water and a second one to the hot water heater. A line coming out of the hot water tank then runs parallel with the cold water pipe as they head off for different fixtures.

Look Out Below!

Find out where your main shut-off valve is located and test it; you don't want to find out it's hard to shut off when you have an emergency. If you live in a cold climate, it's a good idea to shut off your water while you're away for a winter vacation. Otherwise, you could come back to a burst pipe.

Putting the Pressure On

A standard plumbing upgrade in old houses is replacing the service line. Some of these lines were as small as $1/2$-inch in diameter, which was adequate in the old one-bathroom, no major water-consuming appliances days. A 1-inch line is common now; this size is big enough to supply water to a two-story house with a couple of bathrooms or more, as well as the appliances.

The other side of the water-under-pressure equation is the size of the pipes in your house. You want enough water volume and pressure to ensure comfortable use of more than one fixture at a time. The standard rule is to run only two fixtures on a $1/2$-inch line and allot a $3/4$-inch cold water line for each bathroom.

Quick Fix

If your service line is too small, it can always be replaced well in advance of any plumbing-related remodeling. Why not get some interim benefit from the increased pressure?

As an additional measure, many plumbing codes call for the installation of a pressure-balanced tub and shower valve. This slick piece of hardware strives to balance the hot and cold water coming out of a shower head and keep an even temperature.

Get the Lead Out

Lead, the one-time universal miracle metal, was used for both pipes and in lead solder, the stuff that seals up pipe joints. Banned in 1988, lead solder is no longer used, and lead pipes haven't been installed in houses since the 1930s. Our friends, the Romans, started it all—the word plumbing even comes from *plumbum*, which is Latin for lead. Lead pipes aren't so much the problem (relatively few homes even still have them), but lead solder can dissolve and leach into tap water. Some faucets also contain lead—this stuff has got you coming and going.

Lead is a health issue, especially with young kids. To put yourself at ease if you have a house older than 1988 vintage, call your local health department and inquire about water testing. They'll be able to steer you toward a government or private agency that will test your tap water. Meanwhile, you can take a few simple precautions:

➤ Run your tap water for a minute or so if it has been unused for several hours. Mornings are always a good time (standing water contains more dissolved lead).

➤ Only use cold water for cooking and drinking (lead dissolves faster in hot water).

➤ Install a water filter designed to remove lead.

Cleaning Your Water: Filters

We're fortunate to live in a country with such an advanced water-delivery system, naysayers notwithstanding. If you don't believe me, try the local water in a country where water has to be boiled before you can drink it. Nevertheless, to accommodate taste and the desire to remove certain chemicals and trace metals from public tap water, various filtering systems are available, including:

➤ Sediment filters

➤ Activated charcoal filters

➤ Reverse-osmosis filters

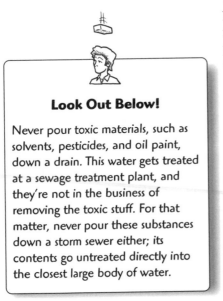

Look Out Below!

Never pour toxic materials, such as solvents, pesticides, and oil paint, down a drain. This water gets treated at a sewage treatment plant, and they're not in the business of removing the toxic stuff. For that matter, never pour these substances down a storm sewer either; its contents go untreated directly into the closest large body of water.

Activated charcoal or carbon filters are the filtering systems most commonly used in households. They either attach to the service line outside your house (these are large units) or are attached as smaller, individual filters at fixtures such as kitchen sinks or refrigerator ice and water dispensers. Periodic maintenance and replacement of the filters, which are usually removable cartridges, is required for the system to continue doing its job. In areas with hard water, a water softener will eliminate lime deposits that gunk up your fixtures and water heater.

Do you need a water filter? Health advocates say yes; municipal water engineers would tell you tap water is safe and clean. It's a matter of taste and beliefs, but filters are rarely an absolute necessity.

Call a Plumber or Two

Plumbers are among the guardians of civilization. Some people can't imagine life without Italian chefs, top-notch dry cleaners, and a good bookstore, but we'd all have problems in a world without plumbers. Apart from minor repairs, it's unlikely you'll ever do any major plumbing work on your own house, but you can always go and practice at the in-laws' place.

You should find a plumber before you need one. Running to the phone book, whether it's for a toilet repair or to get a bid on a new bathroom, isn't the best strategy. Everyone who's owned an old house for a while knows a good plumber—they have to. These homeowners are your best source for referrals.

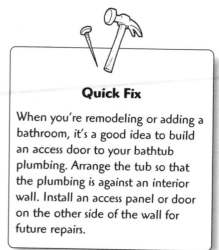

Quick Fix

When you're remodeling or adding a bathroom, it's a good idea to build an access door to your bathtub plumbing. Arrange the tub so that the plumbing is against an interior wall. Install an access panel or door on the other side of the wall for future repairs.

For major remodeling work, get at least three estimates, as you would with any contracting job. One thing you should look at is the type of pipe each plumber proposes to install. Both plastic and copper pipe are used in new construction, and there are strong opinions about each.

Any plumbing repair or remodeling is going to disrupt your water and life somewhere along the line. Plan ahead. Find out when and for how long you can expect the water to be turned off. Unless you're redoing all your bathrooms at once, it would be unusual for you to be without a working bathroom during the course of the work. Get a written work schedule from your plumber so you can arrange your schedule around it.

Last but not least, remember a cardinal rule about plumbers (and electricians): They do not do wall repair. If they have to cut into existing plaster or drywall, they will leave all of their holes for you to patch, unless you want them to line up a subcontractor to do the work.

Pipe Wars

Historically, the world has gone from lead pipes to wood, back to lead, on to iron and steel, then on to copper, and finally on to different forms of plastic. Maybe wood will become super retro and considered chic by hi-tech millionaires who can afford the ridiculous. Meanwhile, copper is the traditional choice of master plumbers. It's flexible, durable, and forms a tight connection with valves.

Copper comes in three grades:

➤ M is the thinnest and is used mostly for interior pipes.

➤ L is thicker and is used for outside water services.

➤ K is the thickest, and it runs between the water main and the meter.

163

*What really goes on
behind closed walls.*

It can be argued that plumbers who automatically prefer copper over plastic are too stubborn to change and get with the new program, but plastic hasn't been without its problems.

Strange Molecules

Rigid plastic pipe includes PVC (polyvinyl chloride) and ABS (acrylonitrile butadiene styrene), and they both make terrific drain and vent pipes. They're both lightweight and don't corrode like old iron and steel pipe.

Add some more chemicals to the brew, and you end up with CPVC (chlorinated polyvinyl chloride), which, because it withstands pressure, can be used to supply both hot and cold water. CPVC is cheaper than copper and easy to cut and fit. Like all rigid plastic pipe, CPVC is cut with a saw, and the ends are glued together.

Tales from the Scaffold

The town of Lake in the Hills, Illinois disliked CPVC pipe so much they banned it a few years ago from being used in new home construction. Building Commissioner David Sellek recommended the action despite complaints from BF Goodrich representative Mike Lipke, who protested that the pipe was a sturdy product. Skeptics of CPVC's durability and compatibility with other plumbing materials won out in the plastic versus copper argument. No word if Lake in the Hills has lifted the ban yet.

The Price of Flexibility

Polybutylene, or "pb" to those who are hip to plumbing, is a flexible type of pipe some local codes allow to be installed to carry water under pressure. Polybutylene has been involved in class-action suits because it's prone to premature failure. Texans received a $750 million dollar settlement resulting from their lawsuit against manufacturers of polybuytlene pipe. An estimated 6 million American homes have this flexible, gray, plastic pipe running hither and yon while it leaks here and there. Manufacturers, including Shell Oil and Dupont, claim the current product is improved and blame most of the leaks on bad installation practices.

> **Look Out Below!**
>
> Galvanized steel pipes, often found in older homes, corrode from water and gradually become restricted as corrosive gunk fills them. Unlike drain lines, water pipes can't be cleaned out. Once they're filled with gunk, you need to replace them.

Polybuytlene is cheaper than CPVC. A major savings is the labor cost of installing it: It doesn't take a plumber to put this stuff in, although a plumber must make the final hookups. Several municipalities in Arizona banned polybuytlene from new construction in 1994. If you're house hunting and run across any plastic pipe, find out what it is and get it in writing. Polybuytlene may be considered a liability in some cities and will affect the value of the property.

What's the homeowner to do? At the risk of sounding like a fuddy-duddy, I say you can't go wrong with copper water pipes, unless your local water supply doesn't react kindly to it, and it may not, due to:

➤ Highly acidic water (low pH)

➤ The amount of oxygen in the water

➤ The mineral content

Check with your local water department before making a final decision about pipe types.

Making the Water Go Away

Potable water is the nice part of a plumbing system. Getting rid of the waste is the part we'd like to forget about, but clogged sinks and toilets remind us that what comes in must go out, even though it gets stuck sometimes. A good drainage and vent system is the critical other half of your plumbing.

Drainage starts at each fixture, which has its own drain line and trap. A trap—look under your sink for a U-shaped piece of pipe—does just what its name suggests. It traps a small amount of water so sewer gases don't find their way into your house. How would they do that? Isn't the sewer outside?

165

Each drain line is connected to your *soil stack*, a series of vertical pipes that run from your basement, where they connect to the sewer line or septic tank, up through your roof. The roof end allows gases to escape and air to be drawn inward, helping to keep your drains flowing—a real-life example of a high school science experiment demonstrating the direct benefits of air pressure.

Quick Fix

Old soil stacks were made from cast iron. Some new homeowners have discovered that plastic soil stacks and some plastic drain lines are too noisy. Despite the advantages of rigid plastic, you might consider using cast iron or a combination of iron and plastic for your second floor drainage.

Running plenty of hot water down your kitchen and bathroom drains will help to keep them clear. You can use an old-fashioned method, too:

1. Pour one cup of baking soda down each drain.

2. Follow with one cup of white vinegar.

3. After 30 minutes, flush with hot water.

If all your drains are running slow, you need to have your sewer line cleaned. Plumbers don't usually do this work, but specialists like Roto-Rooter do. Expect to pay a service charge plus an hourly fee. The technician will come in with a huge power *auger*, which is a big version of a plumber's snake (a flexible coiled cable used for cleaning drains).

Look Out Below!

Bird nests and other debris can clog the roof end of your vent. Make sure the vent is kept clear. For that matter, make sure your vent goes all the way through the roof; sometimes vents stop in the attic—a bad idea!

If you're not attached to a public sewer system, then you're house is connected to a septic tank, which is an in-yard decomposition system. Septic systems need to be pumped out and cleaned periodically and they are not compatible with kitchen disposers. Such is the price of living the good life out in the country.

While You're at It

I'm a big advocate of planning ahead. We may have only the here and now, but tomorrow has a regular habit of becoming the new here and now. Why not give it some thought while you're tearing around inside your walls and adding pipes and drains and you have a plumber on the payroll?

Future projects could include:

➤ Additional full or partial bathrooms

➤ Scrub sinks

➤ Second sink in an enlarged kitchen

➤ Hose bibs (these are faucets for garden hoses)

Running water and drain lines to any probable future locations is a great idea if it makes logical sense while you're doing other work. If you're re-plumbing one bathroom and expect to add an additional bathroom a short distance away a few years down the road, there's certainly no harm in running the pipes while the wall is open. You'll look like a genius when you eventually add the bathroom; if you don't add it, you won't be out any big expense.

Tales from the Scaffold

The earliest water systems used wood pipes! Thick logs, up to nine feet long, were bored out with a 5-foot steel auger, and the joints were sealed with pitch or tar. In some cases, a log would be split, hollowed out, and reassembled with iron bands or lead. If you think wood and water don't mix, you're right; the pipes would eventually rot or get attacked by insects. Ever the traditionalists, Washington state, land of many trees, continued to install some wood piping systems into the 20th century.

How's Your Hot Water Heater?

One of the main energy consumers in a house (besides kids) is your hot water heater. Gas seems to win out in the water heater price war and claims a faster recovery rate (the speed with which it heats up more water). Energy-efficient water heaters come with an ASHRAE (American Society of Heating, Refrigerating, and Air Conditioning Engineers) rating. A rating of 90 tells you the water heater is well insulated and that it won't be necessary to add an exterior insulation blanket. If you have an electric water heater and a gas furnace, compare the cost of keeping your current appliance versus replacing it with a gas water heater. Do the same if you run a gas line in because you're changing to a gas furnace.

Your water heater doesn't ask much from you. A couple of times a year, drain a few gallons of water out of the valve at the bottom of the tank to remove any built-up sludge. This will keep your tank working efficiently.

Tankless or instantaneous water heaters are an alternative to the full-size type. They don't store water, but they heat it as it's needed. More often seen in Europe but also

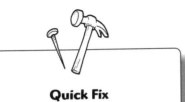

Quick Fix

Ask your local utility if they have a leasing program for hot water heaters. Compare the cost and the terms with buying a hot water heater outright. Some programs can make leasing very competitive with purchasing, and it leaves any repairs up to the leasing utility.

sold in the United States, tankless systems typically attach to single fixtures and are activated when the tap is turned on. Water is heated as it passes through the tank.

Their manufacturers argue that tankless systems are much less expensive to run because they only activate on demand, and you can never exhaust your hot water supply (as long as the unit's working, anyway). Both gas and electric models are available, meaning you would have to run wiring or gas piping to each fixture. Basically, because utilities are cheaper in the United States, we take the bigger-is-better approach: Big hot water heaters and big central furnaces. We like it this way because we like our conveniences. If you've ever been to Europe, you probably found that individual tankless heaters in showers work OK, look a bit odd, and are probably something you'll never want in your house—even if it can be argued (maybe) that they're a good use of resources.

Busted: Frozen Pipes

Hawaiians will never have to read this section, but they're welcome to laugh at those who do. Frozen pipes, whether they're new or old, are a reality. Most plumbers automatically wrap and insulate any new pipes they install, but your existing ones may not be protected against the cold. The problem isn't just that your water gets stuck; when the great thaw comes, the pipe can burst and leave you with a real mess.

To protect yourself and your pipes, here are a few pointers:

➤ In crawl spaces, cover foundation vents when cold weather sets in (remove covers in the spring).

➤ Insulate pipes in any unheated spaces.

➤ Shut off water to individual hose bibs if shutoffs are available; otherwise, cover the faucet or hose bib with a foam cover (available from hardware stores).

➤ Disconnect all garden hoses, drain them, and store them in the garage or basement.

➤ Shut off your water and drain it if you're going away for several days during subfreezing weather.

➤ During severe cold, turn on the faucet furthest from your service line and let it run at a fast drip to keep the water in the pipes flowing.

➤ If your pipes freeze, thaw them with an electric hair dryer or heat lamp, never with an open flame or torch.

➤ When a pipe does freeze and burst, turn off the water at the main shutoff and call a plumber; if the break is on your utility's side of the meter, call them.

Tales from the Scaffold

Every once in a while, Seattle has some frigid winter weather, and pipes freeze all over town. Inevitably, the local papers have a story or two the following day about someone who decided to crawl under the house and thaw out the pipes with a propane torch. At the same time, he (it's always a he) ignites part of the framing, and up it goes. I can guarantee you that a house fire will thaw your frozen pipes out in no time at all.

The Least You Need to Know

➤ Plumbing is a nice logical system of water pressure, air vents, and waste lines; defy its logic, and you'll have problems.

➤ Not all types of pipe are created equal; know what you have and what you're getting before you agree to any plumbing work.

➤ Your waste system (drains and vents) requires some maintenance, monitoring, cleaning, and flushing, or else it may stop doing its disagreeable job.

➤ Water heaters are big energy users; find out whether yours should be replaced or switched over to gas.

➤ It's a lot easier to take precautions against frozen pipes than to deal with one when the first big freeze hits.

Chapter 14

Clear the Air: Heat and Air Conditioning

In This Chapter

➤ Going with gas

➤ Furnace replacement therapy

➤ Maintaining your HVAC system

There's a reason Europeans were always going off exploring: They were trying to stay warm. The British figured that anyplace had to be warmer and drier than an English winter so they headed off to such tropical areas as Canada and Massachusetts. At least the French ended up in Louisiana. Centuries later, working heating systems tempered this wanderlust, and people stayed home and created such cultural delights as Monty Python's Flying Circus, French fries, and the Volkswagen Beetle.

Humans have gone from campfires, fireplaces, and stoves to the first successful central heating, which was developed in 1835 in Great Britain. The stiff-upper-lip English didn't take to it with the same aplomb as Americans; we like being warm and find no virtue in living in cold, damp homes. We've evolved from huge coal and oil-fired furnaces to modern natural gas units, and they're better than ever.

Heating, ventilating, and air conditioning your house is another of your mechanical systems. In the construction industry, it's known as HVAC. Follow the HVAC rules, and you'll be comfortable. All furnaces aren't the same. You have to consider the size of the space you're heating and cooling, the location of the duct work, the type of windows and insulation you have, and the type of fuel or power you choose to use. Your goal is to be comfortable at a reasonable cost. This chapter will give you some ideas for staying cozy and warm without losing your cool.

Way Beyond the Fireplace: Modern Heating Systems

If a house is old enough, say early 1920s, its heating system will have started out as coal, been converted to oil at some point, and then converted once more to natural gas. New houses almost inevitably have forced-air gas furnaces, although some condominiums have electric heat. Oil, once a big seller because of its convenience over coal, is rarely seen much in new residential construction. Old oil systems have left buried, abandoned oil tanks as their legacies. Removal and decontamination of oil tank sites can easily run $1,000 or more.

You have a lot of choices for heating, including:

➤ Forced-air natural gas

➤ Electric furnaces and room heaters

➤ Heating oil

➤ Steam and hot water heat

➤ Heat pumps

➤ Wood-burning stoves

➤ Fireplaces

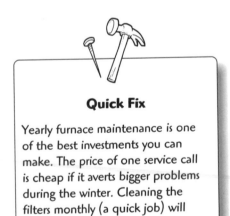

Quick Fix

Yearly furnace maintenance is one of the best investments you can make. The price of one service call is cheap if it averts bigger problems during the winter. Cleaning the filters monthly (a quick job) will help your furnace work more efficiently.

Each type of heating shines in some circumstances and should be replaced in others. Which type is best for you?

Gas Is a Blast

In areas where gas is available, a forced-air gas furnace is the number one choice for heating new homes. Natural gas is economical, clean, and reliable; there's no need to worry about an oil delivery truck getting stuck in the snow. Electronic ignitions have eliminated those pesky pilot lights in furnaces and some gas appliances.

Gas furnaces work on some simple principles. Natural gas is piped into the furnace and ignited inside the fire box, a metal box also called a heat exchanger. A fan forces air over the hot heat exchanger (hence the name, forced-air furnace), through the heat ducts, and into rooms. Cold air is drawn into the furnace through a cold air return. As a bonus, the heat duct work can be used for air conditioning or fan-forced ventilation during the summer.

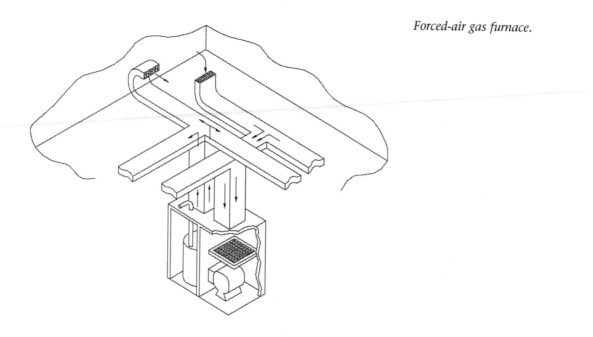

Forced-air gas furnace.

Gas burns pretty clean; you won't see billowing smoke, but there are still exhaust gases to deal with, such as carbon monoxide. These gases are vented outside your house (more on carbon monoxide later).

No Gas or Oil, But at a Price

In an electric furnace, an enclosed coil heats up, and a blower forces cold air across it and into the duct work. Electric furnaces are expensive to run, even here in the northwest where electricity is relatively cheap. Fossil fuels (gas and oil) are so much cheaper than electricity that only exceptional circumstances would dictate the installation of an electric furnace.

Sometimes selective electric heat, or zone heating, is both desirable and a good solution to a heating problem. A room that's tough to heat because of its distance from your furnace or a bathroom, where a little extra heat is welcome, could benefit from electric heaters.

Oil Furnaces

Oil furnaces work similarly to gas furnaces: Fuel is burned, heat is produced, and hot air is forced through the ducts. They are a dying breed in new construction except in areas where neither natural nor propane gas is available. New oil furnaces are a vast improvement over old models and are worth considering if you haven't got access to gas.

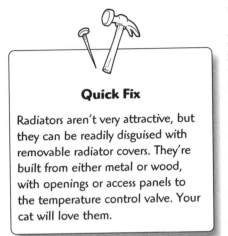

You're in Hot Water Now

If you live in Reykjavik, Iceland, you have a more intimate relationship with hot water heat; most of the homes in this laugh-a-minute Icelandic capital are heated with water from thermal springs. The rest of us with hot water or steam heat depend on a boiler, fueled by gas or oil, that circulates the water or steam through pipes to radiators throughout the house.

Hot water and steam heating systems that use radiators, the part of the system that gets hot and heats your rooms, are rarely installed today. When they are, they are usually modified versions with longer and flatter heating units. If you have a steam heating system, you don't have to yank it out and install a gas furnace. Have your system evaluated by a heating technician and then checked once a year as part of your regular maintenance.

Heat Under Your Feet

Radiant floor heat is a great concept in theory; it doesn't heat the air as a conventional furnace does, but it heats bodies and objects in the room using water-filled pipes embedded in the floor. The first such systems are attributed to the Romans, who heated the public baths and some private residences with hot air circulated in duct work under stone floors. The concept of hot water heat installed in the floor was introduced to American home builders in the 1950s.

Because radiant heat will work with all kinds of floor construction, think of your floor as one big radiator. Unlike radiators, radiant floor heat is more comfortable at lower temperatures than conventional hot water systems. There are no heat registers and no radiators; you can put your furniture anywhere. You have less heat loss because you yourself are being heated, not the air that finds its way to the ceiling and out windows and door gaps.

The drawbacks to radiant floor heating include:

➤ Expense of installation

➤ High repair costs

➤ Difficult access to tubing to do repairs

➤ Longevity of the system

Tales from the Scaffold

Heatway radiant heating systems have been under fire due to leaks that have plagued homeowners. The Goodyear Corporation, which supplied the tubing, adamantly denies responsibility, claiming it produced a tube in accordance with, and accepted by, Heatway's specifications. In a series of lawsuits and counter-suits, a Colorado state judge agreed that Goodyear did not deliver a defective product to Heatway, which doesn't help the affected homeowners too much. There have been indications that improper installation played a part in some of the leaks. If you have a problem or question about a Heatway system, call them at 800-255-1996.

Heat Pumps

If you like forced-air gas heat, you probably won't like heat pumps. Comfort is as much perception and interpretation as it is actual temperature figures, and heat pumps don't make everyone comfortable. Heat pumps depend upon the heat produced when a refrigerant such as Freon changes back and forth from a gas to a liquid. A heat pump system involves a compressor, copper tubing, and a fan to blow air across the changing temperature of the refrigerant.

Heat pumps were more popular in the '70s and early '80s as a less-expensive alternative to fossil fuels.

Wood-Burning Stoves

Also once seen as an alternative to fossil fuels, wood-burning stoves are great if you have a cabin up in the woods, but we're entering the 21st century here and don't need to be chopping down trees anymore to heat our main residence. Earlier versions weren't anywhere near as environmentally friendly as advocates then suggested, although current models have improved. Besides, all that wood has to come from someplace. Leave these out in the woods or up in the mountains where they belong.

Fireplaces: Great for Romance, Not for Heating

Fireplaces give off heat two ways: from the burning of the wood or gas itself and radiant heat from the back and sides of the fireplace as they heat up. Unfortunately, most of the heat goes up the chimney. In fact, if you don't have glass doors or a fireplace cover to prevent your furnace-generated heat from rising up through the chimney, you're even losing heat when the fireplace isn't in use.

Quick Fix

Consider installing a natural gas fireplace insert in your existing fireplace, with gas logs or just a gas grill for burning wood. A gas fireplace with artificial logs requires far less cleaning and maintenance than a wood-burning one. Ask your installer if you have to make any adjustments to your chimney first.

New homes with fireplaces often have gas models with switch-controlled ignitions, glass doors, and fans that blow hot air back into the room. They can produce a lot of room heat as well as a little bit of atmosphere to take your mind off your remodeling. Free-standing gas fireplaces are a lot of fun and don't require a brick chimney for venting. This is one of those luxury extras well worth having and is seen as very desirable when you're selling your house.

Upgrading and Installing Furnaces

Obviously, furnace installation isn't a do-it-yourself job. Your decisions on upgrading should be based on the age and efficiency of your current furnace and the anticipated savings from a new model. Many old furnaces are below 60 percent efficiency; how much wasted, expensive fuel does that amount to?

A new furnace is a good selling point, but not necessarily an investment that will pay for itself, because purchasers expect an adequate heating system. This is one of those remodeling issues that's measured by your own degree of comfort and your savings from lower heating bills, not as a payback when you sell.

Slimming Down Your Old Furnace

A new furnace seems to be about the size of a gym bag. An old "octopus" furnace, so-called because each duct stuck out of the furnace like a tentacle, seems to be the size of a sport utility vehicle. The size difference alone is a reason to replace your ancient furnace; you'll reclaim some of your basement. Changing to a gas furnace is also an opportune time to have your gas installer run gas piping for a gas fireplace, water heater, or range.

What if you've got an oil furnace? How do you convert it to natural gas? First, you have to be on or near a gas line. If your neighbors have gas, you can have gas; you just can't have theirs. Installing a new natural gas furnace and gas service will require:

➤ Permits

➤ The gas company running a service line from their main pipeline to a gas meter outside your house

➤ Installing gas piping inside your house from the meter to your furnace (and any other gas appliances)

➤ Removing the old furnace and installing the new natural gas model

➤ Running new duct work as needed

➤ Having all the work inspected

Look Out Below!

Many old furnaces have asbestos, either on the ductwork or parts of the furnace itself. Asbestos is considered a hazardous material and must be removed and disposed of accordingly. The extra cost can be substantial, so be sure to get an estimate on it before you establish a furnace budget. In some cities, a homeowner is permitted to remove asbestos, but check before doing so.

Hey, I Don't Smell a Thing

Carbon monoxide is a by-product of gas combustion. Like water, it's colorless, tasteless, and odorless. Unlike most water—I'm thinking here of the Cuyohaga River of my Ohio childhood—it's also toxic and a regular cause of poisoning in the United States. Besides your furnace, other sources of carbon monoxide include:

➤ Gas water heaters

➤ Gas appliances

➤ Internal combustion engines (cars, lawnmowers, and so on)

➤ Fireplaces

➤ Wood stoves

➤ Charcoal grills

Carbon monoxide poisoning, according to the Consumer Products Safety Commission, sickens approximately 5,000 people a year and kills almost 200. It does this by inhibiting the blood's ability to carry oxygen—one of those critical elements in our lives, like water and a decent pinot noir. Yearly furnace maintenance should include testing for carbon monoxide leakage.

Natural gas, on the other hand, has an odorant added to it so you *can* smell it. A weaker smell may indicate that a pilot light has gone out. If you detect a strong gas smell, get out of the house immediately—don't light any cigars on the way—and call the gas company. They take leaks very seriously and so should you.

You should know how to get to your gas meter safely and turn it off in the event that you have a leak. Ask your service technician to show you the shut-off valve during your next inspection or repair. Most valves require a wrench to shut them off; if yours does, keep one nearby.

Summertime: The Only Time to Install a Furnace

Winter is not the time to install a furnace, unless it's an emergency, and it shouldn't be if you kept an eye on your furnace and had a technician look at it during the summer or early fall. Furnace replacement is a summer project. Aside from setting funds aside for the work, you'll have to allow for duct replacement; that could mean tearing into some walls to cut some registers. You'll be a lot happier in December if you decide to replace the furnace in July.

Which Gas Furnace?

New furnaces are much more efficient than old models. They are measured by the Annual Fuel Utilization Efficiency (AFUE). The group of furnaces normally called "high efficiency" rate over 90 percent, meaning they convert 90 percent or more of the gas into energy and can be vented directly out a side wall. These furnaces are economical choices if you have long, cold winters. The 80 to 82 percent AFUE furnaces are more appropriate if you have mild winters.

You don't want to overbuy; a furnace larger than your house requires will just keep cycling on and off more often than a smaller one.

Don't Forget the Thermostat

New thermostats come in a couple of flavors: programmable and nonprogrammable. You want a programmable one—this is no place to be cheap. These thermostats can be set to go on and off at various times of the day and maintain predetermined temperatures during those times. You can wake up to a warm house without ever touching the thermostat.

Honeywell makes a wonderful line of these thermostats with varying degrees of sophistication. This is the only way to go with house thermostats; even if they cost more than nonprogrammable models, they can save you money in the long run. Keeping a house at consistent, even temperatures rather than depending on the human responses in your household ("I'm freezing. Who set the temperature so low?" "It's boiling in here; why is this thing so high?") is more cost-effective.

The Other End: Air Conditioning

Air conditioning is one of those technological advances, along with ice-making machines and drive-in burrito stands, that has allowed us to live in places no one in their

Quick Fix

The Consumer Product Safety Commission recommends installing a carbon monoxide detector on each floor of a house and one above a gas furnace and all other gas burning appliances. Carbon monoxide is odorless; a detector will detect leaks and alert you the same way that a smoke detector alerts you to smoke.

right mind would inhabit, like most of eastern Nevada. Air conditioning is simply a system with a refrigerant, such as Freon, that absorbs heat from inside your house and releases it outside at the condenser. A fan blows cool air out of the inside coil or evaporator. At the same time that an air conditioner is lowering the temperature of your house, it's also removing humidity, which is a big comfort plus for you.

Like all of your other mechanical systems, air conditioning requires regular cleaning and maintenance. Filters need to be washed out, and yard debris needs to be cleared away from the unit. Location is important, too; you want the unit out of the sun or otherwise shaded, so it'll run more efficiently.

Look Out Below!

Be careful when you replace old thermostats with new programmable models. Some older units have different voltage requirements, so the new ones may not work. If you've done your own replacement and the new thermostat doesn't work, call a technician. They've seen it all before.

As with furnaces, there's no advantage to installing a bigger air conditioner than you need. One formula calls for one ton of air conditioning (12,000 B.T.U. cooling or British thermal units) for every 500 square feet of living space or, for instance, 5 tons for a 2,500 square foot house. These formulas assume a certain degree of insulation and window space that may not be present in your home, so discuss your needs with your HVAC contractor. Central air conditioning uses the same duct work as your forced-air furnace, so you shouldn't encounter any additional expense on that end.

Unless you're in a part of the country where air-conditioned houses are the norm, you don't need to be in any hurry to install it. You may not be aware (you'd be surprised how many people aren't) that forced-air furnaces come with summer fan controls. Turn the fan on, and the furnace acts as a ventilation system for the whole house by blowing unheated air through all the ducts.

Air Filters

If we could view the microscopic contents of the air we breathe, we'd probably be quite surprised. Every day, we suck up dust, pollen, spores, and dander, both ours and our pets'. Carpet and furniture are great places for this stuff to settle and launch itself from every time we walk or sit down. A standard furnace filter collects only the large particles; an *electrostatic air filter* removes over 70 to 90 percent of airborne particles by producing a static charge to trap them in a polypropylene filter.

Quick Fix

If you're rewiring, go ahead and have your electrician run a wire to the location of an air conditioner you may install in the future. It does not have to be a live circuit, just a wire run from outside your panel box, and clearly marked A/C at both ends. Then you'll have it when you need it.

Maintenance consists of cleaning the filter every few weeks with soap and water.

These filtering systems aren't perfect. They are an added cost to purchase and install, and they lose some of their efficiency as they get older. Some people are annoyed by the noise they make, so be sure to listen to one in action before you buy.

Up in Smoke: Your Chimney

The fireplace isn't the only heat producer in your house that uses a chimney. Some furnaces and water heaters use them as well to vent out toxic by-products of combustion, especially our old friend carbon monoxide. Chimneys also create a draft or air flow for efficient combustion in the furnace or water heater. Like your fireplace chimney, these chimneys need regular maintenance.

Check your chimneys for the following:

➤ Soot and liner deterioration

➤ Chimney deterioration from moisture buildup

➤ Sulfur buildup from oil heat

➤ Birds' nests and broken or loose bricks

Maintenance Schedule for Your HVAC System:

➤ Schedule annual checkup by service technician

➤ Clean furnace filters every four to six weeks when in use

➤ Clean or replace air conditioner filters monthly

➤ Keep debris away from air conditioner condenser

➤ Bleed air from radiators before heating season starts

➤ Have furnace ducts cleaned every five years or so

➤ Check that duct work in the crawl space is secured

Prioritize and Weatherize

Weatherizing isn't an issue with new homes. Insulation and weather-stripping standards are now much higher than they were; old homes leaked like sieves. In some cases, when builders' and building departments' ardor for energy savings overcame their good sense, homes were super-insulated and had so little fresh air exchange that mold developed inside. New housing gets around this problem by having ventilation systems on timers. You should use them for the first year after the house is built to combat off-gassing or curing of carpets, paints, particle board, and floor finishes. Some people don't react well to all of these invisible chemical clouds, even though they aren't considered toxic. These "all house fans" also assist in eliminating any residual radon gas if you live in an area where this is a problem. Older homes can almost always use some weatherizing, including:

➤ Caulking and weather-stripping of doors and windows

➤ Adding storm doors

➤ Installing a water heater insulating blanket (on older models of water heaters, recent ones do not require them)

➤ Sealing leaks around pipes where they come through walls

➤ Caulking around the exterior chimney

➤ Insulating hot water pipes, heating ducts, and crawl spaces

➤ Increasing attic insulation to at least R-19

Contractor Talk

An *electrostatic air filter* works by carrying an electric current through a filter. Positively charged dust is trapped in the negatively charged filter and remains there until the filter is cleaned.

An "R" value indicates a material's ability to resist heat loss. The higher the "R" value, the greater its resistance, which translates into more heat retained inside your home.

It could be that by weatherizing and tightening up your house, you won't have to be in such a hurry to replace your furnace.

The Least You Need to Know

➤ Forced-air gas furnaces are the number one furnace choice for good reasons: They're efficient, economical, and dependable.

➤ Electric heat is normally the most expensive heat you can have, but it's appropriate for select room zone heating or for areas where neither gas nor oil are economically available.

➤ Fireplaces are for atmosphere, not heating (though if you have enough atmosphere, you won't need any more heat).

➤ Programmable thermostats are the only way to go when choosing a new thermostat.

➤ Follow your owner's manual regardless of the heating system you install. Regular maintenance will cut your costs and keep your furnace running on cold days when you need it.

Part 4
Get a Fresh Start: Interior Changes

There are two categories of interior changes we make to our houses: Structural/ mechanical and functional/aesthetic. Structural and mechanical changes, such as a new electrical service or a furnace, aren't any fun at all, something like sour-tasting medicine. We know they're good for the house and they're good for us, but they're expensive and we don't enjoy them as much as, say, a new sauna.

New bathrooms, updated kitchens, an extra fireplace—these we actively and regularly use, but we usually don't need any of them. An outdated, cramped kitchen still does the job, even if it's inconvenient and painted avocado green. But we seek change; we'll take a space we use every day, make it more functional, and dress it up at the same time. Cherry-wood cabinets with brass hardware won't hold the dishes any better than the post-WWII metal ones they replace, but cherry wood and brass add dazzle the metal cabinets will never have.

Interior remodeling offers us all kinds of creative license. Your house becomes a gallery for your remodeling art work and no one can close down the exhibition because your stuff isn't selling. I had a client who was an artist and redid his interior as almost a continual piece of sculpture; this can be a little dangerous when it comes time to find a buyer and move on. In his case, the new owner found it to his liking and the house sold quickly. My client's sales prospects weren't exactly hurt by a hot real estate market, either.

I'd caution you to express yourself, but in the direction of being tasteful—a loaded term, for sure. Not every decision should be based strictly on future resale, but you don't want to go to the expense of remodeling and then find that the house is a tough sell because of the choices you're making today. Strike a balance between your dreams and practicality; make your plans, pick your colors, look at carpet samples, and get ready to enjoy your new interior.

Chapter 15

Cooking Up a Storm: Reworking Your Kitchen

In This Chapter

➤ Getting rid of that cramped feeling when you cook

➤ Appliances large and small

➤ Let there be light: Adding more artificial and natural light to your kitchen

➤ Filling it up with sinks, cabinets, and counters

➤ Finding the perfect floor

Our cave-dwelling ancestors essentially lived in one room: the kitchen. They ate, slept, and played Ice Age board games around the fire, which was the earliest version of a stove. Centuries later, kitchens were often the only warm room in the house, until central heating was developed.

Kitchens have gone way beyond the huddling-to-keep-warm stage; often, kitchens are the most expensive room in the house to remodel. They involve electrical work, plumbing, cabinetry, floors, countertops, windows, and all kinds of finishes. In addition, manufacturers supply a broad range of products, including some real budget-busters, so it's easy to get carried away.

Kitchen remodeling ranges from full-blown gutting, spend-whatever-it-takes, top-of-the-line jobs to the more modest approach of selectively adding cabinets and replacing a few appliances. Take a good, hard look before you leap into this remodeling job. You can improve your kitchen space without draining the kids' college funds; besides, if you spend that money, the kids will never leave home.

The Design's the Thing

Kitchen design can be a tricky business. It's one thing to say you want more storage, more work space, and a sleeping area for your pot-bellied pig (one of my customers wanted just that), but it's quite another to pull it off on your own. The National Kitchen and Design Association (www.nkba.org) makes a big deal of what kitchen design consultants can do with your specific wish list (for a fee). On the other hand, some of the large home improvement stores in your area offer free design services that many people find perfectly acceptable—you sure can't beat the price. I have a stock-design kitchen, and it has worked well for my family, even though a professional may have been able to improve upon the design.

Tales from the Scaffold

My family's last kitchen was small, but usable. We couldn't add on because of limited building lot setbacks, so we invested about $3,500 for new countertops, cabinets, plumbing, electrical upgrades, wallpaper, painting, and floor refinishing. I did the painting and the floors and hired out the rest of the work. Our neighbors spent almost eight times that amount and got a very nice kitchen, including an additional 20 square feet of space, but I could think of better ways to invest $29,000.

I suggest you try the do-it-yourself, complimentary, store-supplied design first. Study the plans you and the in-store designer come up with, then mark off an empty area somewhere in your house (use masking tape on the floor) where you can "walk it" to get a feel for how it will work. Use the masking tape to mark off the locations of different appliances and cabinets. Look at your own list of criteria and decide whether this design addresses most of the items on your list.

If it doesn't, consider hiring a professional designer or space planner. Take your wish list along and establish the terms of the designer's fees and payment schedule at your first meeting. You won't be disappointed with the results, but hiring a designer will be an added expense in your budget, which may mean fewer kitchen toys.

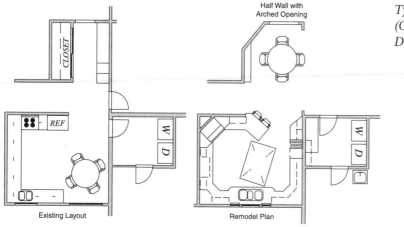

Typical kitchen plan. (Courtesy of Appolloni Designs)

How's the Traffic?

You need room to cook in the kitchen without bumping into family and guests. Even big kitchens can have poorly designed traffic patterns. One of the classic standards for kitchen design is based on the work triangle. Each point of the triangle is formed by the three main cooking appliances: the refrigerator, the sink, and the range.

The ideal work triangle meets these conditions:

1. The distance between the centers of any two appliances is no less than 4 feet and no more than 9 feet.
2. The total length of the triangle's three sides does not exceed 26 feet.
3. The legs of the triangle are unobstructed.

You don't need to gut your kitchen if your work triangle doesn't fit the 26-foot total length requirement for the sides, but use the work triangle concept to examine the working pattern of your kitchen:

➤ Are you walking too far between the sink and the refrigerator? Can the refrigerator be moved?

➤ Does any door run right into your path to the stove?

➤ Does the dishwasher door open against another appliance?

➤ Would the addition of an island increase your efficiency by bringing a working countertop closer to the appliances?

You can get locked in to keeping certain main elements of an existing kitchen, such as the walls and the locations of doors to other rooms or the outside. However, you might be surprised what a good plan and some select wall removal can accomplish.

Look Out Below!

Carefully scrutinize any working kitchen plans. A recurring problem is cabinet or appliance doors and drawers that open in such a way that they get in the way of each other. Some of this is unavoidable, but most of these problems can be fixed in the design phase.

Too Many Walls?

You already know that walls come in two types: load-bearing and nonbearing. You can remove a bearing wall, but you'll have to put up posts and a beam in its place. Nonbearing walls don't require anything to replace them.

You can also remove just a section of a wall or build a pass-through window. Don't limit yourself to interior walls. If your local building code allows you to expand outward, consider pushing out several feet through an exterior wall for added counter and lower cabinet space.

Moving a Door or Two

Moving doors is a more intimidating and involved job. You have to figure out new access to the areas that these doors now provide access to. In some cases, it's easy: You just expand the kitchen into the next room. In other cases, moving doors can be a major job, but it's well worth it if it gives you a more continuous kitchen workspace.

If you have too many doorways coming into the kitchen, such as one from a dining room adjoining one from a hallway, they can cause traffic jams in a hurry. Draw up several scenarios on your planning sheets to come up with the best rearrangement of these problem areas.

Islands Big and Small

Islands are basically freestanding cabinets with workspaces on top. The workspace can be a counter doubling as an eating space or a stovetop with built-in ventilation. Install a second sink, and you create an independent cooking station for a second cook. An island doesn't have to be huge. When existing floor space is limited, something as simple as a rolling butcher block cart for carving and food preparation can do the job.

Hot and Cold: New Appliances

Appliances are long-lasting, but we replace them for the same reason we replace automobiles: We want newer, shinier models with more features. Unfortunately, we don't get any trade-in value for old stoves and dishwashers. To add insult to injury, if they're too old to recycle, we get stuck with the disposal fees.

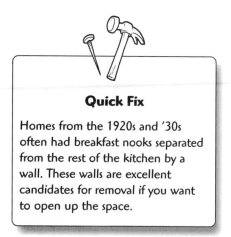

Quick Fix

Homes from the 1920s and '30s often had breakfast nooks separated from the rest of the kitchen by a wall. These walls are excellent candidates for removal if you want to open up the space.

If you haven't had new appliances in a while, or ever, you're in for some surprises. Sub-Zero brand, the god of built-in refrigerators, offers dozens of options, including under-the-counter units. One dishwasher model by Kitchenaid sports a 155-degree, anti-bacterial, sani-rinse option. Thermador has an oven that cooks with three types of heat—convection, microwave, and thermal (radiant)—simultaneously! Whirlpool offers a combination built-in microwave oven and an electric one with a child lockout system.

Built-in microwave ovens offer models that include kitchen exhaust fans, a real space saver and convenience. Smaller appliances can be stored in appliance garages, enclosed storage areas on top of a counter made to match the surrounding cabinetry. The following sections outline some issues to consider when buying new appliances.

Swearing by Natural Gas

Many cooks love natural gas. Gas offers quicker and more precise temperature control than electricity. If you already have a gas furnace or water heater, just run another gas pipe up to your kitchen, and you'll be cooking like Julia Child in no time. Using a gas range also frees up some of your electrical panel because you won't be drawing off power for an electric range, which is a demanding user of electricity.

Refrigerators

Refrigerators with multiple temperature zones and ice and water dispensers are not only more efficient and user-friendly than past models, they're also easier on the eye. Built-in refrigerators come with optional cabinet-matching panels so they blend in more with their surroundings. Some freestanding refrigerators also offer panel options.

A Quiet Dishwasher

Manufacturers are now touting quieter dishwashers with more insulation than older models. The higher you go in price, the quieter the machine. Figure on spending an additional $100 to $150 or so over a mid-range model to get the quietest model in the line.

Lighting Up

The kitchen is one room where you want a lot of light—it's a work room, after all. Houses have come a long way from the single ceiling light fixture and small windows found in old kitchens. The illumination goals are still the same though: to provide sufficient task, general, and accent lighting. How do these three differ?

➤ Task lighting is directed at specific work areas, such as a light over a counter for food preparation; you want to mince onions, not your fingers

➤ General lighting simply illuminates the kitchen as a whole and is in the form of overhead fixtures

➤ Accent lighting emphasizes isolated areas of your kitchen for highlighting, such as a small interior light inside a wine cabinet

Although kitchens demand all types of light, you don't want every fixture to light up all the time. You'll want separate light switches for each grouping of task lighting, for example. Discuss the location of switches with your planner or electrician. Once the drywall is up, you'll have to live with these locations.

Builders and remodelers pay more attention now to both natural and artificial light. You have a couple of sources of each, including:

➤ Fluorescent lighting

➤ Incandescent light fixtures

➤ Skylights and windows

Fluorescent Fixtures in the Spotlight

Fluorescent fixtures have come a long way from old-style hanging ceiling lights. They're now available in more sizes and styles than ever, but according to a 1994 survey by the National Kitchen and Bath Association, they were still trailing behind incandescent lighting in new kitchens and kitchen remodels.

I can't remember the last time I saw overhead fluorescent lighting in a new residential kitchen, but maybe that's just northwest design preferences. Fluorescent lighting advocates will point out its inherent advantages: It's energy-efficient and cooler than incandescent lighting and has long-lasting bulbs—a compact fluorescent bulb can last up to 10,000 hours. Do memories of humming fluorescent lights bother you? The flickering and humming of your youth is now eliminated with electronic ballasts.

Fluorescent lighting is available in the following fixtures:

➤ Small square and round surface-mounted lights

➤ Recessed lights

➤ Lights mounted under cabinets

➤ Lights mounted on top of cabinets to shine onto the ceiling

Compact fluorescent lamps (CFLs) are up to three times more efficient than incandescent lights. Some new 40-watt CFLs put out as much light as an 150-watt incandescent bulb.

In This Corner, Incandescent Lighting

Incandescent fixtures offer a tremendous variety of styles, including antique reproduction lamps and hanging lights. You can't beat them for accent lighting, but it takes more incandescent fixtures than fluorescent ones to provide full general lighting in a kitchen. Incandescent lights also produce more heat, which may be a problem in hot climates (it's never going to be a problem in Seattle).

Look Out Below!

Lighting and electrical outlets don't share the same circuit as a rule. If you're doing your own wiring, don't be tempted to run your lights off a small appliance circuit.

Lighting the Natural Way: Window Ideas

Kitchens are more welcoming when bathed in natural light from windows and skylights. A skylight or greenhouse window placed over a kitchen sink counter can brighten things up on an overcast winter day. Look into tinted glass or Low-E (low-emissivity) glass to cut down on glare and heat gain in the summer months.

One Sink or Two?

Kitchen sinks are no longer simple. They come in a variety of colors and sizes and have all sorts of fun accessories. Consider these factors when choosing your sink:

➤ *Color.* You're no longer limited to white sinks. Try teal, blue, red, sand, or gray if you like.

➤ *Cost.* You can spend a lot, or you can buy inexpensive, perfectly usable stainless steel sinks for under $50.

➤ *Faucet.* You'll need to purchase a faucet separately. Keep in mind that you'll use a kitchen faucet several times a day, so you want to purchase a high-quality one. Cheap faucets will give you cheap results and will require replacement much sooner than quality ones.

➤ *Size.* The size of your sink will determine how large a hole must be cut in your countertop to accommodate it. If you order a sink larger than you originally specified in your plans, make sure your cabinet installer knows about the change so the correct size hole is cut.

➤ *Sink extras.* Sinks have more than one way to dispense water, and they can do a lot of other things. Possible sink additions include sprayers, soap dispensers, and steaming water dispensers that are perfect for tea or hot chocolate.

Some builders and remodelers are installing second, smaller sinks in kitchens when space permits. An extra sink can be a great convenience when you have more than one cook and need to rinse vegetables and wash small utensils. However, you can't just pop a second sink in anywhere! Its drain line must have sufficient slope as it heads for the soil stack and your sewer line. Talk with your plumber or designer to find the best location for a second sink in your kitchen.

The Cabinetmaker's Art

A cabinet is nothing more than a box with either a door hanging on it or drawers inserted into it. Some of these boxes are pretty basic; others are almost exotic in their workmanship and choices of wood. But once they're in, all cabinets function the same, no matter how pretty or ugly they are. (Uh, oh, I can hear cabinetmakers screaming already.) It's easy to get carried away with cabinets, and custom-built ones are the most expensive of all. Separate the function of a cabinet from its role as a piece of furniture, and then find the middle ground.

Here are some cabinet remodeling options:

➤ Refinishing your existing cabinets

➤ Purchasing standard-size cabinetry from a building supply store

➤ Installing custom-made cabinets

Kitchen in progress.

Refinish, Resurface, or Replace?

If your existing wood cabinets are an acceptable design and size, but they've seen better days, you don't have to replace them. Existing cabinets can get a new life at a lower price through refinishing.

Another option is to have the cabinets resurfaced with plastic laminate. This approach is also less expensive than tearing out and replacing your existing cabinets, but be sure to check out a finished job or two. Resurfacing straddles the world between refinishing and replacement, and you may not like the results.

New hardware is the perfect accompaniment to refinished or resurfaced cabinets. Adjustable, hidden hinges do away with the old surface-mounted type. Drawer and cabinet door pulls and knobs come in a dizzying assortment; check out the styles in a local hardware center that specializes in cabinet hardware.

Off-the-shelf or Made-to-order?

Home improvement stores sell ready-to-install kitchen cabinets, but you have to work your kitchen space around the cabinets instead of the other way around. These cabinets can provide an economical approach to kitchen remodeling, but they limit your design ideas. On the other hand, custom cabinets cost far more.

Quick Fix

A few gallons of paint can perk up a kitchen that's had its share of smoky stir-fry meals. Marbling and glazed finishes can dramatically change the appearance of old cabinets.

Count Up Your Countertops

I think it's true that you can never have enough counter space in a kitchen. People not only cook in the kitchen, they also read the newspaper, go through the mail, and help the kids with their homework. Kitchen counters need to be:

➤ Durable

➤ Easily cleaned

➤ Installed at a comfortable work height

New countertops are available in several different materials, including the following:

➤ Plastic laminate

➤ Corian (an acrylic product)

➤ Tile

➤ Stone (granite, marble, and so on)

➤ Butcher block

Plastic laminate, often referred to by the eponymous Formica brand, is the least expensive way to cover a countertop. It's easy to clean and comes in a big selection of colors and patterns, but its finish is not repairable and can be damaged by knives or hot pots and pans. It should be installed by a professional.

If your plastic laminate countertops are in sorry shape, you can always resurface them with another layer of laminate or some other material. With proper preparation, adding a solid surface material like stone or butcher block over your existing laminate will save you the cost of completely new countertops.

Maple butcher block is the traditional cutting surface for butchers, but it stains more easily than other surface materials. You'll need to treat it with mineral oil and wash it down after each use. Butcher block looks great when it's installed, but it doesn't stay that way for long.

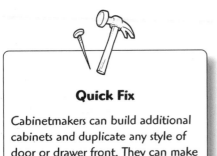

Quick Fix

Cabinetmakers can build additional cabinets and duplicate any style of door or drawer front. They can make your current cabinetry more useful by adding bins, swing-out shelves, sliding wire baskets, and pull-out racks.

Tile offers an amazing array of color and style combinations and offers a hard, permanent surface. The grout can be a nuisance to keep clean and sealed and can be tough to match if any of it needs replacing. Tile, like stone, is cold to the touch, and some people find this uncomfortable. Granite is porous and subject to staining, but has a rich and elegant look.

Corian, a Dupont product, is made from natural minerals and acrylic resin. Since it's the same material throughout, scratches and chips can be sanded out and repaired. Corian comes in a variety of colors and patterns and cleans easily with soap and water.

This kitchen blends in beautifully with the new family room. (Designer: Kerry Rose and Associates; Design follow through: Appolloni Designs; Interior Design: Barbara Madaras; Photo: Castle Studios)

A generous amount of light pours into a family room addition through stepped windows. (Designer: Kerry Rose and Associates; Design follow through: Appolloni Designs; Interior Design: Barbara Madaras; Photo: Castle Studios)

A loft makes good use of empty space in a high ceiling room.
(Designer: Steve Appolloni/Appolloni Designs; Photography: Marble Street Studio)

An enclosed loft.
(Designer: Appolloni Designs;
Photo: Marble Street Studio)

A whimsical fireplace with mosaic tile.
(Designer: Steve Appolloni; Photo: Dick Ruddy Photography)

In progress . . .

Outstanding fireplace additions.
(Designer: Appolloni Designs; Photo: Marble Street Studio)

The sky vault in this new family room lets in ample light all year round.
(Designer: Appolloni Designs; Photo: Castle Studios & David Allison Photography)

A new bathroom with its own sky vault.
(Designer: Kerry Rose and Associates; Design follow through: Appolloni & Associates; Photo: Castle Studios)

This entry features three colors of Navco vinyl wood planking, creating diamond patterns to match the sky vault. (Designer: Kerry Rose and Associates; Design follow through: Appolloni & Associates; Photo: Castle Studios)

This second floor landing doubles as a cozy reading space and storage for the owner's book collection. (Luther Hintz. AIA)

A modern kitchen with stainless steel appliances and hardwood floors. (Luther Hintz. AIA)

Before. . .

After.
Kitchen remodel includes a freestanding island, tile floors, and a skylight within a fluorescent light border.
(Designer: Sharman and Jim Carpenter; Design follow through: Appolloni Designs; Photos: Castle Studios)

A kitchen waiting to be updated. . .

The updates arrive.
(Designer: Appolloni Designs; Photos: Castle Studios
& David Allison Photography)

Exterior renovation, early 1900s duplex. (Architects: Stickney, Murphy & Romine, Seattle; Photo: Michael Romine)

Floor Guidance

A kitchen floor should be attractive and practical, which means it should be easy to clean. As with countertops, you have many materials to choose from, such as:

➤ Vinyl

➤ Tile

➤ Wood

➤ Laminate

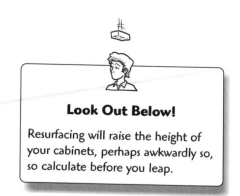

Look Out Below!

Resurfacing will raise the height of your cabinets, perhaps awkwardly so, so calculate before you leap.

Each material—you've heard this before—has its advantages and disadvantages. Your decision to choose one over the others will depend on cost, comfort, and maintenance factors.

Vinyl and Tile

Vinyl floors come in two forms: Sheet and tile. Sheet vinyl has the fewest seams and may not have any, depending on the size of the floor you're covering. A thick, high-quality vinyl is easy on the feet and easy to clean, but holes and tears are not easily repairable and will be visible after patching. Solution? Throw rugs! No one will ever notice the repair. Vinyl tile is easier to repair because you can remove the offending tile and replace it with a new one, but tiles can eventually discolor and even loosen along the edges.

Ceramic tile will probably never need any repair unless you drop one of those heavy, imported, cast-iron soup pots on it. This floor is permanent; once it's in, you're not going to have to replace it, so choose carefully. Tile makes sense in very hot climates because of its cooling effect, but it is unforgiving to stand on.

Reliving the Past with Wood

Many kitchen floors were made from wood, which was never the best choice to resist water, grease, and spilled gravy and still isn't. Nevertheless, wood floors in kitchens are now making a comeback.

Even though wood floors are increasingly popular in new and remodeled kitchens, they're a poor choice, especially around children and pets. They show every scratch made by dragged chairs and barstools, high-heeled shoes, and kids' toys. They only stay scratch-free if you're a single, childless, petless adult who walks around in stocking feet and has no chairs.

Pretend Wood

Laminate flooring uses technology similar to the plastic laminate used for countertops. A melamine laminate layer of material, often printed to resemble wood, is bonded to a moisture-resistant, wood-based core soaked in resins and can be installed over any kind of existing floor. The advantages of laminate flooring include the following:

➤ Long wear

➤ Easy coverage of many old floors

➤ Good looks

➤ Easy maintenance

> **Quick Fix**
>
> Be sure to save any leftover flooring materials or order extra if necessary so you won't go crazy looking for replacement material. A few years down the road, you don't want to discover that the pattern has been discontinued when you need to make some floor repairs.

Another manufactured wood product is engineered hardwood flooring, which consists of various thin layers of wood that are laminated and bonded together with special glues and shot full of resins. These floors come pre-finished and can also be installed over existing floors.

Despite what some manufacturers may imply, no manufactured or laminated flooring product is bulletproof. The same manufacturers make repair kits to cover up scratches and fill small holes.

What Do You Need in a Kitchen?

Before you call the contractor, ask yourself these basic kitchen questions:

1. How much time do you and your family spend in your kitchen? Do you eat there as a family often or grab something on the run?

2. Who does most of the cooking? At what skill level? Does the cook need a lot of specialized equipment?

3. Do you often cook for large groups of guests?

4. Are you and your family warehouse shoppers who need lots of storage, such as a large pantry?

5. Do you need storage for an extensive collection of cookware, utensils, and small appliances?

6. Are the cooks in your house different heights? Will you need some counters to be lower than others?

7. Will you be adding or relocating a sink or major appliance?

8. Do you want cabinets with plastic laminate surfaces or wood? If you choose wood, how will they be finished?

9. How do you want to finish off your countertops? Do they all need to be finished the same way, or will a mix of materials serve you and your budget best?

10. What kind of floor do you want to be standing on while you cook?

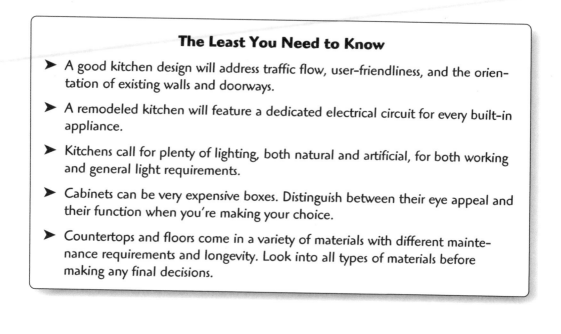

The Least You Need to Know

➤ A good kitchen design will address traffic flow, user-friendliness, and the orientation of existing walls and doorways.

➤ A remodeled kitchen will feature a dedicated electrical circuit for every built-in appliance.

➤ Kitchens call for plenty of lighting, both natural and artificial, for both working and general light requirements.

➤ Cabinets can be very expensive boxes. Distinguish between their eye appeal and their function when you're making your choice.

➤ Countertops and floors come in a variety of materials with different maintenance requirements and longevity. Look into all types of materials before making any final decisions.

Chapter 16

Bathrooms with Bragging Rights

In This Chapter

➤ A few bathroom basics

➤ Picking a tub and shower for low maintenance and high comfort

➤ Personalizing your space with fixtures

➤ The fuss about ventilation

➤ Not all bathroom floors are created equal

In the past, when nature called, humans answered by relieving themselves right out in the middle of it. Apparently, the members of the Bohemian Club in San Francisco *still* do that during their retreats among the redwoods, but that's another story. As a whole, humans graduated from the outdoors to chamber pots, outhouses, and finally to indoor plumbing.

Today, bathrooms go far beyond privacy, convenience, and hygiene. If there had been a bathroom race among the superpowers, the United States would have won it hands down. Bathrooms are a top remodeling priority, but it's easy to get carried away with elaborate fixtures, wall coverings, and tile work. What about your budget? And what about cleaning and maintaining all that tile grout and those brass fixtures? This chapter walks you through the decisions and potential problems of a bathroom remodel without letting you get your feet too wet.

Behind the Scenes and Inside the Walls

Plumbing is a matter of clean water in, dirty water out. Along the way, the water passes through pipes, fixtures, and drains. Incoming water is under pressure and therefore flows through small pipes, and outgoing waste water depends on gravity and larger drain lines. The waste lines and each soil pipe—that's the waste line for a toilet—all enter a vertical pipe called the *soil stack*. The top of the stack is the main vent, and the bottom enters the house drain that leads off to the sewer or septic tank. To complete the plumbing picture, vent lines from each fixture allow gases and odors to escape and provide air pressure to your plumbing system.

Quick Fix

Run some water down any unused drains once a month or so to replace evaporated water in the traps. A simple turn of the faucet ensures that the trap stays full to do its job of keeping gases out of the house.

All these parts have to work together for you to successfully step in the shower, receive more than a dribble of water, avoid being scalded if someone flushes the toilet, and not end up standing ankle deep in waste water waiting for it to drain. Adding a bathroom is more than just extending your pipes to another room of the house. You have to have the following in place:

➤ Sufficient water pressure

➤ An adequate path for drain lines

➤ Water heater capacity to handle the extra demand

You should also include these features in your bathroom design:

➤ Easy access and user-friendliness (rounded corners on the countertop, grab-bars for the elderly, good lighting, ease in cleaning)

➤ Natural lighting (window and/or skylight)

➤ Adequate storage for everyone who shares the bathroom

➤ Adequate ventilation

Under Pressure

Water enters a house through a service line, also called a supply line or supply pipe. The diameter of this pipe is a big determinant of how much water pressure you have. New homes should have a 1-inch service line, the same size you should use if you replace your existing one.

Other factors that can affect your water pressure include your neighbors' water usage habits. During hot spells when water demand goes way up, you can end up with a water-challenged shower no matter how much you've upgraded your plumbing.

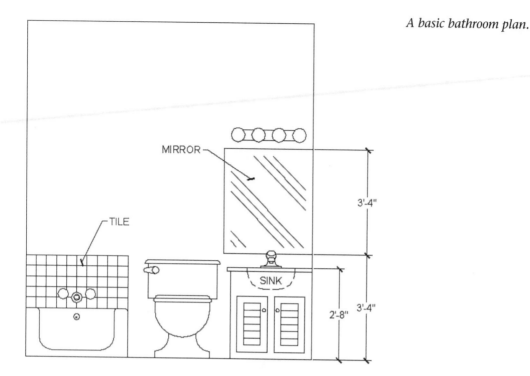

A basic bathroom plan.

MIRROR

TILE

SINK

3'-4"

2'-8" 3'-4"

Coping with Sloping

The more slope a waste line has, the happier it is to do its dirty work. Even though it's possible to run your piping from just about anywhere in the house to your main sewer line, it's not a good idea to pick a route that involves a lot of bends and turns. While your new bathroom is still in the planning stage, talk with your plumber about placement of fixtures and drain lines.

Hot Is Good

You could have the most efficient hot water heater in the world (which would be a natural geyser), but it won't do you much good if you have less heater capacity than you need. Showers, dishwashers, and washing machines all demand hot water, sometimes all at once. The demands of a new bathroom may require a new water heater.

Look Out Below!

In some basement remodels, an added bathroom's drain lines would fall below the existing sewer line. To eliminate waste, a sewer injector can be installed to pump waste liquids and solids up to the sewer line.

Keeping Your Bathroom in Order

Plumbing is another one of your house's mechanical systems (like electrical and HVAC or heating, ventilation, and air conditioning) that acts very reliably when the rules concerning it are followed. Remodeling or installing a new bathroom follows its own order:

1. Demolition and framing
2. Preliminary or rough-in plumbing (remodeled bathrooms may get new pipes, too)
3. Duct work for HVAC
4. Rough in electrical
5. Tub installation
6. After inspections, installation of walls, floor, and ceiling
7. Floor covering, tile work, and painting
8. Plumbing and electrical fixtures installed, inspections called for
9. Taking a bath in your new tub

Tub and Shower Combinations

A Victorian-era hotel in San Francisco called The Mansions has the biggest, most free-flowing shower head I've ever seen in my life (ask for the Barbra Streisand suite). In the

The pipes and drains behind the scenes.

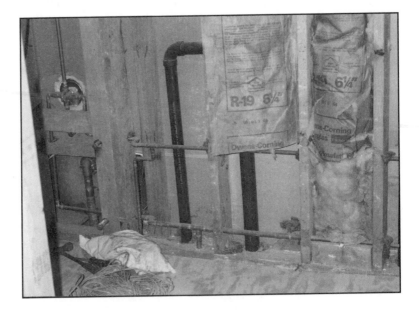

course of one shower, enough water came out to fill Lake Erie, and I loved every minute of it. You may not be able to re-create this Niagara Falls effect in your bathroom, but you have plenty of other options.

The huge selection of tubs and showers available these days includes the following:

➤ Steel tubs

➤ Glassed-in shower stalls with tile walls

➤ Fiberglass tub and shower combinations

➤ Reproduction claw foot bathtubs

➤ Showers with multiple showerheads

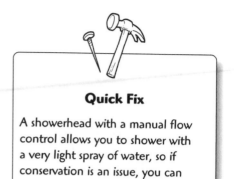

Quick Fix

A showerhead with a manual flow control allows you to shower with a very light spray of water, so if conservation is an issue, you can justify taking a longer shower.

Look at upright square tubs in addition to the traditional rectangular models. The former are made for soaking in a sitting position and are very relaxing. They're normally meant to stand alone, so you would need a separate shower stall.

How Many Showerheads?

In the '70s, there was a slogan: Save water, shower with a friend. Not much water was saved, but more than a few friendships got a little friendlier. The problem with duets in the shower is that you're always maneuvering to catch the spray. The solution? Install more than one showerhead.

The time to install extra showerheads is during the framing stage. At a minimum, consider one showerhead on each end of the tub and make one of them a handheld, personal type. As an added bonus, the handheld showerhead makes cleaning and rinsing the tub and shower area much easier.

Fabulous Fiberglass

Fiberglass tub and shower combinations just keep getting better and better; take a look at the luxurious high-end models when you go out looking at fixtures. Fiberglass corner units are also available for smaller bathrooms where room is limited. I'm a big fan of fiberglass units and recommend them wholeheartedly. What's not to like? Fiberglass units are:

➤ Easy to install

➤ Easy to maintain

➤ Almost leak-proof

Fiberglass isn't maintenance-free—it needs to be kept clean and coated periodically with a sealer—but it's simpler to maintain than tile. A competing material, Lucite HS

acrylic, claims to outlast fiberglass and maybe the bathroom itself. Other manufacturers also offer acrylic-coated fiberglass, which normally comes with a gel coat finish.

You May Not Smile with Tile

Tile is a traditional bathroom material because of its ability to shed water and protect the underlying wall. The problem with tile comes with the grout, the cement-like material that seals the seams between tiles. Grout is partially porous and must be sealed periodically so it will continue to keep water away from the wall studs.

Look Out Below!

Fiberglass enclosures are easy to clean and also easy to scratch if you use the wrong cleaners or abrasive sponges. Use gentle liquid cleaners and avoid any cleanser that doesn't claim to be fiberglass-friendly.

From a cleaning standpoint, grout has a nasty habit of attracting mold and mildew, which has to be scrubbed out and attacked with bleach or bathroom cleaners specifically formulated with fungicides. Another port of entry for mold and mildew is the seam between the tile and the tub or shower stall, which has to be caulked and recaulked from time to time. None of this is a really big deal if you really like tile, but if something as clean and easy as fiberglass is available, why bother?

A Word About Walls

Bathrooms are steamy and wet and bathroom walls need special protection against this moisture attack. If you're going with tile, you want something waterproof underneath it.

Tile works well in this over-size shower, but presents an over-size cleaning challenge.

Drywall comes in different sizes and thickness as well as different kinds of composition. Greenboard is a type of drywall that's better than the regular kind, but not by much; it's not waterproof, so don't even think about using it as a backing for tile.

If you want an alternative to drywall, turn to cement board, the generic name for tile backer systems. Tile backers are typically made from cement and fiberglass mesh and attach to walls with either nails or screws, just like sheets of drywall. The seams and nail heads are covered with open glass-fiber mesh tape and latex-modified Portland cement mortar. Two of the most common brands are Wonder Board and Hardibacker. If you've ever torn apart an old tile wall and found soaked, smelly drywall underneath, you'll appreciate cement board.

Laminated Tub Surrounds

A compromise between tile and fiberglass is a laminated tub surround, a good solution for an existing bathtub when you need to update or repair the surrounding walls. A laminated surround uses the same plastic laminate used on kitchen and bathroom counters. The only areas of concern for leaks are where the laminate meets the tub. This joint is caulked and needs recaulking every other year or so depending on use.

Laminate comes in a huge array of colors and styles; there's something for everyone. It's installed over greenboard, which is OK here because the laminate forms a solid surface. Laminate also needs a full day to dry after it's installed. Installing a laminate surround is not a do-it-yourself job. In fact, there are specialty contractors who do nothing but install tub surrounds and shower doors, and I recommend hiring one for this work.

Beyond the Tub: Sinks, Toilets, and Vanities

The American obsession with bathrooms continues into the world of sinks and toilets, where choices abound. Single sinks, double sinks, one-of-a-kind sculptured sinks, marble, porcelain, steel—it's almost easier choosing a name for your first-born! And we're not even talking about faucets yet.

It's just as easy to get carried away with sinks, faucets, toilets, and vanities as it is with tubs and showers—maybe even more so. Go for quality and functionality first, whimsy and art second. You can always upgrade if your budget allows.

One Sink or Two?

New master bathrooms, which seem to be getting bigger all the time, regularly come with two sinks. Busy couples trying to get out the door in the morning don't have time to wait for the sink to be free. Even if there aren't two of you, figure on putting in two sinks; they're a helpful resale feature.

Look Out Below!

Some toilets use inexpensive tank parts, particularly flappers, the rubber seal at the bottom of the tank. When you're choosing a toilet, ask your plumber or plumbing supplier about the quality of the tank parts. Be aware that some toilets require original replacement parts only and won't accommodate generic parts.

Faucets with Personality

A cheap faucet means problems sooner rather than later. Ask your plumber or plumbing supply store for a few recommendations and test the weight of competing faucets in your hands. More weight and heft means more metal parts versus plastic, and you don't want too much plastic.

The Controversy over Low-flow Toilets

The old, dependable toilets that used water as though the flood gates were being opened every time you flushed are a thing of the past. In 1992, Congress passed the Energy Policy and Conservation Act, a piece of legislation that changed American bathrooms forever. The act called for, among other things, a new standard for the gallons-per-flush (GPF) in new toilets. Gone were the good old days of 3.5 GPF or more, as 1.6 GPF became the new mandated standard.

The original models didn't save as much water as promised because, to put it delicately, they didn't flush away as much as they promised. Flushing two or three times to do what one flush used to do isn't exactly what conservationists and Congress had in mind. Columnist Dave Barry, who apparently has had an exceptional amount of experience with toilets, has written several columns on the subject, including a recent one about an American couple who risked an international incident to smuggle high-volume toilets from Canada back to the United States.

Low-flow toilets have improved greatly since the early models. There are even entire Web pages devoted to this subject (try www.terrylove.com, a site full of plumbing information).

A Vanity That Lives Up to Its Name

Vanities come in all sizes, prices, and finishes—everything from painted particle board to the finest hardwood with a marble top. You can buy premade vanities or order one through your plumbing supplier.

Install as big a vanity as your bathroom will comfortably allow. You'll use all the storage space and then some. If you're an Amish wannabe who doesn't believe in personal adornments, then think about the vanity-crazy people who will buy the house next.

Other Cabinetry and Storage

You have other storage needs to address when you design a new bathroom or remodel an existing one. A large medicine cabinet will handle all those lotions, potions, pills, and dental aids that are part of modern life. How about a cabinet for towels, toilet paper (especially if you shop at a warehouse store), and extra soap? Tight on space? You can always cut out a couple of wall studs and build a narrow cabinet or shelf in the wall. Even a 5-inch deep cabinet can hold a lot of odds and ends.

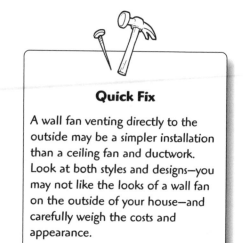

Quick Fix

A wall fan venting directly to the outside may be a simpler installation than a ceiling fan and ductwork. Look at both styles and designs—you may not like the looks of a wall fan on the outside of your house—and carefully weigh the costs and appearance.

Don't Forget Ventilation

Bathroom and kitchen ventilation are big issues. All that steam has to go somewhere, and the best place is outside through the roof or out the wall. The longer steam sticks around, the more likely you are to develop mold and mildew on the walls and tile, and that's more cleaning and painting for you.

You have two choices for ventilation: Mechanical (fans) or natural (an operable window). Ventilation fans are rated by how many cubic feet of air they can move per minute (CFM). Cheap fans mostly make noise to distract you so you won't notice that the steam from your shower is condensing in your bathroom instead of being vented outside. You want the steam out fast, which means you need a top-notch fan. I recommend the Nutone QT series (QT 130/150/200/300); each number is the fan's CFM ability. These fans are guaranteed for as long as you own your home.

An operable window is better than no ventilation, but it is best combined with a fan. A window doesn't draw steam and odors out in any kind of organized fashion, because a cold air current will allow some steam to escape but also will condense some. The window is great for natural light, however. If privacy is an issue, install patterned, obscure glass.

Floor Choices

Traditionally, bathroom floors are covered with tile; it's one place this material works well. Tile installation is labor-intensive because the tile has to set, as does its grout. Vinyl floors require less time and expertise to install and can be laid over a wood underlayment.

Bathroom floor choices include:

➤ Tile

➤ Vinyl

➤ Wood

➤ Carpet

➤ Stone (marble, granite, onyx, and so on)

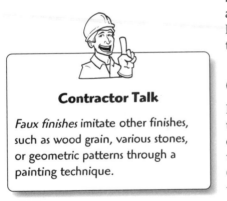

Look Out Below!

Sheet vinyl has one major weak point: Where it abuts the bathtub. Typically, the flooring is installed after the tub, so this joint has to be caulked regularly, or water from your bath will get under the vinyl and soak into the underlayment.

Each type of flooring offers design and comfort challenges and budget ones as well, but tile and vinyl are your best bets for a bathroom. Wood floors in bathrooms are both fashionable and dumb. Why choose a material that can only take limited abuse? Reserve your wood floors for the dry areas of your house, and disregard the enticing displays in home design magazines. Those designers never have to live with the results of their work.

Wood is bad enough in a bathroom, but carpet is worse. Wet carpet is a breeding ground for spores, and you won't even be aware of them. Blotting up the spills from your kids' baths isn't going to do the job. If you want something soft under your feet when you're padding around the bathroom, get some washable throw rugs, and keep a water-repellent floor underneath.

Painting Issues

Bathrooms, and kitchens as well, get painted more often than other rooms of the house. Bathrooms would get painted less often if they had good ventilation, but we've already covered that. After five to seven years or so of steam, soap splatters, and hair spray (the stuff that doesn't go on your hair has to go someplace), many people decide to repaint their bathrooms. Painting in such a relatively small space with so many built-in obstacles is a nuisance. Ignore preparation and paint rules (covered in Appendix B, "Paint and Painting"), and you may end up repainting sooner than you expected.

Contractor Talk

Faux finishes imitate other finishes, such as wood grain, various stones, or geometric patterns through a painting technique.

Clean It First!

Bathroom walls, ceilings, and woodwork should be thoroughly cleaned before painting them. Paint can cover only a certain number of sins, but it prefers that the sinner at least try to do an act of contrition first. Clean all painted surfaces and allow them to dry thoroughly.

Some Styling Ideas

A bathroom is the perfect place for *faux finishes*. One of the best I ever saw looked so much like marble that a single small drip in the paint gave it away. There are several books on the subject, and sometimes classes are offered locally at paint stores, community colleges, and community centers. There are also painters who specialize in these techniques.

The Least You Need to Know

➤ Plumbing isn't all that complicated, but you have to follow a few basic rules for a successful bathroom addition or remodel.

➤ Tile must be installed on tile backer material, not drywall, if you expect any kind of longevity out of it.

➤ Low-flow toilets are legally required for new installations. The newer ones are greatly improved over the original models.

➤ Bathroom ventilation is a big deal and shouldn't be an afterthought in your bathroom design.

➤ A bathroom remodel can be as expensive as you want it to be. In planning and process, functionality and quality should come first.

Chapter 17

Living Rooms and Dining Rooms: Throwbacks?

In This Chapter

➤ Living and dining everywhere but in the living and dining rooms

➤ Spotlight these rooms with more lighting

➤ Shelves, cabinets, and buffets: Improving your storage

➤ Two rooms where hardwood floors make sense

➤ There's always room for a fireplace or two

➤ Painting's special effects

Houses were once designed along very formal lines. Rooms were very distinct and purposeful: You ate in the dining room, entertained in the living room, and cooked in the kitchen. This formality has given way to great open spaces where one room blends into another. We now have bigger kitchens with attached family rooms; in this combo room, we cook, eat, watch the kids play, and entertain. Most of us rarely use our living or dining room anymore. As long as we have them, we ought to put them to good use.

Living rooms and dining rooms have kind of a dual personality. They're separate from the main activity areas of kitchens and family rooms in most newer houses, but they're not so isolated that you can turn them into private office space, for example. But you can change their role in your home. You might extend your kitchen into the dining room area, for instance. You can create smaller, more intimate spaces in a large living room by using glass walls or removable screens. A fireplace in a living or dining room would add a welcoming touch.

There is a trend right now back to more defined spaces and away from the open designs we've had in the recent past. This chapter will help you look at your living and dining rooms as spaces to be used and enjoyed regularly, not just when company comes.

Bringing Out Their Best

The living and dining rooms take up a good amount of space, especially in older homes. From an interior design standpoint, they're usually approached simply, but you can take a broader view. Ask yourself these questions:

➤ Do the rooms have enough outlets for lights, stereo, TV and so on?

➤ Would either room benefit from built-in cabinets or shelves?

➤ Should this space be expanded or given additional windows for natural light?

➤ Should we divide this space differently?

Electrical requirements are pretty basic in these rooms. Unexpectedly, though, the dining room needs a GFCI-protected outlet, usually run off a kitchen circuit, in case you plug in something like a chafing dish. It's a small price to pay for being a fancy host/hostess to your dinner guests.

If you plan on using your living room as your media room, you'll want an abundance of outlets. TVs, VCRs, and stereo systems quickly eat up outlet space. Go over your plans with your electrician to see if you need to add an extra circuit for all your proposed electronic toys.

Quick Fix

New fireplace mantles and trim can be built to cover unappealing brick or old painted brick that won't strip clean. Wood, marble, or other stone can be used to give a fireplace an entirely new appearance.

This Buffet Isn't a Smorgasbord

Up until the 1920s, many homes had built-in buffets in their dining rooms. After we moved to a new house that didn't have one, I began to appreciate the buffets in our previous two houses; unfortunately, new buffets are expensive! Before you furnish your dining room, consider:

➤ The cost of having custom cabinetry built in versus buying movable furniture

➤ Whether you would ever get your investment back if you sell the house

➤ Whether you want permanent built-ins or a more flexible arrangement of furniture

New reproduction buffet.

The same thing goes for bookshelves and cabinets in your living room. Are you better off building something in and getting the size and dimensions that you want or going with finished furniture?

Tales from the Scaffold

I worked on a house whose decorating was under the direction of what was at the time one of the most expensive interior decorating firms in town. It was a late 1930s house with only one potentially operable double hung window in the living room. True to form, the designers paid attention only to colors and fabrics, so without first repairing the window, they had it painted. Of course, it wouldn't open, and the only way to get air to circulate in the room was to open the front door. Talk about looking only at form and ignoring function!

Look Out Below!

Remember, you must run your electrical wires so that they're separate from your stereo, cable, and phone wiring. It's tempting to pull them all through the same holes in the studs and joists when you wire up your living room, but they don't mix well, because one is high voltage and one is low.

Go Toward the Light

Some living rooms need more light, meaning more windows. If you're thinking of adding windows, though, plan carefully; they'll add light, but they'll decrease your uninterrupted wall space and affect your furniture placement. For a dramatic effect, some people add solariums or greenhouse windows to one side of their living room, so they increase the room's natural light as well as the square footage.

Making Your Own Light

Living rooms typically have offered very little in the way of ceiling lights. Remodeling is an excellent time to correct this oversight and add plenty of lighting, especially over fireplaces and reading areas. Installing lights in an existing, finished ceiling can be time-consuming, so talk with an electrician about costs before you get too carried away. Wire has to be fished through the ceiling joists, drywall, or plaster cut out, and patching must be done at the end of the job. Individual recessed lights will take the most work; track lighting, which requires you to run a wire to only one track regardless of how many lights are connected to it, is simpler to hook up.

Another option is to install a circuit of switch-controlled outlets. Each outlet, with its own lamp plugged into it, would be activated at the flick of a single wall-mounted light switch, so all the lamps could easily be turned on simultaneously. New houses usually come with one such outlet in a living room, unless a ceiling light is installed. This way, the house meets code for providing every room with switch-controlled light.

Scoring with Sconces

A sconce was originally a wall-mounted bracket candlestick, and its electric version enjoyed some popularity in houses of the 1920s. Art deco reproductions and other slick designs are available today at lighting suppliers. Sconces are an alternative to ceiling lights and usually easier to wire and install. Sconce lighting is more for mood than for reading, but it can set off a living room or dining room.

Downsizing

Some living rooms are just too unwieldy, but you can knock them down to size. Plan how you want the space used, such as a reading area, a listening corner, and so on, and define these areas with:

➤ Foldable, decorative screens

➤ A built-in or free-standing bookshelf

➤ A short wall

Bookshelves will serve the dual purpose of dividing the space and providing storage. Walls offer all kinds of possibilities and are easy to build. You can use drywall, glass block, even a series of stained glass windows to divide the space. A wall doesn't have to be ceiling height; six feet or so is just enough to alter the sense of space. For easy installation, you can preassemble the framing of two-by-fours in your workshop or garage.

Walls, Floors, and More

The order of events, as you know by now, is to do the disruptive work first, then the patching and preparation work, and finally the finishing details. After you've added to or upgraded the wiring in your living and dining rooms, you have to deal with other parts of the rooms, such as:

➤ The condition of the walls

➤ The windows

➤ Your floor and floor covering

Do your walls have cracks or holes? Get them patched and repaired and caulk any gaps between them and your wood trim.

Picture Window Blues

We've already discussed adding windows, but what about your existing ones? Many a 1920s or 1930s house has found its original front windows replaced with the once hot and popular picture window. Instead of the original three-window sash, one huge, monolithic piece of glass was installed to "modernize" these houses. Like many design elements from the '50s, these windows are well worth replacing with ones that duplicate the originals, assuming the rest of your windows are still original.

It can be an expensive proposition to match up old-style double-hung or casement windows, but you'll be putting a major visual element of your house back in sync with its surroundings. Every time you look at your new/old window, you'll be reminded that it was a good idea.

Quick Fix

Some floor companies are now offering a new dustless sanding process that nearly eliminates cleanup for you. ProSand DCS (Dust Containment System) from BonaKemi USA Inc. captures up to 98 percent of the dust generated by floor sanders and buffers. Floor dust normally goes everywhere, and a containment system can be a big plus.

215

Floors

If you like wood floors, your living and dining rooms make great showcases for them. Because people are normally on better behavior in these rooms, they get less wear and tear than kitchens and family rooms. Many older homes have wood floors, often hardwood, hidden under the wall-to-wall carpet. In newer homes, you'll find a mix of either hardwood or carpet over underlayment or subflooring.

Existing floors can usually be refinished, but what if you've got only plywood or older fir floors, when what you want is oak? Unless your floor is way off level, you can just install new hardwood right over the existing floor. This gives you a lot of options for flooring, including:

➤ Regular strip flooring

➤ Parquet

➤ Wide plank flooring

➤ Choice of woods

If you install a hardwood floor over an existing floor, your installer will have to trim down your doors and door jambs and remove your base shoe, and possibly the base-board as well, and reinstall after the floor is laid. A threshold will have to be installed also to handle the transition between the new, slightly higher floor and adjoining floors.

How About a Fireplace or Two?

Fireplaces seem to hit a chord in just about everyone, regardless of the climate they live in. It must be that primordial, gather–'round-with-the-tribe-to-keep-away-the-things-that-go-bump-in-the-night feeling that humans always carry with them. Fireplace technology is so much more advanced since the days of wood-burning units with unlined brick chimneys. Natural gas has made having a fireplace, and starting a fire, easier than ever. Today, your fireplace choices include:

➤ Multisided models

➤ Inserts

➤ Top vent

➤ Direct vent

➤ Ventless

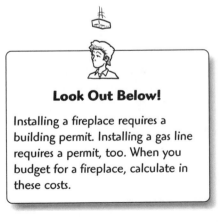

Look Out Below!

Installing a fireplace requires a building permit. Installing a gas line requires a permit, too. When you budget for a fireplace, calculate in these costs.

A multisided fireplace offers a view of the fire from more than one side. These fireplaces are ideal to install between two rooms, such as the dining and living room, because people in both areas can use and enjoy the fire.

Wood-burning fireplace with gas grate.

Inserts are gas units installed in existing fireplaces. They require a chimney liner, which is a 4- or 5-inch round metal pipe, to handle the by-products of gas combustion.

Direct vent fireplaces can be placed almost anywhere. They vent through two pipes in the wall; an outer pipe brings in outside air for combustion, and an inner pipe shoots the by-products back outside. This fireplace just bottles everything up inside itself and doesn't use any of your inside air for combustion.

Is Ventless Also Witless?

Ventless fireplaces are controversial, to put it mildly. Industry proponents claim that they burn so clean (up to 99 percent or more) that they're perfectly safe. They're easy to install, too; after all, they don't require any venting. But there is some concern over indoor pollution as a result of burning in ventless fireplaces; Canadians really don't like them.

Despite being banned in several states (notably California and Massachusetts), ventless fireplaces currently pass both safety and emission standards elsewhere in the country. These units come equipped with an oxygen depletion sensor (ODS) that indicates whether the fireplace is depleting too much of the room's oxygen. Rapid oxygen depletion is a sure sign that you want to get out of the room. Some manufacturers even state that these units are made for occasional use and not as a regular heat source.

Tales from the Scaffold

True to its mission, the November 1998 issue of *Consumer Reports* concluded that ventless or vent-free fireplaces "contribute significantly to indoor air pollution." It went on to recommend that readers choose vented models. Naturally, manufacturers of ventless products have their own opinion on the matter.

Wood: The Real Thing

The only fireplace more convenient than a gas model is one that comes with an attendant, someone like a 19th century English butler who gathers the firewood, builds and continuously stokes the fire, and finally cleans out the ashes. Oh, and he serves a warm brandy and after-dinner cigars, too. Inconvenient or not, wood is a unique fuel.

Wood burns unevenly and changes from multicolored flames to the red glow of hot coals. We mark the passage of the evening as the fire dies down and turns into a pile of gray ash. Tending the fire is a ritual that goes back to the beginning of man's history, but if Neanderthals could have flicked a switch on the side of their cave and gotten a gas fire going, they would have done it in a heartbeat.

That said, nothing quite does beat a wood-burning fire, that is, if you want to mess with firewood, start and tend the fires, and clean the ash pit from time to time. Wood-burning technology has improved tremendously in the last 20 years, and safety has never been better (go to www.woodheat.com for more insights). If you want the mood-setting qualities of wood but the convenience of gas, consider a gas insert. These things will burn logs encased in ice if they have to. If you have an existing fireplace and can't remember the last time your chimney was cleaned, schedule a cleaning and inspection before the next cold season shows up.

Some Finishing Touches

The plainest room can be changed completely with the right trim, paint, and finish package. Your options are endless; wood that's painted or stained and varnished, wallpaper, faux finishes, and fancy wood casings are all readily available. This stuff is the fun work, the time when, after the messy jobs are finished, you can go ahead and be artistic. If your dining and living rooms are off by themselves, you can carry out all kinds of design ideas without having to continue them into the rest of the house.

You can do much of this work yourself with a few good tools: Good quality paintbrushes, a measuring tape, a hammer and nail set, a carpenter's level, and a *power miter saw*. Go to a full-service lumber store and look through their molding and casing selections. Combine two or three pieces if that will give you the look you've been after. Paint stores usually carry samples of their wood stains on different types of wood. Buy some small cans of stain and paint, and see how they look on a sample piece of wood at home.

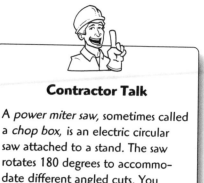

Contractor Talk

A *power miter saw*, sometimes called a *chop box*, is an electric circular saw attached to a stand. The saw rotates 180 degrees to accommodate different angled cuts. You cannot cut a piece of wood by hand as straight as you can with one of these saws, and I thoroughly recommend them if you're going to be doing any finish carpentry.

A Little Trim Goes a Long Way

Our last house had a plain six-inch baseboard throughout. By adding a small piece of cove molding on top (an inexpensive trick), I noticeably changed the look of every room. This simple, yet elegant, touch wasn't used in even some of the more expensive homes of the 1920s.

Newer homes can also benefit from trim additions, such as:

➤ Wider baseboards

➤ Casings around doors and windows

➤ Chair rail

➤ Picture molding

Whatever you do, it has to make sense for the design and style of your house. I had a client who tried adding Victorian era hardware to her 1930s colonial, and it just didn't work. Fortunately, she had only added it to a couple of doors before she stopped.

Tack up some sample moldings and look at them for a few days. If you still like the look, then have at it. You can save yourself some steps later by priming or doing other finishing steps to your wood trim in advance of installing it.

Dress Up with Wainscoting

Wainscoting is wood paneling done with a lot of class. Sometimes just called wainscot, it usually covers the lower section of a wall; the upper section is finished differently. Wainscoting looks like a series of raised or recessed panels separated by vertical pieces of trim and topped with a cap, a piece of horizontal trim that extends out beyond the edge of the panels. The panels are a finished grade of plywood and may be painted or stained and clear-coated. Wainscoting is an especially elegant way to finish off a dining room at a modest cost.

Have Some Fun: Faux Finishes

Faux finishes, the art of making a surface look like something else, was the hot decorating approach in the '80s, but it now seems relegated to the dustbin of yesteryear's trends. Don't let this stop you from trying your hand at marbling or graining techniques. Faux finishing ranges from easy-to-do wash finishes to walls and woodwork that look like serpentine marble. Books and materials on faux finishes are available at art and paint suppliers; one look at the photos in a good marbling book and you'll be hooked.

Not quite willing to use your living room for your apprenticeship training? Try the inside of a closet or even a sheet of loose drywall first. You'd be surprised at what you can do with just a few paintbrushes and some rags.

Quick Fix

Want to do an easier version of wainscoting? If your wall is flat and in good repair, just attach the vertical strips and horizontal cap right to it. Prefer plywood? Buy the cheapest vinyl wall paneling you can find that has a finished wood veneer backing. Glue the vinyl side to your wall with the backside facing out.

Why There Are Wallpaper Hangers

The world is divided into two groups of people: Those who can hang wallpaper (the vast minority) and those who can't. My one experience with wallpapering, a very humbling one, has greatly prejudiced me in favor of wallpaper hangers. A good one not only hangs the paper straight, but also lines up the seams properly so the pattern is consistent. In other words, it won't look like the job was done by The Three Stooges.

Before wallpapering can begin, there's prep work to do on the walls, including:

➤ Removing any existing wallpaper

➤ Repairing any cracks and holes

➤ Cutting out and repairing any bulging plaster or drywall

➤ Using a skimcoat if necessary to produce a smooth wall

Wallpaper will cover only so many sins. Some types of paper will show every flaw underneath it, so you want the walls to be as smooth as possible.

The Least You Need to Know

➤ Living and dining rooms can often be dazzling with some modest remodeling.

➤ Look at all your lighting options in these rooms: recessed ceiling lights, sconces, and switch-controlled lamps.

➤ Adding fireplaces is simpler than ever and doesn't require the traditional brick chimney.

➤ Careful trim and finishing work can easily transform these rooms into fresh spaces.

The Home Worker: Dens and Offices

More and more people are doing some kind of professional work out of their homes—I know I am. A home office used to mean the dining room table, where bills were paid and taxes were figured once a year with an adding machine and legal pad. Today, we need room for a computer, printer, scanner, fax machine, and maybe a copier. The dining room isn't going to cut it any longer.

You may trot off to work every morning and need a home office only for writing the Great American Novel in the evenings. Others need the space because their livelihood depends on it. Just running a household with its bills, the kids' schedules, and other home-related paperwork demands a small office. A well-designed office will satisfy all these needs, but this chapter will focus on creating an office for full- or part-time professional use.

An office is as much a state of mind as a physical space. A small space tucked under a staircase can do the job, as long as you can declare it your private area, not to be shared with the kids, spouse, or cat. A home office won't be quite the real thing if it's not a distinct space, separated from other home activities. This chapter discusses the space planning, construction, and some of the emotional issues surrounding a home office.

Are You Cut Out for This?

Before you build your home-based executive suite for running your new Internet import/export business, ask yourself some questions:

1. Am I disciplined enough to work productively at home?
2. Can I deal with the isolation, and even loneliness, that comes from working at home?
3. Do local ordinances allow me to run a business from my home?
4. If local laws and ordinances allow me to run a business out of my house, do they allow the number of employees I will need?
5. Do I have enough room for employees?
6. Am I easily distracted by the kids, the dog, the television, or the refrigerator?
7. Will my clients view a home office as being less than professional?
8. Are the neighbors going to give me any grief, especially if I have clients or business associates coming by regularly?

If you answered no to the first five questions and answered yes to the last three, then you need to re-evaluate whether you should even bother building an office at home.

If your answers were the opposite, you have all kinds of logistics to consider so you can create just the kind of working office you need. For example, you need to consider these issues:

➤ Will I be here full time or will I telecommute occasionally?

➤ How do I separate business activity from family activity?

➤ What office equipment will I need? Where will I fit it all in?

Quick Fix

A home office can be treated as a business expense and ultimately a tax deduction if it is your principal place of doing business on a regular and exclusive basis. Contact the IRS (www.irs.gov) and request Publication 587, "Business Use of Your Home."

Cost Savings and New Expenses

Unless you've been walking to work, your immediate daily savings from using a home office will your commuting costs: You won't have any. You'll no longer pay train or bus fare or pay for gas, parking, and wear and tear on your automobile. You'll also save the cost of renting an office space, restaurant lunches, and daily trips to your local barrista down at the espresso stand. Your dry-cleaning costs will go way down because every day will be a casual day.

This cost savings extravaganza can't go on forever. You'll also have some new expenses, including:

➤ Construction of your office

➤ Commuting to meet clients

➤ Office equipment and supplies

➤ Additional phone line(s) and phone bills

➤ Office furniture

The Chicken or the Egg Theory of Office Design

Once you've decided to go ahead with a home office, there are two approaches you can take to office design:

➤ Figure out what equipment and furniture you must have and then go about designing your office space around all of it.

➤ Take the only available area in your house and fit your equipment and furnishings into the space.

You can only miniaturize chairs, desks, and computers so much until you get down to children's furniture, which is hardly the right tone for an adult office. If you have a limited amount of floor space, your planning will have to be very creative.

Planning Your Space

Your designated space will determine how you plan out its use unless you have very specific equipment needs. If you must have a mainframe computer, gene splicer, or room for three co-workers, you'll have to come up with the space to hold this mass of people and equipment. If it's just you, a computer, and a telephone, you have all kinds of options for locating your office, including:

➤ A corner in just about any room

➤ Under a stairwell

➤ In front of a bay window

➤ A large closet

Look Out Below!

Building and sharing an office with a significant other can be a real test of a relationship. Allow yourselves plenty of room and designate distinct areas for each of you. You may even want separate phone lines so you can each carry on your work freely without waiting for the phone to be available.

➤ An attic or basement

➤ A small addition

Attics and basements are obvious choices, but they may require a lot of remodeling if they are unfinished space. Installing an office may motivate you to do just that, but what if you're not ready for this kind of task and only need a modest office space for now?

Cornered

A corner of a room will give you only limited privacy, but you can form some borders with bookshelves or movable screens, run up your corporate flag, and declare it off-limits. The advantage of this setup is that you already have two walls built and ready to hold bookshelves and a bulletin board. I would view this setup as more of a casual office for paying the bills or for occasional telecommuting, but it will still do the job, if only while you plan your next move.

Something's Under the Stairs

Some older homes have unused space under their main staircase. A portion of this space may be used as a coat closet, but the rest is walled over and waiting for some clever homeowner like you to discover its potential. Removing the lower wall should have no real effect on the stability of the staircase.

Your office will be only as deep as the length of each stair tread, so plan the purchase of your desk, shelves, and filing cabinets accordingly. It's even possible to close off

A corner office.

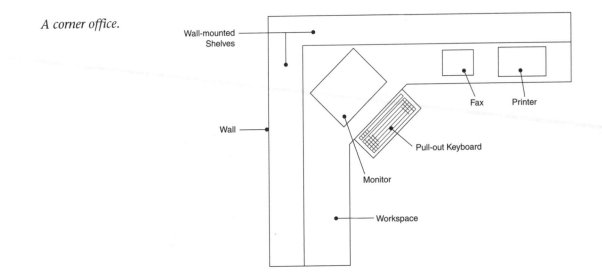

226

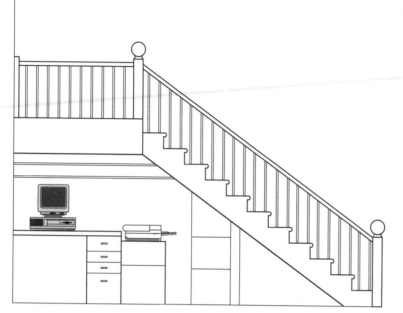

An office under the stairs.

your work area when you're through for the day with a decorative screen or by installing some narrow doors.

My Desk by the Bay

Bay windows will certainly give your office a view, but be careful about too much sun. Glare makes computer work almost impossible, so glass (glazing) selection and window coverings will be a big consideration. Tinted glass is one possibility, but be sure to consider how it will look against your other windows. Installing blinds that open from the bottom of the window up towards the top can provide you with some natural lighting while not interfering with your computer monitor. A bay window office also will limit your immediate storage space and is probably best suited to someone whose equipment and storage needs are minimal.

Closets and Lofts

Spaceunder stairs can be at a premium for apartment and condominium dwellers. Why not use a closet for your office? True, you won't have much of a view, but you could do worse. I've been in apartments where people used closets as bedrooms.

A closet conversion poses no special problems. You may need to extend the door opening, keeping in mind that you'll have some carpentry work to do when you start cutting away wall studs. A pair of bifolding doors will allow you easy access and the ability to close up at any time.

Short on closet space? If you have an old, high-ceiling unit, you can always consider building a small loft. Take another look at your kitchen pantry. Does it look ripe for an office conversion? Remember that you need to clear any such changes with your building owner if you're renting.

Adding On

Adding on a small office space to your house doesn't have to be a major operation. On my last house, I added an additional closet to the master bedroom, and most of the work was done over the course of a weekend. This closet was just over 5 feet long and 20 inches deep, enough to accommodate hangers. Double that depth and you have room for a working desk space. An addition this size wouldn't require a full foundation, just posts, beams, and footings. Once again, you could install folding doors. As a bonus, when you sell your house, you could present your office as a huge walk-in closet. Before you get too carried away, check your local building codes and confirm that you have enough room to legally add on to your house.

Key Considerations

Even if you're working alone, you have to think like a small business with several employees. We live in a communication and technology age, which means fax machines, computers with fax modems, and phone lines. It also means plenty of outlets to plug all of this stuff in and get it going.

Workspace and storage are the other two critical considerations for the home office user. An architect, for instance, will need plenty of room to view and work on plans. A writer may need a modest-sized desk area, but plenty of bookshelves.

Every office user will need a quiet space to work in without the distraction of family chaos elsewhere in the house. Build in enough soundproofing, and you'll forget you have a family. Your kids will have to telephone you to tell you that dinner is ready.

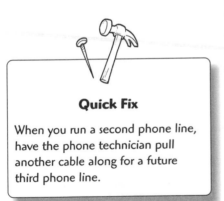

Quick Fix

When you run a second phone line, have the phone technician pull another cable along for a future third phone line.

Will you be meeting clients, suppliers, or other business associates in your home office? You won't want them passing through your dining room or laundry area to get to you, unless they also have home offices and understand your setup. Ideally, you'll want a separate entrance, and this can influence where you locate your office. If you're a pet therapist, for instance, you don't want your clients running into your hyped-up terrier, who's still a discipline problem despite five years of your therapy. It wouldn't be good for business.

You can make do with a windowless office, but unless you find a view distracting, why live like the hapless millions of employees who have no other choice? If you're like most people, there's nothing quite like lots of natural light to get you going at the start of a workday.

Connecting to the Outside World

Your home office has two wiring considerations: telephone and electrical. You want a minimum of two phone lines: One for your fax or fax/modem and Internet connection and one for speaking. You may want a third line if you have to keep your fax machine available at all times.

You will want a dedicated circuit for your computer so it isn't subject to interruptions from users in another room if they cause the circuit breaker to trip. I'd suggest installing a 20-amp circuit for the same reason I'd pull an extra phone wire: You don't know what the future will bring. You may end up with an array of computer equipment that doesn't even exist now. A 20-amp circuit gives you plenty of options.

A standard office copier is the biggest energy user in an office and needs to be on a dedicated circuit. While you or your electrician are running a circuit for your computer, you can pull the wire for your copier at the same time.

Tales from the Scaffold

Technology companies are known for starting out in garages and then moving to cheap offices with equally cheap office furniture. Amazon.com, the Internet bookseller, still makes its work desks out of doors and metal brackets and uses framing lumber for legs. Other companies shun comfortable furnishings in favor of spending their money on more programmers. At least they have their budget priorities in order.

Making the Most of Storage

The Wall Street Journal runs a weekly section on the offices of individuals from all walks of business life. The offices are invariably neat and tidy with no visible clutter. One executive for a major bookstore chain had no paper whatsoever in his office. He had all of his files on his computer, and he was very efficient at getting rid of extraneous stuff he knew he'd never look at again. Your first step in designing home office storage is to lighten your current load and plan on a less-is-more approach for the future.

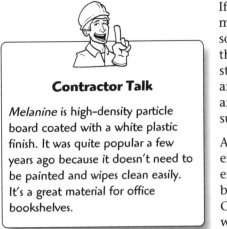

If you're not ready to part with your 10-year-old management training manuals, you can store them somewhere besides your office. Do the same with all those bulk office supplies you buy at the warehouse stores. Store a week's worth of supplies in your office and replenish when you run low. Dry basements are an ideal place to store extra office material and supplies.

After you've cut down the clutter, give yourself an entire wall of bookshelves—you'll fill them soon enough. You can install simple, but elegant, built-in bookshelves using stock materials from a lumberyard. Oak plywood, for example, can be cut into 1-foot widths, which is more than enough to hold binders and files. Easier yet, you can buy *melanine* boards in even longer lengths. Take a walk around your local lumberyard or home improvement store and see whether another type of wood appeals to you.

Your office design should allow for filing cabinets, too. We're still a paper-based culture despite all the hype about an electronic, paperless future. An office supply store can show you an array of filing systems to fit any office configuration.

Quiet Please, I'm Working

It's unrealistic to expect your entire household to revolve around your work needs when you're using a home office—unless, of course, you *are* the entire household. Your best option is to soundproof your work area as thoroughly as possible:

➤ Locate your office as far from family activity as is reasonable.

➤ Pack the walls with fiberglass insulation; two-by-six stud construction will allow you to put in thicker insulation than two-by-four construction will.

➤ Install resilient channel (RC), a light gauge metal strip, on one or both sides of any new or exposed wall studs before installing the drywall; RC holds the drywall $1/2$ inch away from the studs reducing sound transmission.

➤ Install thick carpet in your office and outside of it, especially if you have children who play nearby.

➤ Install a *paneled door* rather than a *hollow core door*.

➤ Replace existing windows with insulated sashes.

A Door of Your Own

If you see clients in your business, installing a separate, outside entrance would be a wise idea. A separate entrance gives you a more professional appearance and maintains a separation of business and personal spaces. Check your local building code. It may require you to have an exit door if you regularly have clients or employees in your office.

Installing a separate entry door may very well determine where you locate your office. What if your office is on the third floor? Do you really want an outside staircase snaking its way up the side of your house? A basement door is more doable and required by code if you convert your basement to habitable space and it doesn't currently have an exit door (see Chapter 26, "Bargain Basements: A Million Uses").

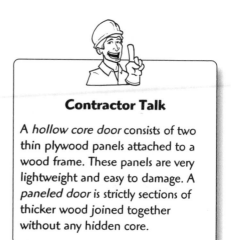

Contractor Talk

A *hollow core door* consists of two thin plywood panels attached to a wood frame. These panels are very lightweight and easy to damage. A *paneled door* is strictly sections of thicker wood joined together without any hidden core.

Lots of Light

A main rule for home offices, especially those located in basements, is to install plenty of lighting. Natural lighting is best if for no other reason than it keeps you tied to the outside world, a relationship you may come to appreciate if you'll be working at home alone. It also has the advantage of being free of charge. Windows can be installed just about anywhere, even in a below-grade basement. A window well or series of window wells can brighten up an otherwise sober-seeming basement office.

I would also recommend recessed ceiling fixtures with individual light switches for every grouping of task lighting. For example, one switch for the lights over your desk, one for the lights over your bookshelves, and so on. These fixtures can be fluorescent or incandescent; fluorescent fixtures give you the most bang for the buck when it comes to delivering general illumination.

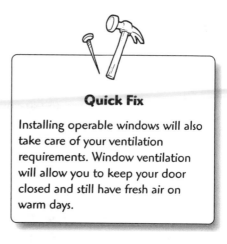

Quick Fix

Installing operable windows will also take care of your ventilation requirements. Window ventilation will allow you to keep your door closed and still have fresh air on warm days.

If You Like a Traditional Men's Club Look

There's nothing quite like the look of walnut or mahogany bookshelves, leather chairs, and a grand desk that would look appropriate in a bank president's office. If this formal, traditional setting is your dream, be prepared to pay dearly for it, or you can do some fancy faking.

I've mentioned marbling and graining techniques in previous chapters, but a home office is where they'll help you look like a big shot at a bargain price. Good graining technique will turn a piece of bland particle board shelving into any wood finish you want, with no one being the wiser. I've seen some graining that was decades old, and I had to look twice to be sure it wasn't the species of wood it appeared to be. Use the same graining technique on wall paneling, wainscoting, baseboards, and window and door trim.

What about that banker's desk? Look around at your local unfinished furniture store for something that suits you, and grain away. You may have to wait on the leather chairs, but you'll be more than halfway there with your faux walnut look.

Do You Need a Restroom?

You may not need a separate bathroom—you're used to sharing the facilities with your spouse and kids—but do you want your clients doing this? Any home-based business that regularly has clients passing through should have a dedicated bathroom (how's that for a new phrase?). This bathroom can be an existing one that's close by and off limits to the family or a new bathroom built specifically for office use.

If you do add a bathroom, look at it in the overall context of the house, not just your business. Ask yourself whether you should stick with a basic half-bath or add a shower, keeping future resale in mind (see Chapter 16, "Bathrooms with Bragging Rights," and Chapter 25, "Special Touches for Special Rooms," for additional information).

The Least You Need to Know

➤ Before you decide to work exclusively at home, consider whether you can handle this lifestyle and its solitude.

➤ The design of your office will be determined by the size of your required office equipment and the size of your available office space.

➤ A wired and connected office will usually require at least two phone lines and a dedicated electrical circuit.

➤ Lighting and soundproofing measures will strongly influence the functionality and comfort of a home office.

➤ A regular stream of visiting clients or business associates will determine where you locate your office within your house. You'll want it as separate as possible from your living space.

Part 5
Street Appeal: Exterior Upgrades

Remodeling isn't limited to the inside of your house. The other side, your exterior, is your statement to the world. Do you like the message that your peeling siding is sending to your friends and passers-by? How about your scruffy deck?

Deep down, even social rebels want some approval from the neighbors.

If a house is well maintained, its siding, gutters, decks, and porches will last indefinitely. Past owners of your house may not have possessed your budding sense duty when it came to painting and repairs, however. Now you're looking at a big investment of time and money to bring your exterior up to grade. This means deciding on materials, colors, design, and choosing contractors for the work you don't do yourself.

The exterior of your house takes a real beating protecting you from the elements. All siding and finishes are not created equal; in fact, some of them can be expensive headaches. The same is true of decks, and even landscaping: Pick the wrong plants and they can overgrow the place in a hurry.

This section will guide you through siding options and deck and porch maintenance, and even show you your garage in a new light. Exterior work is weather-driven: Summer can be a tough time to find available contractors, especially painters. Early planning—think Halloween—will keep you ahead of the game.

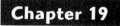

Chapter 19

Taking Sides: Your Exterior Walls

In This Chapter

➤ Traditional wood siding is still a top choice

➤ The trials and tribulations of composite siding

➤ Going the synthetic route: Vinyl and aluminum

➤ Siding the hard way with brick and stone

➤ Keeping it in shape for the long haul

Siding is very much determined by where you live. There's a reason New Mexico has *adobe* and the northwest has cedar siding. Climate and the availability of materials go hand-in-hand. In New Mexico, it's a lot easier to make mud from local dirt than to import cedar trees.

The wood tradition got started in the eastern part of the United States with the early colonists who found dense forests that were theirs for the taking—and take they did. Wood is easy to work with, generally affordable, and very appealing to look at. It's also a nuisance to maintain. As a tree, it laughs at the rain and snow because it sports a thick, protective layer of bark. Strip off the bark and the wood underneath it is on its own unless you keep it sealed with preservative sealers, stains, or paint.

Technology has tried to rescue homeowners with aluminum and vinyl siding products, but they're not the perfect solutions. Composite siding, made from compressed wood fibers mixed with resins, fillers, and binders, has resulted in huge class-action suits against some manufacturers. Even rock-solid siding, such as stone, cast stone, brick, and brick veneer products, requires some vigilance on your part. This chapter details the pros and cons of various types of siding, their maintenance, and what to do if you're considering changing your siding.

Wood, an Old Standby

People have used wood for centuries to side their homes. Cedar is considered the top wood siding choice by many builders, but other woods have also been used, including pine, redwood, and cypress. Siding also comes in a variety of styles or patterns, such as bevel, shiplap, and tongue and groove.

The price of the wood depends on its grade, which refers to its quality and appearance. Clear grades have the fewest and smallest knots and few, if any, splits. Clear vertical grain cedar is the best you can get; #3 common knotty cedar is the most appropriate for tight budgets. Western red cedar, which is the major source of cedar siding today, accepts all exterior finishes well, especially semi-transparent stains. If you have an older house with its cedar siding intact, it's well worth preserving.

Hanging Out Your Shingles

Cedar shingles are another form of this popular wood's siding prowess. Shingles are more labor intensive to install, but they give a house a very rich and appealing look, though they tend to cup or curl on its weathered sides. The Cedar Shake and Shingle Bureau (www.cedarbureau.org) classifies red cedar shakes as the following:

➤ Number 1 Blue Label (premium, 100 percent heartwood, 100 percent clear)

➤ Number 2 Red Label (not less than 10 inches of clear cedar on 16-inch-long shingles)

➤ Number 3 Black Label (utility grade)

➤ Number 4 Undercoursing (utility grade for the starter course or first layer of shingles)

Trying to Be Wood

Composite wood products have had more than their share of woes. Also known as hardboard, in the worst cases the composite wood siding has warped, disassembled itself, and turned black with mold. The most infamous brand is Louisiana-Pacific Corporation's Inner-Seal Lap Siding or L-P Siding, which is subject to a massive class-action, product-liability suit.

Other products and manufacturers include the following:

➤ Weyerhauser Hardboard Siding

➤ Masonite Hardboard Siding

➤ Boise-Cascade Hardboard Siding

➤ Georgia-Pacific

➤ Masonite OmniWood

➤ Stimpson Hardboard Siding (Forestex)

There's even a Web site devoted to problem siding (http://sidingsolutions.com), which has produced a timely publication, *The Siding Book*, for identifying composite siding and assessing damage to it. Louisiana-Pacific has its own site solely for consumer claims (http://lpsidingclaims.com). If you want a thorough technical explanation of the problems with composite wood products in an article that's written in an engaging style, go to www.umass.edu/bmatwt/Alternative_Trim.

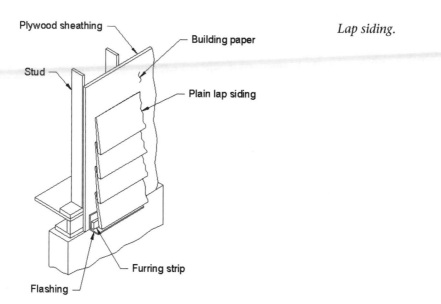

Lap siding.

Plywood sheathing

Building paper

Stud

Plain lap siding

Furring strip

Flashing

Composite siding and wood products are not inherently bad, but they require exacting painting, sealing, and installation procedures to ensure that they won't start unraveling. New generation products by Louisiana-Pacific, for example, have apparently resolved the problems of the early version of L-P Siding, but are you willing to chance them?

The Non-Wood World

Wood has an ageless appeal, but it requires a maintenance commitment and budget outlay that fewer people are willing to make. Wood siding needs to be painted every so many years, and that can be expensive, especially with two- and three-story houses.

The world of chemistry and metallurgy has provided us with some other options. Plastic and metal siding manufacturers appeal to the low-maintenance genes in all of us, but these are not zero-upkeep products.

Plastic World

Vinyl siding is a petroleum-based product. According to its manufacturers, it won't rot, warp, or rust. They don't always mention problems with ultraviolet (UV) light exposure, which can cause the vinyl to become brittle after some years. How many years will it take? The homeowner jury is still out on that one; the product is too new to know for sure.

Vinyl doesn't need to be painted, but it will fade with time. New products are improvements over first-generation vinyl siding and have greater UV protection. Vinyl siding can be installed over existing siding; I recommend that it be done by an experienced installer who is familiar with the nuances of the material.

As a plastic, vinyl siding may resist water, but its resistance against impact, from an errant baseball, for instance, leaves something to be desired. That's especially true as the material ages. This thin, hollow product has little structural strength.

From Recycled Aluminum Cans to Aluminum Siding

Before vinyl siding was introduced, aluminum was the premium alternative to wood siding. Because vinyl is cheaper than aluminum, the latter isn't as popular as it was in the 1950s and '60s, although aluminum now comes in colors other than white and in a wood-grain pattern as well.

Aluminum siding was introduced in the 1950s as a carefree, hose-it-down-once-a-year product, but the passage of time has shown that it has some problems. Aluminum siding fades and oxidizes and eventually needs to be painted. So much for solely hosing it off once in a while, though that's a good maintenance strategy.

Before you paint aluminum siding, it must first be:

➤ Cleaned

➤ Sanded clean of any oxidation

➤ Primed

Ask your paint dealer for a primer specifically made for aluminum siding. Don't use wood primer; it won't stick properly to aluminum.

Look Out Below!

Both aluminum and vinyl can dent if you lean a ladder against them. Run your ladder up to the roof if possible. If not, wrap the ends of the ladders with rags or attach a narrow board across and beyond their span to spread out the pressure.

When Repairs Are at Hand

Finding matching material is a problem when replacing pieces of either vinyl or aluminum siding. Patterns change, and some are discontinued. If you don't have any spare pieces of the original material around, call an installer, who may be able to patch and repair what you have. If you're residing your house, I recommend you get extra pieces of siding for future repairs.

Concrete: a Hardy Siding

Concrete composites, also known as fiber cement products, give you the appearance of wood with the durability of concrete. The best-known of these products are Hardi-Plank and HardiBoard, both manufactured by James Hardie Building Products, Inc. (800-424-3431 or www.jameshardie.com), who has been manufacturing fiber cement in Australia for over 100 years.

Fiber cement is made from wood fiber, Portland cement, and sand; the siding comes in various widths and 12-foot lengths. It holds paint extremely well because it resists absorbing moisture. This interesting siding is increasingly used in new construction. Fiber cement doesn't have the inherent problems of composite wood products, and it has a long history behind it. It's moderately priced, but it's more time-consuming to install than wood siding or composite wood.

Covering Up with Asbestos

Asbestos siding was part of the great wood siding cover-up from years back. As a tough, fire-retardant material, asbestos has found its way into all kinds of building products. You have no compelling reason to remove asbestos siding as long as it's intact and isn't crumbling anywhere (crumbling areas should be repaired); it does become more brittle with age.

If you do remove it, you'll have to follow legal abatement procedures, which include:

➤ Encasing the work area in plastic

➤ Posting signs that asbestos removal is taking place

➤ Keeping children away from the work area

➤ Wearing respirators rated for asbestos

My advice: Paint it and leave it alone. If you think it's a future liability when you eventually sell your house, then weigh the cost of removal against that potential liability. Once it's removed, you'll have to deal with the wood siding underneath. Usually, the wood siding has been covered over for so many years that it's in a preserved state—it's just full of nail holes from the asbestos siding. You'll also find that the ends of your window sills were most likely trimmed off to accommodate the new siding and will have to be repaired.

The Hard Stuff: Brick, Stone, and Stucco

Brick is a material of substance, but it fools most of us in at least one respect. The bricks used to build a house are almost always a veneer or surface application built onto a wood frame, just like wood siding. Occasionally, they're part of the integral structure, but not very often.

Tales from the Scaffold

My Texas relatives have told me that wood-sided houses in the Lone Star state are considered, at least socially, to be second rate and that brick is the construction material of choice. Brick makes good sense in a hot Texas summer, so there may have been more of a practical reason for using it over wood. As you may have guessed, all of my relatives in Texas have brick houses.

Some brick guys—it's always guys—think it's a crime to ever paint brick, though some styles of housing call for it. Most brick should be left unpainted, but that doesn't mean you can ignore it. Brick maintenance includes:

➤ Pressure washing to control moss and clean off pollution

➤ Waterproofing

➤ Tuck-pointing

Waterproofing is somewhat controversial, at least with the historic restoration folks. Masons say it helps preserve the brick and mortar and leaves the surface easier to clean. Opponents say that by sealing the building you run the risk of trapping moisture inside between the brick and the framing. Tuck-pointing is a more straightforward decision, but it's an expensive, tedious, messy process.

A relative of full brick siding is engineered thin brick systems, that are basically brick lite. These narrow versions of regular kiln-dried brick are used when the weight and cost of the siding is a consideration.

Stone

Stone walls are expensive, but just as there's engineered thin brick, there's also an alternative to stone. Cast stone, also called cultured stone, is manufactured from Portland cement, lightweight aggregate, and coloring. Though made to look like stone, it comes in only a limited number of patterns, unlike real stones, each of which is unique.

The process for installing cast stone over any structurally sound surface is pretty straightforward:

1. Install a vapor barrier, such as tar paper.

2. Apply masonry cement.

3. Press stones into place.

Stone can dress up a plain concrete foundation or an addition, if appropriate. It's an easy upkeep material that never needs painting; simply pressure wash as needed to remove pollution and moss. Like any other remodeling decision, you have to weigh its up-front cost against its long-term cost: maintenance, additional resale value, and aesthetic value to you.

Contractor Talk

Tuck-pointing is the process of cleaning out the joints between bricks and removing deteriorated mortar with either power tools or a hammer and chisel. New mortar is then applied.

Stucco, Old and New

Think of *stucco* as a weather-resistant exterior plaster. Old stucco was applied in a three-coat manner like plaster: an initial scratch coat, a second brown coat, and a final finish coat. It was also regularly applied over wood lath, which is not the best material for outdoor use.

Like interior plaster, stucco will crack and need repairs. Please see Appendix G, "Repairs," for a reference to common stucco repairs.

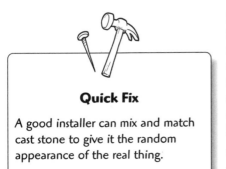

Quick Fix

A good installer can mix and match cast stone to give it the random appearance of the real thing.

Exterior Insulation and Finish System (EIFS) is the stucco industry's legal albatross. This system is a recent development in the building industry. It consists of a plasticized cement stucco applied over sheets of polystrene insulation that are attached to plywood sheathing. The stucco is then sealed with an acrylic polymer. With all that plastic, you'd expect it to be impervious to water, but sadly that hasn't been the case.

Critics say EIFS allows water to enter through tiny cracks and caulk joints. Once it's behind the stucco and insulation, the water has no way to escape and rots out the wood framing underneath. Lawsuits started several years ago and some municipalities have established temporary bans on the installation of this material. Once again, hapless homeowners are caught in the middle, and in too many cases, they're stuck with rotting homes. The EIFS Trade Association has an information line available to builders and consumers at 800-294-3462.

Contractor Talk

Stucco is a siding material that is generally composed of sand, lime, gypsum, and Portland cement.

If You Must Re-side

Re-siding is a big, expensive job. Much re-siding on old homes is done without removing the old siding. Adding on this additional layer of material will change the profile of different building details, especially around windows, and simply covering up problem siding doesn't eliminate its problems. Any rot or structural issues will still have to be repaired; otherwise, they can spread under the new siding. Some contractors advocate removing all the old siding first, but if you're going to go to that much trouble, you might as well repair and restore the old siding, unless it's too far gone to be reasonably repaired. If your old siding is covered with a new material such as aluminum, you may wish to pull it off and restore the original wood siding.

What's Underneath?

In the 1950s and '60s, homeowners who modernized their homes often did so in part by covering up original wood siding with aluminum, asbestos shingles, or asphalt shingles. This last material, a siding version of asphalt roofing shingles, was often done in a fake brick pattern, which fooled absolutely no one.

If you're not sure what you have underneath your siding, carefully remove a small section in an out-of-the-way area of your house, say behind some bushes at the rear or side yard. This will reveal what you're likely to have on the majority of your house, but there are no guarantees that you won't find deteriorated or missing siding in some areas.

Patching and Matching

Exteriors are one big continuum without the kind of visual breaks that individual interior rooms provide. You want to match up siding and other elements as closely as possible. Millwork companies can match any siding, trim, or molding—for a price. You'll pay fees for the following:

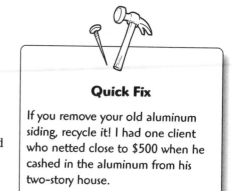

Quick Fix

If you remove your old aluminum siding, recycle it! I had one client who netted close to $500 when he cashed in the aluminum from his two-story house.

➤ Setting up the machines to do the cutting and shaping

➤ The labor to do a custom run

➤ The material itself

To keep your costs down, have all the needed trim run at once (order extra if you're not certain exactly how much you need). You don't want to incur another set-up fee because you need 5 more feet of siding.

Trim that has been hacked at to accommodate new siding can be patched and spliced; you don't have to go to the expense of replacing it completely. You'd be surprised what you can do with some scraps of wood, some glue, and epoxy filler.

Siding Your New Addition

Additions, as a rule, should have siding to match your existing house, but you have some options. A complete new second story can be done in a different material, such as cedar shingles, as long as it complements the rest of your facade.

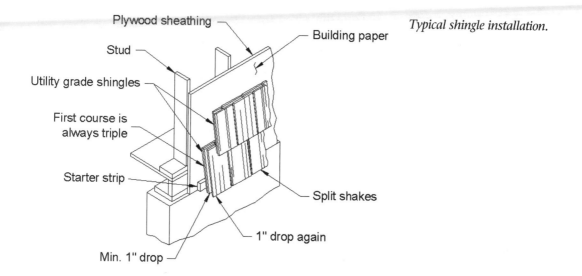

Typical shingle installation.

Plywood sheathing

Stud

Utility grade shingles

First course is always triple

Starter strip

Min. 1" drop

Building paper

Split shakes

1" drop again

What if you have brick and can't match it, or don't want to look at new brick next to old on a family room you're adding on? The same principle of complementary materials applies. Try stone or even narrow cedar siding instead of brick. You're trying to side tastefully and finish your addition so it won't stand out. If you go with wood siding, a careful paint or stain selection will help your addition blend in even further.

Comparing Them Side-by-Side

What's the best choice in siding material? Probably 4 feet of concrete: By the time that stuff deteriorates, it will just about be time for the sun to burn itself out. A more down-to-earth choice will depend on the style of your house, your aesthetic tastes, and the degree of maintenance you're willing to do. The table below compares the most common siding materials.

Siding Comparison

Material	What's Good	What's Bad
Cedar	Attractive, holds paint well, long-lasting, easy to work with	Cost for good material, maintenance
Composites	Affordable, hold paint well, good appearance	Product liability lawsuits
Vinyl	Low maintenance	Looks, long-term unknown
Aluminum	Low maintenance	Dated, needs painting eventually
Concrete composite	Low maintenance, moderate price	Uniform look may not be appealing
Brick and stone	Long life, never needs paint	Cleaning, sealing, tuck-pointing
Stucco	Good looks, durable, easy to paint	New EIFS has product-liability problems

The Least You Need to Know

➤ Old wood siding is often excellent material that can be revitalized with repairs, stripping, and painting.

➤ Composite wood siding is controversial and possibly unreliable as a siding material.

➤ Vinyl and aluminum products are low-maintenance, but no product is maintenance-free.

➤ You can skip the painting with brick and stone siding, but you still need to clean, waterproof, and do mortar repair from time to time.

➤ Fiber cement board is one of the most promising new siding materials, offering the look of wood with greater durability.

Chapter 20

Porches and Decks: Your Outdoor Rooms

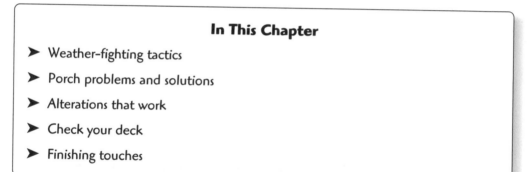

In This Chapter

➤ Weather–fighting tactics

➤ Porch problems and solutions

➤ Alterations that work

➤ Check your deck

➤ Finishing touches

A porch acts as a transition from the public arena of the sidewalk and yard to the privacy of your home. Porches were once a standard feature on American homes of all styles and sizes. As modernist designers decided they were too frivolous and old-fashioned, they banished them without a second thought for their social value. They range in design from the simplest concrete slab covered by an aluminum canopy to grand, wraparound wood structures with tongue-and-groove wood floors and elaborate columns.

Architects, designers, and home buyers have rediscovered porches, and they're gradually finding their way onto homes again. If you have an older home with a porch or two, they could probably use some attention, upgrading, or expansion. Porchless? A good designer can add a porch with street appeal to most homes.

Decks are a simpler version of porches and are usually added to the rear of a house. New decks (see Chapter 28, "Deck Your House with Decks") must be added onto older homes with care; old and new styles clash far too easily. Many existing decks are poorly maintained and often in need of cleaning and sealing. This chapter takes you through the basics of porch and deck maintenance and makes a few comments about porch design, too.

Porch First Aid

A covered concrete slab is not the first image that comes to mind when people think about porches, but they technically fit the definition of a transition area and entrance to a home. Most of us think of the impressive, and even not so impressive, wood porches many homes had going into the 1920s. Wood, as you know by now, tries to fight the good fight against sunlight and the elements, but it needs protection and maintenance or it gets into trouble.

Porch troubles include:

➤ Peeling paint

➤ Loose handrails

➤ Loose and missing balusters

➤ Rotten or decayed columns

➤ Leaky gutters and roof

➤ Rotting, missing, or loose floorboards, joists, posts, and beams

➤ Loose or rotting steps

Remember crawling under your porch during the house tour at the beginning of the book? Now it's time to do any repairs you listed in your notebook.

Look Out Below!

Covered porches are a great place to have a barbecue and an equally great place for an unwatched barbecue to start a fire. Never leave an unattended barbecue or candle on a porch or wood deck. Keep a spray bottle of water nearby to extinguish any errant sparks that land on the decking or floor boards.

Giving a Little Support

The underside of an unventilated porch can be a moist netherworld of insects, bacteria, and fungi happily co-existing without ever seeing the light of day. Your porch foundation may look dry and intact, but poke around for termite damage anyway. If anything is damaged, it will be the posts, because they're closest to the ground. Posts can be replaced, but don't try to do more than one at a time!

A rotted section of post can be removed and replaced with new, pressure-treated wood. This is not a major job, but it's an awkward one because you won't have a lot of room to work in or maneuver. To replace a damaged post section, follow these steps:

1. Raise the affected section of the porch with a screw jack.
2. Install a pier block if needed.
3. Cut out the rotted section a few inches above the damaged area. You must saw the rotted area away with a straight cut (as straight as you can get it anyway).
4. Insert and secure a new piece of wood (see the next set of steps).
5. Lower the porch back to its original position.

To secure the old wood to the new, follow these steps:

1. Apply some exterior wood glue to the top of the new pressure-treated wood before you lower the porch onto it.
2. Drill two angled *pilot holes* on each accessible side of the post from one section to the other; insert and tighten deck screws in each hole.
3. Glue and screw a pressure-treated two-by-four to each accessible side of the post

These posts will last indefinitely and will easily extend the life of your porch.

Contractor Talk

A *pilot hole* is a hole drilled in advance of inserting a screw or nail to avoid splitting the wood. The pilot hole is always smaller in diameter than the screw or nail.

Repairing a post.

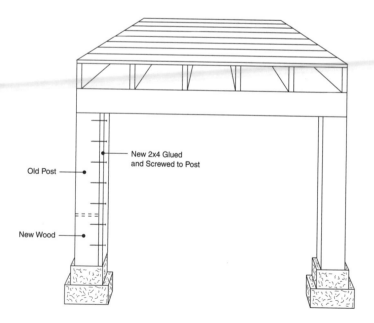

Old Post

New 2x4 Glued and Screwed to Post

New Wood

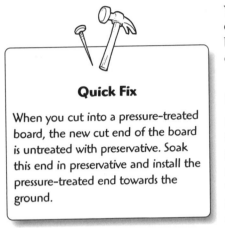

While you're crawling around, install some vents to create cross-circulation. Vents prevent moisture buildup and the scourge of moisture-loving, wood-eating organisms.

Quick Fix

When you cut into a pressure-treated board, the new cut end of the board is untreated with preservative. Soak this end in preservative and install the pressure-treated end towards the ground.

Column Conflicts

Old, intricate columns can also have rot or deterioration at their bases. This is another job that calls for jacking up the porch—in this case, the porch ceiling—so you can remove and replace the decayed wood. After you've removed the base, check for moisture damage on the vertical section of the column. This is a good area to practice your epoxy repair (see Appendix G, "Repairs").

There is some debate about venting a post by drilling a $3/4$-inch hole below the cap at the top of the column. Whether you should do this depends on these factors:

➤ Whether your column is sealed and caulked thoroughly to prevent water from seeping inside

➤ Climate conditions (humidity)

➤ Your appraisal of the column after removing the base

One Step at a Time

A wood staircase is a porch's most exposed and vulnerable section. The staircase is composed of four sections:

➤ The treads or steps

➤ The risers, which are the vertical sections behind each step

➤ The stringers, the framing to which the treads and risers are attached

➤ The railing and its components

Sometimes a wobbly tread can be secured with a nail or deck screw. Old stringers were cut from standard, not pressure-treated, lumber and should be checked for decay. If they're in need of replacement, you're looking at an entirely new staircase. On the positive side, you'll be amazed at how firm and solid a new staircase feels.

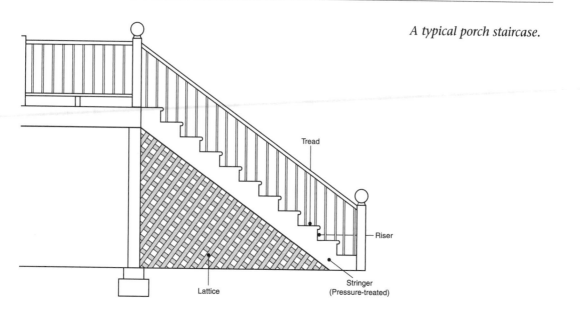

A typical porch staircase.

Tread

Riser

Lattice

Stringer
(Pressure-treated)

Roof and Gutters

A leaking porch roof can cause unseen problems if water accumulates between the wood ceiling and the roofing. You won't know you have any damage until you finally see some rot along the ceiling. Old porch ceilings are typically tongue-and-groove beaded board, the same material sometimes used for some wainscoting. Carefully inspect your porch roof at least once a year for possible leaks. Clean your gutters at least once a year or more often as needed.

Porch Floors: Bring Out the Big Sanders

Old porches have the same kind of tongue-and-groove floorboards as much indoor flooring. In the northwest, fir has been the wood of choice. They were beautiful floors when they were new, but over the years, they got so loaded up with thick layers of porch and deck enamel that it's hard to distinguish one board from another. You can repaint and add to the mess or take the higher road and do a job that will really make your floors stand out. I'm talking about stripping them with floor sanders, which is a big, messy, toxic job worth considering.

Sanding a porch floor is a good dry run for doing your interior floors, if that's your eventual plan. Porch and deck enamel will quickly clog sanding belts, but you should still start out with a very light grit paper until you're used to handling the machine. Just consider the cost of the extra sandpaper as part of your training as a floor refinisher.

Big Lead Paint Evils

There's an excellent chance that some of the old paint on your porch floor is lead-based. Large-drum floor sanders collect quite a bit of the dust they create inside of a dust bag, but you'll still need to take extra precautions:

1. Completely mask off the porch with heavy plastic, sealing the ends with duct tape.
2. Wear protective gear, including a disposable paper suit, respirator rated for lead dust, and ear and eye protection.
3. Vacuum everything, including the walls and ceiling, with a HEPA vacuum cleaner.
4. Dispose of debris according to local regulations.
5. Check that you can legally remove lead paint in without hiring an abatement contractor.

Quick Fix

Consider coating a plywood porch floor with elastomeric finish, a self-leveling, rubber-like material that forms a very tough seal. It's normally used over uniform surfaces such as plywood or masonry.

Paint or Stain?

A covered porch has much better weather protection than an exposed deck and is a good candidate for a semi-transparent stain finish once the floor has been sanded or replaced. Sections of the floor close to the steps or overhangs will receive the worst weathering when rain or snow blow in; these areas will need to be watched for faster wear.

Paint is also a good choice of finish for porch floors for the same reason stain is: The porch floor will be covered and protected and, unlike an exposed deck, has little chance of peeling. If you're a traditionalist, choose paint. You'll need to add some nonslip additive (available at any paint store) to the porch paint to prevent people from slipping on the smooth paint film.

Look Up: Porch Ceilings

Traditionally, porch ceilings were painted in very light colors. One painter told me that light blue used to be used to suggest the sky. Why not carry this one step further? Paint it light blue with white clouds. Hire a set painter from a local theater group. Set painters are highly versatile and can easily reproduce clouds, airplanes, Martians, you name it.

The paint on old porch ceilings is often cracked and flawed. The fastest way to strip it off, short of installing new material, is to take a very sharp scraper and shave it down to bare wood. You'll need a long-handled scraper and a file for sharpening the blade. This is tedious overhead work, but it's faster than sanding.

Adding to Your Porch

Porches regularly get enclosed with windows, screened over, or covered with lattice. Often these additions are done with little regard for design or their effect on the overall look of the house. In historic districts, you'll never get away with these kinds of porch alterations, but you certainly can in other neighborhoods. Plan changes to your porch carefully. Consider removable screens (you'll want them off in the winter), operable windows to maintain an open feeling, and only a modest amount of lattice where you need it for privacy.

Growth Hormones: Extending Your Porch, Adding a New One

Home builders over the years have followed the same formula: Build as much into a house as you must, throw in some modest extras, and don't do anything else. Everything else cuts into a builder's profit, even if it's only $100 a house. Porches began to shrink noticeably by the 1920s, but there's no reason you have to live with this builder parsimony. You can easily add on to existing porches with either a continuation of a covered porch or with an open deck.

Extending or adding on a porch can be done really well or really badly. Ask yourself:

➤ If I extend the roof line, will it conflict with any windows or the existing roof line?

➤ Will a porch block off any basement windows?

➤ Are my planned dimensions in proportion to the rest of the house?

Porch additions are very visible and need to be seen as a plan on paper or computer monitor before you start building.

A Mostly Easy Addition

There are a few things you don't have to worry about when you add on a porch, such as insulation, drywall, and windows. Your biggest problem will be the design, especially on newer houses that were never intended to have porches. If you want a covered porch, but a solid roof won't mesh with the rest of your house, consider an alternative such as glass for a greenhouse-like effect.

Tales from the Scaffold

The most time-consuming porch floor installation I ever read about was featured in *The Old House Journal* some years ago. Normally, floorboards are simply nailed, but the designer had the carpenter caulk every single tongue-and-groove board on the grooved side in addition to nailing. The carpenter found it a time-consuming and perhaps slightly annoying process, but later agreed that it was a good idea in the long run. I think it may have been overkill, but it was a very secure floor by the time he was done installing it.

As long as you're building new, be sure to include:

➤ Plenty of lighting with separate switches for different fixtures

➤ A ceiling fan in hot, humid climates

➤ Awnings or other sun shields

➤ Outdoor outlets

Clear the Decks!

Decks are basically open porches with more imaginative designs. They are seen more as a complement to the house than a matching design element, so decks of all sizes and shapes, including multilevel designs, can be seen on any style or vintage house. Because they're exposed to the weather, decks take a beating all year round: If it's not rain or snow, it's sunlight, which is a wonderful destroyer of finishes.

Existing decks need regular cleaning and maintenance. If yours hasn't been done in a while, don't give up hope. Under all that grime and stain is a fresh deck waiting to show itself.

Deck Fitness Test

Go back to your house survey and read over your deck notes. Does yours need any repairs? Do you have any loose or damaged boards? It's easy to pry loose single damaged decking boards and install replacements. Check your railing: If it doesn't feel safe, secure it with more fasteners or replace it.

Try Cleaning First

There are two areas of disagreement when it comes to decks: how to clean them and how to seal them. Cleaning methods include:

➤ Pressure washers

➤ Home-mixed cleaners

➤ Commercial deck cleaners

Look Out Below!

Bleaches can damage wood if allowed to soak in for too long. Follow the directions that come with your commercial cleaner and rinse the cleaner and its bleach off after the allotted time has passed. With home mixes, rinse off after 10 minutes.

Pressure washers, even in experienced hands, can raise the grain of wood, giving it that fuzzy feeling. Some claim that pressure washing can drive mold spores back into the wood until they reappear later. Advocates claim that pressure washing is an efficient, thorough means of cleaning a deck as long as it's done properly. I've seen it go both ways, but I shy away from pressure cleaning wood.

Home-mixed solutions (such as one gallon of water, two cups of bleach, one cup of powdered soap) are OK for mildly dirty decks, but they won't do much for badly stained, weather-beaten wood. The outer surface of the wood has not only collected dirt and grime, it's also deteriorated.

Commercial deck cleaners clean and bleach the wood. Contractors and homeowners throughout the country swear by certain brands, some of which may not be nationally available. I suggest going to your local paint store and asking for the brand professional painters use in your area. These folks need fast-acting, effective products and will have narrowed the field down for you.

Sanding: Radical Cleaning

There's no better way than light sanding to get the surface of a badly deteriorated board clean; it removes dirt and stains and the top layer of wood as well. But it's a much more laborious process than washing with cleaners, scrub brushes, and a hose.

Decks aren't the best place to practice your floor sanding techniques unless you have a really large deck and a drum sander is the only practical means of sanding it. If you must use a floor sander, use a very light paper (100 *grit*), so you don't tear through the soft cedar and leave depressions.

I've done moderate-size decks with just a disk sander and the job goes relatively quickly without the expense or uneasiness of using a rented floor sander. If you sand, remember to use the finest paper in the recommended range so you leave only minimal sanding marks.

Give It Your Seal of Approval

Sealing is the second area of disagreement among deck refinishers and builders. Every company engaged in deck cleaning has their preferred sealer, claiming it to be the best in the solar system. My advice is to avoid the lowest-priced products and the clear water sealers. Buy a product with UV protection, a high percentage of solids (see the label), and a combination of oils rather than just linseed oil.

Look for a semi-transparent stain formulated specifically for decks, and follow the application directions closely. Don't apply any sealer in direct sunlight or while the deck is still hot. I've found that an old sponge mop makes a great applicator and gets the job done quickly.

Creature Comforts

After you've cleaned and repaired your deck, think about a few additions to it, such as:

➤ Planter boxes

➤ Benches

➤ Lights

Planter boxes have a nasty habit of trapping puddles of water under them, not the best thing for your deck. Set your planter boxes on top of some cedar two-by-two blocks and move them around once in a while so the decking under them can be cleaned.

The Least You Need to Know

➤ Once a common design feature on homes and later discarded, porches are making a comeback with some styles of new houses.

➤ A porch can last indefinitely with routine maintenance and repairs.

➤ Adding a new porch or expanding an existing one must be carefully planned so it matches the house stylistically.

➤ Any structurally sound deck can be cleaned and sealed to look almost like new, regardless of how stained it is.

Chapter 21

Garages: More Potential Than You Think

In This Chapter

➤ Seeing your garage as more than a huge catchall

➤ Making it warm and cozy

➤ Building a portable workshop in a tight parking space

➤ Improved storage for garages

Garages are wonderful spaces that get buried under old bicycles, boxes with unknown contents, and lawnmowers. In temperate climates like Seattle, where freezing weather isn't a common occurrence, people aren't that concerned with garaging cars overnight. That's a good thing, too, because a lot of garages are so stuffed they don't even have enough room in them for the cars they were intended to house.

Your first course of action should be to re-evaluate your attachment to everything you've managed to accumulate in your garage bays over the years. When was the last time you used that rock tumbler you picked up at your local hobby shop's going-out-of-business sale? If you're going to use the rowing machine, how come it's sitting in the garage? Get rid of all the unnecessary stuff, and you will resolve about half of your storage problems; you may even be able to get your car back in the garage.

After the garage is clean, you can deal with designs for storage and shelving and add some lights and maybe even some heat. Garages offer interesting possibilities because they're rarely thought of as having any possibilities. Your garage offers unrealized storage and work space. Some people even turn it into living space. We'll discuss all the possibilities in this chapter.

Look at It as a Small House

I've often said that the perfect guy house would be a five-car garage with a small studio apartment attached to it. Forget this living room and dining room nonsense, just give a car-loving, if-it-moves-on-wheels-I-want-it male a big garage, and he's happy. The family doesn't always go along with this plan, so he reluctantly agrees to buy a house and compromise on the garage fantasy.

Detached garages offer even more possibilities; they often do resemble small houses. Our last 1920s vintage house had a detached, one-car garage in which the previous owner had built a sauna, rendering it useless as a place to park a car. I converted the remaining space into an office, a place to run away to without having to run too far. It worked out great and at a very low cost.

A garage may look like a house, but it lacks the amenities. It's cold and dark and has no running water, and the color scheme usually leaves something to be desired. Why would anyone hang out there? Treat it like your other remodeling projects, and you will want to hang out in it.

Bring on the Power

New garages usually have one ceiling light per bay and one electrical outlet. Older garages, especially detached ones, may have a single light or no lighting at all, and forget the outlet. How much power do you need? What do you want to do out there?

If you want to build a woodworking empire, for instance, with a commercial-size table saw, planers, joiners, and an assortment of small power tools, you'd need as much power as you have in your kitchen. The table saw would require a 240 volt circuit (smaller saws can run on the usual 120 volt house current). Other hobbyists, such as potters with their kilns and jewelers with soldering equipment and polishers, would also benefit from a powered-up garage. There are practical concerns as well, such as running an outlet for an automatic garage door opener—one of civilization's finest inventions.

Put in plenty of light! You may have a hobby or other activity that calls for reading or other close visual work. This is no time to skimp on a few light fixtures.

Quick Fix

The fastest way to brighten up an otherwise sad-looking unfinished garage is to spray out the walls and ceiling with an inexpensive latex paint. Cheaper yet, mix together all your old latex paint and use that instead. It will look cheerier and give you an opportunity to practice your spraying techniques.

Plugging It In

Like any electrical project, you have to get the power where you want it when you wire the garage. You may be fortunate enough to have your electrical panel in the garage, which greatly simplifies your wiring chore. In an unfinished garage, you want to do all your drilling and stringing of the electrical cable first, before you insulate. Once the insulation is in, drilling around it would be a complete nuisance. What if your walls are finished already? Instead of tearing into them, you or an electrician can install surface-mounted *wire molding*.

Sometimes a power line is strung from a house to an older detached garage. Besides looking tacky, this kind of arrangement would never pass code today. Do yourself a favor and bury the line; it will look a lot cleaner when it comes time to sell the house, too.

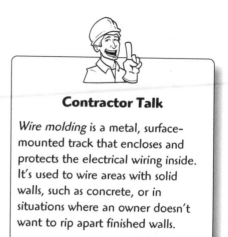

Contractor Talk

Wire molding is a metal, surface-mounted track that encloses and protects the electrical wiring inside. It's used to wire areas with solid walls, such as concrete, or in situations where an owner doesn't want to rip apart finished walls.

Now Insulate

Modern, attached garages are typically insulated and covered with drywall where they interface with the living space of the house. If one garage bay has a bedroom over it and the other bay does not, the first bay will be finished off and *fire-taped*. The other, unless you have a generous builder or you request it, will have open studs and no drywall.

You can choose between insulation batts, which is insulation that comes in precut sections, or rolls. Either will do the job and greatly increase the comfort of a working garage. Another plus would be installing a new, insulated steel garage door; it comes with the added benefit of never needing painting (theoretically, anyway). Get a good-quality door; some are pretty tinny.

Finish It Up

A garage is a great place to practice your drywall hanging and taping skills and carpentry, too. Why not add a window or two while you're in there? You'll want them small enough to rule out break-ins, but a few small windows (even a row of them) would make your garage a more welcoming workspace.

In cold climates, it makes no sense to finish your garage drywall unless the garage is going to be heated. In an unheated space, the drywall tape will shrink and crack.

Finishing Touches

Installing some baseboards and a bit of trim can dress up a garage. Remember, though, that the floor will get wet when you wash it. One solution is to install vinyl baseboard, the same type you see in hospitals, schools, and other cozy institutional settings.

Speaking of Floors

Painting the garage floor changes its appearance for the better, but don't go rushing into it. As you learned in Chapter 9, "Painting: Your House Is Your Canvas," there's a paint for every purpose, including floors. Some just do a better job than others. Your basic floor paint flavors are the following:

➤ Latex, the least durable

➤ Oil-based, which is more durable

➤ Epoxy, which is much better

Basic latex floor paint won't hold up to cars rolling over it, but it is a fast, quick makeover if you're getting ready to sell your house and want to brighten up the garage. Oil is better, but epoxy is the best of the three and is made to withstand abuse. As with any paint job, thoroughly clean the floor according to the paint container's instructions and fill cracks with a paintable masonry caulk.

Making an Artistic Statement

A garage is a good place to practice your remodeling skills. Try faux finishes on the walls or even on the floors. Hire a set maker from your local live theater and have your floors painted in some swanky marble or checkerboard finish (theater people do this kind of thing all the time, or you can buy a book on these finishes). Practice a little trompe l'oeil while you're at it. Install a hanging light over in one corner along with a rug, a card table, and a small stereo for your poker games. For that matter, build some walls in the corner and declare it to be your territory.

Quick Fix

Instead of doing a smooth drywall finish, experiment with texturing. Wet drywall compound can be roughly brushed with a wallpaper brush or rolled out with a thick nap paint roller for some intriguing results. Put it on thick and you'll hide the drywall tape and seams perfectly.

Heating Strategies

An insulated, well-sealed garage (tight-fitting doors, no loose windows) can be heated easily for your working comfort. You'll have to decide for yourself whether it's a wasteful practice. Having grown up in Ohio with a Tudor-style three-bay garage complete with hot running water, floor drains, multiple windows, and a solid concrete ceiling, I can tell you that a warm garage is a real treat. Of course, this also tells you where my inordinate interest in garages originated.

Your garage heat doesn't have to run as often as your house heat. The setback temperature, that is, the lowest temperature at which point the heat will kick in, can be set much lower to provide just enough heat for some basic comfort when you're not working in your garage. Heating options include:

➤ Extending the duct work from your furnace

➤ Electric baseboards

➤ Radiant heat

➤ Gas heater

➤ Wood stove

➤ Gas fireplace

The Easy Choice

Talk with your furnace contractor about running a duct off your current furnace to the garage. Because the thermostat is in the house, it won't sense the garage getting cold every time the doors are opened. Still, it may provide enough heat to take the edge off the cold during the winter.

Quick Fix

One way around any electrical heating limitations is the use of commercial grade, 240 volt, plug-in portable heaters with twist lock plugs. You'll have no trouble getting a permit for the 240 volt circuit (the same one needed for some table saws), and after that, you can do whatever you want with the power.

Electric Heat

Electric heat is an expensive way to go. Some municipalities will want you to meet stringent insulation standards and even then may not approve the use of electrical heat in a garage. (The more power demand, the more the utilities have to put out, and heating your garage isn't a big priority to them.)

A Gas with Gas

An overhead industrial gas heater, the same kind you find in auto mechanics' garages (all right, not in Hawaii), would quickly warm up a cold garage. Talk with your local gas company about sizes, clearances, and mounting height limitations.

The Natural Way

A wood stove, inconveniences aside, isn't a bad way to go for occasional garage heating. The stove would sit on a concrete floor, always a plus. It's also a great way to use up scrap lumber from woodworking projects. Or you could take your garage to a whole new level of garagedom and put in a gas fireplace. That would get you instant membership in the hard-core garage lovers of America.

Storage That Matters

Chances are your garage can use some efficient storage. Shelves, cabinets, and over-head hooks and hangers will organize the stuff of life in a hurry. The cardinal rule is: Get it off the floor! There's little reason why anything other than your car and a snowmobile should be cluttering up the floor. A neighbor of ours even takes exceptions to cars being on the floor: He had a mechanic's lift installed in his end garage bay so he could work on his Porsche.

The Simple Approach

Anyone can fabricate and install shelving; it's just planks and supports after all. You barely have to cut anything, but you will need a few tools, including:

➤ Measuring tape

➤ Level

➤ Drill

➤ Saw

A lumberyard can supply you with boards of any standard width or length you need. You can select from precut boards, or for a fee, the lumberyard will cut sheets of plywood and particle board to order. Metal shelf brackets take care of the rest. If you're feeling more creative, you can make your own wood supports from small boards as shown in the following figure.

Toxic Storage

Paints, thinners, pesticides, and the rest of your chemical parade must be stored securely. An upper shelf is OK, but a locked storage cabinet is better, especially if you're in an earthquake area. By the time your kids are old enough to break into the cabinet, they should be smart enough to understand the labels.

Not-So-Cheap Storage

Preassembled storage units abound in home improvement centers and stores that specialize in home storage solutions. Do a hard cost comparison between buying preassembled units and installing and building your own with lumber and brackets. The problem with any preassembled piece is that the dimensions may not fit your space; they often end up being too small, and you end up compromising.

To give a comparison, I installed shelving the length and width of our three-car garage on two of its sides using delivered boards, cut to my specifications, for $225, including the wood brackets! I even had enough material left over to build a small workbench. I got tons of shelving for a reasonable price and a day-and-a-half of my time (not exactly straining myself to put it all together).

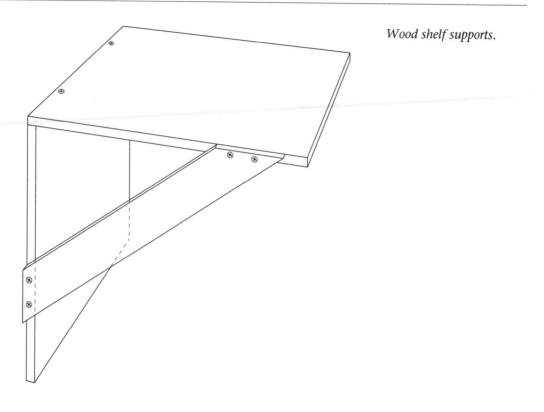

Wood shelf supports.

About That Woodshop

Unless a garage is really short, there's usually enough room at the front of a bay to put a workbench. If not, a simple fold-down workbench will do the trick for very little money. Back the car out, fold the bench down, and you're in business.

The Perfect Place to Pump Iron

Half a garage bay is more than enough space for setting up an exercise area. You can drop all the weights you want on the floor, and it won't make a bit of difference! Lay down a piece of scrap carpet or a remnant and move the rowing machine and the bench press in, and you're ready to go. You'll go a lot further if you've given your garage some creature comforts, such as lights, heat, and finished walls, that will encourage you to work out.

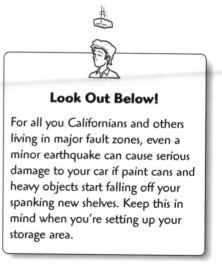

Look Out Below!

For all you Californians and others living in major fault zones, even a minor earthquake can cause serious damage to your car if paint cans and heavy objects start falling off your spanking new shelves. Keep this in mind when you're setting up your storage area.

Fold-down workbench.

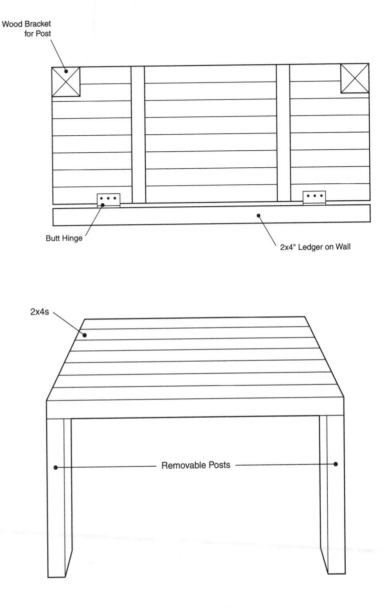

Want to try some kick boxing? There's no better place than the garage to set up a heavy punching bag. If you do it in the basement, you'll be shaking the floor joists every time you give the bag a good kick.

Get carried away and set up an entire gym in your garage: Weights, treadmill, rowing machine, and even a small refrigerator with cold juices. You may want to hold off on sponsoring a body building contest, though.

Living in Your Garage

Some homeowners convert their attached garages into living space. It's a tempting idea. You have an intact room that just needs some finishing up. It seems like a simple way to gain a new family room, office, or guest bedroom. But there are a few problems with this scenario:

> **Quick Fix**
>
> In a converted garage, you'll have a concrete floor to deal with, which is not the most comfortable surface to have under your feet. You'll want an extra comfortable carpet to put over the concrete.

➤ Unless it's done really well, it will always look like a converted garage, at least on the outside.

➤ You still have to put your car somewhere, and carports can look tacky compared to the garage you once had.

➤ Some municipalities have put the brakes on these conversions.

I think garage conversions work if you have room to build another garage. Consult a real estate broker and see if you could be negatively affecting the resale value of your home by doing this work.

A New Garage

Plan a new garage as thoroughly as you would an addition or a house itself. See how far the building code will let you go in terms of size, loft space, and plumbing installations. After mucking around in your yard, wouldn't you rather mess up a utility bathroom in the garage rather than the master bath? Think about installing a scrub sink and a floor drain as well; you'll have the cleanest car in town all winter long (clean cars are another one of those guy things).

Tales from the Scaffold

I knew one proposed garage remodel that got a little out of hand. What started out as "let's just add a storage loft" ended up ($75,000 later) as a two-story, two-car structure, with an apartment on top. It was finished off better than the main house!

The Least You Need to Know

➤ Think of your garage as more than a dead storage area; it has loads more to offer.

➤ Insulating and heating a garage will make it a comfortable area.

➤ Painting a garage floor gives you the biggest bang for the buck; it really cleans up the place.

➤ Garages are the ideal testing ground for some of your remodeling skills.

➤ Before you convert a garage to living space, give it plenty of thought.

Chapter 22

Lights, Walk-ways, Action: Remodeling Your Yard

In This Chapter

➤ Yard strategies, even if you're not a gardener

➤ Fencing yourself—and your yard—in

➤ Getting around: Concrete, bricks, and pavers

➤ Playing house in a house of their own

I'll be the first to admit that I'm not much of a yard person. After I grew up with a yard full of plants whose names I could never remember, but which demanded regular weeding and tending, I kept a distance. These days, I water the yard when I think about it and write a check to the guys who cut the lawn, but that's just my personal preference.

A well-laid-out yard has something for everyone: A play area for the kids, a vegetable garden for the house chef, and a couple of shade trees for napping in a hammock. A variety of plants and blooming periods bring color throughout the year. Maturing plants will gradually fill in gaps and empty spaces throughout your yard. If good fences make good neighbors, good hedges aren't too far behind.

Take a good look at your house and landscaping and ask yourself the same question you asked when you looked at the exterior of the house itself: What message is your yard sending? Could it stand an upgrade along with your house? At least you won't run into as many surprises digging around in your yard as you can digging inside of your walls.

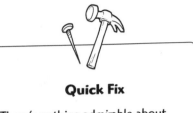

Quick Fix

There's nothing admirable about mowing your own lawn. If you don't enjoy it, hire it out to a licensed mowing service and spend your yard time doing something more enjoyable, like planting bulbs or sitting in an Adirondack chair reading the Sunday paper.

One big plus to landscaping is the cost: Depending on the route you take, it can be in dollars or in your own labor. You can spend a little on simple ground cover and plants grown from seed, or take out a second mortgage to build teak gazebos and a spawning stream for salmon. Plans and a budget, the two constants in remodeling, will lead you out of your landscaping wilderness.

Ideas by the Yard

Unless you're an avid gardener who loves to peruse seed catalogs, you probably want to spend as little time as possible maintaining your yard. You just want a little color and variety that won't strain your budget or your back.

Your yard, like your house, reflects your tastes, values, and willingness to invest time and money in it. A formal house might call for a formal yard with orderly, pruned plants placed in specific beds throughout your yard. A more informal style will be less stodgy with more of a mix of different types of plants. You may prefer more dramatic elements like a rock garden or stone walls that call for fewer flowers and shrubs, but more subtle trailing plants. Decide on a yard style and plan accordingly.

Look at your yard with the same scrutinizing eye that you've learned to use on your house:

➤ Address the big issues, such as drainage, overgrown plants, and trees whose roots are tearing up your sidewalk.

➤ Keep it simple; the more plants and varieties you have, the more maintenance they'll require.

➤ Be honest with yourself about how big a garden space you want to look after.

➤ Use ground cover in areas of your yard that don't cover well with grass.

➤ Use heavy applications of mulch to help keep weeds down and conserve water at the same time.

➤ Fertilize less, unless you want your plants to grow more and need pruning and thinning.

➤ Note where grass is worn from heavy foot traffic and pave these areas with walkways; be sure they're wide enough to accommodate a lawnmower passing through.

➤ Consider planting a hedge for some greenery and a low-maintenance means of privacy (a fence needs painting and repairs, a hedge only needs trimming).

➤ Before you get carried away with vegetable gardening (witness the piles of zucchini people try to give away every fall), start with a small plot and see how much it yields.

➤ Plant flowers in narrow beds for easy maintenance; plant tons of flowers in limited varieties to fill up the beds.

➤ Go native; local varieties have long adapted to your specific environment and will hold up the best.

➤ Buy your plants at a reputable nursery; check out their return policy and inquire about planting and fertilizing procedures for your specific plant selections.

Look Out Below!

It's tempting to hire someone who's unlicensed to do yard work. We've all done it, but if that person has an accident on your property, guess who can be responsible for medical bills, or worse, a lawsuit? You—the employer. Stick with a licensed company and let them deal with any problems.

The Big Picture

What do you need your yard to do? It's easy to define the role of your kitchen, for example: Cooking, eating, storing food, and socializing. You may see your yard as nothing more than a spot of green to be mowed and watered only when necessary, a playground for your kids, or a quiet escape. The function of your yard will determine how you lay it out and what you plant, regardless of the style of yard you choose. This function will determine, among other things:

➤ Whether you plant trees to increase shade in the summer or remove existing ones to improve your view

➤ If you should construct a deck or patio

➤ Whether to plant more grass or more flowers and shrubs

➤ How big the plants you buy should be

Look at your yard from inside your house. Every room gives you a different view. What do you want to see? From an inside viewpoint, your yard will look like a painting through each window. You can be looking at Art 101 or Van Gogh depending on how much work you want to put into it.

Quick Fix

Painters, window washers, and other contractors who work on house exteriors consider bushes, shrubs, and trees planted too close to the house the bane of their existence. When you plant near your house, factor in a few extra feet, depending on the future growth of the plants, to keep them away from the siding. You'll thank yourself the first time you have to paint outside.

Getting Serious

If you have budget constraints, extensive landscaping can take years to complete, but you can save both time and money if you make a well-thought-out plan first. Why? Because you'll avoid having to redo random planting after two or three years when it doesn't work out as you expected it to. Alder trees, for example, grow very quickly, at least in the northwest. Two or three of them may seem like a great idea, but in a few years, they'll be overshadowing your house. That's not the time to find out that what you really wanted were some flowering dogwoods.

Tales from the Scaffold

Take a tip from a contractor I knew who wanted mature plants in his yard without waiting years for them to grow. He had clients who wanted to remove their huge rhododendrons, so he dug around them, removed them with his truck winch, and replanted them in his own yard. When he was done, his yard looked like it had been that way for years.

Vegetables Galore

It's easy to incorporate some vegetables, notably tomatoes, into an existing flower garden, but for all of your vegetable needs, set aside one area of your yard in a sunny location. To enrich your vegetable plot, you may want to include a compost bin in your yard design. It's a great way to use up your grass clippings and leaves from fall cleanups, but you'll have to commit to mixing and watering the decomposing material regularly. Whatever you do, go easy on putting in too many zucchini plants.

Ardent gardeners work on their gardens in the winter, too, by raising plants from seeds indoors. Seeds and potting soil are cheap, so you can have plenty of landscaping material at a bargain price if you grow your own plants. Need advice? Gardeners are a talkative lot. Contact a local gardening club, community college, or university extension class for information on local gardening practices.

Beyond Plants: Walls and Fences

Good fences may make good neighbors, but fences are a nuisance to build and maintain. Many people seem to believe that a cedar fence, for instance, needs little maintenance and let them go unprotected for years. This is exactly why you see so many deteriorated fences in need of replacement. Intricate fences with narrow pickets are very time-consuming to paint, but they're a traditional yard feature and will not be disappearing anytime soon.

Fences serve several purposes, including:

➤ Privacy

➤ Protection

➤ Keeping kids and pets from wandering

➤ Decoration

➤ Defining a particular space

The style and design of your fence is limited only by your imagination. The building code doesn't mandate the technique you use to construct it or the space between pickets or posts, though a permit is usually needed for any fence taller than 6 feet. Check with your building department regarding setbacks (how far you can build from the property lines).

Setting the Posts

Cedar, redwood, and pressure-treated wood are typically used for fence posts, but only ground-contact-treated wood has a decent chance of holding up to a ripe old age. Untreated posts, especially fir or alder, don't last long at all unless the buried sections are first treated with wood preservative. Even then, their longevity isn't terrific.

Your post hole should be dug deep, below the frost line, so it won't heave and move as the ground freezes. Though posts can be set in the ground with gravel and dirt packed around them, you're better off setting them in concrete, especially the corner posts and midway post, which ensure that the fence is supported.

A Clever Fence Idea

I can't take credit for this—it's an architect's idea featured in *Sunset Magazine* some years ago—but here's a great way to assemble a fence:

1. Install and align all the posts.

2. Build a U-shaped wood bracket on each post.

3. Pre-build each fencing section with end pieces that will slip into the brackets.

4. Secure with two small deck screws to each post.

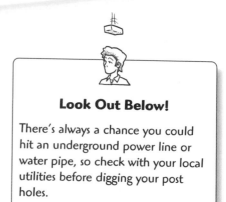

Look Out Below!

There's always a chance you could hit an underground power line or water pipe, so check with your local utilities before digging your post holes.

A cool way to build a fence.

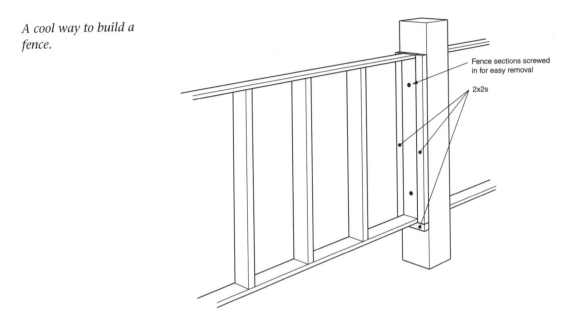

Fence sections screwed in for easy removal

2x2s

The whole idea of the fence is to have removable sections, which are far easier to paint and allow easier movement in and out of the yard for wheelbarrows and other large pieces of equipment.

Tales from the Scaffold

Plastic has hit the fence world, too, with vinyl products that never need painting and, until a polymer-loving termite comes along, won't be eaten by insects. Manufacturers offer a variety of colors and styles, from traditional to modern. Check out your local lumber store or home improvement center for details and samples.

Real Walls

You have several choices for outdoor wall construction, all of them heavy. Retaining walls and privacy walls can be built from these materials:

➤ Interlocking concrete blocks

➤ Brick

➤ Poured concrete

➤ Stone

➤ Boulders

These materials will never rot or need painting, but retaining walls can be pushed out and crack from too much pressure. You also may need to install drains in the soil banking against the wall to keep it from becoming too saturated and eventually moving. Used for a privacy wall, these materials will last forever—all the more reason to be absolutely certain you're not building it on the wrong side of the property line!

Wiring the Great Outdoors

Outdoor lighting adds to your security and comfort and has resale appeal to a future buyer. But keep in mind that any outdoor lighting you install (and I wholeheartedly recommend that you do) has to be done in conjunction with your landscaping efforts. You don't want to dig up a flower garden because you didn't think to bury an electrical cable when you were tilling the soil to plant. Also, all outdoor lights should be on a dedicated circuit.

Be imaginative in your lighting selection (as far as your budget allows). Tiffany Landscape Lighting is on the high end of landscape lighting (www.tifannyll.com), with copper halogen lighting and leaded stained glass globes. See what's available at your local lighting supplier and check their catalogs if you don't see anything in stock that you like.

Tales from the Scaffold

There's outdoor lighting, and there's outdoor lighting. Every Christmas, the newspapers find homeowners around the country who put up very elaborate light displays, using tens of thousands of lights. Some require their own generators. Inevitably, there are lawsuits by neighbors who are seen as spoilsports because they don't like living across the street from a Las Vegas–style light show. The biggest ever? A one-million-bulb display was reported a few years ago.

No More Mud: Real Sidewalks

You always know when a rural area is being gentrified by the appearance of sidewalks. Is it time to gentrify your yard? A well-worn path eventually becomes a muddy path and one ripe for improvement. How do you want to do it? What do you want to walk on?

Concrete is an obvious choice. Aside from a few cracks that may develop as it cures, it's there forever. Sweep it off, and your maintenance is finished.

Before your walk goes in, you or a contractor must do the following:

1. Measure out and excavate the area.
2. *Tamp* and grade the soil.
3. Spread the gravel layer.
4. Build forms to contain the concrete.
5. Mix the concrete or order a load for delivery.
6. Pour concrete.
7. Tamp and screed the poured concrete.

This big job usually requires at least two people, especially if you're mixing single batches of concrete and pouring them one at a time. If you're ordering concrete, the pour site must be ready when the driver shows up; otherwise, you'll be paying a hefty hourly fee for the driver to wait for you to finish up.

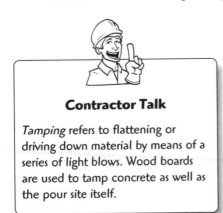

Contractor Talk

Tamping refers to flattening or driving down material by means of a series of light blows. Wood boards are used to tamp concrete as well as the pour site itself.

There are more decorative approaches than plain concrete, but they require more handwork to finish. Special stamping tools (think of them as cookie cutters for concrete) are used to create cobblestone, brick, herringbone, and hexagonal finishes, among others. You can add pebbles to the surface of wet concrete and even powdered pigment for color. With a few hand tools, you can create a flagstone effect or produce a textured surface using a stiff push broom.

Follow the Brick Road

Brick pavers are made specifically for street and sidewalk use. You can lay salvaged building bricks down as a sidewalk, but they won't hold up well to automobile traffic (in case you were thinking of building a driveway out of them). Laying brick requires some of the same steps as pouring concrete, including:

➤ Preparing the site

➤ Tamping the soil and spreading a layer of sand

➤ Laying the bricks and tapping them in place while maintaining an even, level surface

Bricks offer great versatility in design. Lay them about ¹/₈-inch apart and fill the gaps by sweeping sand into them to help keep weeds from growing through (some will anyway). This job is so tedious and time-consuming that concrete doesn't seem so bad after all!

Concrete Pavers

Bricks are basically a mix of baked clay or shale, hardened in a hot kiln. Concrete pavers are formed when concrete is pressed in molds under high pressure. They're available in a great variety of shapes for your sidewalks and patios, and some are interlocking for easier installation. Prepare the ground the same way you would for brick pavers.

Local codes spell out requirements for concrete work, but it's doubtful that you'll find any rules covering the installation of brick or concrete pavers—it's not considered permanent construction. As a precaution, you should check anyway.

If You Live in the Snow Belt

Heated sidewalks and driveways seem to be real indulgences, but maybe not to someone who lives in northern Minnesota, land of the snow, ice, and blood-freezing temperatures. Sophisticated melting systems, consisting of heating cables and built-in

From mud to a paved patio. (Photo courtesy of Dan Thane, Thane Construction)

moisture and temperature sensors, will allow you to put away the rock salt and snow shovels forever, according to the melting systems' manufacturers.

Forever is a very long claim. Before you install any melting system, ask to see some existing ones (5 to 10 years old at least), and ask people who have them how well they've worked. You don't want to make such a major investment only to find that the cables go lukewarm after a few years.

Little Houses for Little People

Some parents—especially architect and builder parents—get carried away when they build a playhouse for their kids. The best playhouse for a child is one that promotes imaginative use rather than determining that use through its design. As your children grow, they'll use their playhouse differently, so it's best to build a flexible design. A four-year-old may see it as a cave one day and a rocketship the next. A 15-year-old, on the other hand, will see it as a place to sneak beers with friends.

You can exercise your construction skills by building a small playhouse. All the principles of design, framing, roofing, and finish carpentry are the same as they are for your own house. You can even wire it for lights and power, but you'll need a permit to do so. Check any covenants that may affect the placement of a playhouse on your property.

The Least You Need to Know

➤ Planning your remodeling is just as important for your yard as it is for your house.

➤ The greater variety of plants you want, the more work you'll have maintaining them.

➤ Good preparation work is critical before installing any type of sidewalk.

➤ Be sure you know where your property line is located before you build a fence. If you're uncertain, hire a surveyor.

➤ Fences, walls, and concrete sidewalks all require permits from your building department. Check with them before beginning construction.

Part 6

And Baby Makes Three: Additions to Your Home

Upgrading a bathroom or adding some kitchen cabinets is one thing, but an addition can be far more intimidating. Besides opening your house to the world by tearing into a wall or removing part of the roof, you wonder how well it will match up with the rest of the house, and if it's worth the expense. In some places, you can buy an entire house or condominium for the price of an addition.

An addition requires more planning and financial projections than just about any other remodeling project. Your design is critical, especially from a structural stand- point. Miscalculate your loads or the size of your footings and you could end up with a Leaning Tower of Pisa addition—a real possibility if you go ahead without a permit and approved plans. Inspectors and architects play critical roles here: They're supposed to catch design and building flaws before you get too far ahead in your construction (and usually they do).

You have to go through just as many steps to add on a new room of 100 square feet as you do for 500, so err on the side of bigness. If your budget allows it, think about going a little bit larger than you need, without building way out of proportion to the rest of the house. Extra space is often a selling point. No doubt you'll find use for it as well.

Chapter 23

The Big Leagues: Adding a Room

In This Chapter

➤ Starting at the bottom with your foundation

➤ Main frame: Walls, floors, and more

➤ Wiring and insulation

➤ Covering it up with drywall, finish floors, and paint

➤ The final details

A first-floor addition is kind of a microcosm of house construction. You'll use all the different construction trades: Carpentry, concrete work, roofing, drywall hanging and finishing, electrical work, and even window-washing. You can pick and choose the work you want to do yourself and the jobs you want to hire out.

Building a first-floor addition is much simpler than going up to the second or third story. You don't have to erect scaffolding, and even the siding work is easier because it can be done from a couple of 10-foot step-ladders. There are few ways to simplify this kind of remodeling, however. A small room may take less time to build than a larger one, but you can't eliminate any of the necessary steps. For instance, you can't hang the drywall until the electrical work has passed an inspection.

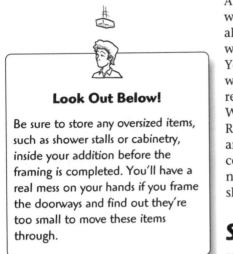

Look Out Below!

Be sure to store any oversized items, such as shower stalls or cabinetry, inside your addition before the framing is completed. You'll have a real mess on your hands if you frame the doorways and find out they're too small to move these items through.

A room addition can be cheaper than moving and will add value to your house at the same time. You already know how to run the numbers (see the worksheet at the end of Chapter 1, "Your Home Is Your Castle—Keep It That Way!") to determine whether your remodeling will pay itself back upon resale. If you've read Chapters 6, "Fixing Your House Without Breaking the Bank," and 7, "Prepare First; Remodel Later," you know how to draw up a plan and specifications, find an architect, and pick your contractors. When you try your hand at building a new room, you'll put all those skills to work.

Seeking Approval

Your work will start with a plan, of course, followed by a visit to your building department. An approved plan will get you a permit; an unapproved plan will take you back to the drawing board for Plan 2.0, the one without any bugs. Why would the building department turn you down? There could be any number of reasons, including the following:

➤ The addition violates setback requirements.

➤ The proposed foundation is inadequate.

➤ Framing, ventilation, or electrical requirements aren't being met.

There could be other reasons, and you want to find them out before you start building rather than during it or afterward. Sometimes it's a question of how the code is being interpreted, and your architect or designer can step in and explain the reasoning for the design. Codes are like any other rules: They seem clear on paper, but they cannot cover all situations.

Every city and town has its own rules on setbacks, or the distance your house is from your property lines. Your zoning—residential, commercial, and agricultural—determines which setbacks you'll have to follow. Within each zoning designation, there are even more distinctions, so confirm your property's zoning designation and plan accordingly.

Floor Thoughts

You need a foundation, but what kind of floor do you want? The simplest is a concrete slab, but it's more uncomfortable to walk on than a wood floor built on joists. Concrete is pretty unforgiving on the feet and knees. A slab is the easier of the two to install if you follow these steps:

1. Compact the soil. Using a rented vibratory rammer is the easiest way to compact the soil. For larger areas, rent a vibratory plate compactor.

2. Level the high spots (where the concrete would be too thin) and the low spots (they require too much concrete to fill).

3. Install drainage to remove existing water and prevent future water buildup.

4. Add a 4- to 6-inch layer of gravel over the compacted soil.

5. Lay two sheets of 6 mil plastic over the gravel to act as a vapor barrier.

If you decide you'd rather have a wood floor, then you can skip pouring the concrete slab; all you'll need to do to prepare the soil is level it out with landscaping tools and lay down heavy plastic to prevent moisture from affecting your wood floor and framing.

Pouring a Foundation and a Slab

The dimensions of your foundation and footings will depend on the size and weight of your addition. Your architect or planner will calculate your foundation's dimensions and order the appropriate concrete.

Once your footing and concrete requirements have been established, you build your foundation by following these steps:

1. Build the forms to contain the concrete.

2. Install rebar (reinforcing steel bars) to strengthen the concrete.

3. Call for inspection.

4. Pour concrete.

5. Install anchor bolts (these secure wood framing to the foundation) in wet concrete.

6. Call for next inspection.

The next step is to let the concrete cure. Concrete cures by means of a chemical reaction with water. To prevent the water from evaporating prematurely, you must do one of the following:

1. Spray the surface with a commercial curing compound.

2. Cover the concrete with wet burlap.

3. Mist the concrete and cover it with plastic.

While the concrete is curing, work on your drainage around the foundation.

Did you decide you wanted a slab? You'll need to reinforce it with wire mesh manufactured for this purpose or rebar. The mesh is laid down in the wet concrete and strengthens your slab as it cures.

Concrete slab construction.

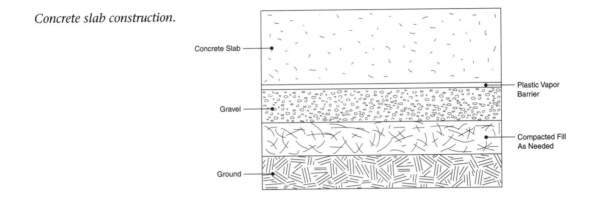

Concrete Slab

Gravel

Ground

Plastic Vapor Barrier

Compacted Fill As Needed

Building a Wood Floor

Concrete slab floor construction is usually reserved for basements or entry-level laundry rooms and inexpensive housing. Given the choice, you can't beat a wood floor for comfort and warmth. Building a wood joist floor is fairly simple:

1. A minimum 18-inch crawl space is maintained between the bottom of the joist and the plastic-covered ground (be sure to build an access door to the crawl space). The foundation wall, individual piers, and beam(s) act as supports for the joist.

2. The end joist are secured to the sill plates (also called mud sills) and are then secured to the remaining joist.

3. Plumbing, electrical, and heating ducts are installed under and through the joist.

4. The building department inspects the work.

5. Insulation is installed and inspected.

6. Plywood or OSB (oriented strand board) subfloor is glued and nailed or screwed to the joist.

7. Depending on the type of finish floor, an underlayment may be installed on top of the subfloor (for example, ceramic tile backerboard would be installed for tile floors).

(Before you go running to your dictionary, joist is singular and plural—I didn't forget the "s"!)

A wood floor gives you some leeway in the future if you ever have to repair it or run additional plumbing or wiring. Admittedly, it is more expensive than a concrete slab, so weigh the costs versus the advantages carefully.

Get the Moisture Out

Your local building code also requires foundation vents to establish cross-ventilation as a minimum requirement for your general health and safety. If you think you need another vent or two, go ahead and put them in. Be sure they have attached insect screens (the smaller the screen the better).

Quick Fix

An architect will designate a nailing pattern in the job specifications, and your contractor must follow it. It spells out the length of nail or screw to be used and the distance that must be between them (every 8 inches, for instance). The pattern will vary with the material being fastened.

One Frame Coming Up

Now that you have something solid under your feet, it's time to start framing. You'll need to cut the existing siding away so your new wall can be screwed directly to the sheathing. Using screws instead of nails to attach these end studs to your existing wall will protect any interior plaster from hammering, which can lead to cracking. You can keep the rest of the sheathing intact until your new addition is closed up to the weather. At that point, you can cut into your existing wall for your new doorway.

Platform framing (the construction of one level of a house at a time) is the most common framing practice in residential construction, and the type of framing you'll most likely be doing. Your plans will call out the dimension of the lumber to be used and the location of doors and windows.

Not as Simple as It Looks

Framing is a science and also a bit of an art form. It looks easy: Just pound a bunch of boards and nails together, and you have a wall. If you don't follow certain procedures, however, you might not have the wall you were expecting. Each wall:

➤ Should be square and straight

➤ Must tie into the next wall in such a way that the drywall will have a nailing surface

➤ Gets a second top plate (the cap plate) nailed onto the first

➤ Needs bracing, backing, blocking, and fire stops installed as required or advised

First-floor addition.

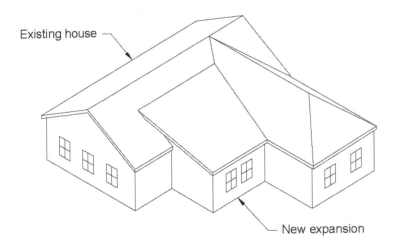

Existing house

New expansion

How you fasten the boards together is important. There are nails for every purpose, so you'll never lack for the correct fastener. Usually, you'll want to use the longest nail you can that won't exceed the thickness of the wood you're fastening. The minimum length of a framing nail, for instance, is $3^1/_2$ inches, which is a 16 *penny* or 16d nail. As a rule of thumb, you should figure on using a nail which is at least equal in length to twice the thickness of the material being nailed. You would use a 1-inch nail to secure a $^1/_2$-inch piece of plywood, for example.

Open Up

Installing a window or door means cutting away some of the wall studs. If you remove studs, you weaken the wall, so you have to reinforce the opening. A door or window opening is strengthened by installing more framing members, including:

➤ A horizontal header over the door or window

➤ King studs and trimmers to support the header

➤ A horizontal sill at the bottom of a window opening

➤ Cripples, or short studs, that run up from the floor to support the sill or run from a header to a top plate

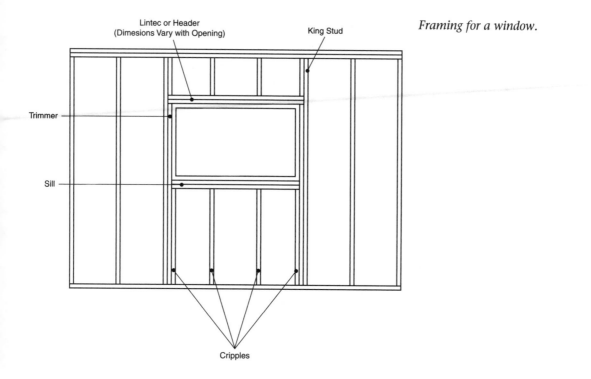

Framing for a window.

A poorly supported header is a problem waiting to happen. If there's a golden rule in carpentry, it's this: You can't go wrong overbuilding when you frame. An extra support, fire block, or bit of cross-bracing will never hurt anything. Sturdiness rules!

Up on the Roof

Prefabricated trusses are increasingly replacing individual rafters that used to frame a roof, though rafters are still used on attic conversions or other designs where a truss would take up too much room. A prefabricated truss is composed of top and bottom chords connected by either a series of triangularly placed braces or a sheet of oriented strand board (OSB).

These roof trusses are made to order and are terrific time savers. You supply your lumberyard with your job specifications (roof style, dimensions, installation of skylights, and pitch), and three weeks or so later the trusses are delivered to your job site. If size or location necessitates it, a crane can lift them to the top of your exterior walls.

Once the trusses or rafters are in place, your roof will need to be sheathed with either:

➤ Plywood (for composition shingles, tile)

➤ Skip sheathing (for wood shakes or shingles)

Your plans should call for a roof that will blend flawlessly with your existing roof. You don't want your addition to look like an add-on. An inspection should be scheduled after the roof and wall framing are up.

Hello Steel, Good-bye Wood

Look Out Below!

Your roof trusses are built according to your plans and specifications. Your wall framing must follow the same plans and be built plumb and straight; otherwise, your trusses may not fit properly. Trusses are engineered supports and cannot be structurally altered without the approval of an engineer or the manufacturer.

Steel studs, joists, and trusses are being used more than ever in residential construction. I suspect they'll eventually surpass wood for framing. Steel has a few advantages:

➤ It's always straight and will not warp.

➤ Insects can't damage it.

➤ Insurance companies like it, and that means lower homeowner rates.

➤ Its pricing has become competitive with wood.

Steel structural framing, such as floor joists, must be welded at the joints by a certified welder. As more framers become trained to install steel, there will probably be quite an increase in its use.

Start Closing It Up

You have the roof on, but what about the walls? Your sheathing can be either plywood or OSB, the two standard sheathing materials for just about everything. The sheathing gets covered with building paper or house wrap (plastic, such as Dupont's Tyvek) as a moisture barrier.

Roof truss.

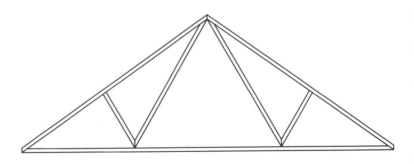

The siding for your addition and your existing siding should match. Sometimes a match isn't possible if you have a discontinued material such as asbestos tiles, but some mills may run custom orders of contemporary facsimiles, such as cedar shingles, to match older style combed cedar ones.

Matching Your Existing Windows

Windows are a major architectural and design element of your house. The wrong window is a dead giveaway that you've added on without thinking it through. Fortunately, wood windows can always be duplicated with new wood versions.

Order your windows well in advance of building your addition and be sure to note the thickness of the wall (two-by-four or two-by-six construction) with your order. New windows will use insulated glass that will stand out against any old, single-pane windows, but that's a minor consideration. What they lack in being the perfect match they make up for in comfort and U-factor.

Paint It and Head Inside

The roof's on, the windows are in, and the siding is up: Now seal the house with paint or stain. The later in the year you work, the more important it is to get this done. I say this as someone who lives in the Seattle area, where, in early 1999, we had over 7 feet of rain in a period of 105 days. Try to paint in that kind of weather!

An Inside Job

Your addition's interior work can be put off indefinitely if need be, but you'll probably be anxious to get started. Now you can cut through your existing wall and connect the two rooms. Remember, this wall is a load-bearing wall! Any studs you remove must be replaced with new supports in the form of a header, trimmers, and king studs. Depending on the size of your opening, you may have to install temporary supports against the ceiling until your doorway has been framed.

Your room still has open walls at this point, which makes wiring and any plumbing a breeze. But if you decide to heat the room using your existing furnace, running a duct can be a problem. There's no easy way to do it, so consult with your architect and heating technician about your options.

> **Contractor Talk**
>
> The *U-factor* measures a window's conduction of heat, that is, the total window efficiency, not just the glass. The lower the rating is, the more efficient the window.

Quick Wiring: Electrical, Cable, Phone, Security, Internet

Wiring your addition is simply a matter of hooking up with a power source. You will most likely have to go back to the panel and run your circuits, but always check the existing circuits first. If one of them has room to safely add the outlets in your addition, consider tapping into it instead of fishing wire back to the panel.

Phone and cable wiring can run from the nearest existing outlets. Not sure who's going to win the future cable/phone/Internet access wars? You may not be ready to sign up with the current front-runner, but as long as you have an accessible crawl space, you can always pull cables later. In the meanwhile, go ahead and install the most promising contender.

> **Quick Fix**
>
> You can save some time by ordering primed siding for the exterior of your addition. If you have the room in your garage, spread out the siding and apply the first coat of paint prior to installation.

Most wires and pipes running through wall studs need a metal plate hammered into the edge of the stud to prevent nails and drywall screws from damaging the wire or pipe. These protective plates are an absolute necessity and come with a prong in each of the four corners for easy installation. After your rough-in electrical work is done, it's time to call for an inspection.

Insulation in Open Walls

Fiberglass insulation in either pre-cut batts or rolls is the way to go when you insulate your addition. These rolls are manufactured to fit between wall studs and joists of varying sizes and spacing, and all you or your installer have to do is measure, cut, tuck the insulation into the wall or ceiling, and staple the edge of the paper or foil to the studs.

When installing fiberglass insulation, keep these issues in mind:

> **Look Out Below!**
>
> Your house temperature must be at least 55 degrees, and preferably warmer, before you do any taping. A warm temperature must be maintained so the mud will dry; otherwise, it will dry unevenly and crack.

➤ In cold climates, the foil side or vapor barrier faces the interior of the room; in warm climates, it goes against the sheathing.

➤ Buy the correct size insulation for the framing, wall, and ceiling you are insulating.

➤ Wear a protective mask, long-sleeve shirt, and gloves while installing insulation.

Insulation requires a separate inspection.

It's a Cover-up: Installing Drywall

After all of your wiring, plumbing (if any), and insulation has been inspected, you can cover your walls. Drywall may be easier to install than plaster, but it isn't *that* easy. Three groups of workers are involved in the drywall trade: stockers who deliver drywall, hangers who install it, and tapers who do the finish work. If you're going to be the hanger and taper, make sure you read the tips about installing drywall in Appendix G, "Repairs." Schedule the delivery of the material as close to its installation date as possible.

Taping and finishing drywall is a three-to-four-step process. Several layers of joint compound are needed to hide and smooth over the joints. Sanding the joint compound or mud is a dusty, messy process, so be sure to tape a sheet of plastic up in the opening between your addition and the adjoining room.

Prime and Paint

Once your drywall work is finished and the room is clean, you can prime and paint the walls and ceiling. You can apply two finish coats of paint before installing your trim, but often for a top notch job you'll need to put your final coat of paint on the walls after all of your woodwork is installed.

Trim Time

To trim a room out means to install the finish woodwork: baseboards, door and window casings, and the doors themselves. Just as you tried to match the exterior features of your house, try to match the interior trim in the addition to the trim in the rest of the house.

Drywall that's almost ready to paint.

Quick Fix

Pre-hung doors come fitted in their own door jambs. Install the jamb correctly and you don't have to worry about the door fitting. Take advantage of technology and use a pre-hung door. Custom-made doors can also be ordered pre-hung.

The five most important tools you'll need to trim off your addition are these:

➤ Measuring tape

➤ Power miter box or chop saw

➤ Level

➤ Hammer

➤ Nail set

Your choice of flooring will have some effect on the rest of your finish work. If you choose carpet, for instance, you won't need to install a base shoe. Hardwood will have to be installed before your baseboards and door trim, with the base shoe to follow.

Finishing Touches

If all your work was done in an orderly manner, you have only a handful of tasks to finish now:

➤ Install the lights, sconces, cover plates for the outlets, and the switch plates.

➤ Put a final coat of finish on your wood floors.

➤ Touch up the paint.

➤ Wash the windows.

Is That It?

Building a single-room addition involves a lot of tasks, coordination, and finish work. Can you do this yourself? Sure, if you have the time and the temperament. But it's a lot easier to fit a job like repainting your bedroom into a busy schedule than it is to add on a new family room.

The Least You Need to Know

➤ Even a modest addition will require many building skills and inspections by your building department.

➤ Stay ahead of the weather when you add onto your house by completing the framing, siding, and roofing as quickly as possible.

➤ Carefully weigh the costs and attributes of a concrete slab floor versus a wood floor when you design your addition.

➤ None of the individual construction trades is an easy one. When work is done by an inexperienced homeowner rather than a talented contractor, there will always be a tradeoff in results.

Chapter 24

Going Up: Second-Story Additions

Adding a second story to a house is one of the most dramatic remodeling jobs you can do. Everything changes: The roof line, the views, bathroom availability, and your degree of privacy (all that extra room gives you a place or two to hide). First-floor bedrooms can now be used for other purposes. Unlike a ground-floor addition, a second-story addition won't take away an inch of your yard space.

A second-story addition is a complicated job that can run into snags such as height limitations, complaints from neighbors, and your possibly having to relocate during part or all of the work process. If you stay in the house and listen to hammers and electric saws all day, you'll never complain about the neighborhood kids playing basketball again.

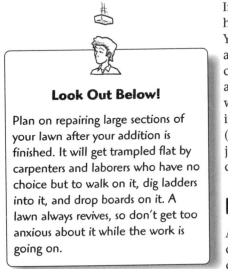

Look Out Below!

Plan on repairing large sections of your lawn after your addition is finished. It will get trampled flat by carpenters and laborers who have no choice but to walk on it, dig ladders into it, and drop boards on it. A lawn always revives, so don't get too anxious about it while the work is going on.

If you're considering adding this much space to your house, a real estate broker will be a valued consultant. You have to calculate whether your neighborhood and its projected property values will support the current price of your house plus the expense of the addition. If you're the first kid on your block of post-war, one-story homes to grow into a two-story house, it could be years before you get your investment back (if ever). But if all signs point to proceeding with the job, be prepared for a load of work and a greatly changed house.

Design Considerations

Adding a second story gives you the opportunity to change the entire style of your house. The usual candidates for these additions are old bungalows and post-war one-story houses. You don't have to stick with any of the original architectural elements, though many people do. Your design decisions will be guided by these factors:

➤ Your neighborhood

➤ The appeal of the original design

➤ The cost of altering the first-floor features to match your new second story (instead of the other way around)

If you decide to go the fake French chateau route, owners of a neighborhood full of turn-of-the-century Craftsman homes will shun both you and your remodel. Plain, unadorned, working-class houses are the ideal choice for total makeovers, in part because they have so much to gain. A new second story is the perfect excuse to redo the exterior of the first floor by replacing the windows, siding, and trim to match the addition.

Giving It Some Structure

Building up means that all your support is down below at the foundation, which wasn't expecting the extra responsibilities. You need to have an engineer or architect calculate the load and ascertain if your foundation can handle it. You may also have to alter or add to your load-bearing walls to carry the increased weight. Your existing attic joists probably won't be big enough to support a habitable space, which means adding new, bigger joists across the floor span. Don't assume anything until you've had an analysis done. The last thing you want is to start an addition of this size only to find out that your foundation footings are undersized.

What Will the Neighbors Think?

When you increase the height of your house, your neighbors can be your friends or your foes. Possible neighborhood complaints to a building department or city architectural oversight committee can include:

➤ Views will be blocked

➤ The resulting house will be out of proportion to others in the neighborhood

➤ The changed architectural style no longer matches the neighbors' houses

➤ Privacy issues are raised (looking down on nearby houses from a second-floor vantage point)

These concerns are very real and have blocked upper story additions in neighborhoods everywhere. The city or local municipality has the final power of approval, and yours might have a habit of listening to disgruntled neighbors. Accommodating neighbors won't fight your request for a *variance*, but if any neighbors oppose your plans, a variance will just add fuel to the fire. Variances can take months to be approved, so start the process early. If public meetings are required to review your request, winter is a good time to file it: Lousy weather may keep everyone away. When opposition rears its ugly head, maybe you should ask yourself if you want to stay in a neighborhood that disapproves of the way you want to live.

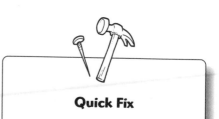

Quick Fix

Minor design changes can get an otherwise unapproved plan passed. For instance, neighbors complaining about a loss of privacy may not have an argument if you remove side windows facing their house. Replace the windows with skylights for natural light.

Contractor Talk

A *variance* is an exception to the zoning regulations. You may apply for a variance if your plans don't meet these regulations. A variance request may be followed by a period for public comment.

Upgrading the Entire House

If a house is old enough to be upgraded by a second-story addition, it's probably old enough to need substantial upgrading elsewhere. Major remodels like this have a way of moving downward and affecting the rest of the house, so you may have to make the following changes as well:

➤ Install a new service panel

➤ Replace the existing plumbing

➤ Replace the HVAC

➤ Upgrade the windows

➤ Repaint the exterior

When you plan such a big job, always figure on upgrades to your existing structure. Otherwise, when you're through, you'll regret not having done them because your new work will look so much better than the old. Plan and budget for such changes ahead of time, or you'll end up with a series of snowballing change orders and add-ons.

Look Out Below!

Some additions get way out of hand to the point where there isn't much left of the old house. Some building departments let this slide and still consider it a remodel of an existing structure. Others may not be so flexible; they could declare your entire project new construction, which could affect your permits.

What Will You Do with the Space?

Most economically feasible second stories are added to take advantage of views or to accommodate a growing family that wants to stay in the neighborhood. You have almost free rein to design the rooms and bathrooms any way you want. The three major encumbrances to your second floor remodeling are your soil stack, the location of your staircase, and any chimneys that may be present.

You can always work with a chimney or soil stack by building a wall around it, but you usually have few choices when it comes to the location of the staircase installed for the construction. It has to go somewhere, and somewhere may be an existing bedroom or hallway on the first floor. Make up your mind that, while you're working on gaining space on the second floor, you're going to have to lose some on the first floor for a while.

Getting Started

A second-story addition is a more intrusive version of a first-story one, but the steps are the same. You still need to be paranoid about the weather, your plans are more critical than ever, and your checkbook will record its biggest withdrawals ever. Your yard will need more TLC at the end of the job than after a first-story remodel, and you'll have to get used to walking up the stairs to get to your bedroom. When you finally move back in, however, you'll wonder how you ever managed in the old space.

A second-story addition means tearing off your roof; that means exposure to the weather and dealing with rolls of plastic and tarps to keep the weather out. Adding a second story isn't a job you want to start in November unless you live in Arizona. You also want written assurances from your contractor that once the job has started, a crew will be on the job daily until the house is closed off to the weather or dried in. *This is why you have a contract!* Be sure to spell out provisions for crew levels and supervision. (See Appendix F, "Contracts," for information on contracts.)

The traditional approach to this job is to tear off the roof and start framing. All the mechanical systems—wiring, plumbing, and HVAC—are then installed. Plastic or no plastic, you want the briefest possible exposure to the weather. Another approach is to build the addition in pre-assembled sections that are trucked to the job site and installed in less time than standard platform framing. You can find one example of this technique by going to 2ndstorysolutions@valpart.com, the Web site for Hemphill and Coupard, architects and builders.

Tearing off a roof produces piles and piles of debris, and contractors aren't known for kinder and gentler demolition. A site in the yard or driveway is used for a garbage container that will be hauled off as soon as it's full; you're renting it by the day, so you don't want it sitting around any longer than necessary. Contractors typically place plywood over basement windows and landscaping near the trash site to prevent damage from falling debris, but discuss their intentions and methods before the demolition begins. Otherwise, your prize roses may be a distant memory by the time the job's finished.

Your driveway will also be a delivery and storage point for lumber and plywood. Inside your house, if there isn't an existing stairway to the attic, a new one will be built and used regularly by carpenters and laborers until the framing is finished. They will be followed by electricians, plumbers, drywall hangers and tapers, painters, finish carpenters, and carpet layers. In other words, your house will be full of people trampling up and down the stairs with tools and materials.

The way to prepare for this invasion is to do the following:

1. Clear a wide path for the contractors and remove anything of value.
2. Cover the floor with clean, heavy drop cloths (thin ones can slide around too much and are dangerous to workers).
3. Remove anything hanging on the walls near the stairs.
4. Designate one bathroom for contractor use or pay for the rental of a portable toilet.

Adding on.

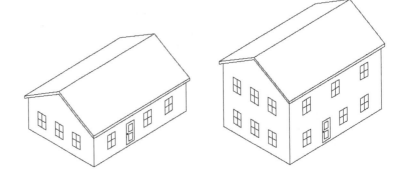

Life in a Noise and Dust Factory

If you're willing to put up with the disruptions of a big time remodel, you could live in your house while the work goes on (and on . . .). In addition to noise and having strangers walking around your home, you'll have to prepare for the following:

➤ Dust

➤ Depression

➤ Cracked plaster

➤ Some disruption of water and electricity

➤ A strong desire to run away and not return

> **Quick Fix**
>
> If you're uncertain about whether to stay in your house during such a major remodel, use your children as a gauge. If they're really young, you won't want them exposed to the noise and dust, so just assume you'll have to live somewhere else. With older kids, use your judgment. If you or any family member has special health concerns, consult a doctor.

Once the pounding begins overhead, decades of accumulated dust will start filtering down from the attic, and there's no way you can stop it. Older houses produce a not so lovely fine, black soot, albeit in small amounts.

After the first few days, you'll know how much time you're going to have to devote to daily cleaning.

You will get depressed at some point—all right, happiness-challenged—but it'll pass, unless your contractor is still with you at Christmas. The cure? A weekend away does wonders; any longer and you might not come back. One thing you can do is keep your living area clean and tidy to help you maintain some semblance of normal life.

Safety Reminders

Safety is always a priority when you remodel. It's even more critical when you're working on a second floor because a fall can be fatal. You or your contractor should ensure everyone's safety by:

➤ Installing guard rails

➤ Keeping children and guests out of the construction area

➤ Installing safety lighting

➤ Adhering to the rules for safe use and storage of ladders (see Appendix D, "Ladders")

➤ Picking up the work area daily

All workers, including you if you're doing some or all of the remodeling, need to wear safety harnesses and be tied off securely when their job calls for it. As the owner, you must insist on this safety precaution. An injured worker can always try and sue against your homeowner's policy if the general contractor's own insurance has lapsed.

A sloppy work site isn't necessarily the sign of a bad contractor, but it's a bad habit that you don't have to put up with. You can specify in your contract how much regular cleanup you expect. A messy site is not only unsafe because of tripping hazards, it also slows down the work when workers have to maneuver around extension cords and scraps of wood while trying to do their jobs.

Look Out Below!

Never throw anything off a second floor work site without looking below first. People (and pets) have a tendency to wander around exactly where you want to toss an extension cord or piece of lumber, even if you have caution tape posted.

This Stuff's Heavy

Conscientious builders hate working around an occupied house. There are too many opportunities to break things or scrape a wall with a piece of lumber, so they'll try to pass most building material up to the second floor from outside the house. The drywall is always delivered that way by special delivery trucks with telescoping forklift attachments that allow the driver to lift it up to a window opening. The stockers or your contractor then remove the drywall and stack it inside.

The roof trusses will most likely be delivered to your rooftop by a crane, and the roofing shingles will probably be delivered by a truck-mounted conveyor system. The largest items that will have to be taken up through the inside of your house will be the plumbing fixtures, windows, doors, and rolls of carpet.

Don't Be the Noisy Neighbor

Your neighbors may be your best friends, but they'll count the days until your work is over. Your project doesn't just affect you: Everyone has to listen to the trucks pulling in and out, the noise, the carpenter banter, and the radios, especially the people next door. You can't muffle the noise from the tools, but you can control the volume of the radios by establishing some ground rules with your contractors before they start.

297

Remodeling is perfectly legal work, of course. As long as you're not violating *noise ordinances* or neighborhood covenants regarding work hours, you can do whatever's necessary to finish the job. Staying on good terms with your neighbors should be on your list of things to do. Let them know your time frame for completion and how the work is progressing. Regular communication will keep your face off their dart boards, even if you can't make everything quieter.

Wiring, Plumbing, and HVAC

Once your addition is closed in, your framers will have to share the space with electricians, plumbers, and a HVAC contractor. Don't worry, they'll arrive in order and stay out of each others way. Besides, many subcontractors know each other from regularly working for the same general contractors.

Sub-panel to the Rescue

Your addition is going to require at least four electrical circuits including:

➤ One for general lighting

➤ One for the bathroom outlet

➤ Two for bedroom and hallway outlets

It's bad enough having to fish one wire up from the basement or garage, let alone four of them. And who wants to run all the way downstairs if a breaker trips? The easy solution is to install a sub-panel on the second

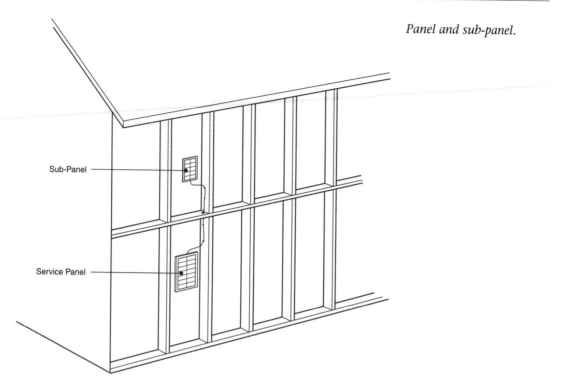

Panel and sub-panel.

Sub-Panel

Service Panel

floor. A sub-panel is a miniature version of your 200-amp house panel. One cable is run from the main panel to the sub-panel, which will then distribute electricity to your addition.

Fishing a cable through an old house can be frustrating. It has to be pulled between wall studs and up through the plates. An electrician can drill down from the second floor easily enough because the framing at the top of the wall is exposed. Drilling from the first floor to the basement means cutting away part of the wall in order to get the drill bit positioned against the bottom plate of the wall. Remember, electricians don't do wall repair.

If all goes well, this process isn't too complicated. When it doesn't go well, the electrician will run into fire blocks in the middle of the wall or barely accessible framing in the basement (a furnace duct might be in the way). In particularly difficult circumstances, you may elect to run the cable in metal conduit on the outside of the house.

At Least the Stack Is Nearby

A full-size addition calls for fresh pipes and drain lines. How do you go about getting water up there? You have two choices of how to run the hot and cold water pipes to your second floor bathroom(s):

➤ Tie into an existing bathroom's water supply.

➤ Go directly to your basement or crawl space and run them from there.

The bathroom is closer, but it may mean tearing into an existing tile wall, hardly an easy repair job. The kitchen isn't going to work because the sink is almost always in front of a window. Running the pipes around the window, behind cabinets, and then up is more work than running them out of the basement.

Unlike wires, pipe isn't very flexible, and it has to be secured to a stud as it runs through the wall. Plumbers have to remove a section of drywall or plaster to do their work, which means more wall repair downstairs (plumbers don't repair walls, either). Wall repair leads to painting the patched-in section of wall, and that leads to painting the entire room. And you thought adding a second floor would be the end of your work!

HVAC

You'll want your addition to be tied into your heating and air-conditioning system. It's one thing to heat a single room addition with electric heat or even a gas fireplace, but you don't want to try that with an entire floor. When you make your plans, ask yourself one vexing HVAC question: Does my current system have the capacity to heat and cool our proposed addition?

A furnace is built to produce a certain amount of heat output. Your existing system may be more than adequate for a one-story house and less than adequate once you double the floor space. When you're in the planning and budgeting stage, be sure to consult with a heating company; a new furnace can easily add on $2,000 or more to your costs.

Now That You're Finished

Your house is more valuable now that it has a second story, which has two financial implications for you: You'll have to increase your homeowner coverage, and your property taxes will eventually go up when the property is reassessed.

As a condition of your home improvement loan, you'll be required to maintain adequate insurance. At the beginning of the job, your policy was based on the value of a one-story house. Your carrier will need to re-appraise your policy in view of your home's added value and increase your premiums accordingly.

> **Quick Fix**
>
> Unless your local laws state that you have to contact your tax assessor in the event that you do any work that changes the value of your property, I wouldn't necessarily announce it to the state. Let the law take its course; if you think a new assessment is too high, you can always contest it.

The Least You Need to Know

➤ Carefully calculate the cost of adding on a second story against the increased value of your house. It may be a better idea to move.

➤ Major work to the second story always causes you to do some upgrading on the first floor as well.

➤ Weather considerations and the speed of your contractors are more critical than ever when you tear the roof off your house for an addition.

➤ Dust and noise go hand-in-hand with such a major remodeling job. You may be better off living somewhere else until the work is finished.

➤ Keep on friendly terms with your neighbors—they're living through this, too.

Chapter 25

Special Touches
for Special Rooms

In This Chapter

➤ How your baby sees the nursery

➤ The master bedroom as a private retreat

➤ A Kids' retreat

➤ Solariums and sunrooms: All-season additions

By now, you have a few repairs under your belt and a better idea about what's involved in major additions to your lair. Getting space added is a big accomplishment, but how about doing some custom-finishing? For instance, why not turn your new or existing master bedroom into a sanctuary to get away from the activity of the household?

If you bought a new house, chances are you found the setup pretty perfunctory: No extra shelves or windows, no cabinetry, or not even additional phone jacks. You can build these extras into any house you build for yourself, but if you buy new housing, you have to add them after the fact.

You're beyond the basics now: Your roof isn't leaking, and the furnace is running. So start stretching your visions! Take another look at the rooms you already have and see how they can be improved.

Baby Boom Means a Baby Room

Politicians, the stock market, and fad diets all come and go, but babies are a constant. (They have to be; otherwise, we wouldn't be here.) When we can, we indulge infants. *Our* kids aren't going to grow up telling stories of how they shared a one-room, five-story walk-up with a family of five and slept in an open dresser drawer when they were infants. We want our kids to have their own rooms, if for no other reason than to get them out of our bedrooms.

What about size? An infant doesn't need a big room, even after reaching the crawling stage (most of that will go on in the family room anyway). A baby's room can be a very modest size, enough for a crib, diaper changing, and the standard rocking chair. If you're short on bedroom space, you could add an alcove off a hallway or even at the top of a staircase and close it off with folding doors. A skylight can bring in natural light if you don't have access to an outside wall to install a window.

Tales from the Scaffold

I've seen all kinds of creative uses of space to build a nursery. One couple converted a cold, drafty, second-floor sunroom into a wonderful, cozy space by weather-stripping the windows, insulating the ceiling, and adding heat. Another family removed a built-in set of drawers and a window at the end of a hallway, cut through the outside wall, and added about 60 square feet of room with windows on two sides. As an added bonus, it was right outside the master bedroom, so the parents were close by. This inexpensive addition made a nice bonus room when they sold the house two years later.

Cheerful Says It All

Parents usually decorate and fuss with a baby's room according to their notions of what would appeal to someone so young. Most of your nursery's interesting touches will come from your use of furnishings. Baby furniture and accessory stores catering to new parents are plentiful, so you should be able to find something to suit your tastes.

Your job with the room itself is to make the color theme as inviting as possible. Keep in mind that although you may see elephants and clowns and circus theme wallpaper, young babies just see shapes and colors, because their vision doesn't have sharp focus until after the first year of life. You may choose to produce a cheerful room with stimulating colors or decide to go with the more traditional pastels, which can be soothing to a frustrated baby and frazzled parents.

Exceptional Walls for Wallpapering

Smooth, vinyl wallpaper—the washable kind you want in children's rooms—isn't very good at hiding problem walls. Before you start hanging the happy farmer wallpaper with smiling cows and chickens, make sure your walls are in tip-top shape:

➤ Repair all cracks, even minor ones (they can always get bigger).

➤ Remove any nails, screws, or hooks and patch the holes.

➤ Repair any large patches of loose plaster or damaged drywall.

➤ Remove or repair any existing wallpaper.

If you have several layers of wallpaper, you're usually better off removing it before you paper again, but it's a lot of work and can entail unseen wall repairs as well. Removing wallpaper from drywall is especially difficult because you can pull the paper cover off the drywall if it wasn't primed before the wallpaper was put up.

Plenty of Windows

New home builders are a little stingy when it comes to installing windows. I can't entirely blame them; bedroom dimensions have shrunk, and too many windows can make furniture placement problematic. I don't know for sure whether babies necessarily like a lot of windows, but natural light will add to your enjoyment of the room, especially during feedings. If you have room for more windows or a skylight, consider adding them.

Did You Hear Something?

Wireless baby monitors are very popular. One unit goes in the nursery, and one goes with you. You can then listen in and know whether junior is safe or needs a changing. Unfortunately, in some circumstances, your neighbors can hear what's going on, too, if they have their own

Look Out Below!

You may be tempted to insulate the interior walls of your nursery in order to sound-deaden it to noise from the rest of the house. This measure can create an artificially quiet environment for your baby, who can then have trouble adjusting to the regular routine of the house. Don't go to any sound-proofing extremes, just keep the excessive noise down during nap time.

monitor. It's a phenomenon similar to being able to pick up cellular phone conversations if you have an appropriate scanner (something Prince Charles found out the hard way).

Consider installing a hard-wired intercom system that will allow you to monitor one or more rooms and keep your privacy private. New systems on the market can perform these functions and, in some cases, incorporate AM/FM radios as well.

Master Bedrooms and Master Bathrooms

For some people, a master bedroom is a miniaturized version of the rest of the house. Nearly all new master bedrooms come with their own bathrooms, and it isn't unusual to find decks, saunas, fireplaces, Jacuzzis, and cable television as well. Throw in a small kitchen or wet bar, and you can spend a few days in there before emerging to replenish your food supply.

Master bedroom suites are almost like hotel suites, especially if you install a minibar, microwave oven, and coffee maker. Set its timer and you'll wake up to fresh, hot coffee instead of an alarm clock. This may seem like overkill, but it is the direction some higher-end homes have been going in. If you have the room and the budget, you, too, can add a few of these amenities to your master bedroom.

It's like living in a hotel: Your own minibar.

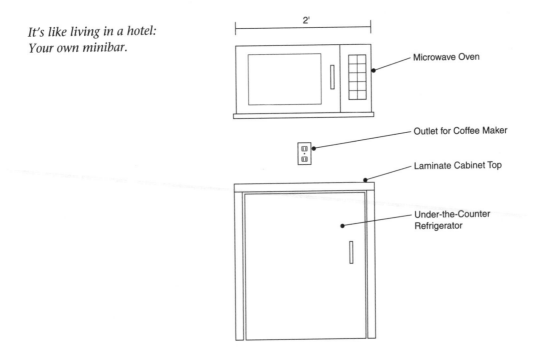

About That Minibar

Hotel minibars are lots of fun to look at, but the prices are a deterrent to everyone who isn't on an expense account (even then you'll have some explaining to do if you munch on a $4 bag of potato chips). Install your own minibar, complete with an under-the-counter refrigerator, microwave, and coffee maker, and you can have the conveniences of a high-end hotel without the prices (you can always leave a price list out for visiting relatives). One trip to a warehouse store will stock your bedroom minibar for months.

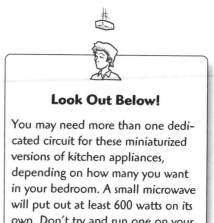

Look Out Below!

You may need more than one dedicated circuit for these miniaturized versions of kitchen appliances, depending on how many you want in your bedroom. A small microwave will put out at least 600 watts on its own. Don't try and run one on your bedroom circuit.

An under-the-counter refrigerator requires less than a 2-foot-wide by 2-foot-deep space. It could be housed in a simple cabinet with a coffee maker on top and a compact micro- wave oven overhead. A custom cabinet could be made to match your bedroom set.

How much will it hold? You can pack a Sanyo SR-172 Cube Refrigerator with 87 12-ounce beverage cans. Prefer wine? Try a Sanyo SR-2404 Wine Cooler, which holds 24 750-milliliter bottles and comes with glass doors for easy viewing.

Planning It Out

Like a broken record, or CD if you prefer, I keep coming back to the importance of planning. You may want to install a direct vent gas fireplace, for instance, but how will you get the gas pipe to your bedroom? What's the least convoluted way you can route it from your basement or garage?

The routing of pipes is also important if you're considering adding a bathroom. The easiest approach is to build on the other side of an existing one. If that forces you into an awkward location, routing the pipes and drain lines to the location you want will mean tearing up the floor. Tearing up your floor may mean destroying vintage hardwood that would be difficult to replace. Laying this all out in your plans first will give you the opportunity to reconsider a bathroom location (or a fireplace or closet) before you commit yourself too seriously.

Rules for any New Bathroom

Adding even a small bathroom to a master bedroom in an old house will increase your home's resale value and add to your convenience while you own it. Figure out the maximum square footage you'll have available and add known fixture sizes to your plans. Remember the cardinal rules of bathrooms:

➤ They need plenty of ventilation.

➤ A tile shower stall requires more maintenance than a fiberglass or acrylic one.

➤ The building code requires a GFCI outlet.

➤ Your drain lines must have sufficient slope between the fixtures and your soil stack to allow water to flow out.

➤ You must have sufficient water pressure and a large enough hot water tank to handle the demands of an extra bathroom.

➤ Whenever possible, a bathroom should have a source of natural light (either a window or a skylight).

Contractor Talk

A *pocket door* is a sliding door stored inside the wall on either side of a door jamb. The space inside the wall is called the pocket. Doors hang on overhead tracks and slide on pulleys.

Tight Space? Try a Sliding Door

Increasingly, new houses have fewer doors and walls between the master bathroom and the master bedroom. These open arrangements have the tub, shower, and vanity exposed to the bedroom, with the toilet closed off on its own, reminiscent of an old-style water closet. Open relationship or not, a door provides some privacy when you want to take a hot bath and close yourself off to the rest of the world. If you don't have the room for a standard-size, swing-in door, install a sliding *pocket door* (if you're building new walls) or a bi-fold door in the door jamb instead.

Pocket doors.

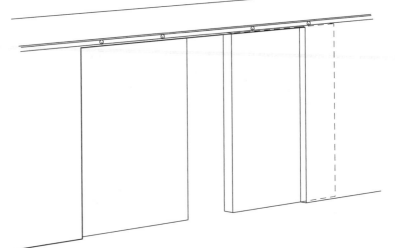

One More Fireplace

A master bedroom is the perfect location for a gas fireplace. You don't have to bother with hauling logs in or building a brick chimney. Small corner units are unobtrusive, yet provide heat and atmosphere. The question remains: How do you route a gas pipe from your basement or garage up through existing walls without making a real mess of things? You do it carefully.

You want to run your gas pipe through open spaces where you won't mind looking at it, or you can box it in and disguise it with wood trim or molding. Running the pipe along a laundry room ceiling and then up through a coat closet, for instance, will avoid tearing up living room walls to get it to your bedroom. When you've gotten through to your attic, the pipe can be run horizontally along the joists until it can be dropped down into your bedroom. You'll have some wall repairs to do, but this approach can keep them to a minimum and out of the main rooms. Discuss the routing with your general contractor or gas appliance subcontractor.

Kids' Rooms

Kids and the accumulation of stuff go hand-in-hand. Toys, books, rocks, dolls, clothes, posters, and stickers are the debris in the ongoing battle over clean rooms. It's easier to organize your child's bedroom if you have storage to organize it around.

The cardinal rule for a child's room is this: You cannot build or add enough shelving. The "less is more" philosophy doesn't work here: Go ahead and install floor-to-ceiling shelves across an entire wall and include wider shelves near the bottom. Incorporate a desktop for art projects and homework (be sure it's near an electrical outlet for a lamp and radio). Melamine shelves (see Chapter 18, "The Home Worker: Dens and Offices") are among the easiest to take care of; you can just wipe them clean, and their plastic finish means they'll never need painting.

A Good Greenhouse Effect

Most of us are naturally drawn to the sun. Northwesterners have been known to go out and stare at it the two or three times a year it shows itself out here. Solariums and sun-rooms allow more of the sun inside your house than standard window arrangements do, but you must be thoughtful with your design. Sticking a great pile of glass on your house without any thought to how it will affect the rest of your exterior can easily result in an ungainly addition.

Tales from the Scaffold

You've probably noticed the unevenness and distortions in old glass. Although glass behaves like a solid, the atomic structure of glass is more like that of a liquid (it's manufactured by cooling a hot liquid). Old glass isn't as stable as new because, over the years, gravity pulls at it, and it gradually migrates downward like a slow-moving liquid. A new glass solarium won't have this problem, if you consider it one; many people find distorted glass charming.

A solarium is an extension of an existing room and involves removing the connecting wall between them. A sunroom is an addition to an existing room or space without the removal of a connecting wall. Solariums feature floor-to-ceiling windows as well as clear ceilings. Sunrooms typically have two or three walls of tall windows; just think of them as rooms with windows for walls. Adding either type of room to your house will follow the same standard construction details any new room requires: permits, proper framing techniques, weight and stress considerations, and sealing the addition to the weather.

Solariums offer you several building options, including:

➤ Ready-to-assemble kits

➤ Polycarbonate or other plastic windows

➤ Insulated glass windows

➤ Aluminum or wood framing

➤ Custom-made or ready-made sizes

Each option has its advocates and detractors. Your decisions will depend on your budget, working space, and personal likes and dislikes of the different materials.

Make It Their Way or Your Way?

Ready-to-assemble solarium kits look like ready-to-assemble kits. You wouldn't build a kitchen or bathroom that way, so why do it with a solarium? The advantages of cost and convenience may be undone by a design that doesn't blend with your house in any way, shape, or form. Remember, the best additions are the ones that don't stand out when seen from the exterior of your house.

Naturally, a custom-made solarium will cost more than a ready-to-install, one-size-fits-all model because all the framing has to be custom cut and the glass has to be made to

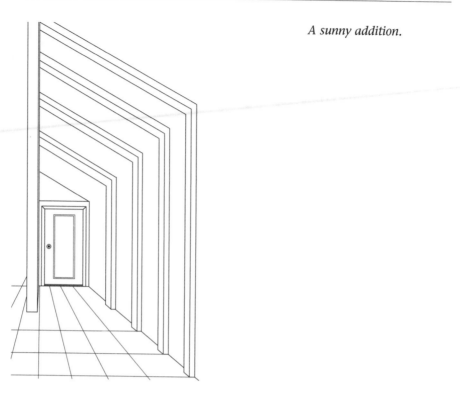

A sunny addition.

size. You'll get exactly the size and detailing that you want, resulting in a solarium that blends in with your house instead of one that noticeably sticks out. Is it worth it to you? Is your budget screaming? There aren't any guidelines to making this decision other than your own tastes and judgment.

Windows to the World

A solarium has quite a task. It must have a leak-proof, mostly glass or plastic surface and keep water out despite all of its exposed joints and sealants. No matter how high-tech a sealant you use, it's always subject to deterioration. Plastic or polycarbonate solariums may have a cost and weight advantage over glass, but look at an existing one (find one that's at least five years old) and decide for yourself how well the plastic has held up. Glass doesn't scratch and doesn't deteriorate from exposure to sunlight and UV light as plastic can.

Insulated glass or not, solariums can get hot in the summertime and cool in the winter after the sun disappears. Window coverings help some, but they're not cheap. This room will have to be heated if you want to use it on cloudy, winter days and cold evenings. Discuss this with your furnace technician. Because you're heating a room without conventional wall and ceiling insulation, you may need to run two heating registers into it or consider adding supplementary heat, such as a gas fireplace.

Wood or Metal: The Debate Goes On

An aluminum-framed solarium with a baked-on finish is very efficient and pragmatic, but in my humble opinion, it has almost zero visual appeal in most houses.

Some solariums combine materials by using wood framing on the lower sections and aluminum for the overhead glass area. Wood finishes and the wood color itself will fade and deteriorate more quickly inside a solarium because of all the sun exposure; that's the big maintenance difference between wood and aluminum. You'll need to choose carefully between the two, and I strongly suggest you go to some manufacturers' showrooms, sit down in different models, and decide which one you can live with.

Look Out Below!

Before you install your solarium—especially one on the second floor—consider how you're going to keep the glass clean. The room could lose its appeal in a hurry if the overhead glass is regularly covered with leaves or pine needles, and you have no easy way of cleaning them off.

Sunrooms

A sunroom is kind of a compromised solarium. You have a real roof overhead with maybe a skylight or two, but the two or three walls of windows give the room its defining name. Sunrooms have some advantages over solariums:

➤ They're easier to blend into your existing architecture.

➤ You have no overhead windows to clean.

➤ There's less chance of the roof leaking.

Historic districts and neighborhoods with building covenants will take a dim view of solariums, but may accommodate a tastefully executed sunroom. As always, check your building code and zoning requirements before you start tearing any walls out.

The Least You Need to Know

➤ After the functional work on your house is done, you can think about the extras that will make your home more livable.

➤ All kinds of modest-size spaces can be converted into a nursery as long as you keep it bright, warm, and cheerful.

➤ A master bedroom can be turned into a wonderful retreat and private space for a modest cost.

➤ When you think about a room for your child, think storage!

➤ Solariums and sunrooms are great additions if they're planned carefully to fit with your home's design and style.

Chapter 26

Bargain Basements: A Million Uses

> ## In This Chapter
>
> ➤ Dealing with code requirements for basement remodels
>
> ➤ Addressing those pesky moisture problems
>
> ➤ You can never have enough lighting
>
> ➤ Hiding the overhead utilities
>
> ➤ Bathroom considerations

A full basement offers square footage equivalent to that of the first floor of your house; why waste it all filling it up with debris you'll throw out or give away when you move? Pare down your belongings with a garage sale and recapture your basement for a better use.

The recreation rooms and faux Polynesian wet bars of the '60s are giving way to higher quality finished basements. If you add enough windows and overhead lighting, you can convert your basement into a play area for the kids or a play area for yourself, with a pool table, guest quarters, home theater, and even a partial solarium.

Houses are more expensive than ever, so it just makes sense to make the fullest use of your home until you have to move on to something larger because you had twins. A finished basement will also add to the value of your house when you do sell. Yet despite the opportunities they present, basements pose some special problems that you won't face in your main living areas including:

➤ Height restrictions

➤ Moisture and water seepage

➤ Egress

➤ Lack of natural light

➤ Pipes, wires, and duct work running through the ceiling

Unlike other parts of your house, basements don't hide their flaws; what you see is pretty much what you get, which means fewer surprises. As you tackle these issues one at a time, you'll be well on your way to turning your downstairs storage locker into solid living space.

It All Starts with Headroom

Headroom is a major consideration in the basement and attic. Most building codes require a minimum ceiling height of 7 feet, 6 inches for at least half the area of a habitable room. No, this doesn't mean that your uninhabitably messy children's rooms can have lower ceilings. New construction has a minimum of 8-foot-high ceilings.

Tales from the Scaffold

Some people accept the limitations of a basement and capitalize on them. I came across a Web site that featured a reproduction of an English pub built in a windowless basement. Pubs aren't known for abundant natural lighting, so the homeowner skipped installing any additional windows and concentrated on other details, such as the bar itself, walnut-stained woodwork, and illuminated, stained-glass panels. The homeowner wanted authenticity, and he got it. What a great idea! The site didn't say if he was applying for a liquor license.

Some common exceptions to these height requirements include the following:

- Hallways, bathrooms, and utility rooms can have minimum ceiling heights of 6 feet, 8 inches.
- Suspended ceiling panels can have a 7-foot height.
- Beams installed 4 feet apart (on center) can be a minimum of 7 feet above the floor.

If your basement doesn't meet these requirements, you probably can't turn it into living space. Basements that won't pass for living space can still be upgraded for storage, wine cellars, and such uses as woodworking shops.

Moisture, the Main Stumbling Block

I've brought up moisture issues several times in this book, but it bears repeating here: Clear up moisture problems before you do any basement remodeling! You don't want to deal with wet carpet and drywall later because you didn't think about seepage problems earlier.

Suppose it's June, you've just bought your house, and you're ready to turn the basement into headquarters for your Internet start-up company. You haven't lived through a wet season yet, and the former owner didn't mention anything about water problems. Do you take a chance and go ahead with your remodeling plans? You can go ahead with the remodel, but do some investigating first. With a bit of testing and observation, you'll have a much better shot at ending up with a dry, comfortable office.

Water leaves a trail. In your basement, look for the following:

- Water stains on the floor and walls
- *Efflorescence*, the white mineral deposit water leaves behind on masonry surfaces as it evaporates
- Cracks in the foundation

> **Look Out Below!**
>
> Homeowners are supposed to disclose any known defects to prospective buyers. If occasional basement puddling is a common occurrence where they live, some people may not consider it a defect, so be sure to raise the question of moisture in the basement as a specific issue when you're considering a house purchase.

Use your nose: Does your basement smell musty? It's not necessarily a sign of leaks, but it's probably a sign of dampness due to poor ventilation or lack of heat. In some cases, a dehumidifier may be needed to extract water vapor.

Check the soil outside. Is it moist while the rest of your yard is dry? This moisture suggests that you have a leaking pipe or even an underground spring. Test dry soil by soaking it with a hose and then checking inside for leaks. Even occasional water problems need to be resolved early so you don't end up damaging your finished work (see Chapter 3, "Judging a House by Its Cover").

Tales from the Scaffold

There is such a thing as a permanent wood foundation, or PWF. These foundations are built from wolmanized wood, a process in which wood is soaked under pressure in various copper arsenate solutions. Wolmanized wood is moisture-, rodent-, rot-, and fungus-proof. The American Plywood Association built a house using a wood foundation in 1938, un-earthed it 52 years later, and declared it to be in perfect condition. The state of Pennsyl-vania has used wood basements for over 80 years; over 300,000 homes in the United States and Canada have these foundations. Manufacturers claim these foundations hold up as well as concrete and install faster. Go to www.woodbasements.com for product information.

Plans from the Underground

Basements offer you the opportunity to have one large, open room for entertainment or several individual rooms; smaller basements lend themselves better to fewer rooms. Regardless of your plans, you have to figure in *egress*. Below-grade basements pose particular egress challenges, especially if you have to cut through the foundation in order to install a window or an exit door (required in a habitable basement).

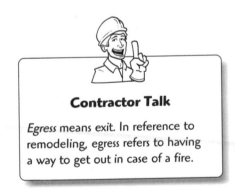

Contractor Talk

Egress means exit. In reference to remodeling, egress refers to having a way to get out in case of a fire.

She Came in Through the Basement Window

An egress window must be large enough to accommodate an adult passing through it, and the sill has to be less than 42 inches from the floor. What if you have to cut through the concrete to meet the 42-inch requirement? Before you call a contractor who specializes in concrete cutting, ask your building department or architect about some alternatives, such as:

➤ Raising the section of the floor under an existing window with a large platform

➤ Permanently attaching a small ladder to the wall

➤ Building a small two-step staircase up to the window

Looks like we made the 42-inch cutoff.

I've seen these solutions used with the approval of my local building department. The last thing you want to do in your basement is cutting unnecessarily through the foundation.

Of course, windows provide more than egress in a basement; they provide a certain amount of natural light, which is required by your local building code. They also meet ventilation requirements, though a HVAC system can meet them, too.

Unfortunately, basement windows also provide entry for burglars, who prefer to break in less noticeably at a conveniently short distance from the ground. Short of an alarm system, your best bet is to install security screens on the windows and remove all bushes and shrubs that obscure the windows.

Outside Entrance

In habitable basements, windows are a secondary means of egress because an outside door is required. There's no way around this one; if you don't currently have a door, you'll have to cut through the concrete foundation. This complicated job includes these tasks:

➤ Locating the opening (away from pipes, electrical panels, and so on)

➤ Excavating a 3-foot wide staircase and outside landing down to your foundation's footing

➤ Installing a drain outside the door

➤ Building the forms for the stairs and landing and pouring the concrete

➤ Cutting through the foundation for the door opening

317

➤ Framing the opening and installing the door

➤ Installing a railing around the top of the stairway and one down the steps

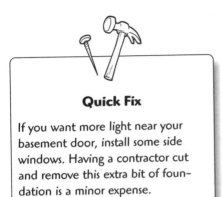

This is a lot of work! Some suggest that you can cut through a foundation with a regular circular saw using a masonry blade (or several blades), but this is unrealistic. You may be able to get away with it if you're cutting through concrete block, but not through solid concrete. Besides, it's a great way to burn out a saw. Professionals use heavy-duty masonry saws (some rental stores carry them) and are experienced at making clean, straight cuts. Are you prepared to cut out a stairway and then pour nice, even stairs and risers? Hire this job out; it's not worth the frustration of doing the job yourself. If you need to keep your spending down, do the work on the inside.

Moving the Utilities

Basement ceilings are a great place to run pipes, heat and air-conditioning ducts, and wiring. Most of your mechanical systems are located there, and the ceiling provides you and your contractors access to them to make additions and changes. But that doesn't mean you want to look at all that stuff all the time.

It's unrealistic to move all of your existing plumbing, but if a HVAC duct is running down the middle of your basement or inconveniences your plans and design, consider rerouting it to the top of a wall where headroom isn't critical. Concealing pipes and duct work can be problematic; your efforts may lower the ceiling and put you out of code compliance.

Generally, basement ceilings are *furred out* with two-by-twos attached to the bottom edge of the floor joists.
This furring provides a slightly lowered ceiling (by 1¹/₂ inches) that clears most small pipes, and ceiling panels or drywall can then be attached to the two-by-twos. Before you choose drywall, consider this: Drywall elimi-nates easy access to the ceiling joists for future wiring or plumbing work. Basement ceilings are good candidates for remov-able panels.

Speaking of Furring Out

Most basement remodeling involves covering over the foundation wall with drywall. If your foundation wall goes all the way up to the ceiling joists, follow these steps:

1. Install a plastic vapor barrier over the concrete.

2. Install rigid foam insulation over the vapor barrier.

3. Attach furring (either wood or metal) to hold in and secure the insulation.

4. If wood furring is used, avoid contact with the slab by running it an inch short of the floor.

5. Attach drywall to the furring.

Contractor Talk

Furring out means adding building material to walls, wall studs, or joists to form a level, uniform surface to which to attach cover material. Typical furring materials are wood, strips of drywall, and metal.

Some basement walls are a combination of concrete on the lower section and standard wood framing on top. In these cases, you can frame a new wall directly in front of the foun-dation wall. This eliminates any unevenness in the concrete and gives you a nailing surface, the studs, for the drywall. The sole plate or bottom section of the wall must be pressure-treated wood because it's in contact with the concrete slab.

The sole plate is secured to the floor with either a stud driver, also known as a nailing gun, or construction adhesive. The stud driver uses an explosive charge, similar to a bullet, to drive nails through the wood and into the concrete. Hand-driven concrete nails are available, but they're not as effective as using a stud driver, especially on old concrete. This wall should maintain a 1-inch minimum distance from the foundation wall.

You May Need to Change the Stairs

Check your local code for staircase requirements in finished basements with habitable space. You may have to widen your existing stairs or even relocate them, which is a big expense. If you do have to change the stairs, consider some grand plans and build an elaborate, open staircase to the first floor. It would tie your basement more directly to your first-floor living area and make it easier to keep an eye on the kids.

Making the Grade

Some local codes spell out how high the exterior grade of your yard can be in relation to the level of the habitable basement floor space inside. In other words, you can only have so many feet of dirt above the level of the inside floor. Ask your building department if they have any such regulations and how they are to be calculated.

Electrical and Plumbing

Electrical requirements in a basement aren't any different from those for the rest of the house as far as the amount of lighting and outlets per given room area. Plumbing is another issue. You must have enough slope for the toilet, sink, and shower/tub drain lines to flow properly. The closer you can locate your new bathroom to your existing plumbing, the better it will be for your budget. If you can't get the required slope, you'll have to break up the concrete floor, bury your new drain lines, and then hook them up with your sewer line. Look at the bright side: You or your contractor will get to practice your concrete finishing skills.

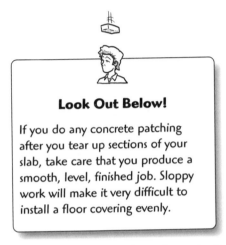

Look Out Below!

If you do any concrete patching after you tear up sections of your slab, take care that you produce a smooth, level, finished job. Sloppy work will make it very difficult to install a floor covering evenly.

Warming It Up

Basements are naturally cool in the summer and make a great place to escape to on hot days. For the rest of the year, however, you need to heat the basement. You have several options, including:

➤ Running ducts from the furnace

➤ Electric heaters

➤ Gas fireplace

Running ducts from the furnace is convenient, but the thermostat is upstairs—not the most responsive situation if the basement is cooler than your first floor. Electric heaters with wall-mounted thermostats do a good job in basements and are relatively inexpensive to install. You have to look at the long-term costs, however; electric heat is expensive in most parts of the country, and the heating bills from a regularly used basement can add up. A gas fireplace with an electric blower will heat your basement up in a hurry, but it cannot be left on unattended. A combination of furnace ducts and supplemental electric heat may be the best choice.

Floor Thoughts

Concrete is a tough work floor, but it leaves a lot to be desired in a play or living area. There is some controversy about how to finish a basement floor. One school of thought says you should never install carpet or hardwood flooring below grade be-cause of the inevitable moisture problems. Even a small amount of dampness can cause wood floors to separate or turn carpet into a breeding ground for mold. The anti-carpet/hardwood group asserts that the only safe flooring is vinyl attached directly to the concrete slab or paint on the slab's surface. Advocates of wood and carpet say it'll work if precautions are taken first.

I'll Raise You a Couple of Inches

Installing a raised floor over concrete allows you to install any kind of flooring over it. A multistep procedure is involved:

1. Seal the concrete slab with a commercial masonry water sealer.

2. Cover the slab completely with heavy plastic, which acts as a vapor barrier.

3. Secure pressure-treated two-by-fours (laid flat, not on edge) with a stud driver; space them at 16 inches on center, just like a wall.

4. Install a plywood subfloor that is at least $1/2$ inch thick.

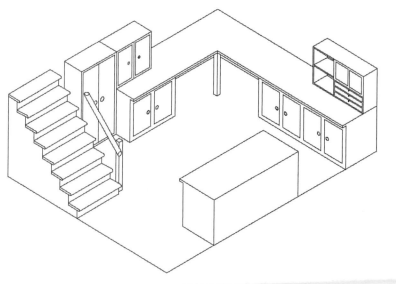

Simple utility basement.

Now you're ready to install carpet, vinyl, or hardwood as you choose. However, even some advocates of this system say that it works only if you can vent and drain the slab floor under the raised one; in some cases, you can even have insect infestation under it and not know it. Your final decision will probably depend on your local climate and the experience of local contractors in this problematic area.

Sticking with Concrete

Vinyl flooring applied directly to the existing concrete slab is usually a safe route in a dry basement. Insects can't get under it, it won't rot, and the worst that any seeping water can do is to loosen the glue. If you're installing vinyl, the slab must be as smooth as possible, which may mean you'll have a lot of patching to do. Sheet vinyl rather than vinyl tiles will cover an uneven floor best.

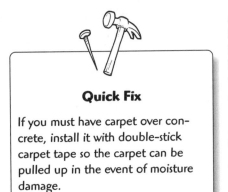

Quick Fix

If you must have carpet over concrete, install it with double-stick
carpet tape so the carpet can be
pulled up in the event of moisture
damage.

Another option is to just paint the floor. Basement floors can be tricked out with special painting effects to look like just about anything: marble, checker-boards, and even wood. Putting down large area rugs that can be removed periodically if you have moisture concerns will increase your comfort level.

Starting from Scratch

Some houses that have nothing but a crawl space are candidates for new basements. Building a new base-ment is a major job that may involve raising the house and building a new foundation. Consult a local real estate broker or two and see if this work makes sense for your house and your neighborhood. Major basement additions cost tens of thousands of dollars and can be difficult to justify financially.

The Least You Need to Know

➤ The two major preliminary issues facing your basement remodeling plans are ceiling heights and moisture.

➤ Another remodeling obstacle is egress if your basement is going to be habitable. Building an exit door is a major job and one best left to a contractor.

➤ Furring out the ceiling is the first step in hiding all those ugly pipes, wires, and ducts running through your basement.

➤ There are no easy answers when selecting a floor covering over a concrete slab. Ask around locally and see what works and what you should avoid.

Chapter 27

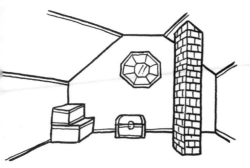

Turn Your Attic into a Penthouse

In This Chapter

➤ Making headway with headroom

➤ A sturdy floor is a must

➤ Bringing light (and ventilation) to a dark (and stuffy attic)

➤ All year round comfort

Attics have a long history in popular culture as hiding places for ghosts, bats, and deranged relatives. They're more than that, of course: They're storehouses of family and national history (someone is always finding an old presidential document in their great-grandmother's attic).

Attics and storage go hand-in-hand. Large, older houses often have attic storage accessible by a staircase; smaller houses may have a drop-down folding staircase or a removable panel in the ceiling for occasional access. New homes usually have shallow attics crisscrossed with roof trusses, which makes them unusable for storage. If you have an attic with storage room, then you also have a future guest suite, master bedroom, or office away from the household hubbub. An attic conversion can turn a dark, dusty, underutilized space into a valuable addition to your house, and as a bonus, you'll have some new views to enjoy.

Attic conversions can be more complicated than second-story additions because you're working around an existing roof instead of removing it and starting fresh. The changes to a roof line that attic conversions can entail must be planned carefully. Ceiling joists from below, which will become the floor joists when you remodel your attic, usually

Look Out Below!

Before you get too far into your attic plans, check your local zoning restrictions. If your local code considers your finished attic a third-story or even fourth-story living space, it may be subject to tougher code requirements (fire becomes more of an issue the higher the habitable space).

Contractor Talk

A *collar tie* is a structural member, usually a two-by-four, that connects opposing rafters supporting different sides of a roof. It acts as a brace as well as a nailing surface for drywall.

will have to be reinforced to carry the load imposed by the new living area. In addition, attics are often used for routing electrical wiring; it may have to be rerouted or otherwise concealed as you remodel. Despite these obstacles, attic conversions are terrific projects: All you have to do to get started is look up!

A Plan with a Higher Purpose

Before you write up your plan, decide what you want out of your attic. Are you looking for office space or a master bedroom? Do you feel that your family will be safe sleeping on a separate floor? Maybe you're planning on turning the attic into a playroom; how will you dampen the noise your kids make running around? If you turn it into a guest room with an added bath, will you want to listen to water running overhead at odd hours? You can take steps in your design and planning to address these and other issues before they become post-project problems.

This One Starts with Headroom, Too

Attic conversions have one thing in common with basement remodels: You must have sufficient headroom in order to meet the building code. The most commonly enforced regulations include:

➤ A ceiling height of 7 feet, 6 inches, as measured from the bottom of the rafters or *collar ties* to the top of the finished floor

➤ A minimum of 50 percent of the attic floor space must meet the ceiling height requirement; the remaining 50 percent can be as little as 5 feet in height

➤ Room size, except in the case of bathrooms, must be a minimum of 70 square feet and no less than 7 feet in length or width (floor space with less than 5 feet of headroom does not count towards the 70 square foot minimum room size)

When you measure for ceiling height, remember to allow for a finished floor as well. That means adding at least $^3/_4$ inch for the subfloor plus carpet and a pad, or another $^3/_4$ inch for a hardwood floor. If your existing floor joists can't support the load and you have to put in larger ones, the change will also affect your height dimension.

In an ideal world, an attic conversion takes place without any adjustments to the roof except for the installation of skylights. In reality, a roof may have to be raised to meet the height requirement; this work can add substantially to your costs. If you do have to raise your roof, you'll probably have to redo the rest of it with new shingles in order for your remodeled section to match with the existing roof. And this is just the preliminary expense in order for your conversion to meet the building code!

Other Framing Considerations

An attic meant for storage but not for living space may not have enough joists—or may have joists that are too small—to support a habitable area. Storage is one thing, but living space brings more weight with it because of:

➤ Extra lumber, drywall, and flooring

➤ Furniture

➤ People

Look Out Below!

Be sure your footings and foundation can support the increased weight and stress of a finished attic. You must have a structural engineer or architect assess this situation before you get too far along in your planning.

If your attic floor joists are too small (two-by-sixes, for example) and spaced too widely (24 inches on center instead of 16 inches on center), you'll have to reinforce the floor with additional, larger joists. You can nail the new joists next to the existing ones if they are already spaced at 16 inches on center.

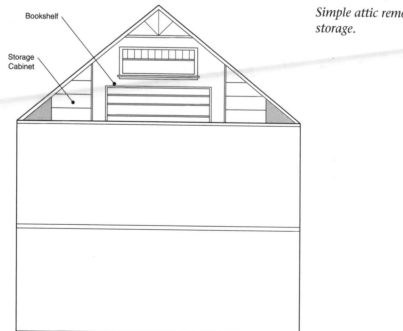

Bookshelf

Storage Cabinet

Simple attic remodel, with storage.

Roof rafters run from the top of your outer walls to the peak(s) of your roof. They are sometimes supported by two-by-fours or even a short knee wall nailed to the joist. This arrangement allows all kinds of maneuvering in your attic because the center or core of the area is free and open. Even with rafters, you'll need talented framing work to assure any new roof work ties in appropriately with your existing roof design.

Conversions rarely work if you have roof trusses (see Chapter 23, "The Big Leagues: Adding a Room"), which are engineered supports running across an attic space as they support the roof. You cannot alter them without jumping through all kinds of engineer-approved hurdles.

Stairway Requirements

When you change your attic into habitable space, your staircase requirements change. Your existing staircase may not meet these requirements and may not be altered easily. A newly located staircase will take up room from existing living space, either a room or a hallway. Most staircase requirements include the following:

➤ The staircase must be at least 36 inches wide.

➤ The minimum headroom has to be at least 6 feet, 8 inches.

➤ There are minimum and maximum heights for risers and depths for treads (these vary with local codes).

➤ A handrail must be installed on at least one side of the staircase; open staircases and landings call for railings on all open sides.

Contractor Talk

A *dormer* is a box-like structure that projects out from a sloping roof. Its main purpose is to frame one or more windows. Without the dormer, skylights would have to be installed for natural light.

Check with your building department if you want to install a spiral staircase. Such staircases may be restricted due to their narrow passageway.

New Openings

Attics are dark by nature. In the past, a builder would see no point in installing more than a small window or two in unoccupied storage space. You, on the other hand, will want windows and skylights everywhere. The question is, what's the best approach? Attic walls (except for end walls under the roof peak) are rarely tall enough to accommodate windows, which means you'll have to build *dormers* or add a lot of skylights.

Attic conversions must have windows for the same reasons other rooms have them, including:

➤ Natural light

➤ Ventilation

➤ Fire escape

At least one window must have a minimum opening of 20×24 inches for egress. This requirement is normally for bedrooms, the idea being that you can be unaware of a spreading fire and find yourself trapped. You should maintain this kind of egress in your attic anyway because you could still be unaware of spreading flames if the attic door is closed. Check with your local building code to determine the maximum distance from the floor that you can install a window (if it's too high, egress will be too difficult). Usually, the maximum distance is 44 inches. The total area of windows and/or skylights has to equal at least 10 percent of the finished floor area and not be less than 10 square feet of glass.

Skylights from the Outside

You have to be careful when installing skylights. A perfectly acceptable location inside your attic space may look ghastly from the outside. On traditional, older houses you want your skylights on the back side of the roof so you don't unduly destroy your home's street appeal. Locate your skylights away from chimneys, roof valleys, and plumbing vents.

Skylights come in two flavors: Operable, or ventilated, models and fixed models. An operable skylight can help fulfill your ventilation requirements as well as provide natural light. Some models come with electric controls for opening and closing them and even sensors that close them when it rains.

Breaking Out with Dormers

Think of installing a dormer as you would think of installing a window or door in an existing wall; only in this case, you're cutting through rafters instead of wall studs. The cut rafters are doubled up, headers are installed, and the dormer is built and butted up against them both. You have a choice of several dormers, including:

➤ Gable

➤ Shed

➤ Hipped

➤ Extended

A gable dormer has an A-shaped roof that is perpendicular to the existing roof it butts up against; a shed dormer's roof has a downward slope in the same direction as the roof it intersects. These two styles are the most popular styles of dormers. A hipped dormer fits with a hipped roof, which has four sloping sides. An extended dormer is basically a long shed dormer. If you put the wrong style dormer on your house, the dormer will stand out like aluminum picture windows on a Federal period mansion.

Look Out Below!

Dormers are acceptable additions to historical housing, but follow the rules! Stick with small dormers away from the street side of the house. If you're in a historic district, you'll probably need to get your plans approved. You can have serious compliance problems if you add on an inappropriate dormer.

Dormers galore.

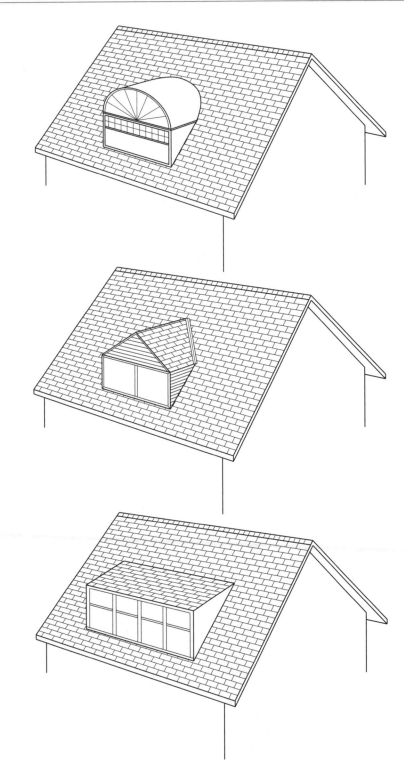

Dormers normalize an attic by providing space for installing windows. Every dormer takes away some wall space, however, and limits your placement of furniture, so use them judiciously.

Keep Your Cool: Temperature Control

Left to their own devices, attics become hot in the summer and cold in the winter. When you convert an attic to living space, you'll want to reverse this scenario, at least to a point. The biggest single factor in controlling the temperature of your attic is insulation.

Your local building code determines how much insulation you need in different areas of your house. If you live in Warmer-Than-Thou, California, you won't need to pad your walls and ceiling with the same amount of material you'd need in SubZero, Montana. The code should state the minimum *R value* for insulation in the attic; minimum insulation requirements usually range from R-19 to R-38 (there isn't a maximum end of the scale).

The easiest insulation for most homeowners and contractors to install is fiberglass, which fits be-tween the rafters and between wall studs. The insulation should not block the roof venting, and there should be a gap between the insulation and the roof sheathing so air can flow along the underside of the roof.

Cool winter air, the theory goes, circulates up from the soffit vents and through the rafters, equalizing the temperature along the roof. This prevents snow from melting on the top of your roof and freezing into ice dams further down at the eaves. This theory came into question when studies by the University of Illinois Champaign/Urbana and the Florida Solar Energy Center showed that the color of the roofing material, not the presence or absence of ventilation, controls its temperature. Watch for the counter studies to come out any day now.

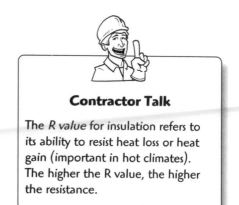

Contractor Talk

The *R value* for insulation refers to its ability to resist heat loss or heat gain (important in hot climates). The higher the R value, the higher the resistance.

Heating It Up

An attic conversion has to be heated according to the building code, not that you wouldn't want to heat it anyway. Your contractor can cut into existing ductwork in a bedroom or hallway and run a new duct up to the attic, but one heat duct and register isn't going to adequately heat, say, 500 square feet of additional living space. The size of your attic conversion will determine its heating needs. Consult with your heating technician and consider installing electric baseboard heat with wall-mounted thermostats as a supplement.

If you want a more elegant solution, try a gas fireplace for coziness; install one with an electric blower, and you'll get cozy and get heat delivered at the same time. New versions of gas fireplaces come with temperature controls, even remote ones! On the other hand, electric heat gives you the option of maintaining constant heat without the worry of having an unattended fire burning (even if it is contained behind tempered glass doors in the fireplace).

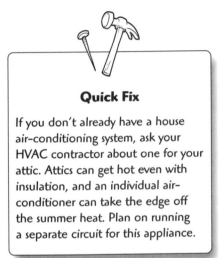

Quick Fix

If you don't already have a house air-conditioning system, ask your HVAC contractor about one for your attic. Attics can get hot even with insulation, and an individual air-conditioner can take the edge off the summer heat. Plan on running a separate circuit for this appliance.

Cooling It Off

If you're already extending the ductwork for heat in the attic, your attic will be included in your in-house air-conditioning—a welcome comfort in the summer heat. If your climate doesn't quite justify the need for air-conditioning, install your attic windows so they establish a cross-breeze and use ventilated skylights to release hot air that accumulates near the ceiling.

Putting It Together

Remodeling your attic will be similar to adding a second floor, with a few exceptions:

➤ You won't be exposing the rest of your house to the elements in such a big way (although you will be exposing it some).

➤ You may not have a readily available opening to the outside through which to move building materials.

➤ If you don't have an available opening to the outside, you'll be hauling more materials through the house.

You or your contractor will have to bring in power, water, drainage (if you're adding a bathroom), and HVAC from the lower floors, and you know what that means: at least some wall repair in the rooms below. Picking the least invasive routes may be more time-consuming on the front end, but it will save repair time and costs later.

An attic conversion is weather-dependent work because you're cutting out sections of the roof. You're exposing your house to rain even in the middle of the summer. Concentrate on finishing any work involving skylights, dormers, or raising the roof while the weather is good. The interior can always be done later.

A Few Details

Attics are unique spaces in houses that involve different remodeling considerations than those regarding the rest of the house. For example, when attic roofs get close to intersecting the floor they create a certain amount of dead space. You can change it from dead space to living space with a small effort. This space is the perfect place to tuck away a bathroom with a fiberglass shower stall, for example, which can be installed easily. The following sections provide more helpful hints for remodeling an attic.

An Attic with All the Trimmings

As much as I like wider trim and baseboards in the rest of the house, they can be overwhelming in a converted attic. Sloped ceilings visually shrink the space, and wide woodwork breaks it up too much, shrinking it further. You don't want to call too much attention to the room's dimensions, so stick with narrower moldings, casings, and baseboard.

Walk Softly

Hardwood floors are very handsome, but you don't necessarily want to be living underneath them when an insomniac guest paces around in high heels at 2:00 a.m. I'm a big fan of thick, fat carpet in attic conversions, both on the floor and on the stairs. Exposed floors are bad enough, but wood stairs sound even worse if a guest or family member is using them late at night.

Lighting the Way

Midnight snacks and the call of nature will drag people out of an attic bedroom and down to the kitchen or bathroom. Fumbling down the stairs in the dark isn't much fun nor is the rude awakening you can get from turning on a glaring light over the stairs. Speak with your electrician about installing some low-wattage recessed lights as a series of night lights just above the stair treads. This kind of lighting is an especially good idea if you have children or older relatives sleeping in a converted attic.

View Deck

A remodeled attic, especially one on the third floor of a house, can offer some awesome views. If you really want to take advantage of them, consider installing a small deck with a fancy French door. What better place to get some distance from the neighborhood activity and read the Sunday paper?

Adding on a third-story deck will involve some high ladder work and careful flashing against the siding. You want the deck to be as unobtrusive as possible given its visibility from the yard

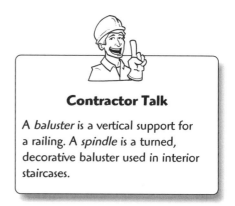

Contractor Talk

A *baluster* is a vertical support for a railing. A *spindle* is a turned, decorative baluster used in interior staircases.

and street. Instead of installing a standard railing and balusters, for instance, wrap the deck in siding to match the rest of the house. If you have a brick house, consider a custom-designed steel or wrought-iron railing.

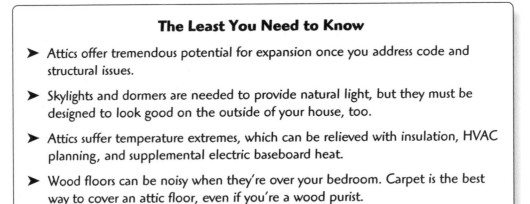

The Least You Need to Know

➤ Attics offer tremendous potential for expansion once you address code and structural issues.

➤ Skylights and dormers are needed to provide natural light, but they must be designed to look good on the outside of your house, too.

➤ Attics suffer temperature extremes, which can be relieved with insulation, HVAC planning, and supplemental electric baseboard heat.

➤ Wood floors can be noisy when they're over your bedroom. Carpet is the best way to cover an attic floor, even if you're a wood purist.

Deck Your House with Decks

Decks are an interesting phenomenon. As we've eliminated the front porch, which gave us a view of the neighbors and provided an impromptu gathering place, we've increasingly added decks at the rear of our houses. I'm sure sociologists have something to say about this retreat to privacy, but from a builder's standpoint, the reasoning is simple: Decks are cheaper to build than most porches. If you already have a deck (see Chapter 20, "Porches and Decks: Your Outdoor Rooms"), your main concern is maintenance, refinishing, and upgrading.

Both porches and decks require the same basic floor framing, but then they part company. A porch needs a roof and a finished ceiling in addition to a solid floor. Traditionally, the floor was tongue-and-groove fir, at least on the west coast; it was never all that cheap to buy or install, but these days it costs a fortune. Porches also need walls finished with the same kind of siding used on the rest of the house.

A deck, on the other hand, doesn't need a roof or siding and is pretty simple to assemble, though decking material, usually cedar or sometimes redwood, can be pricey.

The absence of a ceiling means more maintenance for you: All that rain, snow, and hot sunlight have to go somewhere, and your wood deck is a perfect target.

Despite their high maintenance, decks are built all over the country in all kinds of climates—they seem almost mandatory in California. This chapter gives you a few alternative building ideas and points out some potential maintenance red flags. I'll try and keep your work to a minimum, so you can enjoy your place in the sun—on your deck, of course.

Deck Fundamentals

Decks come in two basic versions: those that sit on or close to the ground and those that are elevated a story or two. The higher you go, the more attention you have to pay to structural matters. Because elevated decks are usually made with post-and-beam construction, it's critical that the posts be sized correctly to carry the load and that they be secured at the base. An 8-foot-long, six-by-six post, for instance, can carry almost twice the load of one that's 12 feet long.

Deck planning and construction will include:

➤ A foundation

➤ Framing

➤ Choice of decking materials and finishes

➤ Railing details

Basic deck.

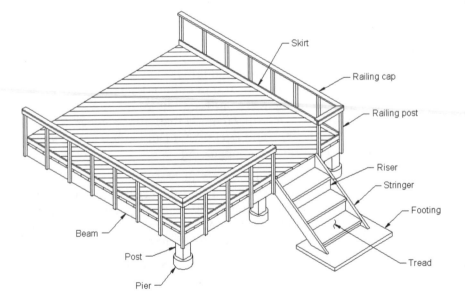

334

➤ Stair locations

➤ Electrical outlets and lights

Concrete Pier: Instant Foundation

Wood and dirt are a worse combination then wood and water; at least with water the wood can get a chance to dry out once in a while. Dirt holds water, and wiggly, squirmy microorganisms that see it as one big vacation resort. To drive these freeloaders away, pressure-treated wood was developed. But even pressure-treated wood isn't impervious to wet dirt. (Some grades of it can be used for wood-to-ground contact, but I don't recommend using it this way for deck construction.) Concrete piers will keep your pressure-treated posts dirt-free and give your deck proper support.

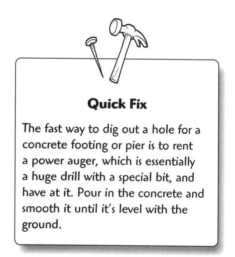

Quick Fix

The fast way to dig out a hole for a concrete footing or pier is to rent a power auger, which is essentially a huge drill with a special bit, and have at it. Pour in the concrete and smooth it until it's level with the ground.

Piers are baby-size, precast concrete foundations made specifically for supporting posts and columns. You want the ones that come with post anchors, which are U-shaped metal saddles that secure the post. One pier gets one post; and the spacing is figured according to the joist span and the size of the beam that sits on top of it. Your local building codes will tell you the spacing of your piers as well as their size and the depth of their footings. Another approach is to pour concrete in a form to the desired height and insert a post anchor in it while it's still setting up.

Frame It Up

Think of your deck as a floor just like any other in your house. You have joists, posts, beams, and some kind of flooring to walk on—in this case, decking. The same construction principles apply:

➤ Posts support beams that themselves support joists

➤ Joists are attached with metal joist hangers

➤ Decking is secured to the joists

A deck that's attached to your house will need a ledger, which is essentially a rim joist to which other joists are attached. The ledger is the deck's reference point; it must be positioned correctly so your finish decking isn't too high, like higher than the door sill (a great way to leak rain and melting snow into your house). All of your framing material should be pressure-treated to protect it from the weather.

Decking Decisions

Decking, the boards you walk on, has to put up with a lot of grief. Weather, spilled barbecue sauce, and scratchy chairs all leave their marks. Your choice of decking and your regular maintenance of it will determine its longevity.

Many people prefer the look of natural wood, but technical advances have brought some new choices:

➤ Plastic lumber

➤ Composite lumber

➤ Pressure-treated decking

Cedar: A Deck Tradition

Cedar has long been the decking wood of choice because of its natural ability to resist insects and decay (cedar has its own preservative oils). This lightweight wood is easy to handle and shape and accepts all types of finishes.

Natural oils or not, cedar needs protection, too; otherwise it will eventually decay from exposure. Cedar is also expensive, especially if you get the good stuff with a straight grain and only minor *knots*. Your deck will look absolutely beautiful, at least for a while, if you build with top-grade cedar, but it requires a lot of maintenance.

Cedar decking.

A Plastic World

We have plastic cars, plastic violins, and plastic body parts—why not decking made from plastic? Plastic lumber sounds like a contradiction in terms, but it will probably be the deck-ing of the future. The history of building and finishing materials is one that goes relentlessly towards lower cost, quicker installation, and lower maintenance and upkeep. Plastic lumber certainly fits into the picture.

Plastic lumber is made from high-density poly-ethylene(HDPE), which comes mainly from recycled plastic milk jugs. (Maybe plastic lumber manufacturers are the guys who sponsor all those "Got Milk?" ads.) Old milk containers are cleaned, dried, ground into small flakes, and then blended with pigment and other fun additives. There is no surface coating; the color you see goes all the way through.

According to various manufacturers, plastic lumber's properties include:

➤ Durability

➤ Resistance to cracking, chipping, peeling, warping, and splintering

➤ Imperviousness to many chemicals, rot, and insects

➤ UV resistance

➤ Ease in cleaning—just hose it down

Plastic lumber comes in several colors, including white, cedar, gray, and sand. When stored prior to installation, it should be well supported and kept out of the sun to prevent any possible warpage. Depending on the manufacturer, you even get three ways to fasten it to your deck joists:

➤ Conventional deck nails and screws

➤ Deck glazing tape

➤ Clips

Deck glazing tape is an adhesive system for attaching plastic lumber. Clips attach to the joists, and the plastic lumber slips into the clip. You never see any surface fasteners with either of these systems.

Plastic lumber is practical, efficient, easy to clean, and, well, plastic. You can build most of your deck out of it except for the structural parts. It makes a lot of sense; you just have to decide how sensible you want to be. What if you want something practical, but you'd rather be looking at wood instead of old milk cartons?

Look Out Below!

Some consumers have commented in on-line newsgroups that some plastic lumber, such as trellises, can warp in extreme heat and become brittle in extreme cold. Ask a supplier or installer in your area who's used these products if they've encountered such problems.

Compromise with Composites

Composite woods are made from recycled wood and plastic—a nice way of saying sawdust and old milk cartons—and can be used for everything you need to finish off the deck: posts, rails, balusters, mounting brackets, and caps. Composite lumber, like plastic wood, is designed for everything but structural use.

Composite wood isn't perfect. Mildew and mold can grow on it just as on regular wood, and it needs regular cleaning with a commercial deck cleaner. It can accept standard deck finishes. Before you decide composites are for you, check out a one- or two-year-old deck that was built with it. See how it's aged and whether you like the results. You want to build this deck just once.

Tales from the Scaffold

Contractors I knew were called out to a house by a homeowner who wanted someone to finish building a second-story deck that he had started. It still needed railings and stairs, but he had done all the framing, post work, and decking. They took one look at it and quietly informed him that none of it was up to code and it would all have to be rebuilt. He had used undersized posts, beams, and even joists. The decking was spaced too tightly, and he'd used the wrong fasteners. It looked like he'd built it intuitively rather than by following the code. They never did hear back from him.

Under Pressure: Pressure-Treated Wood

Pressure-treated wood is also used as decking. Unlike ground-contact-treated wood, which has deep cuts in it to allow the preservative chemicals to penetrate further into it, decking undergoes a different pressure treatment that results in a more-finished look. Wolman is a big producer of pressure-treated lumber and plywood. Pressure-treated wood is the decking material closest in appearance to regular wood, though the treatment process does discolor it and affect how it will absorb a deck finish or preservative coat.

Building and Maintenance Tips

Decks involve more than just strong framing. Decking can't be tacked on as an after-thought. Spacing, fasteners, and finishes must be considered. Railings and balusters have to meet code requirements. Regular maintenance is also essential if you want your deck to have some longevity; even plastic ones have to be hosed off one in a while. A few construction and upkeep rules should keep your work to a minimum.

Doing Decking Right

Leave a space—up to ¹/₄ inch—between deck boards to allow for water drainage; remember, a dry deck is a happy deck. Keep these gaps clean of leaves and other debris that can hold water and prevent it from draining. Hint: It's a lot easier to sweep this stuff out when it's dry. Surface fasteners should be either galvanized finish nails or deck screws.

Railing Safety

Your top railing has to be a minimum of 36 inches high from the decking surface. The bottom rail can't be more than 2 inches off the top of the deck. Also—and this is a big one—the spacing from one vertical member to another (posts and balusters) cannot exceed 4 inches. The idea is to prevent a baby or small child from getting his or her head stuck between the posts or possibly even falling through them.

Railings not only make your deck safe; they play a key design role in its construction. Be creative: Try to match an architectural element of the house or even go freeform. On my last house, I matched the railing and balusters to the geometric design in a leaded-glass window. Lattice, sold in sheets of various design, can easily take the place of balusters and provide privacy at the same time.

Deck Coatings

Outdoor wood needs protection, and that means some kind of coating. Even pressure-treated wood can benefit from a coat or two of sealer. What are your options for decks?

There's always paint, which isn't such a good idea unless your deck is the budget variety. Paint applied to flat exterior surfaces eventually starts flaking, which means more work every time you repaint.

You want a finish that repels water, contains a fungicide, and protects against ultraviolet light. Your choices are:

➤ Clear sealers

➤ Semi-transparent stains

➤ Solid-body stains

Look Out Below!

Keep your pets off your deck until all finishes are completely cured. Dogs and cats lick their paws, and you don't want them licking off toxic deck finish.

339

Clear sealers will leave your wood looking the most natural. Semi-transparent stains are basically clear sealers with added pigment and more UV protection. A solid-body stain has even more pigment, but not as much as paint. Clear sealers and semi-transparent stains have to be reapplied every year, maybe every two years if you don't get much rain or snow.

Getting There: Staircases

Deck staircases should be built out of the same materials as the rest of the deck. The stringers (the supports for the treads, the section you walk on) should be pressure-treated because they'll have contact with a concrete base on the ground. Plan the locations of your staircases carefully! I've seen instances where clearances weren't figured correctly and stairs didn't fit where they were expected to, causing both the owner and the contractor more grief than anyone deserved. On large decks, consider two staircases, one on each end, for easier access.

Deck Power

Always plan on at least one electrical outlet for your deck and some lighting, too. The exposed joists are a perfect pathway for wiring and conduit. The more comfortable the deck, the more time you'll spend on it, so allow enough power for lights, radios, and barbecue rotisseries.

Extras

You can stack your deck with all kinds of extras: planter boxes, benches with built-in storage, tables, even furniture to match your choice of decking. When you're in the planning stage, be sure to allow enough room for any built-ins because they'll take away from how much of the deck area you'll have to walk on. Your building code allows for a certain percentage of your building lot to be covered with structures, including decks. Say you figure on a 10 foot by 20 foot deck, but then start adding benches, planters, and maybe a barbecue. Say good-bye to your 200 square feet of roaming space.

The easiest way to get a sense of deck space is to mark off the proposed dimensions of your deck in your yard and then mark off the built-ins. Feeling cramped? This is the time to reconsider your plans and maybe expand them.

Deck Alternatives: Patios

Patios get a bad rap. They're too often associated with conformity and boredom. Some people even build decks over their old patios—talk about taking a zero-maintenance yard space and turning it into work!

An artistically constructed patio—it can be concrete, brick, pavers, or any combination of stone materials—can accomplish everything a ground-level deck can, but without the hassles of cleaning and sealing it every year. A patio gets cleaned every time you water the plants and hose it off. Patios can feature rock gardens, fountains, ponds, and outdoor furnishings, and you don't have to rotate the furniture as you do on a deck, because the patio's surface won't be altered by water.

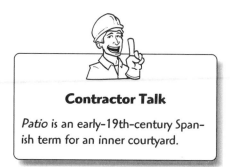

Contractor Talk

Patio is an early-19th-century Spanish term for an inner courtyard.

If you have a problem with the term *patio*, call it your terrace instead and consider all the advantages of this outdoor space. With careful planning and construction—the soil has to be compacted and drainage issues addressed— you can be on your way to easy outdoor living. You'll never, ever have to replace it or repair a deteriorated piece of wood. Contrary to popular wisdom, there isn't any virtue in hard work when the hard work could have been avoided.

The Least You Need to Know

➤ Deck plans and construction must follow code requirements.

➤ Pressure-treated wood is the best choice for deck posts and supports.

➤ The best way to decide on decking material is to look at some existing decks, especially ones that are a few years old.

➤ All wood decks—even those built with pressure-treated wood—will benefit from regular coating with preservative sealers.

➤ Every deck requires some maintenance, and wood decks require the most.

➤ Consider putting in a patio instead of a ground-level deck. They offer a lot of advantages, especially low maintenance requirements.

Part 7
Fantasy Time: Your Dream Projects

When we think of remodeling, we often see medium to large scale projects with one unifying theme: Practicality. We build larger kitchens, add a garage to the back of the house, or install a new heating system—sober projects all. We need these improvements, but are they really any fun?

It's easier, I think, to appreciate smaller scale, more defined remodeling jobs that stand out for their artistry or appeal to our individual interests. It's one thing to show off the new kitchen, but an unexpected wine cellar tucked away in the basement will really spark your friends' interest. A cigar room would bring even the most secretive smoker out of the closet.

Remodeling doesn't have to be all large, loud, dust cloud-producing work. Carefully installed cove moldings will dress up just about any room—without the need to tear it up in the process. Adding a closet could be a week-end job that wouldn't even require your moving into another bedroom.

If you live in an older home, you may wish to take some direction from the past and restore it. This is some of the most challenging remodeling of all—and most rewarding. And, if you're interested in developing your repair and building skills, you couldn't want for better circumstances than a house restoration. I promise you'll never lack for something to do.

Chapter 29

The Finer Side of Remodeling

You don't have to make every remodeling project a monumental event that will become a legendary tale in the family folklore. Simple jobs have an impact, too. Adding a track light in a hallway can change it from a dim passageway to an at-home art gallery. Install a floor-to-ceiling corner cabinet in the living room, and you have a home for all the skateboarding trophies you now have stuffed into your closet.

There are bigger projects, of course, such as adding a fireplace in a family room or installing a tile entryway floor. The scope of these jobs is very contained and doesn't involve filling the house with dust, having a dozen different contractors wandering around, or your living in the basement until the work is finished. Yet these short-term projects bring long-term results.

As you read through this chapter, take a look around your house. Could you use another closet? How about dressing up the living room with some cove molding? Consider one of these budget-friendly jobs to give your house a special touch.

There's Always Room for Another Closet

You don't have to be a clotheshorse to need more closets; most people could use more closet space for general storage. Closets run the gamut from wide enough for their doors to clear a standard hanger to small rooms complete with recessed ceiling lights, wood shoe racks, and a live-in tailor. Walk-in closets are no longer a rarity in new homes, but small closets are still far too common. The master bedroom makes out OK, but the other bedrooms are often short-changed when it comes to closet space.

Builders make the most of bedroom space by building long, narrow closets with sliding doors. It takes only a 20-inch-deep wall recess to do the job, and that's easy to plan into new construction. It may be an efficient use of space, but does it do the job for you?

Store-bought, Custom-made, Built-in, or Added On

Think of a closet as a box, just like a cabinet. A box can be installed just about anywhere in a bedroom or spare room. Your closet remodeling options include:

➤ Buying an armoire or freestanding wardrobe closet

➤ Having a freestanding closet built to your specifications by a cabinetmaker

➤ Constructing a closet using an existing wall as the backside

➤ Cutting through an outer wall and building a closet flush with the interior drywall or plaster

Armoires and wardrobes are the easy way out, and you can select between antique and new. But you'll be buying a pre-assembled unit made to a manufacturer's dimensions, not yours. If you have specific size requirements, a better option is to contract with a cabinetmaker and get a freestanding closet made to your measurements.

Armoires, wardrobes, and freestanding closets should be secured to a back wall, especially if you live in an area prone to seismic activity. Use 3-inch or longer wood screws and always screw them into a wall stud.

Building In

You can assemble a closet to your dimensions out of $^3/_4$-inch, cabinet-grade plywood by using an existing wall as its back. Metal cleats or brackets can secure the sides and top to the wall. With an open shell inside, you can build any configuration of shelves and clothes rods that suits your needs.

Building Out

If you prefer a built-in closet that's flush with your wall, then be prepared to build out. This structural work will require a permit. You'll also need to check property line setback regulations.

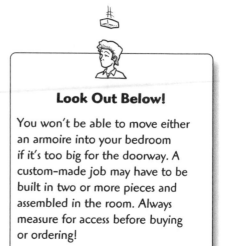

Look Out Below!

You won't be able to move either an armoire into your bedroom if it's too big for the doorway. A custom-made job may have to be built in two or more pieces and assembled in the room. Always measure for access before buying or ordering!

Your choice of closet supports will include:

➤ A ledger support on the outer wall

➤ Posts and beam

➤ Angled supports off the outer wall

Your support system will depend on whether the closet is on the first or second story and the design elements of your house. Building this closet means some outside work with sheathing, siding, and roofing. Try to do as much of the framing as you can from

New closet addition.

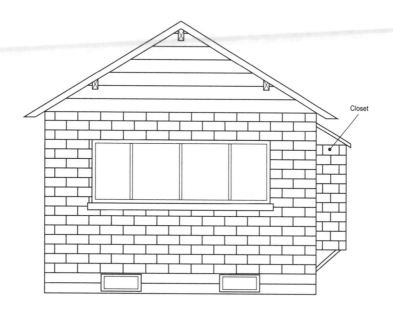

inside your house. This strategy keeps you off ladders when you have to hammer the stud walls together.

Cedar Lining for a Touch of Class

There's cedar, and then there's aromatic cedar, a tree unto itself. The fragrance of aromatic cedar is an appetite suppressant to moth larvae, which damage clothing. This species of cedar is available in paneling and planking, which is easily installed as a closet liner.

Don't worry that your clothes will smell like the cedar shavings in a hamster cage (when the shavings are fresh anyway); they won't. When you take your clothes out of the closet, the cedar aroma will dissipate. Over time, the cedar can lose its fragrance as it's exposed to air, and the cedar oil on the surface of the wood solidifies. A light sanding with 150-grit sandpaper will remove the solidified oil and allow fresh oil to take its place.

Quick Fix

Order enough aromatic cedar to install a finish floor in addition to the walls and ceiling. In small, add-on closets, the floor is used only for storage and won't have any foot traffic, so the thinness of the cedar won't be a problem.

Instant Bedroom

William L. Murphy, apparently tired of living around a standard bed in his turn-of-the-century San Francisco apartment, came up with the idea of a folding bed and had no problem selling them until after World War II when returning veterans rushed to buy new, large homes. Sales began climbing again in the 1980s as cheap housing disappeared; Murphy beds were seen as an inexpensive way to turn a spare room into a bedroom when guests showed up.

Beds made by Murphy's company and its competitors offer a simple way to turn any room—OK, not the kitchen—into an extra bedroom with a bed that doesn't tie up floor space when it's not in use.

They're easily installed and are available in a variety of finishes, sizes, and configurations. Go to www.murphybedcompany.com for further information.

Enter Here: Vestibules and Tile Entryways

A vestibule is an enclosed area between the entry door of a house and the interior. The second door's purpose is to keep cold air out of the house when the entry door is open. Vestibules are a great idea and aren't included much in new construction, but that doesn't mean they can't be revived. As cold and damp as Seattle gets in the winter, they just don't build vestibules out here, not even in restaurants: If you get a table near the door, it's your tough luck.

Look at your entry. Would you be more comfortable in the winter if you had a small, glassed-in room between you and the front door when guests visit? This project is not complicated to build and shouldn't require a permit (check anyway). Your design can include custom-made windows, perhaps leaded ones for elegant results.

A vestibule design must be crafted carefully so it blends flawlessly with its surroundings. If you skimp on the details, it'll be painfully noticeable. These details include:

Look Out Below!

Depending on the design of your vestibule, you may have to install safety glass. Check the local requirements with your building department.

➤ Matching the baseboards, casings, and any wood moldings to the existing ones

➤ Keeping the size of the vestibule in proportion to your entryway

➤ Matching the wall texture to the existing drywall or plaster

If a vestibule is a bit much, reconsider your entryway anyway. Does your front door open onto a hardwood floor or carpet? In such a high-traffic area, you may want a more permanent material.

An Entry to Stand the Test of Time

You can have both an artistic and practical entryway floor if you install a longer-lasting and lower-maintenance material, such as tile, marble, or stone (granite, slate, limestone, and so on). These sound choices will stand up to dirt, wet shoes, and wet paws. A well-chosen slab of marble or stone can dress up your entryway and protect your floors, but how complicated is the installation?

Tile is very rigid, and it doesn't like any movement underneath it, so your subfloor and underlayment must be well supported and secured tightly to the joists. Acceptable underlayment, in descending order from the best to good, would be:

➤ Mortar or mud bed

➤ Concrete backerboard or cement board

➤ Exterior plywood

A mud bed is the very best approach; it's a professionally installed layer of mortar troweled over roofing felt and wire mesh. A tile setter then levels and finishes the mortar in preparation for the tile or slab. A good tile contractor can adjust the level of the mortar to any unevenness in the surrounding floor.

More goes into a tile floor than meets the eye.

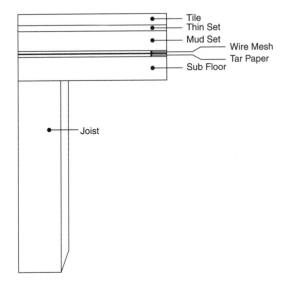

Measurements Are Everything

Your entryway has two critical dimensions that can affect your installation of a tile, marble, or stone floor: the thickness of your floor (the subfloor, any underlayment, and the floor covering, such as carpet or hardwood) and the distance between your floor and the bottom of your entry door. Ideally, you want your new floor to remain flush with the surrounding area, but that may not be possible. Consider the following:

➤ A subfloor is at least $^3/_4$ inch thick

➤ Hardwood flooring is up to $^3/_4$ inch thick

➤ A marble slab is $^3/_4$ inch thick

➤ Tile averages $^3/_8$ inch in thickness

➤ Cement backerboard is $^5/_8$ inch thick

➤ Thin set, in which tile or a slab is set, is $^1/_8$ inch thick

As you can see, there's more than one thickness measurement to calculate into this job. Removing a section of hardwood flooring gives you some room to install your tile or slab, but your door may not clear it as it opens. That means trimming to accommodate the height of the tile, and adjusting the door threshold as well. This complicated job may be best left to a tile setter.

Trim Time

In the 1830s, wider dimensions for baseboards were the standard of the day in higher end houses, and they've been diminishing ever since. If you trace home construction over the years, you'll find that interior trim and molding have been shrinking and that some types have disappeared completely. But that trend shouldn't stop you from dressing up your house with some cool-looking trim.

Out with the New, in with the Old

The best way to view traditional woodwork and trim is to visit some older houses and see what appeals to you. You'll have to go back at least 60 years or more. Your choices will depend on how your house is currently trimmed out. Some new homes are dressing up again, but usually the builder holds back by not trimming out all the windows or by installing a narrow, plain baseboard. The main floor may get the full treatment, but the bedrooms get ignored.

Mixing the style of a new house with more traditional wood molding can bring mixed results, so pick your woodwork pattern carefully. Bring a piece of baseboard home, lay it against a living room wall for a few days, and see whether it makes sense visually.

Where Do You Start?

Before you experiment in your highly public and visible living room, try trimming out a bedroom. Bedrooms are great places to experiment with different styles and shapes. Finish one room and live with it for a month. If it doesn't strike you—or it strikes you the wrong way—quit while you're ahead and decide whether you still think it's such a good idea for the rest of your house.

See whether you can add to your existing woodwork instead of completely removing it. You may have wide, but plain, baseboards and door and window casings. What would happen if you added a piece of *cove molding* to the top of the baseboard? You can add more molding directly onto the face of your casings, increasing their thickness and making them more interesting at the same time.

What about those old flush mahogany doors? You can't exactly turn them into six-panel ones, but you can disguise them by gluing molding on their face to create the illusion of a panel.

Take a look at your ceiling. Would cove molding, crown molding, or something simpler add

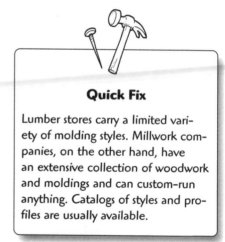

Quick Fix

Lumber stores carry a limited variety of molding styles. Millwork companies, on the other hand, have an extensive collection of woodwork and moldings and can custom-run anything. Catalogs of styles and profiles are usually available.

some appeal, or would it make the room seem smaller by breaking the continuity between the walls and the ceiling? If there's absolutely nothing you can do with your existing woodwork, carefully remove it and replace it with new work.

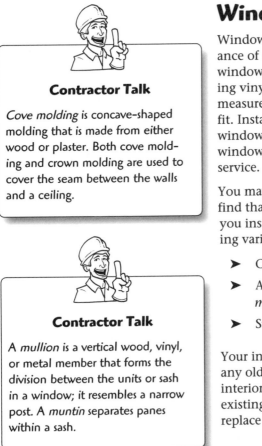

Windows

Windows are a big influence on the exterior appearance of a house. Replacing your old metal or wood windows is a fairly painless process if you're installing vinyl windows in their place. Your openings are measured, and new windows are manufactured to fit. Installation crews remove and haul off the old windows and pop in the new windows; trimming the window out with new casings is usually an optional service.

You may already have relatively new windows, but find that they detract from the looks of your house. If you install new wood windows, you have an unending variety of designs available to you, including:

➤ Casement, double-hung, and awning windows

➤ Any configuration of glass, *muntins*, and *mullions*

➤ Stained glass and leaded glass

Your installer will have to build a wood frame around any old embedded metal frame and finish it off with interior and exterior trim, but if you think your existing windows are ugly, that's reason enough to replace them if your budget can handle it.

A Welcoming Front Door

An entryway door is an important part of the exterior look of your house. You have dozens of choices for a replacement door and three materials to choose from:

➤ Wood

➤ Metal

➤ Fiberglass

Wood doors are traditional, awesome to look at, and in need of regular maintenance. A wood door works best when it's under an overhang or porch and isn't directly exposed to the weather. With regular painting or clear coating, it'll last indefinitely.

A hybrid wood door uses laminated lumber veneer for the frame and wood composite, which can be painted or stained, for the surface wood or skin. The core of the door is full of polystyrene insulation, which also adds some sound-proofing value.

It's a Steel

Next up on the door food chain is the steel entry door, complete with its own core of polyurethane insulation. Steel has obvious advantages, such as weather and decay resistance, but it's not the perfect door. Steel doors have their own problems, including:

➤ Denting

➤ Rust

➤ Heat buildup

Stanley, the tool company, makes a line of both steel and fiberglass doors. They warn against excessive heat absorption by steel doors if they're painted with a dark finish or placed behind a nonventilated storm door. Either action will void the door's warranty.

If someone wants to break into your house, a steel door can be sprung or forced open the same way as a wood one. Steel may offer an illusion of worry-free security, but I'd still lock up the jewelry collection if I were you.

Fiberglass

Outside of a custom-built door, fiberglass doors are the most expensive of the three door types and are particularly suitable for the weather in coastal areas. Fiberglass can be either painted or stained and comes with the longest warranties of all door types; Stanley, for example, offers a limited lifetime warranty on its models. They won't dent, rot, or rust, and they are constructed with a polyurethane foam core for insulation. Some manufacturers even offer fiberglass French door systems with security glass.

Look Out Below!

Factory-finished wood doors may come with an exterior lacquer finish that soaks deep into the grain of the wood. If the door needs refinishing, the lacquer must be completely stripped out of the grain with paint remover, steel wool, and a lacquer thinner rinse. Otherwise, the wood will stain unevenly, resulting in a splotchy finish.

The best way to take advantage of both fiberglass and steel door engineering is to install door jambs made from the same material as the door. Look into engineered systems that combine the outer door material, the core insulation, and weather-stripped jambs.

Decisions, Decisions

Wood looks terrific, steel is economical, and fiberglass has the best warranty—which do you choose? It's a case of the dreams of the artist running up against the realities of everyday life. If you're willing to pamper a wood door with regular varnishing or

painting, then by all means install wood. If you'd rather ignore it and want a top-notch door, look into fiberglass. If you're indifferent, but need to replace the door, consider steel.

Quick Fix

Uncertain about floor colors? Find a color you like and then go one shade lighter. An entire room can appear darker than you expected once all of the flooring is laid; a lighter shade will compensate.

Hung Up

When you replace an entry door, in addition to the cost of the door itself, you'll incur two other costs: The labor to hang or install it and the cost of a new lock set and its installation. The installation fee will depend on the type of door and the extent of the adjustment needed to fit it. For this job, I would strongly suggest that you hire someone who specializes in door installation. Ask your dealer for some recommendations, or call a weather-stripping company.

Wood Floors

Wood floors can dress up a room. They can be in-stalled just about anywhere you have a flat, level surface. You can even install them over other types of floors, such as vinyl tile, without stripping out all of the old flooring material. It isn't uncommon to install hardwood floors over existing floors of fir or other soft wood.

If you're doing only a single room, you or your installer will have to place a transition strip of some kind between the new wood floor and the adjoining floor at the door-way(s). If you want to keep the mess and dust down, install pre-finished flooring instead of raw wood, which would have to be sanded and finished.

The Least You Need to Know

➤ A remodeling project doesn't have to be big and messy to be effective. Small, well-executed jobs can add value and comfort to your house, too.

➤ You can always find a use for an additional closet.

➤ It's easy to dress up a room with a change in wood trim and molding.

➤ Replacement windows and doors should blend flawlessly with the style and design of your house.

➤ The finer remodeling touches should come after your major work is completed.

Chapter 30

Really Fun Additions

In This Chapter

➤ Adding a wine cellar in an under-used basement

➤ A media room needs quiet and plenty of outlets

➤ Heat things up with a sauna or steam room

➤ Adding a politically incorrect smoking room

Remodeling can dredge up many lessons of childhood, but one in particular stands out: You can't go out and play until you've done your chores. You have to do your remodeling chores—repair the foundation, replace the roof, update your plumbing—before you can address your creative, fun side. You can build a new sauna, but it won't do you much good if you haven't got enough juice in your electrical system to run it.

If your budget will allow it, indulge your whims. When you're remodeling fun rooms, you're limited only by your imagination, dollars, and available space. Picture yourself in a high-tech leather recliner, surrounded by stereo speakers and sound-deadening walls so you don't hear anything that's going on outside your musical sanctum. Consider sewing rooms, poker rooms, and even a separate space for a video game parlor.

Treat these new spaces as seriously as any other remodeling project:

➤ Write up a plan.

➤ Be sure your project fits into your overall house plans.

➤ Apply for the applicable permits.

➤ Research materials and contractors.

➤ Enjoy it thoroughly.

This chapter highlights some popular additions, but it's only a starting point for your own imagination and inventiveness.

For Oenophiles Only: Wine Cellars

The wine cellar is an increasingly popular home addition. Wine storage includes anything from a cardboard wine box turned on its side and placed under a bathroom vanity sink (don't laugh, this works and the wine stays cool) to a full-blown, climate-controlled room complete with a tasting table, glass storage, and a small refrigerator for cheese. Even warehouse stores sell self-contained wine-storage units with cooling systems; just plug them in and walk away.

Look Out Below!

Remodeling can be less stressful if all parties communicate clearly and of-ten. These are indulgent projects, so tread carefully with your significant other before blowing a few thousand dollars on a video game room.

As you move up in the world of wine appreciation, so will your definitions of proper storage. Laying a bottle of Chardonnay on its side in the vegetable crisper before dinner just won't do it anymore. You're ready to enter the world of serious wine storage.

A Natural for Your Basement

The wrong temperature and humidity can take its toll on a quality wine. A windowless section of your basement, already a naturally cool area, is an ideal location for wine storage. Pick an out-of-the-way corner and consider how you'll use the space:

➤ Will it be for storage only?

➤ Will you do wine tasting?

➤ Do you expect your collection to grow?

The larger the wine cellar, the more expensive it'll be to keep cool. If you expect to expand your collection, don't shortchange yourself on the dimensions; be realistic, but build as large a room as you expect to use in the future.

Keep these guidelines in mind when you write up your plans:

➤ Completely insulate the room for the most effective use of the cooling unit.

➤ The sole plate or bottom section of your new walls must be pressure-treated wood because it's coming into contact with the concrete floor.

➤ Install a lock on the door.

➤ Install sufficient overhead lighting.

➤ Consider a dedicated circuit for the cooling unit.

Rack 'em Up

Wine racking is a big deal if you go by what you see in the brochures and on the Web sites of companies that manufacture storage racks. They extol the virtues of clear redwood or western cedar racks, which are carefully assembled like fine furniture and have prices to match. Elegant-looking wine racks won't store your wine any better than homemade racks made with #3 pine, the cheapest of the cheap.

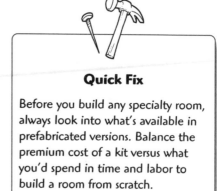

Quick Fix

Before you build any specialty room, always look into what's available in prefabricated versions. Balance the premium cost of a kit versus what you'd spend in time and labor to build a room from scratch.

If you're not inclined to go the bargain route, you have some alternatives:

➤ Contact companies specializing in wine cellars (try www.customwinecellars.com or do an Internet search under wine cellars).

➤ Order premade wine racks.

➤ Purchase and assemble modular wine racks.

You can order 72-inch high, ready-to-assemble storage units from www.wineenthusiast.com (or call 800-377-3330). These units come in all shapes and types, including individual bottle holders, diamond shapes, and case racks. The staff will even help you design your own wine cellar. Just fax your sketches and dimensions to 800-833-8466 or contact the Web site.

A Chilling Experience

For many novice collectors, an insulated room in a basement would probably meet most wine storage requirements. If you want to go a step or two further, you'll need a

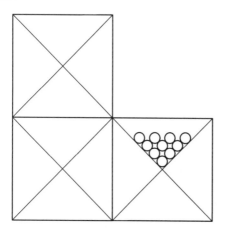

Typical wine storage.

cooling unit to control both temperature and humidity. Keep a few things in mind before you make your purchase:

➤ Refrigeration units aren't cheap; depending on the room size, you could be looking at $1,000 or more.

➤ Cooling units make noise, so consider their location before you build your wine cellar; listen to one before ordering.

➤ These units are most effective when they vent outside the wine cellar itself.

Refrigeration units range from a Breezaire self-contained, 110-volt, wall-mounted model to their 2000-cubic foot, ducted system with remote compressor.

Tales from the Scaffold

A local wine store was quoted thousands of dollars to install a cooling and ventilation system in its modest-size store. They were assured that this was the only way to cool the store properly. Instead, the owners decided to install a single air-conditioner in the window over the entry door. For a few hundred dollars, even on the hottest days of summer, the store was cool and comfortable; the wine was happy, too. There are always alternatives if you're willing to explore them.

Finishing Touches

You have your room, racks, and refrigeration. What else do you need besides wine? You've gone this far, why not consider the following:

➤ Overhead storage for wine glasses

➤ A tasting area

➤ Wine-related software

You could keep a handwritten journal and record vintages and the results of tastings. Or you could haul down your increasingly worthless four-year-old computer and set it up with software made specifically for wine lovers. You can even download a sample of a program called Wine Cellar by going to www.geocities.com/NapaValley/5996. Your plans should allow for an electrical outlet in your wine cellar even if you don't see bringing in a computer any time soon. Given the rate at which technology is changing and prices are dropping, there'll eventually be something you'll need the outlet for.

Your Own Movie Theater

My idea of home entertainment is a good book, Scrabble game, or standard, off-the-shelf TV and VCR. Video/audiophiles have a much broader viewpoint, which explains the growing popularity of home theaters. If you sprinkle your conversations with terms such as pre-amps, surround-sound decoders, and subwoofers, then a home theater is right up your alley.

Your media room can be as elaborate as you can afford it to be. Possible equipment includes:

➤ Big-screen TV

➤ Projection video

➤ Satellite integration

➤ Computerized lighting

➤ Motorized screen

➤ Dolby Digital, DTS, or THX sound systems

➤ Theater seating

➤ Home concession stands

Your equipment choices will influence where you build or house your home theater. *Video Magazine* is one source of equipment reviews.

Location, Location

Theideal theater room is very much like a commercial theater: It's dark and quiet and has seating with clear views of the screen. You'll need a room that's large enough to accommodate the equipment you've chosen. If this is starting to sound like your basement again, you're right: The basement is an ideal setting. You'll have sound-deafening concrete walls on up to three sides, depending on the size of your theater, and a concrete floor underneath. Add insulation to the remaining wall(s) and ceiling, and you'll have an optimum home theater sound experience.

Quick Fix

According to the Consumer Electronics Manufacturers Association (CEMA, January 9, 1997), more than 80 percent of home theater owners installed their systems themselves.

Add a Circuit or Two

You'll need many outlets to service planned and future equipment. The outlets should be on a dedicated circuit, and cable service and satellite cables should enter the room close to the location of the equipment. Install and hide in the walls as many equipment cables as possible during the framing stage of construction. Buy the best cables you can and be sure they're sized for the distance they'll have to run to reach your speakers (the longer the distance, the thicker the cable).

Making Arrangements

Keep your seating in mind when you locate your TV or projection screen. Will this location give you the best viewing area? As a general rule, the distance between the viewer and the television should be about four times the size of the screen. If you have a 25-inch TV screen, for instance, your seating should be around 8 feet away.

You can order and install real theater seating, but this can be expensive. It may be appropriate for large home setups, but you can easily get by with a comfortable couch and overstuffed chairs. Plus, these seats are movable if you ever change addresses and have to say good-bye to your home theater.

Speaker locations (you'll have at least six of them) are another concern. Movie theater sound results from a complex relationship between high-resolution film, multiple speakers, and encoded soundtracks that coordinate movement on the screen with the sounds you hear. Home theaters use front speakers, a central speaker that reproduces a movie's voice track, and rear channel speakers; some home theaters have additional subwoofers that can be used to enhance movie soundtracks.

Tales from the Scaffold

When George Lucas, the Star Wars guy, became dissatisfied with commercial theater presentations of his films, he developed THX, a greatly improved sound system for theaters. The home version, THX Home Cinema, competes with other speaker systems, notably Dolby.

Your Own Casino

Surprisingly, some states allow you to own your own gaming-style slot machines. There is a big caveat, of course: You cannot use them for gambling or commercial purposes. Fourteen states allow such slot machines; some of the remaining states allow older machines (15 years or more, depending on the state), and others prohibit any and all such machines. Be sure to check with your state gambling or attorney general's office before you get outfitted as a croupier.

One version of a slot machine for home use is not considered a gaming device, though it works like one. It takes tokens instead of money, and you can stop the spinning reels manually by pressing buttons on the front of the machine; that classifies it as a game of skill. If your fantasy is to be a floor manager in Las Vegas and still keep your day job, a casino room is for you.

You'll build this room like a home theater: In the basement behind insulated walls so the electronic cacophony doesn't drive everyone else in the house batty. Once again, install a dedicated circuit for your one-armed bandit(s). Fake security cameras would add an authentic touch. Allow room for poker tables and storage for cards, poker chips, and green eye shades.

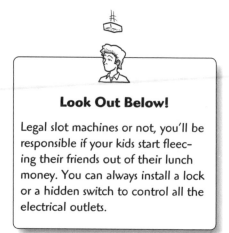

Look Out Below!

Legal slot machines or not, you'll be responsible if your kids start fleecing their friends out of their lunch money. You can always install a lock or a hidden switch to control all the electrical outlets.

More Noise Makers

If you want something more wholesome than slot machines, look into other amusements such as:

➤ Pinball games

➤ Jukeboxes

➤ Video games

➤ Arcade games

Your children will not understand your attraction to pinball and will disparage restored Pac-Man games as being extremely lame, but it's your room, so you can do what you want. Pinball will drive unappreciative family members even crazier than a slot machine, so be certain to install insulation in the ceiling. One source of this coin-operated entertainment is www.vintagegames.com, located in Austin, Texas.

Hot Stuff

Sauna is apparently the only Finnish word in an English dictionary. All right, Helsinki is in there, too, but it's in the geographical names section, so it doesn't entirely count. All kinds of health claims are made about the benefits of using a sauna, but the fact is that a sauna just feels cathartic, especially if you go directly to a cold shower after you're through taking the heat.

A sauna is an obtainable fun room for any house. The size of your sauna will be determined by how many people you want it to hold at a single sitting. Saunas produce dry heat, despite the water coming out of you, and do not present a major moisture problem for walls and ceilings.

Saunas can be built according to your own plans, assembled from precut sauna kits, or installed as prebuilt units. Your choice will depend on your size requirements and limitations, your budget, and your carpentry skills if you'll be doing the building yourself. The easiest way to go is with a prebuilt unit: All you need is a location and a dedicated electrical circuit.

The Sum of the Parts

A sauna consists of the same parts and pieces regardless of how you buy it. These parts include:

➤ Wood walls, door, and benches

➤ Heater

➤ Thermostat controls

➤ Stones for the heater

➤ Ceiling light

Quick Fix

A sauna requires about a half hour to heat up. Infrared saunas use radiant heat and have virtually no warm-up time. Try both models before making your purchase.

Sauna kits are advertised as made from the finest furniture-grade western cedar. The selection of the cedar is critical: It must be first-rate and knot-free. Any knot can ooze out sap when heated and burn someone sitting on that board.

Building from Scratch

It's a good idea to build your sauna close to a bathroom so users can jump into the shower and wash off. You'll need to insulate the walls and ceiling (be sure to use insulation with a good vapor barrier). Use only the clearest tongue-and-groove cedar for the walls. Don't leave any nail heads exposed in the benches; they can burn you if you sit or lean against one. Build a wood heater guard to keep you and your family from bumping into the heater. Go to a sauna supplier to get some ideas on design and styles. Compare the cost of a precut, ready-to-assemble unit versus building your own.

If You Like the Wet Look . . .

Steam rooms were once the province of health clubs and often left something to be desired in the sanitation department. These rooms are traditionally done in tile, but you can take an easier, less expensive, and lower maintenance route.

Tongue and Groove Cedar

Studs

Sauna wall elements.

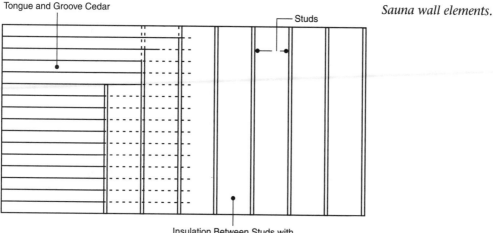

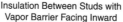

Insulation Between Studs with
Vapor Barrier Facing Inward

Home steam rooms consist of a steam generator, electrical and plumbing hookups, nozzles, controls, and the room itself. Some manufacturers suggest you convert an existing shower into a private steam room, but I wouldn't recommend it. Others suggest building your own room with tile, granite, or marble walls, but this kind of room is both expensive and a future maintenance headache. Steam rooms produce a lot of moisture and should be built in as part of a large bathroom.

The best solution is to install an acrylic steam room. I've seen these units in Europe, and they're wonderful. Each unit comes complete with:

➤ Ceiling and wall panels

➤ Seating

➤ Vapor-proof glass door

➤ Steam generator and controls

Best of all, there's no grout to clean or maintain. Cleaning is a snap because of the plastic surface.

Lighting Up in Style

In an article dated December 4, 1998, *The Wall Street Journal* declared a retro smoking room to be the new status symbol. New York tobacconist Nat Sherman International, Inc., according to this article, has designed smoking rooms starting with a $7,000 walk-in humidor all the way up to a $150,000 reproduction of an English hunt club. A smoking room addition is definitely guy territory, despite the number of women cigar smokers.

Look Out Below!

There are plenty of statistics on tobacco-related health risks. Second-hand smoke is a real issue that you must address if you build a smoking room. If you have children or asthma sufferers in your home, be sure that your smoking room is well sealed and ventilated.

The key consideration when designing a smoking room—spousal, family, and health issues aside—is ventilation. The best and most expensive approach is a fast-working, dedicated ventilation system to remove smoke and odor from the smoking room only that is not tied to the house's air circulation. Claims made about negative ionization and ozone-generating systems with removable filters may go up in smoke when you compare them with a fresh-air ventilation system.

Finally, no smoking room would be complete without smoking room toys: Mahogany paneling, leather chairs, cognac glasses, and, to make a fashion statement, a smoking jacket and fez.

Seamstresses and Tailors Only

Sewing projects often end up on the dining room table, which makes formal entertaining a little tough. A designated sewing room allows you to leave projects spread out and undisturbed until you can finish them. This room should include:

➤ Large, counter-style workspace

➤ Lighting for close work

➤ Shelves for patterns and cloth

➤ Storage for small items (thread, needles, buttons, and so on)

➤ Full-length, three-way mirror

➤ Raised platform for fittings

The Least You Need to Know

➤ Do the necessary remodeling and upgrades before you work on the strictly fun, optional rooms.

➤ Wine cellars are a natural for unused areas of your basement.

➤ Pay special attention to insulating media rooms, wine cellars, rooms with amusement machines, and saunas.

➤ Smoking rooms require a dedicated ventilation system to effectively clear out smoke and odors.

Restoration or Remodeling?

Historic restoration can be a slippery concept. No one who is going to take an 1890s brownstone back to its "original condition" means they're going to put in lead pipes and a coal furnace, so just what does restoration mean?

It's a judgment call for one thing. You want to strip all the paint from what was originally varnished woodwork, for example, but will you strip out the linoleum that's always covered the old fir floors in the kitchen and then sand and refinish them? Most restoration work is a return to the design and aesthetic origins of a house while introducing modern conveniences. You shouldn't fall into a lock step with the past if it doesn't meet your needs for some modern comforts.

Don't limit yourself to a cramped kitchen or poor floor plan simply because they're original to the house. Take a reasoned approach to your renovation work. Find some books about similar period homes for guidance. Check your local property records for any early photos of your home's exterior (you'd be surprised to find what's on file). Pick the best of the old and combine it with the best of the new. The results will be both charming and practical, which is an excellent combination for any old home.

Tales from the Scaffold

Some years ago, the *Seattle Times* did a feature on a local architect's home. He'd spent over 17 years restoring an 1890s Victorian house, even going so far as to install the type of windows and wainscoting he thought, based on his research, a Victorian should have. He made the house more Victorian than it had been to begin with!

Historical Accuracy Is the Guiding Light

Most homeowners, by my observations, try to stay within the spirit of the restoration laws by being faithful to a lot of the visual details—refinishing floors, tearing off wood paneling, repairing old plaster, and finding reproduction window hardware—but upgrading all the mechanical functions. Even then, there are compromises:

➤ Do you replace the original wood single-pane windows with new matching wood windows that have insulated glass, which will give the outside of the house a different appearance?

➤ Wall-to-wall carpet didn't exist 75 years ago, but going back to the wood floors in the second-story bedrooms is noisy and more work to clean. What should you do?

➤ A new reproduction claw foot bathtub costs a fortune and can't be built with a shower surround to protect the walls. Your kids will get water everywhere unless you go with a more modern tub.

➤ The trim throughout the house is no longer a standard pattern or size. How can you match it for your addition? Should you even bother?

Some issues are simpler to deal with. When you're doing historic renovation, choosing colors, deciding whether an arch is original to the house, and finding out what your missing original doors looked like is not difficult; let history be your guide. Old paint can be analyzed for colors, and just walking through a house or two of the same vintage as yours will tell you what the doors are supposed to look like. In that respect, your decisions are kind of easy.

I Have Nothing Better to Do

There are always overboard remodelers. Here's a case that stood out to me.

In the 1980s, a certain state capitol building—let's just say it's west of the Mississippi—underwent a major, multimillion-dollar restoration. Locally, it was probably known as the Contractor and Artisan Full Employment Act, because just about everyone in town got a job working on it. This building has very tall, heavy entry doors that originally only opened inward—not the best situation in the event of an emergency evacuation. The new reproduction doors followed suit, as if hanging them to open outward would have somehow torn the historic fabric of the building and negated the restoration efforts.

When I took a tour of the building and asked the tour guide about the door issue, she apparently took me for a restoration Philistine, retorting curtly that it was irrelevant, and all that was important was saving the building. I almost suggested that we have a fire drill to see how irrelevant it was, but I thought better of it.

Quick Fix

Need some matching hardwood flooring strips to patch a visibly damaged section of your floor? Look inside your closets. You can buy new wood, but you may not match the patina of the wood as closely as you'd like. You can always patch the closet floor with plywood and carpet it.

Tales from the Scaffold

Clients of mine made a perfect blend of old and new in a turn-of-the-century bathroom. They wanted a large, claw foot bathtub with a shower, but it would have required the tub to be surrounded by a shower curtain—hardly the way to show it off. Instead, they built a tile surround on three of the walls, hung a shower curtain on the remaining side, and installed a tile floor underneath with a floor drain. It was a very clever approach, and it worked like a charm.

How Far Back Do You Go?

Some features of a house should never be resurrected because they don't fit with modern living. My old bungalow originally had a cedar shake roof that had since been covered with two layers of asphalt shingles. If I were still living there, I would never consider replacing the existing asphalt roof with high-maintenance cedar.

Some original wood finishes and colors are just plain ugly—how's that for being objec-tive? One such finish from the 1920s was a type of glazing, a thinned-out coat of paint lightly brushed on to woodwork and then wiped off with a rag dampened with thinner or turpentine.

Clues

Your old house offers you a number of clues to its original condition if you know where to look. For example, attics with charred rafters indicate a past fire and rebuilding, perhaps not to the original plans. If a utility room at the rear of the house or the rear section of a kitchen has a slant to the floor, it's a strong indication that the room was a porch that was enclosed.

Thinking of refinishing your wood floors? Remove a piece of *base shoe* first. You'll usu-ally find that it's intact and that the section of the floor underneath it was not sanded. The difference in thickness between the floor under the base shoe and the sanded areas will give you or your floor contractor some idea of how many times the floor has been sanded and whether there's enough floor left to do it again.

The Hazards of Hazards

I suppose there are worse fates than living in a culture that attempts to remove all presumed toxic menaces and safety hazards from our lives at any cost. Over the years, lead-based paint, asbestos, wayward oil tanks, and frayed electric wiring have found themselves in a large red circle with a slash through it.

Here are some of the ways the presence of these hazards can increase your remodel-ing costs:

➤ Asbestos has to be abated according to regulations from plumbing and heating fixtures and pipes before contractors can work on them.

➤ Lead-based paint and lead pipes cannot be removed unless a contractor follows established government guidelines.

➤ Oil tank removal must be carried out according to the rules of the municipality.

➤ Old wiring can be a fire hazard and should be inspected and sometimes replaced.

Still want to fix the place up? You'll need a crash course in hazardous material removal and disposal.

Go by the Rules

The same officials who've made such a mess of regulating industrial and nuclear waste all these years have few qualms about establishing and micromanaging certain restrictions on the residential level. Add some state and local regulations, and you'll have to stay on your toes as a remodeler of an old house. Check with your local building and health departments regarding these issues:

➤ All regulations that may affect your dealings with lead-based paint, asbestos, and oil tanks

➤ A clear understanding about which work you can do yourself and what must be done by a certified contractor (such as an asbestos abatement contractor)

➤ Disposal requirements

Look Out Below!

Mishandling lead or asbestos can result in big fines for you, even if your contractor was the one who messed up. It also can slow a job down if an inspector issues a stop work order until proper cleanup and removal has been completed.

The following information is only advisory:
Read all the necessary government pamphlets (see Appendix H, "Safety") for more information. Oil tanks are considered a liability when selling a house; if a tank has leaked and contaminated the soil under or around it, removal can be expensive.

Adios to Asbestos

Asbestos is a naturally occurring mineral with great fire-retardant qualities that used to be used in residences to wrap hot water pipes for heating systems and tap water and to wrap heat ducts. The degree of danger asbestos poses is controversial, particularly the mass removals of it from schools. In one study by the Harvard Medical School, the conclusion was that exposure from the process of removing the asbestos ceiling tiles in schools posed a greater danger than leaving them in place.

Before you attempt to remove asbestos yourself, check with your local building department officials to see whether it's allowed or whether it must be done by a certified abatement contractor.

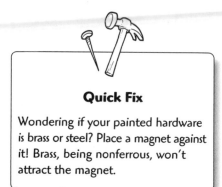

Quick Fix

Wondering if your painted hardware is brass or steel? Place a magnet against it! Brass, being nonferrous, won't attract the magnet.

Lead: It's Everywhere

Long term, heavy exposure to lead is a problem. The law is very specific about its removal and containment, especially around children. I could write a book about it (actually, I am), but for your purposes, treat lead the same way you would asbestos: With great precautions. Safety tips for both lead and asbestos can be found in Appendix H, "Safety."

Unpainting Your House

Original paint and wood finishes can be easy to identify, especially if all your door hinges and other hardware have been painted over as well. Past painters and homeowners too lazy to remove them when they painted have left you an easy way to identify the wood's original finish.

If your woodwork has been painted, remove a doorknob or two and the round metal plates behind them. Gently scrape the paint off with a putty knife or the blade of a pocketknife. You may find:

➤ Varnish underneath (this is good)

➤ Shellac (this isn't as good)

➤ Primer (this can be bad)

Stripping paint is standard procedure for owners of old houses. The original finish will determine whether your job will be cursed or blessed.

Look Out Below!

Never assume how your woodwork was originally finished based on the type or age of the house; always do a test patch first by scraping off the paint. I ran across one Tudor whose mahogany had been painted since it was new—a highly unusual case and very disappointing to the new owner.

Strip Show: Going Back to Varnished Woodwork

Paint that has been applied over a varnished finish can be stripped off pretty cleanly because the varnish prevents it from soaking into the wood. Few people ever properly prepare varnish for painting by sanding and deglossing it first. Shellac also prevents the wood from absorbing the paint, but it's harder to strip off. Primer indicates that the woodwork has always been painted, and all you can do is clean it up and repaint it. You cannot strip and refinish it completely be-cause there'll always be bits of primer in the grain of the wood.

Don't believe me? Follow my cardinal rule and do a small sample first, such as a couple feet of baseboard. Strip it and stain it. When you see bits of white primer coming through, especially on highly detailed pieces of trim, think kindly of me for stopping you before things got out of hand.

Shellac was also used as a clear-coating finish material. It's much gummier to remove regardless of which method you use. It dries much faster than varnish—minutes as opposed to hours—allowing a painter to finish sooner and not worry about dust. Unlike paint or varnish, which use mineral spirits as their solvent, shellac demands denatured alcohol.

Stripping It Off Before You Strip

The easiest way to strip most woodwork is to carefully remove it from the wall first. After you remove it from the wall, you can take all the pieces to a garage or workroom, seal it off, make your mess, and then reinstall the trim. This process will also give you a cleaner job than you'll get if you strip the woodwork in place.

With the woodwork flat on a work surface, follow these steps:

Quick Fix

To remove woodwork, carefully insert a wide, stiff putty knife between the edge of the woodwork and the wall, working your way up and down its length. Pry back slightly from the wall until the nails are exposed. Cut the nails with a hacksaw blade or clip them with wire cutters and pull the board out with a small pry bar.

1. Scrape the bulk of the paint off.

2. Apply one thick coat of stripper.

3. Remove the stripper with a putty knife.

4. Clean the residue off with steel wool and lacquer thinner (varnish), denatured alcohol (shellac), or water (water-rinseable strippers).

5. Sand the woodwork when it's dry.

Tank-dipping operations, that is, immersing your woodwork in a tank of either chemical stripper or hot water and lye, are other options to consider, but do a test piece first. Dipping causes its own problems by discoloring wood and raising the grain, giving it a rough, hairy feel and look.

Varnished woodwork that's never been painted strips pretty fast and does not need to be removed. Wide baseboards are tough to remove without splitting them and are best worked on in place.

You're only removing the trim, not the door or window jambs. Old, double-hung and casement window sash can be removed completely, however. Be sure to carefully mark and code any woodwork you remove, including doors. It all has to go back in its original location. You can even line up the old nail holes for a precise reinstallation.

Paint Removal Is Never Fun

You can remove paint either mechanically by scraping and sanding or chemically with paint remover. A combination of the two approaches is usually the fastest and least messy, lead issues not withstanding. I've found that scraping the worst of the paint off first and then using chemicals to remove the residue and varnish/shellac makes the process tolerable.

Scraping requires some control on your part, so you don't gouge the wood by digging in too deeply. You need the right tool: Red Devil manufactures a paint scraper with a carbide blade that gives you fantastic control without tearing up the underlying wood. It's the perfect tool for scraping paint off varnish, but it's not commonly available, so you'll probably have to order it from any Red Devil dealer (try your local hardware store). They're not cheap at around $25 each, but they're well worth the investment.

Refinishing

Now that you've stripped off the paint, you'll want to finish the wood. Wood stains come in an array of colors, but you should always test a piece of wood first before you commit to a color or type of stain. You may not want any stain at all, preferring just to clear-coat the wood, so do a sample of that as well. A little stain goes a long way, so brush on only a small amount until you get the tone you're looking for. Brush it on, let it sit for a few minutes, and wipe off the excess with a rag. Apply polyurethane, varnish, or oil over the stain for protection.

Exterior Paint: Loads of Lead

For years, exterior paint has been scraped, sanded with big electric disc sanders, and torched off with propane torches, sending dust and vaporized lead everywhere. New rules put an end to that, and painters and homeowners are being fined for such activities. Old, peeling lead paint has to be handled more carefully.

Tales from the Scaffold

A few years ago, a painter sanding a house exterior in Seattle made the front pages of the paper (maybe it was a slow news day) when he failed to contain any of the dust from his work. The next-door neighbor called various authorities as well as a lead abatement contractor to come and inspect her house and yard for contamination. He told her it would costs thousands and thousands of dollars for him to come in and clean and abate her house and grounds, much to the chagrin of the offending neighbor and his painter. There was no follow-up article on how they settled the problem, but it's safe to say that the painter rethought his sanding methods after that job.

As in interior stripping, the work area must be sealed off. That means encasing each side of the house with plastic, top to bottom, and sealing all the edges. All lead debris and plastic has to be properly disposed of.

Cheaper to Replace the Siding?

Badly peeling siding can be a real headache to prepare for painting, and you can even be subject to lead abatement regulations for simply removing it, because you're dispersing lead paint chips and dust.

New cedar siding—if you want to faithfully replace the old siding—isn't cheap. It's still worth considering if the overall cost is competitive to stripping off a lot of your lead-based paint. On the plus side, you won't have any preparation work to do at all; your new siding will be ready to paint. As an alternative, some homeowners successfully cover their old siding with new cedar shingles. This alternative obviously changes the original appearance, but it may still look historically appropriate.

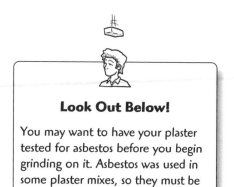

Look Out Below!

You may want to have your plaster tested for asbestos before you begin grinding on it. Asbestos was used in some plaster mixes, so they must be handled carefully.

Safe Ways to Strip

There are some safe ways to strip exterior paint, but you'll still have to be careful if it's lead-based. Safe approaches include:

➤ Using a heat gun with a low enough temperature so it won't vaporize the lead (under 1100 degrees Fahrenheit)

➤ Using chemical remover

➤ Using sanders with dust collectors and vacuum attachments

Plaster and Lath: The Days Before Drywall

Plaster walls and ceilings were the standard up until the 1940s, and different eras of plaster work produced different results. Some Victorian-era material, for instance, is relatively fragile and crumbly. Plaster work from the 1920s and 30s is much harder. All of it is subject to cracking and falling away from the lath.

There are relatively few journeyman plasterers around these days, and most of their work involves repairs and restoration. You don't need this level of skill to do some basic repairs, but you do need a few tools.

Mostly Permanent Crack Repairs

Most home repair books call for taking a tool like the sharp, triangular end of a beer can opener—remember those?—and scraping out and widening any cracks in your plaster before filling them with Spackle or new plaster. I say, take it one step further

and rout or grind the crack completely, so it doesn't come back. You won't need a fancy router, just an electric drill and a small grinding wheel about 2 to 3 inches in diameter. This is a dusty job, so be sure you
have plenty of plastic for sealing off the room and a heavy dust mask or respirator for yourself. Wear eye protection, too.

To repair your cracks, follow these steps:

1. Grind the cracks out with your drill and grinding wheel, going all the way down to the lath or until you hit solid plaster.

2. Brush away all loose dust and plaster.

3. Following instructions, press in one or two applications of patching plaster, such as Fix-All, with a medium-width putty knife.

You can fill the cracks with a three-coat process of regular plaster (the scratch, brown, and finish coats), but few people are going to go to this much trouble. As a compromise, if you want this treatment, go ahead and clean the cracks out yourself and then call a plasterer.

Skim Coating

A skim coat is a thin coat of drywall compound spread over entire walls and ceilings for a smooth, consistent appearance. It can be done over plaster or drywall. This big job requires the practiced hand of a drywall taper. All cracks and holes in the underlying wall must be repaired first. Professional plasterers recommend skim coating with a coat of finish plaster instead of drywall compound because the latter is softer than plaster. If you decide to take this route, you'll have to hire a plasterer to do the work because drywall tapers rarely do any plastering.

Resolving Window and Door Problems

Windows are a main defining element on the exterior of a house. Mess with them, and the whole look of your house can be thrown out of whack. In the '50s and '60s, original wood windows were replaced by picture windows; now these old picture windows are themselves getting replaced by reproduction wood windows.

The main problems with old doors and windows amounts to:

➤ Poor fit

➤ Inoperable windows

➤ Missing or broken hardware

➤ Inadequate door locks

➤ Deteriorating paint or finish

Tales from the Scaffold

Clients of mine had a 1940s house with a single, originally operable, casement window in their living room. It hadn't been opened in the 18 years they'd owned the house; on hot summer days, they would escape to a finished basement for relief. They asked me about replacing it with something that worked. Instead, I got it opened, stripped off the paint, and reinstalled the sash, all in about an hour and a half. It had been painted shut so long that it was perfectly preserved. I didn't ask them how they felt about having lived in discomfort for 18 years when they could have figured out how to do such a simple repair.

I've repaired thousands—yes, thousands—of old wood windows, and it's highly unusual to find one that can't be refurbished. These windows can be refinished, weather-stripped, have their broken glass replaced, and their locks upgraded. Consider these questions:

➤ What is the cost of repair versus replacement?

➤ Does the replacement look appropriate for the style and design of the house?

➤ Will I be satisfied with the results of a repaired unit?

➤ How badly do I want the energy savings of new windows and doors versus the appearance of the originals?

Restoration: Unknown Budget Territory

Restoration is expensive if you hire out all the work. Contractors will tell you that they can build a new house for less than the cost of some extensive restoration projects. I've worked on some of these types of projects and wondered what some owners were thinking when they were making their plans. Emotions take over, and dollar figures can add up.

Labor-Intensive, Labor of Love

Owners of old houses who restore them and move to another and do it again and again will tell you that it isn't about dollars, it's a true love affair with their home, its craftsmanship and detailing, and the distinctive style and design that stands out from the perceived homogeneity of today's new houses. They'll also tell you that, in the case of big restorations, being a little crazy helps.

375

Although it isn't true that owning an old house means there's always something else to do—once it's whipped into shape, maintenance shouldn't be abnormal—there's plenty to do to get it to a point of standard maintenance. The costs aren't too bad if you can do a lot of the work yourself to keep them down, but remember, your time is worth something, too.

It Will Never Be a New House

No matter what you do to an old house—even if you gut it completely and rebuild—it won't deny its identity. You'll always be aware, if ever so subtly, that it's not a new house. This is just as well with old house advocates, because they obviously don't want a new one. There's something about convenience and modern building codes that must not be very appealing!

Enjoy your old house, carefully consider your remodeling options, and try not to get carried away with duplicating the past. Previous owners accommodated modern changes, and you can, too.

The Least You Need to Know

➤ Strive for a balance between historic accuracy and modern convenience when restoring your old house.

➤ Restoration work is very labor-intensive and can cost more than building new.

➤ A house should adapt and change with the time and its owner's needs, not be a prisoner to the past.

➤ Old houses pose certain hazards in the form of asbestos, lead-based paint, and possible oil tank contamination. These hazards must be dealt with according to regulations.

➤ Restoration work is more a matter of taste and commitment than practicality; test your commitment by doing a small project first before taking on the entire house.

The Contractor Talk Glossary

ABS   Black plastic pipe commonly used for waste water lines.

alkyd paint   Paint that contains synthetic resins and uses mineral spirits or paint thinner as a solvent, often referred to as oil-based paint.

allowance   Money set aside in a remodeling or construction contract to pay for labor or materials not specified in the contract (for example, an allowance for cabinet hardware if no specific hardware has been selected).

amperage (AMPS)   A unit of electrical current or volume; a service panel is referred to by its amperage (a 200-amp panel, for instance).

anchor bolts   In foundations, the L-shaped bolts that are set in wet concrete and used to secure the framing of the house to the foundation.

architect   A state-licensed architect typically has an undergraduate degree in architecture and has served an internship under a licensed architect; on large construction jobs, this person is often seen as the bane of a general contractor's existence.

asbestos   A fire-resistant, fibrous form of magnesium silicate used in housing construction to wrap pipes and furnace ducts; it's considered a hazardous material if inhaled and is linked to lung cancer and asbestosis.

asphalt   Bituminous material with waterproofing properties that is used in roofing shingles.

baluster   Vertical support for a handrail; a spindle is one style of baluster.

beam   Horizontal framing member that supports joists or a roof across an open space.

bottom plate   Bottom, horizontal framing member of a wall.

casement window   Hinged window that swings open like a door.

caulking   Flexible sealant used to fill a gap between two surfaces (for example, a door casing and drywall).

change order   A modification, which should be in writing, that changes the scope of work and usually the price of a remodeling or construction contract.

circuit breaker   A switch-type device inside a service panel that limits the amount of current flowing through a circuit and trips when the demand for power exceeds what the circuit can safely carry.

concrete   Typically, a mixture of Portland cement, sand, and aggregate used to build residential foundations and slabs.

concrete board   Concrete and fiberglass panel used as a backing material for tile (for example, Wonderboard).

condensation   Water changing from vapor to liquid when warm, moist air comes in contact with a cold surface.

contract   A written agreement between a contractor and client spelling out work to be performed and the terms of payment.

contraction joint   a joint which controls the cracking that results from the tensile and bending stresses in concrete slabs.

contractor   Normally, a state-licensed individual or company qualified to perform remodeling or construction work; there are general and specialty contractors.

cost-plus contract   A time and materials contract.

covenants and restrictions   Rules, normally regarding publicly viewed changes to a property, agreed to by homeowners in certain neighborhoods.

cripple stud   Short stud used between a sill plate and a windowsill or a header and the top plate; also known as a cripple.

designer   A house designer who is not a licensed architect.

dormer   A box-like projection that frames a window from the sloping plane of a roof.

double-hung window   Window with two sashes, which slide up and down.

downspout   Pipe connected to roof gutters for drainage into a standpipe or onto a splash block.

dry rot   The misnamed result of fungal rot.

drywall   Gypsum plaster panels used as a wall covering.

eaves   Horizontal overhang of a roof beyond the exterior wall.

estimate   An educated attempt to price the cost of labor and materials necessary to complete a remodeling job.

expansion joint   A joint that allows for expansion and contraction during temperature changes; an important component of concrete pouring.

fascia   Board nailed to the ends of roof rafters, usually a backing for gutters.

felt   Fibrous material saturated with asphalt and used as an underlayment or sheathing paper.

fixed-price contract   Contract with a set price for labor, materials, profit, and overhead.

flashing   Sheet metal used to waterproof roof valleys, hips, or the space between a chimney and the roof; also used between a deck and siding and on the tops of doors, windows, and siding to lead water away from the wall.

fluorescent lighting   Tubular bulbs containing mercury vapor.

footing   A below-ground concrete base used to support foundation walls, piers, and some slabs.

forced-air heating   Furnace that uses a fan to blow hot air through a system of ducts; although typically associated with gas furnaces, it's also used with electric and oil systems.

framing   Structural wood and/or metal components that form the skeleton of most houses.

French drain   A gravel- or stone-filled trench or hole covered with grass or other ground cover, which collects water from drain lines.

fungal wood rot   Wood-munching organism resulting from the exposure of wood to moisture for an extended period of time, without an opportunity to dry out.

furring   Applying thin wood or metal strips to studs, joists, or walls to create a level surface.

fuse   The predecessor to the circuit breaker; not reusable after circuit is overloaded and the fuse burns out.

gable dormer   An A-shaped dormer.

Ground Fault Current Interrupter (GFI or GFCI)   Either an electrical outlet or circuit breaker designed to trip almost instantaneously when it detects a short-circuit; required by building codes in settings such as bathrooms, kitchens, and outdoors.

grout   Mortar used to seal gaps between tile.

gutter   Trough that carries water from the edge of the roof to the downspouts.

header   Horizontal beam that supports the wall above a door or window opening.

historic district   Neighborhood whose covenants and restrictions revolve around maintaining historically accurate homes.

incandescent lighting   Light bulbs with filaments.

jack stud   Partial stud nailed next to full studs to support the header at door or window openings; also called a cripple or sometimes a *trimmer*.

jamb   Window or door frame.

joint compound   Soft, plaster-like material used to fill drywall joints.

joist   Framing member that supports a subfloor and runs perpendicular to beams.

knob-and-tube wiring   Two-wire system that predates modern grounded wiring; it was used until the late 1940s.

latex paint   Paint that uses water as a solvent.

lath and plaster   Main predecessor to drywall; wet plaster is troweled onto thin wood strips that are nailed to wall studs and ceiling joists.

lintel   A header.

load-bearing wall   A wall that supports an overhead structure.

mudsill   Also known as a sill plate; the bottom framing member of a wall that is attached to the foundation (should be pressure-treated wood).

Oriented Strand Board (OSB)   Plywood substitute made from wood chips and glue; sometimes known as wafer board or chip board, though this term isn't entirely accurate.

overhang   Portion of the roof structure that extends beyond the exterior walls of a building.

payment schedule   Predetermined and agreed-to schedule for paying contractor for work performed and materials purchased; usually based on percentage of work completed.

permit   Local government OK to proceed with remodeling or construction.

pier block   Concrete block used to support foundation members, such as posts.

pitch   The slope of a roof (ratio of the rise over the span, or run, in feet).

post   Vertical framing member, usually designed to hold a beam.

pressure-treated lumber   Lumber impregnated with chemicals to resist decay, insects, and moisture.

primer   The first coat of finish used to seal a surface before paint is applied.

R value   The measure of insulation's resistance to heat loss or heat gain; the greater the R value, the better.

rafter   Framing member that holds up and supports roof sheathing.

rebar   Reinforcing steel for concrete.

ridge   The peak of a pitched roof where the two sides meet.

riser   Vertical member between two stair treads.

rough opening   Any framed, but unfinished, opening.

sash   The frame that holds the glass in a window; the movable section of a window.

setback thermostat   Programmable thermostat that can be preset to go on and off at different times of the day as well as days of the week.

shake   A thick wood roofing product, usually made from cedar.

sheathing   Exterior-grade boards used as underlayment for roofing shingles; also panels that lie between the studs and the siding of a structure.

shed dormer   A dormer with shallow sloping roof.

shingle   Machine-sawed wood roofing and siding product, usually cut from cedar; there are asphalt and fiberglass roofing shingles as well.

shutoffs   Valves that shut off water from either an entire building or an individual fixture.

sill plate   The bottom member of a wall that is secured to the foundation of a house.

skip sheathing   Boards used as nailing surface for shakes and shingles.

slab on grade   A concrete slab poured onto prepared ground or subgrade (it's quick and cheap).

slope   The degree of a slant; the incline angle of a roof.

soffit   Finished underside of the eaves.

Sparky   A sometimes-accurate name for an electrician.

specifications (specs)   These spell out materials to be used on a remodeling job; they include sizes, colors, and models. They also state methods and procedures for job tasks. Specifications supplement the plans and design.

splash block   Fin-shaped concrete or plastic pad that diverts water from the end of a downspout and away from your foundation.

soil stack   The main vent pipe that extends out through the roof.

stucco   Plaster-like finish usually containing cement, sand, and lime.

stud   Vertical member of a frame wall usually placed between a bottom plate and a top plate and spaced every 16 inches or 24 inches apart. Plaster lath and drywall are nailed to the studs.

time-and-materials contract   This contract specifies a base price (such as costs per hour) for a job, but it has no maximum ceiling unless one is written into the contract.

tongue-and-groove   Lumber machined to have a groove on one side and a protruding tongue on the other; the tongue of one piece fits into the groove of the other.

top plate   The top horizontal framing member of a wall.

trap   Section of a drain that holds a small amount of water to prevent sewer gases from entering the house; the most commonly referred to type is a P-trap which goes under a sink.

truss   Engineered roof support that takes the place of individual rafters and joist.

underlayment   Waterproof or water-resistant material installed under roofing shingles, or panels installed over subflooring for specific flooring materials such as vinyl or tile.

UV rays   Ultraviolet rays from the sun.

valley   Inward angle formed by two intersecting, sloping roof planes.

vapor barrier   Substance that prevents the transmission of water vapor; it can be a special paint, plastic, or paper/foil backing on insulation.

voltage   Measure of electrical potential.

watt   Measure of the electrical demand of an appliance.

zoning   Assignment of specified use of property, such as commercial or single-family.

Paint and Painting

Today, you can choose from a mundane flat interior latex to an exotic, two-component epoxy with gene-altering solvents. There are paints made for every purpose, and the choices can be confusing. How do you pick the right paint and still keep your DNA intact?

Almost all of your painting will involve latex paint. You'll probably never use any of the following finishes:

➤ Epoxy

➤ Lacquer

➤ Shellac

You might use one or more of the following:

➤ Alkyd paint

➤ Varnish

➤ Polyurethane

➤ Interior wood stain

➤ Danish oil

You will probably use one of these finishes:

➤ Latex paint, especially acrylic paint

➤ Exterior wood stain

Which One's Which?

Epoxy is used only for specialized purposes such as coating certain metal surfaces or some high-traffic floors. It's toxic and difficult to apply, and you'll never use it in your house. Lacquer is a very fast-drying, clear finish that must be applied with a sprayer, and you won't be doing that, either. Most lacquer is highly toxic, and you won't want to be around it while it's drying, let alone be the one applying it. Shellac is a clear finish (there is also orange shellac) that was once used on interior woodwork, floors, and furniture. It's diluted with alcohol and has been around for ages, and almost no one but historical restorers and refinishers use it much anymore.

Alkyd paint is the modern version of oil-based paint. This genre of paints contains pigment, a vehicle to hold the pigment (either oil or the alkyd, which is a synthetic resin), and a solvent such as turpentine or mineral spirits. The solvent keeps the paint in a liquid state until it's spread on a surface. Once the paint is exposed to air, the solvent evaporates, and the alkyd or oil forms a film on top of the surface to which it is applied. Alkyd and oil-based paints have a long drying time and smell worse than latex, but they form a durable interior finish. They are never used on new construction anymore, but they are sometimes used for recoating any old woodwork that has previously had this type of paint applied. Alkyd and oil paints are gradually disappearing from the marketplace except for use in specialized industrial applications.

Varnish is something like a paint without any pigment or color; it's a combination of oil, resin, a drier, and solvent that produces a clear, protective film when dry. Varnish has typically been replaced by polyurethane, a clear finish that's formulated with synthetic resin. You might use one of these if you're refinishing woodwork or furniture or even a wood floor.

An interior wood stain is essentially a very diluted paint or a combination of solvent, a small amount of pigment, and oil (for oil-based stains) or water (for latex stains). Stains aren't considered to be film-forming substances because they're made to soak into the wood and impart color from within, as opposed to on the surface. However, any idiot should know if it's got oil or any amount of acrylic as an ingredient that a stain can form a film.

Danish oil sounds like a massage product, but it is a generic name given to any of a number of clear oil finishes that are thin enough to be applied with a rag and wiped down. Essentially, these are very diluted varnishes and don't form much of a protective film unless you apply multiple coats. Their ease of use has made them very popular, however.

Latex paint is the one product I can guarantee you'll be using if you repaint any room in your house—log cabins and caves excepted. Like alkyd or oil-based paint, it also consists of pigment and solvent (in this case, the solvent is water), but it does not use oil or alkyd as its vehicle or film-forming substance. The best latex paints use liquid acrylic resin, which is emulsified or suspended in water. Latex paint does have one similarity to alkyd paint: You spread it on a surface, and it will form a film as its water component evaporates.

Latex, first introduced in 1949, is now the king and queen of the paint kingdom. It's easy to use, dries quickly, and cleans up with soap and water. Early formulations left something to be desired in terms of durability, but current latex products will outlast alkyd paint on most exterior applications, and you can apply it faster. What's not to like?

Exterior stains, called semi-transparent stains, come as both latex and oil-based. Like interior stains, they're diluted, penetrating finishes that form very little film. These stains are popular because they're easy to apply, dry quickly, and require no priming, but they don't give the longer term protection that paint provides. This leads to an author-observed rule of painting: If a finish is really easy to apply and doesn't form much of long-lasting film, you'll have to reapply it sooner rather than later.

To add to your information overload, there are also solid-body exterior stains, both latex and oil-based, that are more like a paint than a stain. They form a film that dries quickly after it's applied, and they're not always as durable as paint, but check with your paint supplier. The Flood Company sells a Solid Color Deck & Siding Stain that contains a bonding oil and a quality latex paint (talk about mixing oil and water) and comes with a 15-year guarantee for siding and a 5-year guarantee when used on decking. Read the label carefully; the conditions outlined in guarantees can be subject to broad interpretation.

So Much Paint, So Little Time

From this point on, unless I note otherwise, I'll be talking about latex paint. Now that you know what kind of paint you'll be dealing with, you need to know a little more about it. Paint comes in different finishes, including:

➤ Flat (dullest and softest finish)

➤ Satin and eggshell

➤ Semi-gloss

➤ High-gloss (shiniest and hardest finish)

Each finish works best in different situations. Flat paint, for instance, hides a lot of imperfections on walls because it reflects relatively little light. It does not clean all that well and makes a bad choice for bathroom or kitchen walls or any other high-traffic area.

Satin and eggshell have a slight sheen (satin is a little shinier). Either one is a good choice for higher traffic areas such as hallways or children's rooms because it cleans more easily than flat paint, but isn't too reflective. You still want to hide any imperfections in the walls. It's often used in kitchens and bathrooms in new construction.

Semi-gloss is harder yet and was once regularly used in kitchens and bathrooms, as well as on woodwork throughout a house. These days, residential use of semi-gloss paint is mostly restricted to woodwork. Both semi-gloss and high-gloss are hard, washable paint surfaces.

High-gloss is the champion of shine, but this shine means it shows any imperfection on the surface it's painted over. If you like the looks of a shiny yacht and yourself wearing a cap that reads Skipper, then high-gloss paint is for you. Glossy paints are usually classified as enamels; a flat oil enamel is also available.

Paint technology has entered an unprecedented era of new products and development, much of it in response to the phasing out of petroleum solvent-based products due to environmental issues. Maybe you have a unique painting problem or are looking for an unusual finish. Talk it over with your local paint supplier. There's a product solution for every painting problem.

Putting It On

Your main painting tools will be a roller, roller pan, and a brush or two. Before you start slapping it on your living room walls, here are a few guidelines to make the job easier.

Rolling Along

Follow this process when you're rolling on paint:

1. Empty the room of all movable furniture, knickknacks, pets, and children; cover everything else, including the floor and light fixtures, with plastic and drop cloths.

2. Remove cover plates from light switches and electrical outlets; also remove or cover with masking tape any window or door hardware.

3. Paint the ceiling first. Where the ceiling meets the walls, cut in the paint with a brush. Roll out about a four-inch section across the shortest dimension of the ceiling. Apply the paint in a series of diagonal strokes in the shape of a W, followed by vertical strokes from one end of the ceiling to the other. Overlap each newly painted section with the previous section.

4. Slip the roller cover off the frame an inch or so, and roll it along the edge of the ceiling to obscure the brush marks. Don't let the roller get too dry, or it will spatter as you press against it.

5. Paint the walls next. You'll have to cut in with a brush where two walls meet at a corner, just as you did where the ceiling met the tops of the walls. If you're very much a novice and are concerned about getting the wall paint on the woodwork, you can mask around it with blue masking tape. Then you can run the roller right close to the tape without getting any paint on the woodwork itself.

6. Roll on enough new paint to thoroughly cover the old finish, but don't put it on so heavily that it begins to sag. If the old color bleeds through or you're not satisfied with the coverage, you'll have to apply a second coat. Surprisingly, this can happen when you attempt to cover a light color with a dark one.

7. Paint is ready to use out of the can and normally doesn't need any diluting or thinning. As the job goes on, if your paint doesn't seem to flow quite as easily as it did at the start, add a small amount of solvent. It doesn't take much, just a tablespoon or two per gallon (use water for latex paint or mineral spirits for alkyd paint) thoroughly mixed into the paint.

8. After you paint a section, lightly coat the roller with paint and roll it gently until all the roller marks are obscured and evened out.

Better Your Brushwork

For brushwork, it's best to use only a partially filled paint can or other container, one-third filled will do nicely. You can't brush as fast as you can roll, so paint has a tendency to thicken slightly as its solvent evaporates in the can. Follow these guidelines when using a brush:

1. Dip your brush into the paint until you've saturated the bristles halfway up from their tips. Lightly whack both sides of the brush against the inside of the can to knock off excess paint (another reason to use only a partially filled can).

2. Brush the woodwork or other surface in long strokes, turning the brush sideways as needed to work the paint into grooves or depressions.

3. When you've completely painted one section, tip off the finish by lightly brushing it smooth using just the tips of the brush and painting in long strokes.

More Painting Pointers

Here are a few more painting pointers:

➤ A small amount of interior wood stain goes a long way; practice on a scrap of wood before you tackle your entry door. Work the stain quickly before it sets up on you and wipe off any excess with a rag. It gets worse if you do your staining under hot, sunny conditions. Remember, use the weather to your advantage even when you're working inside your home.

➤ Alkyd paint is tougher to brush out than latex paint, so keep some Penetrol or mineral spirits around for thinning purposes.

➤ When applying a clear coat such as varnish or polyurethane, dip a section of a clean, lint-free rag slightly into the can, remove it, and fold it over a couple of times to distribute the varnish. This is a homemade tack cloth (commercial versions are cheesecloth immersed in a waxy, sticky substance). Run your tack cloth all over the surfaces you're about to clear coat to remove any remaining bits of dust or dirt you may have missed. In clear coats, everything shows up, so the surface must be as clean as you can get it.

➤ Disposable foam brushes work OK on flat surfaces where you don't have to cut in, that is, paint very closely to a line or edge. They don't hold much paint, but they work well for quick touch-ups.

➤ You can make Danish oil and similar products form more of a surface film by brushing them on heavily and allowing them to set up, but the finish won't be as tough as a varnish or polyurethane finish.

➤ Interior wood stains can also be brushed on heavily and allowed to set and dry without wiping them down. This is beneficial when you're trying to match some old, dark wood finishes. Brush the stain on very heavily and tip off with your brush, very lightly, until the stain sets. Allow it to dry for several days before you put any kind of clear finish over it.

Paint Preparation

Some writers and painters claim that preparation work is 90 percent of a painting job. I wouldn't go that far, but it is a big part of the work. The best paint job won't stand up to poor preparation. You'll need soap, water, and sandpaper before you ever open up a can of paint.

Scrub-a-Dub-Dub

What needs to be cleaned? Kitchens should be cleaned if the walls are greasy—don't kid yourself, they're always at least a little greasy. Besides, it's kind of gross to know you're painting over old bacon grease or olive oil spatters. Any strong household cleaner that won't leave a residue, such as Spic 'n Span , mixed with hot water will do the job. In case you were wondering, use a sponge mop to clean the ceiling. Bathroom walls are another place that usually need a good scrubbing.

What about walls in other rooms? Unless you've been cooking with your electric wok in the living room, you should be able to paint right over the existing finish—after you've done any plaster or drywall repairs, of course. Exceptions to this paint-and-go policy are marks, usually in the form of children's artwork from crayons, ink pens, and felt markers. If you paint over these marks, you'll see them again and again as they bleed through the paint. It's best to coat these areas with a sealer (sometimes called a primer/sealer) first. Sealers are normally very fast-drying (under 30 minutes) and can be purchased in quart-size cans. Look for them in aerosol spray cans as well if you have only a few marks to prime.

Working on the Woodwork

Woodwork throughout the house should also be washed down before it's painted; you'd be surprised how much dust, dirt, and general goo accumulates on it. Unlike plaster or drywall, woodwork also gets sanded because it's usually coated with glossy paint or a clear finish such as varnish. Washing isn't enough to knock down the sheen and give the woodwork that toothy feel that paint likes so much.

Paint that's in pretty good shape can be hand-sanded with 120- or even 150-grit sandpaper (the lower the number, the coarser the grit) just enough to rough it up. Heavier paper can leave sanding scratches that may not be covered up after painting.

Woodwork that needs more aggressive sanding is best handled with an electric sander. Signs that you need an electric sander include:

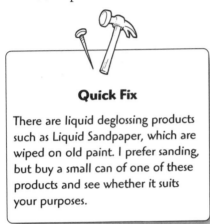

Quick Fix

There are liquid deglossing products such as Liquid Sandpaper, which are wiped on old paint. I prefer sanding, but buy a small can of one of these products and see whether it suits your purposes.

➤ Chipped paint in need of feathering

➤ Rough finish

➤ Finish that has paint drips and sags from the last painting

Look Out Below!

If you hire the work out, be very clear with your painting contractor about what kind of preparation work you are expecting. This is an area of real contention, especially on older homes, which often need extensive cleaning, sanding, and scraping (see Chapter 31, "Restoration or Remodeling?"). A painter may propose two or three different levels of work. Have a sample of each done, review them, and agree to one before signing a contract.

Sanders greatly cut down on your preparation time, especially on doors and cabinets. My recommendation? A Makita speedbloc sander, which is a small, lightweight finish sander at a bargain price of a little over $40. I've used these for years and have never been disappointed.

The use of sanders does lead to another painting rule: Latex paint does not like overly aggressive machine sanding. The problem is that the orbiting sandpaper heats up the paint, which softens and starts to come off in little, gummy balls, giving you more of a mess than you bargained for. Go ahead and use the sander over latex, just don't get too hostile with it. Keep the sander moving after you've knocked off the gloss and dulled the surface. Keep a light touch and don't bear down on the sander.

If you're sanding alkyd or old oil-based paint, both of which form a harder film than latex paint, you can sand as much as you want—after you've tested for lead content as discussed in Chapter 31, "Restoration or Remodeling?". Sand one piece of trim before you make a career out of the rest of the house. These paints can be sanded to very smooth, polished finishes, and it's easy to get carried away with the job.

Wallpaper Woes

You see painted-over wallpaper all the time in older homes, and it's not always pretty. Try and paint directly over some old, non-coated wallpaper, and it will absorb the water from the latex paint and start coming off in small pieces right on your roller, or it will start lifting and bubbling later.

Newer papers, such as foils, mylars, and vinyls, can be painted if they're prepared correctly. This preparation involves cutting out and spackling any torn or loose sections and priming all the wallpaper with a primer/sealer like Kilz. Do a test section first! Prime and paint a three-foot square section and let it dry overnight. Rub and scratch the paint to see how well it sticks. If the paint doesn't hold, try lightly sanding another section of wallpaper with 120-grit sandpaper and then redo your test.

Wallpaper removal can be a real chore, especially if it's not a strippable kind of paper that is made for easy removal. In some older homes, even the ceilings were papered. After you strip off the wallpaper, you'll have to patch up the walls—what a mess!

You have an alternative called skim coating (see Chapter 31, "Restoration or Remodeling?"), which gives you a won-derful, smooth wall to work with without all the stripping. Skim coating is the application of a thin layer of drywall compound or even plaster over an existing wall. Because both of these materials contain a lot of water, you'll have to seal the wallpaper first with an oil primer before skimming. I've done this a number of times on older homes, and it always works. Skim coating is done by drywall tapers, or you can tackle it your-self. Try a small section of wall first before you commit yourself to a big project.

Outside Washing

Exterior preparation on newer homes is usually a matter of washing the old paint to remove dirt and car pollution. Old homes with multiple layers of paint are subject to more problems than simple dirt and often need extensive preparation work (see Chapter 31, "Restoration or Remodeling?").

Exterior washing is easy with a rented pressure washer. In fact, it's too easy to become careless with the wand or nozzle. Aim it too close to the siding, at the wrong angle, or in the same spot for too long and you can shred or splinter the wood or force water inside your house.

The key to using pressure washers is to wash from the top down so the siding will shed the water as naturally as it sheds rain. Rinsing back and forth from the side is OK as long as you're not aiming in a upward direction, which can force water behind the boards. Pressure washing removes most surface dirt, but it is not as strong an action as scrubbing.

An alternative to pressure washers is to buy a house washer, which is a series of aluminum or plastic poles that attach to each another and then to a garden hose. House washers come with scrub brush attachments for the end opposite the hose and have a soap dispenser near the hose. Water and soap are continually fed through the poles to the scrub brush, which you move back and forth against the siding. This inexpensive, low-tech solution doesn't have the operator problems (that's you) that can come with pressure washers. House washers are slower and require more elbow grease to clean your house, but they shouldn't be ruled out entirely if you feel more comfortable using them.

Ladders

Unless you live in a pup tent, you're going to need some ladders to do your painting. Ladders come in many flavors, but the only two you need to be concerned about are the following: Extension ladders and stepladders.

Extension ladders are two single ladders combined in one. The narrower of the two ladders slides out, extending the ladder's overall length. A 32-foot extension ladder will comfortably access most two-story houses and can be set up by one person. Home-owners typically buy lightweight models that professional painters would never be caught using. Heavier-duty commercial models are made to hold painters, planks, buckets of paint, and tools without giving painters that queasy feeling that they should have chosen another profession. Commercial-grade ladders can be rented at tool rental outfits along with planks and ladder jacks, which support and hold the planks.

Stepladders open up to form an inverted V. They come in standard sizes, starting at 2 feet in height up to 12 feet—although even taller ones are manufactured. A 12-foot stepladder is very convenient for painting one-story houses.

Little Giant Ladders (www.littlegiant.com or 888-865-4577) sells an interesting ladder that "does it all." This combination ladder unfolds to become multiheight stepladders, extension ladders, and even a scaffold system. It exceeds OSHA (Occupational Safety and Health Administration) standards and folds up for easy storage.

Ladder Unease

Setting up a pair of extension ladders, ladder jacks, and the plank that runs between them usually requires two people, but that's not the hard part. What's hard is walking the plank: Climbing off the extension ladder and onto a plank 15 or 20 feet off the ground. This activity is not natural; I avoid it whenever I can. Your alternative is to use one ladder and move it as you work, even though it's awkward and slows the job. Don't worry about that, you have to do what's comfortable for you.

Most house painters don't wear safety harnesses and tie themselves off to something sturdy (like a chimney) to hold them in case they fall, but you should. On top of that, you need to take all ladders and planks down at the end of the day; you don't want to be held liable if someone climbs up and falls off while you're not around. You don't want them falling off while you are around, for that matter.

Safety Rules Rule

The old saying "as easy as falling off a log" could just as easily be "as easy as falling off a ladder," except you fall a lot farther from a ladder. According to the National Safety Council, more than 30,000 people are injured each year in falls involving ladders. Follow a few rules and you should stay on solid footing:

➤ Check the locking mechanisms on your extension ladder—even if you're renting it—to be sure they lock properly and tight; check fasteners, hinges, braces, and rungs or steps on extension and stepladders.

➤ The foot of the ladder must be level and secure. If the ground is uneven, you can put a block of wood or brick under the affected leg. Stand on the bottom rung of the ladder and bear down to be sure the leg doesn't slip.

➤ Pound a stake in front of each leg of the ladder to prevent slippage.

➤ The foot of an extension ladder should be one foot away from your house for every four feet of height to the point where the top of the ladder rests against your house.

➤ Only one person should be on a ladder at a time.

➤ Climb the ladder carefully with both hands on the side rails; keep yourself centered between the rails.

➤ Never climb above the third rung from the top of an extension ladder or the second rung from the top on a stepladder; these are great places to fall from.

➤ Don't carry more tools than you can fit in one hand; better yet, carry your tools in a tool belt or put them in a bucket and pull them up with a rope (paint stores sell special hooks, which hang on the ladder rungs, for holding buckets and cans).

➤ Don't overreach to the sides when you're working; get down and move the ladder instead.

➤ Be sure your ladder has been certified for complying with ANSI (American National Standards Institute) and is listed by Underwriters Laboratories (it should display a UL label). Commercial ladders complying with OSHA standards are better yet.

➤ Wood ladders don't like being left out in the rain, so keep them under cover when the weather turns bad and you're not using them. Never paint a ladder, or use one that someone else has painted.

Hiring and Working with a Contractor

Acting as your own contractor—whether you're supervising others or doing the work yourself—is time consuming and not always a great money saver. It all depends on how you would otherwise be spending your time, especially if you could be earning money at something you're competent at and for which you're well paid. Do you want to spend 20 hours a week pounding nails in order to save $25 an hour to hire a carpenter, or spend 10 hours a week doing your own contract computer programming work for $50 an hour?

Some people find remodeling labor refreshing because they already do more programming, legal work, and corporate management than they can stand. You may not be one of them. You want to do what you already do best and hire out the bedroom addition to someone who knows how to get it done efficiently and, preferably, while you're not around. These people exist in the form of general contractors and subcontractors such as builders, plumbers, and roofers.

How do you find these guys? And what are they like to work with? Do you really want them running around loose in your house while you're at work all day?

Referrals

Ask every homeowner you know if they have the name of a contractor they would recommend. Personal referrals aren't absolute guarantees that your job will be problem-free using the same contractor, but they're a good start. If one name comes up several times as a referral, all the better.

Some are Busier Than Others

Remodeling and building contractors' business cycle seems to be one of continual feast and famine. When times are good, they're busy, sometimes difficult to get a bid from, let alone an agreement to do the work. In bad times, they'll get back to you by dinnertime.

Contracting differs from other businesses in that the work can usually be put off by most homeowners. Your roof may be looking a little patchy, but as long as it isn't leaking, you can always replace it later. When you're making your phonecalls to contractors, ask them up front whether the proposed job is of any interest to them, and how soon can you expect to meet with them. If someone cannot commit or doesn't make a follow-up call to you to schedule an appointment, then keep looking. I've known many competent and well thought of contractors who got so busy they simply didn't respond to phone calls, which they regretted later when new jobs were few and far between.

In many respects, house contractors are among the last cowboys; they're very independent and not always the best business managers, but they try the best they can in a constantly fluctuating market. Markets fluctuate for all businesses (ask any car dealer) but this market fluctuation affects you more personally because it's dealing with your home environment and your desire to improve it. The relationship you enter into with a remodeling contractor is a little more personal than the one you have with your water company.

The Bids

Keep one rule in mind: The price of the bid is not an indicator of work quality or reliability on the part of a contractor. Most are professional and bid the work appropriately, so they can earn a profit, and you can get a fair price. Some bids are too low for various reasons:

➤ The contractor may really need the work, giving you an advantage in the negotiations.
➤ The bidding contractor is an incompetent estimator.
➤ The low bid is intentional, with the contractor expecting to make up for it with change orders or substitution of cheaper materials.
➤ A contractor may have much lower overhead than competing bidders.
➤ The contractor is new to the business and trying to establish a clientele and reputation.

As a rule, you should be leery of low bids. You could be buying problems instead of solutions. I've had clients who took low bids from new contractors whose enthusiasm made up for their lack of experience, and the jobs came out just fine, but this strategy can be risky.

Bids that seem far too high are suspect as well, but for different reasons. The contractor may have so much business that there has to be enough money in a job to make it worth the bother. However, a very high bid just may be the only accurate one in the bunch. That contractor may be onto something that the others missed. How do you tell?

Each competing bid must be based on your plans and specifications. This is the only way to compare prices fairly. For large jobs, have each contractor break out the costs for labor, materials, overhead, and profit; then you can compare bids realistically. You'll be able to ascertain, for instance, if a high bidder has a more expensive labor rate or is allowing more time to do the job.

Small, single task jobs, such as refinishing floors, painting, or installing a new garage door, don't need this kind of breakdown, though you might ask for one if the bids are all over the board, a fairly unlikely occurrence.

On most jobs, given enough bids, a cluster will fall within 10 percent or so of each other. Given the above caveats about high and low bids, the ones in this cluster are the ones you should consider. On $3 million commercial jobs, I've seen the final bids come within 2 percent of each other!

How Many Bids?

Contractors build their bidding and estimating time into their general overhead. On large commercial jobs, a general contractor can spend thousands of dollars in time putting together a bid that may prove unsuccessful. It's your right to get as many bids as you want, but this can turn into an abusive waste of contractors' time if you get carried away. I had one client, for instance, who solicited over a dozen painting bids for the exterior of his house when four or five would have been more than sufficient.

The nature of the job will determine how many bidders you need. Refinishing an ordinary oak floor might require three bids. Floor refinishing is pretty straightforward it's usually based on square footage, the type of finish requested, and any required repairs. Ten bids won't produce a magical insight from the tenth bidder that will suddenly cut the price in half. A major remodeling job calls for more attention and careful selection, but even then, five bids from competent general contractors should be suitable.

Going Shopping

Shopping the bid refers to taking confidentially submitted bids and showing them to another contractor in an attempt to get the second contractor to lower his or her bid. This practice is not ethical. It's one thing to say to someone, "This estimate is about 15 percent over what I anticipated. Is there any way you could lower the price?" and see whether a bidding contractor can suggest some changes in the scope of the work or material selections. It's quite another to take an estimate submitted in good faith as a final price and use it as leverage to get someone else to lower a competing bid.

Qualifying Your Contractor

In some states, it's not very difficult to get a contractor's license: You pay a registration fee, show proof of insurance and a bond, and off you go. How do you know if someone is competent or even licensed?

It's entirely reasonable for you to require proof of a contractor's credentials; on large remodeling jobs, it's critical to do so. You don't want to be getting angry phone calls from building materials suppliers demanding payment for lumber and fixtures delivered to your job site. It shouldn't be your problem, but it can become your problem in a hurry if your contractor hasn't been paying the bills.

Expect the following from your contractor:

➤ The legal name and business address

➤ The name of the legal owner of the business, along with a home address and phone number

➤ State license and registration number

➤ City license and registration number

➤ Proof of insurance, including liability and worker's compensation (if the contractor has employees)

➤ Proof of bond

➤ Federal tax identification number or social security number

➤ If the contractor is unknown to you, some recent customer references

In addition, if the job is sizable—and this dollar figure is up to you, but $15,000 on up could certainly qualify—you can request bank and credit references. Contractors will understand your need for information, but you could run into some problems; a large, well-established, busy roofing firm may not want to bother with any requests beyond its state registration numbers. But maybe that roofing company is in the midst of a bankruptcy—wouldn't you want to know?

On the other hand, just because someone doesn't want to comply with your requests doesn't mean that they have anything to hide. If they have tons of work, why should they bother with what may be viewed as pesky demands to confirm that they're legitimate? Your need for self-protection is real, but you may end up limiting your pool of cooperative contractors. In 17 years in business as a small contractor, I was never once asked by a residential customer for any proof of license, bond, or insurance, and I think this is true for a lot of small contractors.

Making a Choice

You have your bids, and a couple of prices fit your budget and appear to cover the plans and specifications. Short of flipping a coin or bringing out the Ouija board, how should you decide?

At this point, all things being equal, you'll go by personalities. After all, this is a hiring process, just like any other job interview, except that you're on the hiring side of the desk. Look for:

➤ A personality compatible with yours
➤ A listener first and talker second
➤ Humility instead of grandiosity

You're Being Looked at, Too

A contract is a two-way street. Contractors size up clients all the time and ask themselves:

➤ Will this be an agreeable client or a problem one?
➤ What kind of budget figure do they have to work with?
➤ Am I going to be micro-managed during this job?
➤ Will payments be made on time?
➤ Are they going to be unrealistically picky with the results and expect the impossible?

Timely payments are a big deal with self-employed contractors, and a payment schedule will be spelled out in your contract. Honor it and pay promptly unless you have a dispute. A well capitalized general contractor will have the reserves to get by with a late or even missed payment, but it's not fair treatment. If the contractor is holding up his end of the contract, you should hold up yours as well.

Living with Your Contractor

Establish some ground rules with your contractor up front regarding the following issues:

➤ Job hours
➤ Use of those parts of the house not being remodeled
➤ Use of the bathroom (you may want to pay for a portable toilet to be used on the site)
➤ Smoking
➤ Radios
➤ On-site safety
➤ Material storage and cleanup expectations

Residential construction normally starts between 7:00 and 8:00 a.m. (good luck getting anyone to start that early in Hawaii) and ends between 3:30 and 4:30 p.m. for work crews on weekdays. Contractors who are self-employed will work longer hours, but both you and local noise ordinances can have something to say about that. You'll have to be flexible here if you want the job done on time. Some days call for a long, hard push into the early evening, and this should be respected.

People who like their privacy will go nuts during a major remodel if they keep living in the house. Types you may never have run across in your normal working life will be tramping around your house in heavy work boots carrying piles of lumber and wearing large tool belts. It's within your rights to limit access to the rest of your house, and to be honest, most contractors don't want to wander around where they may damage something. They'll need a warm, dry place to escape to for lunch and coffee breaks if the weather is bad.

The bathroom is another matter, especially if you have only one that's working. If the contractor has to rent a portable toilet, it'll be added to the contract fees, but it may be worth it to you if you don't want a dozen people tromping through your bathroom throughout the day.

Contractors, at least their crews, often like loud music and cigarettes—not that the two are related. You're not going to find a lot of holistic, vegetarian demolition laborers these days. Your neighbors, whom you should talk with and prepare if you're about to do a noisy remodel, don't need to listen to a drywall hanger's choice of music blasting away at top volume, and you probably don't want any smoking in your house. Make sure you so clarify these issues before anyone starts on the job.

Remodeling job sites are dangerous: Floors with holes in them, walls with holes waiting for windows to be installed, and stairways without rails, to name a few hazards. You want the site safe for yourself and your housemates, as well as the workers. State departments of labor and industry along with OSHA have well-outlined safety procedures that you should expect your contractor to follow.

Cleanup can be an ongoing battle. Some contractors are neatness-challenged, and others pick up and sweep nightly. Clean-up can also extend to your yard; you don't want it becoming a dumping ground. A contractor's choices for disposal of construction debris include making regular "dump runs" or renting a Dumpster (an open steel box, delivered to the work site and later hauled off when it's full). There's a slowly growing movement to recycle construction waste, including lumber, concrete, and drywall and some contractors have found this an economical alternative to regular disposal. Regardless of the method chosen, make it clear how clean you expect the work site to be kept and if it's not being kept up to those standards, remind the contractor. There'll always be some days when someone working late may not get around to cleaning up very much, if at all, so be prepared to yield on this point occasionally.

A major remodel is something like turning your home into a rooming house except that, at the end of the day everyone leaves instead of coming home. With planning, patience, and not a small amount of good grace on both sides, you can get through it—you might even invite the contractors back for your first open house!

Contracts

Contracts protect both you and your contractors. You need to guard against poor workmanship, law suits for non-payment, unfair price increases, and damage to your property, among other things. Your contractor needs protection in case you decide not to pay, or you sue without just cause over workmanship or other contractual agreements. These contracts should not be one-sided documents favoring one party over the other.

You're Not Signing Your Life Away

A contract should include the following:

- ➤ A description of the job with a cross reference to the plans and specifications
- ➤ The contractor's license, bond, and insurance information
- ➤ Detailed financial information, including a payment schedule, fees, adjustments to the fees, an interest rate for unpaid billings, a stated daily fee charged to the contractor in a penalty clause for late completion, and retention
- ➤ A time frame for the job, including start and completion dates
- ➤ A liability clause
- ➤ A description of warranties for both labor performed and materials installed
- ➤ An arbitration clause
- ➤ A cancellation clause

You must reference the plans and specifications or, for smaller jobs, list them in the contract itself. A roofing contractor, for instance, will spell out the material to be installed, the removal of existing shingles (if necessary), start and completion dates, and debris removal. All this information adds up to one or two paragraphs in a roofing contract. A large remodel, however, should refer to the most recent version of your plans and specifications.

Bonds

A contractor's bond or surety bond is required by many states in order for a contractor to obtain a license to operate. The bond guarantees that the contractor perform as per the signed contract. Surety bonds are for relatively small amounts; here in Washington state, for example, they run $6,000 for a general contractor. This bond means that if work is not completed satisfactorily, you can put a claim in against the contractor's bond. If your claim is successful, the most you can collect against a general contractor's bond in Washington is $6,000, regardless of the amount of your claim. A subcontractor's bond is even less, $4,000 in Washington, for example.

You can obtain even greater protection by requiring your contractor to take out a separate, one-time performance bond (standard with large commercial jobs) equal to the price of your remodel. If your contractor does not have sufficient credit or bonding ability to obtain a performance bond, you want to find out before the job starts.

Paying the Price

Money should be dealt with in a straightforward manner. Fair price or not, no one likes writing those checks for thousands and thousands of dollars. The contract should spell out progress payments—at what point a certain percentage of the fee should be paid—and a total amount due. Change order rates should be outlined (special fees or an hourly rate or both). Penalty fees, usually a stipulated daily amount, are levied against the contractor if the work is not finished by a certain date. This normally is the "we cannot go beyond this date because we're hosting a wedding reception, OK?" date.

Retention means the client or homeowner retains or holds back a certain amount of money from each payment, usually 5 or 10 percent, which is paid when the job is completely accepted and signed off. A job is signed off when the punch list, a final list of unfinished items or items that need correction, has been completed. Retention is a well-established practice of giving the client some leverage in case problems arise with the contractor.

Liability

You don't want to be held liable for a worker's injury on the job. A liability clause holds the contractor liable, which is appropriate.

Arbitration

An arbitration clause mandates that you and the contractor resolve any major disputes through an arbitrator rather than going to court and litigating. The American Arbitration Society provides both arbitrators and arbitration language for contracts.

Canceling Out

If your state doesn't require a three day right to cancel a contract, you can always write it into your own contract. Normally, a period of three days from the time of signing is allowed if you have reason to cancel. Use this time to read over and review your contract. Never sign any agreement you don't fully understand. Ask plenty of questions; it's a good idea given the legal boilerplate you'll be wading through.

A Few Things You Shouldn't Do

Standard construction and remodeling contracts, such as those available from the American Institute of Architects (AIA), are written by lawyers. They are, by nature, complex and seemingly excessive, but that's for your protection. A contract cannot protect you from yourself, though, so be aware of the following:

➤ A down payment will be expected, but it shouldn't be excessive. Check with your state consumer protection agency to find out if your state limits the amount of such down payments.

➤ Pay for work that has been performed, not for future work.

➤ Don't sign off on any work as completed unless you're satisfied that it's been done according to the contract.

➤ Get all warranties in writing, including the contractor's warranty and those from material suppliers where appropriate (appliance warranties, for example).

➤ Be sure to get lien releases as you make your progress payments.

Liens

A lien or, more accurately, a mechanic's lien (it sounds like "lean," which is appropriate in this case) is a claim against your property until a legal debt is paid to the individual placing the lien. Every contractor, architect, and supplier who works on your remodel can place a lien against your home until their fees have been paid. This protects them against deadbeat customers who don't pay.

A lien can be initiated if a claimant files a Notice of Intent (or Right) to Lien; the term varies from state to state. This notice is nothing more than the claimant saying, "Hi, we're working on your house, and even though we don't expect to have any problems with payment, we have this legal insurance policy in case we do have a problem. OK?" The time frame in which the notice must be filed for the claimant to retain a legal right to put a lien on your property also varies from state to state. You can figure a notice to be sent within 20 days from the time someone starts working on your project or provides materials for it. Other timetables for filing and recording a lien must also be met by the claimant in order for the lien to be valid.

Ultimately, you, the homeowner, are responsible for full payment to your contractor, subcontractors, laborers, and suppliers—even if you already paid your general contractor. You will be the one receiving the lien notices, including one from your general contractor. Note who sent them and file them away.

Protecting Yourself from Liens

Liens protect the rights of contractors and suppliers and rightfully so, but what about you? You need to be sure everyone is being paid by the contractors you've been making progress payments to. Several standard options are available to you:

➤ A lien release can be issued as payments are made.

➤ You can make your checks payable to both the contractor and whomever has sent you notices of intent to lien.

➤ You can contact a title company about taking out a title policy that would protect you from construction liens.

A lien release is another piece of legalese issued by anyone who gave you a notice of intent to lien. The release states that you have satisfied all or some of your contractual obligations—in other words, you've paid your bill. Partial lien releases are typically issued with every payment. If you've paid $10,000 out of a $50,000 job and receive a partial lien release for that amount, a future lien could not include that $10,000.

Lien releases come in two flavors: Conditional and unconditional. A conditional lien release states that upon payment for a current billing, the claimant can no longer impose a lien for that amount. After your check has cleared, the conditional release usually ceases to have any conditions attached to it. An unconditional release means that the claimant is giving up any right to hit you and your property with a lien. You want an unconditional release at the end of the job from everyone who sent you a notice of intent to lien so they don't come after you later on. You should also get a list of any contractors and suppliers who didn't file notices, and verify that they have been paid by the general contractor.

Checks made out to two parties are not usually welcome by contractors. You're hiring them to manage the accounts, not share bookkeeping chores with you. On commercial jobs, I've only seen this type of arrangement with marginal subcontractors who, it was discovered, were not paying their bills promptly.

What It All Comes Down To

In the end, contract or no contract, the success of your remodeling job will come down to the integrity of your contractor and suppliers. Do your very best to prequalify your contractor by checking all references, including the Better Business Bureau, for any history of complaints, and you should do all right.

Hold up your end of things as well. Communicate clearly, pay your bills on time, and keep your change orders to a minimum. It's also your responsibility to protect your family and your possessions from mishaps on the construction site. Finally, send pizzas over to the crews once in a while. Contractors will go out of their way to do an exceptional job for exceptional clients.

Repairs

One home repair book lists 79 pages of tools, everything from measuring tapes and drywall hatchets to plywood saws and glass cutters. You'd need to double your remodeling loan to buy all of this stuff (and build an extra room to store it). In reality, you don't need a lot of tools unless you're in the construction and remodeling business. Specialty and power tools can always be rented for one-time usage. If you foresee future remodeling work, weigh the purchase price of a tool or piece of equipment against rental fees.

The basic homeowner tool kit should consist of the following:

➤ Medium-weight claw hammer
➤ 25-foot measuring tape
➤ Needle-nose pliers
➤ Channel lock pliers
➤ Wire cutters
➤ An assortment of screwdrivers
➤ Utility knife
➤ Flashlight
➤ Assortment of putty knives
➤ General purpose hand saw
➤ Paint brushes and roller
➤ 50' 12-2 extension cord
➤ Plunger

And then there are the power tools, including:

➤ A circular saw

➤ A 3/8-inch drill

➤ A finish sander

➤ An electric leaf blower (great for getting rid of sawdust and drywall dust)

You'll also need the following safety equipment:

➤ Plastic safety glasses

➤ Ear protectors (muff style or disposable plugs)

➤ Elbow length rubber gloves (when using solvents)

➤ Disposable plastic of latex gloves (when painting)

➤ Heavy duty dust masks

➤ Respirator (for solvents, contaminated dust)

➤ Knee pads

Rudimentary Repairs

The flip side to the privilege of homeownership is the annoyance of home repairs. There are many well-illustrated books (see Appendix I, "Resources") on home repair and I only intend to touch on a few of the common repairs here. You'll keep your repair time down to a minimum by simply adopting a regular maintenance schedule around your house.

The most common repairs involve:

➤ Plumbing

➤ Walls

➤ Sticking windows and doors

➤ Squeaky floors

Plumbing Fixes

We've summed up plumbing as clean water in, waste water out. If either of those functions doesn't go well, it's time to do some work.

Problem: Clogged sink drain

Solutions: Use a plunger; disassemble and clean the trap; or use a plumber's snake or auger

Plungers are great low tech tools that solve a lot of drain problems. Buy a good one—it's a cheap investment. To unclog a sink:

1. If there isn't any water in the sink, add a couple of inches (this helps the plunger seal more completely).

2. Seal the plunger over the drain and push hard several times; on the last plunge, pull the plunger up and out.

3. Repeat until drain flows free.

What happens if your drain stays clogged? Your next step is to disassemble the trap, the "J" shaped waste pipe under your sink. Plastic traps can usually be disassembled without the use of tools while metal ones require a wrench or channel locks. *Place a bucket under the trap to catch the waste water!* Clean the gunk from the trap and check for further obstacles in the rest of the drain line by inserting a metal coat hanger and rooting around a bit. If it comes up clean, carefully reassemble the trap and hand tighten the slip-joint nuts that hold it together. Over tighten and your trap will start leaking.

If your blockage is further down the drain line, you'll need a plumber's snake or auger. Small snakes are made from narrow spring steel which can be fed down a drain line to poke, probe, and pull at blockages; larger snakes and augers are made from coiled steel and are used on more serious drain problems.

Problem: Clogged toilet

Solution: Plunger or toilet auger

Toilets can get clogged with anything from paper to small toys. Often, it's the former and is easily pushed on with a plunger. *Don't try and clear it away by flushing the toilet a second time!* In fact, just to eliminate the temptation to try this, you should turn the water off at the shut-off valve near the floor. Larger obstructions will need to be cleared with a toilet auger, also called a closet auger. Remember, your toilet—unless you have one of those stainless steel prison models—is made out of porcelain. If you get too aggressive with an auger you could end up needing a new toilet.

Problem: Toilet runs when not in use

Solution: Adjust the float arm

Toilet tanks fill after each use. If the water runs higher than the overflow tube inside the tank, it's getting too much water. The tank stops filling with water when the plastic ball or float sitting on the end of a brass arm reaches the correct level. If the tank continues to take in water, the float has to be adjusted by either screwing the ball tighter to the float arm or, if it's already tight, gently bending the arm so the ball sits lower in the water. If neither of these remedies work, you may have to replace the ballcock valve inside the tank (kits are available at hardware stores and plumbing suppliers).

Leaky fixtures can require a variety of repairs depending on their type and age. Any number of parts can need replacing including washers, valve seats, O-rings, and cartridges. This is where a illustrated repair book comes in particularly handy.

407

Problem: Toilet bowl leaks where it's attached to the floor

Solution: Replace the wax seal at the bottom of the bowl

You'll have to remove the toilet bowl and tank to do this job. First, shut off the water to the toilet at the shut off valve; flush the toilet to empty the tank. Disconnect the water supply line from the tank, unloosen the bolts which secure the tank to the bowl, and remove the tank. Next, remove the bolts which secure the toilet to the floor. Carefully remove the toilet from the floor flange (there will still be some water in the bottom of the bowl).

Stuff a rag into the drain hole to keep the sewer gases out. Take a putty knife and scrape all of the old wax seal from the flange and from the bottom of the bowl. Wipe both surfaces clean with a rag dipped in alcohol. Press a new wax ring into the base of the bowl, place the toilet back onto the flange, and tighten the bolts. Reinstall the tank, attach the water supply line, and check for leaks.

Problem: Leaky pipe

Solution: Turn your water off, either at the affected fixture or at the main shut off. Depending on the severity of the leak, you can use:

➤ Repair kit

➤ An old inner tube

➤ New pipe

Hardware stores carry several kinds of compression repair kits for leaky pipes (they tighten around the leak). These work for small leaks or as temporary fixes. In a pinch, a small leak can be tightly wrapped with a section of a bicycle inner tube and then secured with duct tape, the universal fix-it material. Severe leaks will have to be repaired with a new section of pipe. Individual supply lines to toilets and sinks can be removed and taken to a hardware store or plumbing supplier for replacements.

Disposers

Garbage disposers are a great convenience, but occasionally get stuck. Disposers usually have an Allen fitting on their bottom side which takes, appropriately enough, an Allen wrench which usually comes with the disposer. This fitting is installed so you can manually turn the disposer and dislodge any obstructions (be sure the power is turned off first). Disposers also have a reset button, usually on the bottom, in case it has stalled due to an overload.

Walls

Cosmetic wall repairs consist of patching up either plaster or drywall. Plaster cracks were covered in Chapter 31, "Restoration or Remodeling?"; larger repairs are a bit more time-consuming. Plaster is a flexible medium when it's wet and needs lath or some type of mesh to hold it tight after it dries.

Problem: Damaged plaster

Solution: Remove damaged section of wall down to the lath, brush away all loose pieces of old plaster, lightly wet the surface with a spray of water, and apply a thin coat of patching plaster. *Don't try to match the thickness of the existing plaster in one application!* If you do, it can crack as it dries. Figure on applying at least two, if not three, coats of new material with a clean putty knife. Smooth out the last application so it's flush with the existing plaster. Plaster dries quickly so work fast.

Drywall is a different animal. It cracks along its taped seams. Damaged tape needs to be cut out and usually patched with a new layer of tape—it's easiest to use the self-sticking nylon tape—and recoated with drywall joint compound. Repairing larger holes or damaged areas require a patch with new drywall.

Problem: Replacing a damaged section of drywall

Solution: Either cut out the damaged section all the way to the closest wall studs or cut a smaller section, install a piece of backing, and attach a new piece of drywall

Cutting to the studs gives you a solid nailing surface. You'll want to make as even a cut as possible in the damaged area and then install a new piece of replacement drywall. If you don't want to cut away to the studs, then do the following:

1. Cut away an even rectangle or square from the damaged area

2. Cut a piece of plywood or OSB larger than the cut-out piece, but small enough to insert diagonally through the hole; put a long drywall screw in the center of the board, apply glue or construction adhesive along the outer face of the plywood, insert it into the hole, and pull it against the drywall by holding onto the screw. Insert four drywall screws through the drywall and into the plywood to hold it firm.

3. After the glue dries, remove the center drywall screw. Measure the hole and cut a new piece of drywall as your patch. Apply joint compound to the back of the patch and push it against the plywood.

4. Apply joint compound across the entire surface of the patch—go at least 3 to 4 inches beyond the seam—and then sand when dry.

You may have more than just patching to do—you could be hanging an entire room full of drywall.

It's a Cover-Up: Installing Drywall

Drywall may be easier to install than plaster, but it isn't *that* easy. There are even three groups of workers involved in the drywall trade:

➤ The stockers who deliver drywall

➤ The hangers who install it

➤ The tapers who do the finish work

Schedule the delivery of the material as close to its installation date as possible. The last thing you want is a pile of drywall getting in the way of your other work. Drywall is heavy and cumbersome, especially if you're not use to handling it. If you're going to be the hanger and taper, here are some tips:

➤ Consider renting a drywall lift, a manual machine which will move and hold drywall while you attach it to walls or the ceiling (www.telproinc.com for more information).

➤ Use full sheets of drywall whenever possible.

➤ Hang the drywall perpendicular (long side horizontal) to the framing.

➤ Hang the ceilings first, then the walls.

➤ Always try and line up the finished factory edge of the drywall with another factory edge; the edges are beveled, causing a slight recess to receive joint compound.

➤ Keep your taping knives clean; any hardened joint compound on the edges will give you a marred taping job.

Taping and finishing drywall is a three- to four-step process. Several layers of joint compound are needed to hide and smooth over the joints. Sanding the joint compound or "mud" is a dusty, messy process. Be sure to tape a sheet of plastic up in the opening between your addition and the adjoining room.

Stucco

Stucco repairs very much like plaster; it's an easy material to maintain as long as water doesn't get behind it and cause the underlying framing to rot. When cracks occur from normal settling and movement of the house, repairs are straightforward:

1. Lightly scrape out any cracks.
2. Fill cracks with either a high quality latex caulking or paintable, brushable elastomeric sealant; brush either material in with an old, slightly dampened, latex paint brush.
3. Larger cracks can be cleaned out with a putty knife and filled with urethane sealant.
4. Prime and paint all caulk and sealant after they've cured.

Painting is also easy: Lightly wash the stucco, allow to dry completely, and paint with a high quality latex paint or even an elastomeric finish.

Sticking Windows and Doors

Doors and windows stick when they expand with temperature and weather changes or when there is some settlement in the house. The simplest solution for doors and casement windows? Rub the sticking area with a piece of paraffin or a candle. A bar of soap is OK, but paraffin is longer-lasting.

If your door or casement is beyond the paraffin trick, you'll have to either plane or sand down the offending area or scrape the paint from the window or door jamb. Scraping the jamb is a good solution when the vertical side or stile is sticking, but more work when the top or bottom rail is the problem. These out of sight areas can be quickly sanded with a small belt sander. Remove just enough wood so the window or door will close easily.

Double hung windows, the type that slide up and down, can be lubricated with spray silicone or WD-40.

About Those Double Hung Windows

Double hung windows are mechanically simple. The old versions used weights attached to window sash with either rope or sash chain. The rope passed through a pulley to facilitate movement. Newer versions use metal tape or cable contained in metal cases installed in the window jambs.

99% of the problems with old windows, particularly double hung models, is due to excessive paint build-up. Break the paint bonds or remove the paint and the windows will move easily again. If your windows are painted shut, you can break the paint seal between the sash (that's the portion of the window that holds the glass) and the jamb or stops by inserting a wide putty knife and tapping with a hammer. Do both the interior and exterior sides and gently force the window up from the sill (if it's a double hung) or out from the jamb (if it's a casement).

Old windows are a book unto themselves. They are almost always repairable and worth reusing if you want to maintain historic accuracy.

Weather-stripping

New windows and pre-hung entry doors come with integral weather-stripping. You can increase the efficiency of old wood windows and doors as well as metal windows with the addition of weather-stripping. Your choice of materials includes:

- ➤ Metal (brass or bronze)
- ➤ Foam
- ➤ Vinyl

Spring bronze is the most popular and adaptable metal weather-stripping. It's installed by nailing to either a window or door jamb and flares out against the door or window sash to form a taut fit. It's normally sold in $1^1/8$-inch-wide roles (one role is enough to weather-strip one door). You can order larger widths and roles up to 100 feet in length from such manufacturers as Pemko.

Foam weather-stripping is available in a variety of thicknesses and widths. The closed cell variety is thick, dense, and longer-lasting than the open cell type. Both are self-adhesive and will stick to either metal or wood.

The most common vinyl weather-stripping is the v-shaped variety. It's shape allows it to flare against a door or window sash to form a seal (one edge is self-adhesive). The v-shaped vinyl works well in tight areas and is less likely to prevent a door or window from closing completely then the foam material. Attach self-adhesive weather-stripping to clean surfaces only.

Leaky Windows

Windows will usually leak from one of two places:

➤ The glass seal
➤ At the sill

Glazing compound, an elastic, clay-like material, is usually used to seal glass in older, single pane windows (both metal and wood). Over time, especially if it isn't kept painted, the glazing compound will dry up and begin to fall off of the sash. It's important that this seal be maintained. To replace deteriorated glazing compound, first gently scrape away all loose material and brush away the small fragments and dust. Empty all the contents of a one quart or one pint can of glazing compound and completely knead the material until it has the consistency of bread dough. Apply it to the glass, following the bevel of the intact glazing, and smooth it out with a clean glazing knife or putty knife.

This takes some practice in order to produce a smooth, straight line. Thoroughly kneaded, soft glazing will make your job a lot easier. Newer, insulated windows are sealed with caulking and rarely leak. If a small leak does develop, seal the area with a clear silicone caulking (the factory caulking takes more expertise to apply, but clear silicone will do the job for minor leaks).

Leaking sills can often be cured with a bead of silicone caulking. Deteriorated wood sills can be repaired one of three ways:

➤ The rotted wood can be cut out and the damaged area filled with epoxy or fiberglass filler.
➤ A piece of fitted sheet metal can be fastened over the sill.
➤ The sill can be replaced.

Fiberglass and epoxy fillers are great materials for wood repair. They are available at both auto and marine parts stores. Some paint stores carry similar materials. The damaged area must be dry before you pack it with any of these fillers. Several applications may be required. After the final coat has cured, sand it flush with the rest of the sill, prime, and apply two coats of paint.

Sheet metal panning simply covers up the problem and can make it worse if it isn't a good fit with all edges caulked. If any water gets under the sheet metal, it won't get a chance to dry out and will really deteriorate the wood underneath.

New sill material is available in several profiles from millwork suppliers. You'll have to saw and chisel out the old sill—which is nailed up vertically into the window jamb—and fit a new one in its place. This can be a frustrating job which even carpenters avoid doing.

Squashing Those Squeaks

Floor squeaks are always irritating, but we often don't get around to repairing them. You can address your squeaks from above or below the floor.

Problem: Squeaky floor boards or subfloor

Solutions: If you have access to the underside of the floor, have a friend walk around overhead on the floor until you find the exact location of the squeak. Nail a small, glue-coated wood shim between the floor joist and the subfloor until the shim is taut. Larger gaps between the joist and subfloor can be repaired by screwing a two-by-four (be sure it's cut longer than the length of the gap) to the joist; be sure you use glue or construction adhesive on the side against the joist and push it up against the subfloor while attaching. The joist themselves could have cupped slightly over the years and may have pulled away from the subflooring. If you suspect this, install some diagonally placed cross-bracing.

What if you don't have access to the joist? You can always nail through a wood floor into the subfloor and then putty the nail holes. If you have carpet over plywood, you'll have to go through the carpet to fasten the subfloor to a joist. There are screws available made specifically to go under carpet and through subflooring. When they're completely tightened, the head snaps off so the top of the screw is flush with the subfloor.

Finding the joist under carpet isn't easy. You can try and measure from an outer wall, but this isn't a reliable method. You can also remove a light fixture—it will be attached to a joist—from the ceiling below and use that joist as a reference point.

Speaking of Floors

Vinyl floor repair can be as simple as throwing a washable rug over the offending area to hide it or carefully cutting out and matching a new piece of material with the existing floor covering. A carefully installed patch will mostly be noticeable to you, but less so to anyone else.

Problem: Damaged vinyl floor

Solution: If you have vinyl tile, take a propane torch or heat gun and warm the tile and the adhesive until the tile can be removed. Clean all the old adhesive, apply new adhesive, install the new tile, and weigh it down overnight. Sheet vinyl is a little trickier. You'll have to cut out an even section of the old material and cut a patch to exactly match it. Remove the old material and install the patch the same as you would for vinyl tile.

Danger Ahead

Old homes present unique remodeling challenges, not the least of which are the presence of asbestos and lead-based paint. You're going to end up working around them—or paying someone else to—so you might as well know what you're dealing with.

Adios to Asbestos

Asbestos is a naturally occurring mineral with great fire retardant qualities. It was used in residences to wrap hot water pipes for both heating systems and tap water and also to wrap heat ducts. The degree of danger asbestos poses is controversial as is previously mass removals of it from schools—a Harvard Medical School study concluded that kids were getting more exposure because of the removal of the asbestos ceiling tiles than from leaving them alone (the tiles, not the kids). Before you attempt to remove it yourself, check with your local building department officials and confirm that a home-owner can do his or her own removal. Some rules call for certified abatement contractors—the sound you here is your money flying away—to do the removal.

The rules aren't simply an example of the big, bad government interfering in your natural right to remodel your home: They're for your own protection (and your family, too). You'll need to wear appropriate protective clothing and a respirator if you intend on doing your own asbestos removal.

When removing your own asbestos from pipes or furnace ducts:

1. Wear a disposable paper suit, plastic or rubber gloves, and a respirator; tape the ends of the sleeves and legs with duct tape to form a complete seal.
2. Don't wear the suit while eating or in leaving the work area (rules actually call for changing into a new, clean suit every time you step out of the work area for a break and then re-enter later).
3. Tape off all doorways, windows, and heat registers in the affected area with heavy plastic; put plastic all over the floor and mark the work area as under abatement.
4. Wet the asbestos down completely—use a spray bottle of water—to keep any fibers from flying off during the removal.
5. Continue to wet it as you cut through the asbestos.
6. Double bag all asbestos in heavy duty plastic trash bags and mark as toxic disposal.
7. If you're removing entire ducts or cutting away sections of pipe, wet the asbestos first and then wrap and tape with several layers of plastic.
8. Place all plastic and used paper suits in plastic bags as well.
9. Dispose of all waste according to local regulations.

And this is only a modified guide! Professionals follow the regulations very stringently all the while just loving this business. And no wonder: Abatement pays very well, it can't be avoided on commercial jobs, and isn't all that physically taxing. Balance the pros and cons carefully before hiring this one out.

Lead-Based Paint

Long term, heavy exposure to lead is a problem. The law is very specific about its removal and containment, especially around children. I could write a book about it (actually, I am), but for your purposes, treat lead the same way you would treat asbestos: With great precautions.

You are suppose to do the following when removing lead paint:

1. Seal off the area with plastic.
2. Wear a protective disposable paper suit, respirator, and gloves.
3. Avoid scraping and sanding of lead paint.
4. Double bag all refuse and dispose of as toxic waste.
5. Vacuum the area with a HEPA vacuum and wet mop.

Government regulations and guidelines won't even recommend scraping to remove lead paint, let alone heavy sanding or torching. No scraping? How are you suppose to get the paint off? There's the rub: it's preferred that you *don't* because that disperses lead dust into the air. The rules have been established for contractors so neither their employees—who even have to have their blood monitored for lead—nor anyone else working on a job site are exposed to lead. As a homeowner, you can eat the stuff for lunch and it's no one's business as long as you don't expose anyone else to lead's evils while you're removing it.

Safety

Remodeling is fraught with potential and actual hazards including toxic chemicals, sharp tools, dust, and extreme noise. Short of dressing yourself up in a suit of armor with a built-in breathing apparatus and massive ear protectors, there are some precautions you need to take.

Safety Rules: The Always and Never Series

- ➤ Always wear protective gear related to the job you're doing (see section below on safety gear).
- ➤ Never work when you're too tired to pay full attention to a dangerous job.
- ➤ Never carry on a conversation while using a power tool that needs your full attention.
- ➤ Always wear shoes, preferably sturdy work shoes, at the work site.
- ➤ Never let children or pets play or wander around a work site unattended.
- ➤ Always install guard rails where needed to prevent falls.
- ➤ Never drop trash or debris out an open window without checking for other workers below and yelling, "Look out!"
- ➤ Always wear heavy, long-sleeve rubber gloves when using harsh chemicals and paint thinners.
- ➤ Never climb an unsecured or unsteady ladder.
- ➤ Always keep trash and other stuff (extension cords, extra boards, and so on) at a work site from getting underfoot.
- ➤ Never come up behind and surprise or startle a worker who is concentrating on a task, especially if it involves a power tool.
- ➤ Keep a first aid kit on the job site and be sure everyone knows where it's located.

Safety Gear

An endless amount of safety gear is available, but these are the basic items every home remodeler should have:

➤ Plastic safety glasses

➤ Ear protectors (muff style or disposable plugs)

➤ Elbow length rubber gloves (when using solvents)

➤ Disposable plastic of latex gloves (when painting)

➤ Heavy-duty dust masks

➤ Respirator (for solvents, contaminated dust)

➤ Knee pads

You Say Something?

I cannot emphasize hearing protection enough. Everything from the whine of electric saws to the reverberations from hammering in a closed room can affect your hearing. The fact that you attended rock concerts and sat two feet away from speakers the size of a bus is no argument—you should have worn ear protection then, too. If you don't believe me, just look at Peter Townsend of the rock group The Who. He has ringing in his ears all the time due to severe tinnitus.

Disposable foam plugs, which fit inside your ears, are the cheapest way to go, but they're less convenient than protective ear muffs. I recommend the muffs, but keep a few pair of the disposables on hand (they can be washed and reused).

Masks and Respirators

Our nose usually tells us when the air is foul or stuffy, but we often ignore the warnings. It's one thing to put up with a stinky locker room, quite another to breathe in drywall dust or paint stripper fumes.

Masks and respirators are made for every purpose, and should be worn. Some people will have immediate reactions to lung irritants while for others its cumulative. Respirators and masks include:

➤ Light paper dust masks for low level, non-toxic dust

➤ Thick disposable masks (such as 3M series 8710) for heavier volumes of dust

➤ Half-face rubber respirators with a variety of cartridges for dust, smoke, and organic vapors (such as paint remover, mineral spirits, paint)

I'll be the first to admit that respirators are not comfortable, but they beat the alternative. Respirators and dust masks are available at paint stores, home improvement centers, and safety equipment supply companies. Be sure that the brand you purchase has readily available cartridges for your specific tasks—dust, vapors, etc.—before you buy it. For the most extensive selection of equipment, go to a safety equipment supplier.

Dangerous Encounters: Asbestos and Lead–Based Paint

Old homes present unique remodeling challenges, not the least of which are the presence of asbestos and lead-based paint. You're going to end up working around them—or paying someone else to do it—so you might as well know what you're dealing with.

Adios to Asbestos

The rules for asbestos removal aren't an example of the big, bad government interfering in your natural right to remodel your home: They're for your own protection (and your family, too). You'll need to wear appropriate protective clothing and a respirator if you intend on doing your own asbestos removal (and can legally do so according to local laws).

When removing your own asbestos from pipes or furnace ducts, follow these rules:

1. Wear a disposable paper suit, plastic or rubber gloves, and a respirator; tape the ends of the sleeves and legs with duct tape to form a complete seal.

2. Don't wear the suit while eating or when leaving the work area (rules call for changing into a new, clean suit every time you step out of the work area for a break and then re-enter later).

3. Tape off all doorways, windows, and heat registers in the affected area with heavy plastic; put plastic all over the floor and mark the work area as under abatement.

4. Wet the asbestos down completely—use a spray bottle of water—to keep any fibers from flying off during the removal.

5. Continue to wet asbestos as you cut through it.

6. Double bag all asbestos in heavy duty plastic trash bags and mark them as toxic disposal.

7. If you're removing entire ducts or cutting away sections of pipe, wet the asbestos first and then wrap and tape it with several layers of plastic.

8. Place all plastic and used paper suits in plastic bags as well.

9. Dispose of all waste according to local regulations.

And this is only a modified guide! Professionals follow the regulations very stringently, loving it all the while. Abatement pays very well, can't be avoided on commercial jobs, and isn't all that physically taxing. Balance the pros and cons carefully before hiring this one out.

Lead-Based Paint

Long term, heavy exposure to lead is a problem. The law is very specific about its removal and containment, especially around children. I could write a book about it (actually, I'm doing that), but for your purposes, treat lead the same way you would treat asbestos: Very cautiously.

You are supposed to do the following when removing lead paint:

1. Seal off the area with plastic.
2. Wear a protective disposable paper suit, respirator, and gloves.
3. Avoid scraping and sanding of lead paint.
4. Double bag all refuse and dispose of as toxic waste.
5. Vacuum the area with a HEPA vacuum and wet mop.

Government regulations and guidelines won't even recommend scraping to remove lead paint, let alone heavy sanding or torching. No scraping? How are you supposed to get the paint off? There's the rub: It's preferred that you *don't*, because that disperses lead dust into the air. The rules have been established for contractors so that neither their employees—who even have to have their blood monitored for lead—nor anyone else working on a job site is exposed to lead. As a homeowner, you can probably eat the stuff for lunch, and it's no one's business, as long as you don't expose anyone else to lead's evils while you're removing it. Check your local regulations before doing your own lead-based paint removal. In Massachusetts, for example, you cannot do it yourself if any child under the age of six lives in the dwelling.

Resources

You'll never find a shortage of books, magazines, Web sites, or TV and radio shows devoted to remodeling and home upkeep. Add local classes at community colleges and one-day affairs sponsored by historic associations, garden clubs, and homebuilding stores, and you'll be kept too busy to do any remodeling!

Books

Homeowner-oriented books fall into several categories: Repairs and maintenance, remodeling, building new homes or additions, and historic restoration. I'll include some references to all categories. Check your local lumber or homebuilding store for free handouts and videos for rent on such topics as deck building.

The Reader's Digest, Time-Life, Ortho, Better Homes & Gardens, and Sunset are basic series that have many clearly written and well-illustrated books on all phases of home remodeling.

Additions: Your Guide to Planning and Remodeling. Better Homes & Gardens Books, 1997.

The Complete Book of Kitchen and Bathroom Renovation. Time-Life Books, 1998.

The Complete Idiot's Guide to Trouble-Free Home Repair. David J. Tenenbaum; Alpha Books, 1996.

Home Improvement 1-2-3: Expert Advice from the Home Depot. Benjamin Allen, editor; Meredith Books, 1995.

New Complete Guide to Home Repair and Improvement. Better Homes & Gardens Books, 1997.

The New Fix-It Yourself Manual. Reader's Digest Group/Putman Publishers, 1996.

Ortho's All About Kitchen Remodeling. Larry Hodgson et al; Better Homes & Gardens Books, 1998.

Renovating Woman: A Guide to Home Repair, Maintenance, and Real Men. Allegra Bennett; Pocket Books, 1997.

Web Sites

When it comes to Web sites, remember that we're in the early days of the Internet; sites come and go, addresses change, and some material can be dubious at best. By all means, surf around and see what's out there. Many sites are excellent and answer common homeowner questions submitted by readers just like you. I guarantee you that you'll find plenty of useful and pertinent information.

www.aha.com   The American Homeowner's Association site provides much miscellaneous information.

www.askbuild.com   This site answers many common remodeling questions.

www.bbb.org   The Better Business Bureau site provides some information on hiring a contractor and checking with your local office to check out a contractor's record.

www.bhglive.com/homeimp/dogs   The site for the *Better Homes & Gardens Encyclopedia and Tool Directory* provides good basic information.

www.build.com   The building and home-improvement products network.

www.builder.hw.net/guide   The interactive guide to building products and their Web sites.

www.builderweb.com   Directory for the builder industry; this site lists manufacturers, dealers, design software, and building specialists.

www.contractornet.com   This site has a Q&A section, home and garden information, and expert tips.

www.doityourself.com   The name says it all; contact this site for the e-mail newsletter.

www.homedoctor.net   This site offers free e-mail newsletter, information on repairs, and so on.

www.homemeas.com   Provides information on planning and researching projects around the house.

www.hometime.com   This excellent site is tied in with the *Hometime* TV show; it covers just about everything.

www.improvenet.com   Finds and prescreens local contractors; it also has an "Ask the Pro" feature.

www.info-s.com/build.html   About 700 links to everything house or remodeling related.

www.kitchenet.com   Offers manufacturer links and free information on the kitchen and bath industry.

www.livinghome.com   This site is an online remodeling magazine.

www.nahb.com   The National Association of Homebuilders' sit which provides facts and figures for homeowners and builders.

www.naturalhandyman.com   Lots of general remodeling information.

www.paint.org   The National Paint & Coatings Association's Web site has more information about paint than you thought existed.

www.remodeling.hw.net   Offers a little of everything, including designing and financing the job, computer technology, books, and remodeling plans.

www.remodelingtoday.com   The home page for the TV show of the same name.

www.soundhome.com   This free newsletter covers various remodeling topics.

www.yournewhouse.com   This site provides free e-mail tips and is based on a TV show.

Magazines

To figure out which magazine might best suit your needs, look through recent copies at your local public library before subscribing:

➤ *Better Homes and Gardens*
➤ *Home*
➤ *Metropolitan Home*
➤ *Old House Journal*
➤ *Sunset*
➤ *The Family Handyman*
➤ *This Old House*
➤ *Today's Homeowner*

Free Remodeling Information

"Home Improvement: Tools You Can Use" is a free kit put together by a team of business, government, and consumer advocates to educate the consumer on the remodeling process. It's available by contacting:

Federal Trade Commission
Consumer Response Center, Room 130
Sixth Street and Pennsylvania Avenue NW
Washington, DC 20580
www.ftc.gov

Index

A

ABS (acrylonitrile butadiene styrene), 164
acrylic paint, 383
Additions: Your Guide to Planning and Remodeling, 421
additions. *See* room additions
adobe, 236
aha.com Web site, 422
AIA (American Institute of Architects), 403
air conditioning systems, 178-179
    attics, 330
    electrical wiring, 179
    maintenance, 179
    second story additions, 300
air filters, 179-180
    electrostatic air filters, 179-180
    maintenance, 180
airless sprayers, 118
alkyd paints, 108, 383-385
aluminum gutters, 142
aluminum siding, 238-239
    finding replacement materials, 239
    painting, 239
    recyclable products, 38
American Arbitration Society, 402
American Institute of Architects, 403
American National Standards Institute. *See* ANSI
Annual Fuel Utilization Efficiency (AFUE), 178
appliances
    repainting, 190
    replacement of, 189-190
        dishwashers, 190
        gas stoves, 189-190
        refrigerators, 189-190
arbitration, contractors, 402-404
    canceling projects, 403
    liability, 402
    liens, 403-404
architects, 88
Architectural Digest, 82
asbestos, 177, 414-415, 419-420
    removal, 414, 419
    siding, 239-241

ASHRAE (American Society of Heating, Refrigerating), 167
askbuild.com Web site, 422
assembling fences, 271-272
attics, 324-326
    air conditioning systems, 330
    ceilings, height requirements, 324-325
    decks from, 331-332
    dormers, 327-329
    egress, 327
    electrical wiring, 151
    floors, 331
    framing considerations, 325-326
    heating systems, 329-330
    inspecting, 28
    insulation, 329-330
    lighting, 331
    skylights, 327
    staircase requirements, 326-327
    ventilation concerns, 136-137
    windows, 326-327
auger, 166, 407

B

Backorders, effects on remodeling, 98
balusters, 331
baseboards, garages, 259
basements
    building with crawl space, 322
    ceilings, height requirements, 314-315
    covering walls, 318-319
    egress, 316-320
        windows, 316-317
    electrical concerns, 320
    floors, 320-322
    heating systems, 320
    inspecting, 26-27
        leaks, 52
    moisture problems, 315-316
    moving utilities, 318
    outside doors, 317-318
    plumbing, 320
    staircases, 319
    windows, 316-317

wine cellars, 356-358
    cooling units, 357-358
    finishing touches, 358-359
    wine racks, 357
wolmanized wood, 316
bathrooms
    floors, 207-208
    increasing resale value, 9
    inspecting, 27
    master bedrooms, 307-308
        sliding doors, 308
    offices, 232
    painting, 208-209
        cleaning, 208
        styling ideas, 209
    plumbing, 200-201
        ordering tasks, 202
        sloping, 201
        water heaters, 201
        water pressure, 200
    sinks, 205-207
    storage needs, 207
    tiles, 204-205
    toilets, 205-207
    tubs. *See* tubs
    vanities, 205-207
    ventilation, 207
    walls, 204-205
bathtubs. *See* tubs
bearing walls, 57
bedrooms
    inspecting, 28
    kids' rooms, 309
    master, 306-309
        bathrooms, 307-308
        fireplaces, 309-310
        planning, 307
        sliding doors, 307
    Murphy beds, 348-349
Better Homes and Gardens, 423
bidding, contractors, 396-399
    time and materials bid, 76
bird droppings, removal of, 7
bleaches, deck cleaning, 255
bonds, contractors, 402
books (resources), 421-422
bricks, 240-241
    inspection of, 38-39
    maintenance, 240-241
    sidewalks, 274-275

429

433